A REDCOAT'S KISS

He edged closer to her and the salty tang of the air was replaced by a fresh scent of rose water, of Hannah. "Good Lord, I've died and this must be heaven."

He reached one finger out and traced Hannah's delightfully furrowed brow, then cupped her chin and turned her to face him square on.

Hannah watched his face come closer, his smoky grey eyes wearing creases of merriment at the corners, and glistening with a joyous sheen. "Art thou sporting with me, Redcoat?"

"Nay, Brown Eyes. 'Tis no game."

Yet it felt more like a game to Hannah than something serious. Until his lips touched hers.

"Oh! 'Tis like feathers. Soft."

Vincent growled and pulled her head closer. This time his lips moved more forcefully on hers, to let her know that he was not feathers, and he had more hardness in him than she dared know.

Her heartbeat bounded, keeping apace with his, until she was left gasping in wonder. From this simple thing. A kiss.

Simple no more.

More complicated than a King's maze or a tangled fishing net. More complicated than the mysterious working of her own body as it rested against his . . .

CAPTURE THE GLOW OF
ZEBRA'S *HEARTFIRES!*

BARBARA CUMMINGS

WILDERNESS FLAME

ZEBRA BOOKS
KENSINGTON PUBLISHING CORP.

ZEBRA BOOKS

are published by

Kensington Publishing Corp.
475 Park Avenue South
New York, NY 10016

First Printing: April, 1993

Printed in the United States of America

For Julie, Sandy, and Kerry.
Time passes but doesn't diminish
the joy of knowing and loving you,
not as my daughters and daughter-in-law,
but as women in your own right.
You make me proud.

And to Ariel,
the next generation of Cummings women.
Enjoy.

Part One

Vows

Prologue

Pennsylvania-Ohio Territory
October, 1760

He muttered under his breath at the humiliation of it!

Ordered by his mother, Acoha, to fetch and carry, merely because she thought she had glimpsed berry bushes, fungus rings, and sassafras trees in last night's trek through the woods.

His mother!

No brave was ever ordered by his *mother!*

And he, Cuppimac, was first son to the leader-chief of their remnant Wappintauk band. By his birthright he should not be ordered by a mere woman to do anything! Especially not now, when he had passed his fifteenth summer and was ready for his testing by the elders.

But the hunting had been poor during these years of skirmishes and wars with the fur-trappers and growl-talkers. The Wappintauks had been pushed from place to place so often that the communal pot was never filled more than half to the top. In his wisdom and worry, Cuppimac's father, the great sachem Abwenak, feared another hungry night. And with more a wish and prayer than certainty, had concurred with his wife's visions.

What else could they have been? She was the only one who had seen anything! The only one who could think that in these last days before winter set in there would be food to be found in abundance in the wild.

So here Cuppimac was, sent by visions into the deep woods to gather berries, fungus, and roots, as if he were his baby sister and not an important hunter.

Scowling now, but with a determined glint in his eye, Cuppimac lashed the gathering bag *and* his bow and quiver to his back. After all, there could be game in the woods and he could bring back something for the communal fire as well as the communal pot.

Which would demonstrate most effectively to his father that he was meant for better things, as befitted the next sachem.

More than an hour Cuppimac toiled through the thick underbrush, following the directions of his mother. Rage built inside him when he found the bushes, trees, and brown-tinged mounds exactly where Acoha had said they would be.

Visions!

He shuddered. He was yet to have his first vision. That would come, the elders jested, when he was brought deep into the woods at the next full moon and left with only bow and quiver and one mantle. Left to survive or perish, he would soon see visions! And, they had warned, he had best not ignore them: Cuppimac understood that kind of vision—the kind where his personal totem would come to him, to guide and protect him through the harshness of the weather, the barrenness of the land, the emptiness of his belly, the terrors of the night.

Yes, a brave's visions Cuppimac knew well. But this kind . . . a woman's kind . . . he knew not at all.

And it frightened him more than the loneliness of his impending initiation. This vision was mysterious, since it chose a *woman* to guide, when everyone knew a woman must be guided by her husband's totem. This vision was suspect, since it was not tested.

What if it were an evil vision?

The thought left him breathless, shaking, cold. A lesser son would have turned back empty-handed then. But Cuppimac was not the lesser son. He trusted his instincts . . . and his eyes.

At first sight of the heavy-laden branches he knew he could not now return with the excuse that his mother had been mistaken, nor that he feared this vision of hers. Nor could he return buried in his anger . . . because he remembered the hunger which kept the children whimpering through the night. Berries and roots would assuage the gnawing in their bellies—a gnawing he had long ago taught himself to ignore.

The roots came first. They would cushion the fungus, which would in turn cushion the berries, so their black flesh would not burst before he got them back.

It was hot, dirty, sticky work . . . fit for women. But he did it quickly.

He dug as many of the roots as he dared take and left the others to give nourishment to next year's growth.

11

The fungus came in four shapes. The purple-headed variety, whose tops resembled sun-shades the color of wampum, he tucked into the right of the bag. His mother loved their delicate flavor and he hoped to save some for her.

The large, brown-flecked, yellow variety covered the roots on which they fed to a depth of his hand. They would add strength and a good savory broth to the food that night.

On top of those Cuppimac dropped in the small grey fungus with its shaggy coat. He smirked. The braves had a name for this fungus . . . "happy stick" . . . because it reminded them of their man parts.

The last fungus he added to the bag was his favorite, and very rare. That he found any at all astonished him, since it usually grew in open ground. He tickled the soft, ruffled tops as he dug them. They felt almost like the doeskin he had been saving for a wedding gift for his wife . . . when the time came.

Though Cuppimac's hands and arms were soon cut and scratched from the thorns on the berry bushes, it took no time at all for him to strip the branches clean. As he tied his bag and turned to leave, he heard the rustle of leaves and looked up.

"What!"

His eye stung from whatever had struck him and he groped for the thing which had fallen from the sky. When he found it, he squinted out of one eye.

Apple! Small, hard, and wizened. But apple, nonetheless.

Here? In the woods? How had that happened?

He shrugged. What did it matter? It was a gift from the great god and would bring him favor. So he

12

unslung the gathering bag from around his shoulder and hung it on a high branch where it would be out of reach of animals.

He would have to use his mantle or breech clout to carry the apples but it didn't trouble him. He had been naked in the woods before. In fact, he preferred it.

Hastily, he found a hand-hold and hoisted himself into the tree. Hand over hand, he climbed until he reached the high branches where the sparse fruit still clung. Then he shook each branch, dislodging the apples.

"Probably sour," he murmured.

But stewed with the mint the women had gathered from the banks of the small stream where they camped, the apples would give them a good ending for their meal.

As he finished his task, the wind picked up and the leaves scraped back and forth against each other. Rain pattered, then splashed fiercely against oak and beech and pine and hemlock and sassafras. The forest sentinels bowed their heads as the wind roared.

"Yes," Cuppimac muttered. "Of course! Doomed to do woman's work. Doomed to get caught in a storm. Doomed to walk back naked through the muck. What else can go wrong?"

Thunder crackled and he craned his neck to the sky, which was now dark as dusk, yet it was but a little past noon.

"Manitou, you great god . . . have you no pity for this not-yet-brave? Sending thunderbolts will light my way back. But they would also fry me. I would not like to be a bear's charred dinner."

Cuppimac scampered down from the tree, gathered

up the apples in his mantle, and tied it into a bundle. The apples were so small, they spilled out of the sides; but with diligence—and his breech clout—he managed to secure a place for every last one.

As he plodded through the wind, rain, and mud, he heard a peppering of thunder in the distance, in the direction of his people. His head snapped up.

Pop! Pop! Pop-pop-pop-pop!

He watched the sky as the sounds continued. No bolts flashed. *No bolts flashed!*

Pop! Pop! Pop-pop-pop-pop!

Pop! Pop! Pop-pop-pop-pop!

He ran . . . stumbling over exposed roots . . . crashing to the wet ground . . . blood pounding in his temples, coursing through his limbs, propelling him onward to . . .

Hell.

There was no rain here. Only fire and smoke and ugly smells.

He searched through the mounds which had once been his people and never found his mother. How could he? Every woman and girl . . . even his baby sister . . . was naked. Blood ran from between their legs. The women's faces had been slashed and burned, their breasts hacked away.

When he stumbled over the mutilated body of his father, Cuppimac cradled Abwenak's head, closed his rage-filled eyes, and propped him against the entrance post of their wigwam.

Then one by one, he dragged each body . . . all sixty-three of them . . . into the center firepit, heaped wood and stones around the base, topped the burial mound with his father, and set fire to it.

He could not sing the burial songs because he was not a medicine man. He could not dance the burial dance because he was not yet a tested brave. He could not sprinkle the holy herbs because he was not a sachem. So his people would meet their destiny unheralded, unblessed.

As the sixty-four souls were released by the flames, Cuppimac screamed to the still-thundering heavens in the East. He gathered his rage from deep inside him and flung it in the face of the setting sun. It bounced from tree to tree, gathering momentum, and echoed back to him in waves of agony.

He tended the burial fire for four days, eating nothing, drinking only when he felt faint. When there was nothing left in the fire but smoking bones, he dug a pit and scooped them into it. He did not mound the earth, but left it level. As the bones became part of the earth from which they were formed, the ground would depress. And the depression would mark their graves for all eternity.

Hours later, he gathered what he would need from each wigwam. The horses were gone, of course. They had been the only thing of value in the camp. But the growl-talkers had not left much else.

Yes, the growl-talkers. White growl-talkers with great muskets and rifles. He knew that as well as he knew *he* was breathing and his people were not.

Wars were honorable things among Indian bands, tribes, and nations. Even the dreaded Mohawks warned their enemies when to expect an attack. Even the feared Pequots were not defilers of women and children. They, too, would have sent a war tomauhauk as signal of impending attack. And if they vanquished.

15

the men, they always took the women as slaves.

No. No *Indian* he knew would have raped the young girls. No *Indian* would have left Indian bodies unrecognizable to the great god in the land to the Southwest, the hereafter. That would have seared an indelible mark on an Indian's soul, one he would never be able to explain away after death, when he had to defend the life he had led on earth.

But there was one thing an Indian was required to do . . . and would be proud to defend . . .

Vengeance demanded reparation for great wrongs.

Vengeance demanded a singular vision, a great totem, unending sorrow, and relentless determination.

Cuppimac was not yet a brave; but this savagery had burned a brave's heart into his breast. Somehow he would survive. He would have his vision. He would find his totem. He would follow it through his life. And every growl-talker in the land would know his name, the name of his band, the name of his tribe.

And be filled with dread.

Not in the sweet fire of rage, but in the sour ice of vengeance, he whispered into the abyss. "This, I promise, Acoha . . . my mother. This, I will do, Abwenak . . . my father. Man for man. Woman for woman. Child for child. Blood for blood. This, I promise."

Chapter One

The Netherlands
March, 1772

Promise. You must promise me, child . . . though you've not been brought up in the true Faith . . .

Hannah Yost ached with the effort it took for her mother to get out the words in her pain. Ague, the doctor had called it. Though she was only sixteen, Hannah already knew ague didn't leave skin like parchment. Didn't leave rattling in the lungs. Didn't leave a body of skin, bones, and little else.

Hilda Yost clutched her daughter's hand, her nails biting into Hannah's wrist as she forced another whispery sentence. *You must promise me . . .*

"I promise, *Mutter.* I promise."

Anything. She would have promised anything. She would have given anything to keep this moment from happening. But it *was* happening. And Hannah could do nothing to stop it.

"I promise, *Mutter.* I promise."

17

Good girl, Hannah. You will . . . stay . . . with . . . the Church. Her mother reached up and brushed the tiny wisps of flyaway corn silk blond hair from Hannah's heavy white prayer cap. Suddenly, Hilda's thumb made the sign of the cross on Hannah's head, and Hannah jumped as if scalded. Then a warmth surged through her. Surely this was a long-remembered gesture from a newly-abandoned faith. If Hilda were in her right mind, she would not have done it. But Hilda was dying. Hannah wanted to weep, wanted to scream . . . but knew it would discomfit her mother. And she would do nothing to bring more discomfort to an already-wracked body.

The sign of the cross once again as Hilda all but ordered, *"You will . . . you will . . . will shun the world . . . and Gott, himself, will bless you . . . as I bless you . . .*

They were the last words of Hilda Yost. A blessing, accompanied by what Hilda believed in her heart was a futile gesture.

But as Hannah tugged at the bundle of clothes at her feet and looked around the teeming docks of Amsterdam, she had great difficulty keeping the blessing uppermost in her mind. The futile gestures of *this* world dominated.

Pushcarts of foodstuff. Hawkers of every flashing ornament.

And the people! Publicans. Soldiers in spanking bright uniforms. Fancy men. Fancier women.

Hair dressed in heights which should have toppled over had they not had some stiffening inside. Hair powdered and curled at nape and forehead. Hair twisted and turned into unfathomable shapes, which would confound God. Hair uncovered, mostly. But when hatted, embellished mob caps with ribbons and lace predominating . . . though some wore shepherdess hats and some wore straw brims much like those her companions wore.

But there the comparison ended.

For her companions were dressed as plainly as she.

Not for them, eyes lined with black, eyelids swiped with some kind of paint or powder. Cheeks boldly reddened. Mouths twisted or frowning . . . but mostly enhanced. *How did they do that?* Not for these plain people, the red and green and blue embroidered bodices. Not for them, birdcage undergarments over which yards of silk or satin or velvet emphasized a woman's form.

Not for them, the wares piled on barrels and tossed into trays. Not for them, lace—bold or finely woven or shot with sparkling threads. Not for them, feathers from exotic birds. Fans of painted paper or delicate lace. Gold. Silver. Jewels.

Nor for her.

She trudged behind these people she did not know, into whose hands she had been entrusted, as they searched for the ship which would take them across the sea to America . . . to William Penn's colony and its promise of religious freedom. To land to farm . . . snug homes in which to worship . . . isolation to practice the faith of Menno Simons . . . to escape the martyrdom which had been their lot since the first Anabaptist decree which called into question the centuries-old Roman Catholic rites.

They called themselves Mennonites now. Proudly, they said it. Factually, and sometimes passionately, they embraced the faith for which the name stood.

But, Hannah wondered, was this land called America ready for such as they?

Not if this quayside in Amsterdam was any indication of what they were to find. This, she had been told by the elders, was what they could expect in the new land . . . was the reason they were headed far west, away from the city and the vices they must avoid to keep their faith pure and holy.

She had already come far west. From the Palatine in Germany, southwest to Switzerland, then northwest to Holland. She had already left much behind, so much she wanted to remember. Before it was too late, her eyes and ears and nose drew in the scene and fixed it in her mind, to be savored later, when the hours of Mennonite prayer services threatened to send her into trance.

Here was every tongue of every nation. Truly, the Tower of Babel enclosed her, crushed her.

But she didn't hunch her shoulders for fear of contamination if touched, as did the other women in the small Mennonite party. She didn't keep her eyes on the ground or fixed on the long two-tailed coat of the man in front of her. She didn't seek out the safety of the center of the group. She trailed behind, using the heaviness of her belongings as an excuse and knew she exaggerated their weight enough to come close to a lie.

She loved it! She loved the noise and confusion and whirling, swirling colors! She loved the smell of fish too long in the sun and heavy cologne on bodies unwashed. She relished the bewildering, comical sight of painted women and bewigged men. Her body rang with each clang of steel on steel. Her mind raced to paint pictures of those shiny rifles held at the ready by sentries ranged alongside the dozens of ships pulled up to the docks. She imagined the snug warmth of the soldiers' long leather boots, black breeches, and red coats with their silver or gold braid.

Most of all, she reveled in the medals. What were they for? How had they been won? There were so many possibilities . . . the Thirty Years War . . . the new war in the Americas . . . war . . . always war . . .

It was for this she was "orphaned," her father having been taken into custody five years ago when he refused induction into the Palatine forces. She had not seen him again. Her mother . . . *Mutter, how I miss you!* . . . warned her not to hope for his return, but to build a new life with the Mennonites, to pray, to await their family's reunion in another life, in the hereafter.

But she only knew *this* life, the here and the now. She had not had years to accumulate knowledge of these Swiss and Dutch and their older, Obbenite zeal. She was a child growing into a woman. What did she know?

Except . . . she knew she would miss all of this . . .

Her head swiveled and she sighed. And out of the corner of her eye she saw a small boy with a huge tray held by a leather strap round his neck so he could balance the goods he offered for sale. In his tray were books. Small books. About the size of her hand. Leather bindings. Tooled gilt edges. Not the *Ausbund*, the hymnal without music found in every Mennonite family. Not the great German Bible, which, it seemed, was the only reading material allowed in these Swiss

21

and Dutch homes. Not the new *Martyr's Mirror*, the collection of stories about a passionate profession to a faith she hardly understood. Each copy of the *Mirror* was precious to the fledgling communities.

Her fingers traced the spines and she turned over a few of the tiny books. She was a true European and knew a little of the old Catholic Latin from missals long burned by her father; a smattering of classical French taught by her dead *grossmutter's* servant; more Dutch, some English. There were books in all of these languages, and many German titles. She recognized Shakespeare's *Sonnets*, the *Decameron, Canterbury Tales* . . .

"Hannah! *Was ist das?* You dawdle behind, for what? For to look at things best left behind?"

Jacob Lendle grasped the wide shoulder straps of Hannah's apron. She shrugged the young man off, took one last lingering look at the precious books which tugged at her heart, and pulled her belongings closer to her.

"Give it to me, here. I will help," Jacob said. "But you must stay with us, Hannah. And you must not the *Englishen* or their worldly wares examine. Say a song from the *Ausbund*, Hannah. Keep your mind on the purpose, the vision."

"Some vision, all right," Geoffroy Parkson hissed to his mate, Lieutenant Vincent Scott.

"Aye. But not the kind he means."

Hair so blond it was almost white, and the biggest brown eyes he had ever seen . . . yes, truly a vision. But the eyes had been so filled with sorrow! No girl should know that much woe.

The girl named Hannah turned back to catch one last sight of the books she had been examining, and a heavy sigh escaped her. Then she straightened her shoulders, stuck out her chin, and trudged valiantly after the German in the long coat.

Suddenly—he didn't know why—Vincent knew she deserved something from that meager store. He broke rank.

Geoff whistled. "Scott, are you daft? Get back here. Montmorency will return any minute."

"Cover me. I'll only be a second."

"It only takes a second to be hanged for desertion, you twit!"

Vincent didn't stop to read the titles, he merely grabbed up three of the small volumes and threw a half-crown into the tray—far more than called for—then sprinted after Hannah. When he came alongside, he thrust the books into the deep pockets in her white apron.

She gasped and whirled, but Vincent merely smiled, held a finger to his lips, and bounded back to the line. He watched while she felt in her pockets; he imagined her fingers brushing against the bindings and pages. When her head jerked up and a broad smile streaked across her face, a warmth such as he had never felt made him stand tall and proud. He couldn't help winking broadly, smiling in return, and throwing her a snappy salute.

"At your service, Hannah," Vincent said when she raised her fingers in a tentative gesture of thanks. As she hurried to catch up with the tall German and the others in the same stark, dark uniforms, Vincent chuckled. "That *Deutsche* man will not easily tame that girl."

Geoff laughed. "Not as easily as she tamed you. Your reputation will be ruined forever, Scandalous Scott. Being nice to a woman! You? Thought you only took, not gave."

"She's hardly a woman."

"Hah! Under that severe black skirt, purple bodice, and white apron is every curve that proclaims her a woman. As if you didn't notice."

Oh, Vincent had noticed all right. He had also noticed a trim ankle and delicate hands. A heart-shaped face with a widow's peak. Gently curving brows. Blond eyelashes so thick they looked made of pussy willow fuzz. Delicate bones supporting rosy cheeks the color of ripe peaches. A nice straight nose. A mouth rounded with generous, very kissable, lips. And a neck so graceful it should have belonged to an aristocrat.

"Company! Attention!"

Vincent snapped upright as Captain Montmorency gave the marching orders for King George's Second Fusilliers. Geoff and Vincent fell out of rank and took command of their unit.

Vincent felt a great satisfaction that day—and not only because of what he had done for Hannah. He inspected his unit and even his critical eye could not find one of the men out of step. With Geoff as his second, Vincent had been able to ready these untried men in record time. They looked smart, marched eagerly.

But if the rumored war in America were truly to come, Vincent knew they wouldn't look so smart, nor be so eager after their first skirmishes. His first taste of war had been in '68, *after* the Treaty of Paris. But try to get peace with the damned French and their Indian cohorts, who had made life miserable for the settlers on the American frontier. He had been only sixteen then, and the sight had sickened him—and hardened him. Every manjack he had fought with had been killed. He was not looking forward eagerly to another. No, now that he was seasoned by several other battles here on the continent, he was more cautious, though not less loyal. The King needed him and his new recruits to keep order in the colonies. And if the King needed him, he would go.

Unlike Geoffroy, who, as the fourth son, had few prospects other than a military career, Vincent had not had to enlist. He was a respected second son of Scotsman Pryce Spencer Scott, the Baron of Byrne, and King's Councilor. Vincent could have stayed at the manor house, helped manage the estates, and lived off the trust his grandfather had set up for him, while waiting for his sickly elder brother Byron to die. His younger brother Fenton had done just that, and was happy in his station.

But from the days of nursery stories about Richard and Henry's armies, Vincent had ached to put on the uniform which too often chafed him, though it did not chafe at him. Even in the midst of the carnage caused by gunfire, arrows, and tomauhauks, he hadn't regretted his decision to become the best damned officer of the best damned fusillier regiment in the best damned infantry in the world.

Once aboard ship, he got his men billeted below, in their central quarters, and readied for sailing.

The English sailor is the best in the world—as long as the Spanish are ignored. But the British soldier! As soon as he sees water, his stomach heads for the sky, its contents with it.

Vincent didn't know where he had heard it first, but heard it he had. He had made five trips across the Atlantic and in each one, his men had rushed to prove the axiom. This time, he provided each of them with sturdy buckets, then headed up on deck to watch the crew raise the sails and get them underway.

This was the best part of the trip, the only part which made it bearable. Though he had learned to school his own stomach, it, too, preferred land as its home base. But watching the well-trained crew as they leapt from sail to fighting cock to topmast, then shinnied down the stays—he had learned long ago not to call them ropes—was more entertaining than the theatre. And the bite of the cold sea air filled his lungs, settled his stomach, and cleared his head.

He needed to clear it. It was too crowded with images of biscuit-sized brown eyes sparkling with the fire of topaz.

He went to the gunwale and looked at the horizon. Another ship made for the open sea. He could just make out the name carved into the stern. *Sorcière de Mer.* He smiled when he recognized the people milling about the decks of the *Sea Witch.* That dark clothing was very distinctive. He laughed aloud. Dear God! The good people were aboard a ship named for a *witch.* Enough of Hannah's people had been burned at the stake. Perhaps they had an affinity for witches.

*   *   *

26

Hannah lost sight of the other ship only a short time before she lost sight of the coast. One minute the ship was there, the next minute it wasn't. One minute she was still connected to land, the next, a tiny dot adrift on water which stretched beyond her vision.

It frightened her.

It frightened the lot of them. Children wept and buried their heads in their mothers' aprons. Men paced the deck, getting in the way of the crew.

After a firm word from the captain, Bishop Stultz rounded them up for prayer. As usual, he brought out the worn leather German Bible and read from Luke, Chapter Eleven, the prayer Jesus had taught his disciples to say. Then, uncharacteristically, he immediately followed that with several psalms praising God and asking for guidance in their new life. He ended with David's twenty-fourth psalm, immediately followed by David's twenty-third.

Well, founding the earth upon the seas was certainly appropriate. But if the Bishop thought this Atlantic akin to David's still waters, what would he call roiling?

And there were other things which confounded her.

These Mennonites certainly sought the face of the Lord. But they omitted the part about "mighty in battle." They did not fight. They did not take up arms. And for this her father had been ripped from her mother's arms. Yet the Lord fought battles. Robed in gold and glory.

She looked down at the drab of her clothing and sighed. She had much to learn, and it was her mother's hope that she would learn it. She would try. As hard as she could.

But she was not blameless. She did not feel she had a

27

clean hand and a pure heart. She had lifted up her soul unto vanity. And she had sworn deceitfully.

Well, not exactly sworn. Merely omitted telling about the books in her pockets.

She hoped this wasn't her day to ascend into the hill of the Lord.

Bishop Stultz handed off his duties to an elder, who led them in more readings and prayers. Then hymns . . . those chanting melodies without real music which were sometimes discordant because they had no accompaniment. But they were pleasing to God, Hannah had been assured. Everything was pleasing to God, as long as it was of the faithful. And naught was pleasing to Him when it came from the worldly.

She wondered how this was so.

And the wondering took up much of her time during the first week's travel. The wondering and the deceit.

Because she couldn't tell them about her books. He . . . that tall Redcoat . . . had given her Shakespeare and Milton and Molière. She was almost sure the elders would approve of Milton . . . or not disapprove mightily because he wrote about lost paradise and the divisions of hell. But not disapproving was different from approving . . . and she knew it.

But the not disapproving ended with Milton. Shakespeare's sonnets? Or Molière's comedies? They were of the world. Absolutely of the world. The elders would frown on them. There was no doubt of that.

Of course, until she professed her faith and declared herself a believer and became baptized into the Mennonite church, she was allowed more latitude than those who had already chosen the way and the vision. So, she justified not telling and hid the books in the

28

bottom of her travel bag until she could find a place to bring them out into the open to read them.

She set about finding that place immediately after the first night. By asking lots of questions and appealing to the captain, she was allowed to accompany the young cabin boy as he made his rounds. Hans, they called him. Hans and Hannah. The crew and the Mennonites laughed at the two, laughed and told wickedly funny stories. But Hannah didn't care. She wanted to find a hidey-hole to curl up in with her books.

As she followed Hans about, she helped him with his chores and he told her about his life. He was twelve. Only twelve!

"How can a boy so young be on his own? Why aren't you at home, helping your parents?"

"All seamen, they start out young. The boy who came before me was only ten when he started. And now, up there, he is, in the rigging, sewing up the holes in the sails."

Hannah squinted and took in a young man who straddled both rigging and a cross beam, and who did it without a guideline around his middle. With no thought to his own safety, he pulled a great needle through the sails. And again and again and again. Monotonous. It was very monotonous. But, it was also dangerous . . . and Hannah knew that the danger was the reason Hans had such envy in his voice for his predecessor.

"You couldn't find similar work in your town?"

Hans snorted. "My town, it is naught but one street and four houses. For what should I stay there? For to be a dredger of canals? Or for to fill them? That is what they do in my country. Fill or empty canals. Stupid!"

"But my *mutter* said you Nederlanders were making more land. That you needed it."

"How can you make more land? Look at the ocean! It is strong. Fearless. Do you think it can be tamed by skinny little boys filling it with sand? Never!"

Hans took her to every section of the midship as he fetched and carried water, food, dirty and clean clothing, garbage, medicine, supplies, and written orders. And there wasn't a corner which suited Hannah's purpose.

"Could I not see the hold?"

"'Tis only filled with cargo. Naught but rats and foul-smelling water there."

But it was the only place where she could hide, because the rest of the ship was teeming with men. So, when the others were in their cabins or at their meals, she slipped down the ladder into the dark, dank hold. She had a candle and tinder and struck a light quickly. Holding it high to throw as much light as possible, she edged her way past barrels and boxes until she found a small opening where sacks of flour or meal were stacked to either side. Just behind the smallest pile was a wedge-shaped area which would hold her nicely.

The spot was close enough to the ladder so she could get to it quickly, and far enough away so she could hear if anyone was coming.

But Hans was right. There were rats. And it was foul-smelling.

And there was no place to sit.

On her rounds with Hans the next day, she found an unused stool, a stack of pallets, and the cupboard where they stored the blankets. When she took them later, she pushed down her conscience. This was *not* stealing. She was merely borrowing what she needed until the ship docked, when she would return everything.

Carefully, she prepared her "sitting room." First, she laid pallets on the floor. Over them, she tugged a heavy sack of meal, which she topped with blankets. The pallets were to keep the rats from nibbling their way up to her. The sack, to make a soft seat. The blankets, to keep out the damp which constantly seeped through the walls of the hold. On two pallets atop other sacks, she grouped three candlesticks. When they were lit they gave off enough light for her to read reasonably comfortably.

For nine days she sneaked away from the group and went to her hidey-hole. They hardly missed her, anyway, since she had no relatives to care for her. Her only aunt and uncle were in a community in Pennsylvania awaiting her arrival. And each Mennonite family was large. Three of the women were expecting new additions to their families. They had more than enough on their hands . . . too much to watch out for a girl who could claim none of them as kin.

It was no wonder she chose books over the companionship of the group.

For nine days she read . . . first from one book, then from another . . . in disjointed sections . . . merely to get a feel for what the authors were saying. It was hard work. Her French was not good and she agonized over every one of Molière's words, trying valiantly to translate the written word into the spoken tongue so she could understand from sound. And the English!

31

The sentences seemed back to front and she had a hard time mastering their tricky construction. Once she did, she decided she liked Shakespeare better than Milton. Why did Milton use such big words which made her head ache and her eyes water? She much preferred the simple cadences of the younger poet. Small words, but such large ideas they contained!

On the tenth day, she was safely ensconced in her hideaway . . . reading through Shakespeare's fiftieth sonnet for the second time.

> *How heavy do I journey on the way*
> *When what I see, my weary travel's end,*
> *Doth teach that ease and that repose to say,*
> *"Thus far the miles are measur'd from thy friend!"*
> *. . . For that same groan doth put this in my mind:*
> *My grief lies onward and my joy behind.*

Shakespeare must have had many friends. At least one he loved dearly.

She frowned. She was on a "weary travel;" her miles were measured far from her parents. But she had no friends . . . unless you counted the Redcoat who had given her the books. But she did not even know his name! How could she count him as a friend?

Did, then, her grief lie onward and her joy behind? Or was it the other way about?

The grief of burying her mother and leaving her father in the great unknown was real. But so was the uncertainty of what she faced.

She closed her eyes and tried to imagine the kind of land America would be, the kind of colony Pennsylvania was. But all her mind conjured up were the raucous sights and sounds she had left behind in Amsterdam.

So she reveled in them.

Then her stomach gave a great whoosh and her head spun. Her eyes flew open. The candles toppled and gutted in the bilge in the bottom of the hold. The timbers above her head groaned and cracked. The ship tilted one way, then another. She clearly heard the wind, where she had never heard any sounds other than footsteps overhead. It roared. She didn't know wind could sound like that. Furious. Threatening.

Like a head of rye in a fierce storm, she was pitched from side to side. Had she not been securely stationed in her hiding place, she would have been tossed to her feet.

She tried to stand and couldn't. The rats, her only companions for days, were screeching, now . . . clamoring up and down the sacks and barrels . . . fighting with each other to find safety where none was.

Something crashed above her head. She smelled smoke. Not gunpowder, for she had smelled that when the captain had test-fired the cannons. Smoke.

And then the voice . . . loud . . . terrifying.

"Stand by to abandon ship!"

She tried once more to stand; and this time she managed it.

Drunk. She looked like the town drunkard. No purchase for her steps. Naught but pitching and rolling wet boards to grasp.

She jammed her precious books into the inner pocket of her skirts and stumbled, fell, pitched, staggered, and sometimes crawled through the muck and mire to the ladder. What should have taken only three minutes took what seemed a lifetime. Twice, she fell from the rungs. And when she got to the top, she pushed on the closed hatch cover. It was heavier than she expected and she pushed some more, then slammed her hands against it with all her might.

The hatch was securely closed.

She was trapped by a storm in a ship that was going down. She was trapped—and no one knew it.

Chapter Two

When the storm hit, Vincent remembered his second crossing and the gale which had swept away three unseasoned travelers. He found Geoffroy and together they rounded up some heavy lines and brought them to their unit.

"Tie this around your middles," he ordered. "We'll anchor you to cross timbers, so you can ride out the worst of this."

One of his men backed away. "And go down with the bleeding ship? Are ye daft, man?"

"Can you swim?"

"A wee bit."

"If you think the sea is the best place to be during this howler, then good luck to you. You'll have to try to get into the water without being bashed to bits by flying masts and stays. The water will be so cold, your arms will go numb in thirty minutes. Your legs soon after. And if you can manage to find some flotsam to hold onto, you'll have to share your watery quarters with *sharks.*"

"Blimey!"

"Or, you can take your chances that the ship is tight and can withstand this storm."

"I'll take me chances, Lieutenant."

"Thought so."

He and Geoffroy played out the line bit by bit. First one man tied it round his middle, then they played a little more line, then another tied it round his middle. With every third man, he and Geoff secured the line round a great cross beam or strut.

"Stay here," he ordered Geoff, and made certain that he was securely lashed as well. "I'm going above to find the captain."

"Don't play sailor, Scott."

"I've no intention of playing anything." He lowered his voice so their men wouldn't hear. "I want to know how bad this really is."

Buttress had an efficient crew. Naught a one raced round with panic on his face. It calmed Vincent.

But the sea and the sky made his breath falter and his heart pound.

Sea and sky were one color. Grey.

Rain was hard as a prison lash. He raised his hand to his cheek, expecting to see blood, and was astonished there was naught but rain mixed with seawater.

He found the captain at the helm, his first mate beside him. Each was tied to stays held secure on the gunwales. The mate put a spyglass to his eye and swept the horizon. He faltered, then swept once more. And faltered again.

Shouting to be heard above the wild winds which slashed icy water into the very bones of a man, the mate said, "Have a look, captain. Thirty degrees off the starboard bow. Am I seeing things?"

They exchanged places and the captain scanned the area the mate had designated. Vincent didn't know what they were looking for, nor could he imagine that they could see *anything* in this foul weather.

"God help them!"

The captain—Royce was his name—plucked a passing crewman by his shirt and shouted something in his ear, something even Vincent couldn't hear. The man took one terror-sticken look towards the starboard side and lurched forward into the demented wind until he disappeared down the scuttlebutt hatch. Immediately, dozens of crewmen swarmed topside. Some readied thick, huge lines, tying them into nooses. Others pulled down the two rowboats atop the scuttlebutt and tossed oars into them.

Royce gave orders and the ship screamed against the wind and waves. At Royce's insistence, Vincent grabbed hold of a line and tied himself to the largest timber he could find, one of the secondary masts on the ship. He watched dumbfounded as the captain sweated and strained against the wheel until great blood vessels on his neck and head popped out. And strained more. His mate helped and together they somehow managed to turn the ship.

Vincent stared in the direction the mate had indicated, yet could see naught but more rain, feel naught but more wind, smell foul salt air and . . .

Smoke!

And then he saw it.

Fire. It could only be fire.

Aboard another ship.

His mind made a leap of logic. They had been

keeping sight of *Sea Witch* for days, sometimes coming close, sometimes surging far ahead. In this storm, they had slowed, both of them. The ship carrying Hannah and her people was ablaze and they were full in the force of a fierce gale.

"God help them." His whispered echo of the captain's words made his head snap up. He yelled to Captain Royce, "What can I do?"

"Can you swim?"

"Yes!"

"When we come alongside, you may have to!"

With each roll of the waves, Vincent mentally urged the ship forward. They had already crested half the distance. Still, they had a long way to go.

But now he could see through the rain, and he blanched at the sight which greeted him.

Everything that could float had been thrown overboard. Only one rowboat was in the ocean, and that was upside down. Previously starched white stringed caps were sodden, bobbing on the waves, but he couldn't tell if they topped heads or had merely been blown away in the wind.

As *Buttress* crept closer, Vincent watched *Sea Witch's* crew battle the storm and the fire. Why didn't the rain put it out? What kept it blazing, biting into sodden wood with a whoosh here, and a crackle there?

He ran his hand down the sides of Royce's ship and a sticky black mass came away on his finger. Pitch. The cracks and crevices were filled with pitch to stop leaks. But in stopping leaks, it had left the ship open to slow, steady blazing, which flared whenever a flame licked out to catch a pocket of it.

Jesus! There was pitch all the way to the hold, and its dry cargo. All the way to the magazine, and its gunpowder stores. On this ship, and on *Sea Witch*.

"God help them!"

"Help me! Help!"

Hannah beat on the hatch cover. But her cries were muffled in the pounding footsteps and crashing timbers above. She sank onto the uppermost rung of the ladder and felt her heart try to batter its way out of her chest.

She screamed again but the sound was swallowed in the fear-filled litany of chanting psalms and shouted prayers which seemed to seep into her skin and set it rippling with terror.

She had to get out of there!

She examined the hatch cover. It fitted down like the cover of her mother's coffin. There was a lock of some kind on the other side. She had seen it when Hans had taken her round the ship. If she could smash it off . . .

She needed timber. And found a short board and large rock being used as weights to hold down the lid of a pickle barrel. If one didn't do the job, the other might.

She scampered down quickly and hefted the rock. It was heavy as sin but she managed to maneuver three of the rungs. As she began to ascend the fourth, her breath caught in her throat. Was that . . . ? Oh, God! A tiny lick of flame flashed between two boards on the left side of the ship. Starboard, the seamen called it. No, larboard.

Why was she worrying about that? And how, by all that was holy, was a fire spilling its way below the water line?

When another spark flashed over to her right, she didn't stop to wonder any longer. She threw herself up the ladder and bashed the hatch cover with the rock. For a time which seemed like eternity, she kept up her efforts. But all she succeeded in doing was chipping away at the wood, little by little. At this speed, it would take her a week to get through the heavy, thick cover. But if she could pry it up . . . ?

Back down she went to get the board. She examined it carefully, aware of the sputtering fires which filled the cracks all around her, beginning to bite through to the heart of the wooden ship's sides. It was hard to breathe, but she had no choice. She had to get out of there, and the only way was through the hatch.

Unless . . .

Her head snapped up when she remembered the other hatch, closer toward the bow. It was bigger, with a double cover. Perhaps one of them . . . ?

She picked her way carefully around the cargo, avoiding the rats scampering everywhere. That they also avoided her showed how terrified they were. As she hurried, she kept her head down because tongues of flame seemed to lick out toward her.

The forward hatch was larger. And the ladder, which was sometimes above on deck, was in place. She gave thanks and hastily checked the cover. Also in place. The captain obviously hoped to contain the fire above the hold. Why else protect his cargo by keeping it bottled up tight? But there *was* some light here, a tiny hole where smoke seeped through. Here, she might be

40

able to pry with the board.

But it was too thick. She needed something much thinner . . . and stronger.

She had seen the crew using iron bars. If there were any in the hold . . .

She stood in the center and scanned the boxes and barrels. The pry bar would be near them, she was sure. *If* it were here at all.

Pickle barrels, naught.

Corned beef barrels, naught.

Water barrels. Medicine boxes. Apple barrels. Furniture crates. Muslin boxes. All naught.

Then a rat screeched to her left and she heard something clatter to the floor. She stumbled round several flour and coffee sacks, slipping in the muck on the decking. Once she fell. Her hands cushioned her fall, but several splinters ripped through her palms. She moaned and hoisted herself.

And froze.

Three rats sat not a hand's breadth from her nose, their whiskers and teeth twitching as their eyes flicked over her. One stood on his hind legs and pawed at the air, coming within a hair's breadth of her face. She screamed and pushed herself all the way up. The prying bar! She had to get to the prying bar!

Shuddering at the thought of what the other frightened inhabitants—who outnumbered her more than a hundred to one—could do to her if she weren't careful, she searched frantically for whatever had made that telltale sound.

She stepped on it and turned her ankle. The iron bar was in inches of water which lapped at the top of the pallets, and she plucked it up greedily. Black and long

41

and tapered at one end, it would fit that hole in the hatch.

As she turned to hurry back, what seemed like lightning bolts radiated from her ankle to her back teeth. She sucked in the pain, refusing to allow it to defeat her. She *would* get out of this. She would! But each step was agony and the way back to the hold took longer than finding the pry bar. By the time she arrived, she was bathed in sweat and her hands shook. Spots swam in front of her eyes. Watery eyes, stinging from the smoke beginning to fill the spaces round the hatch.

She looked below and saw that the smoke had not yet floated into the hold. It would be easier to breathe down there, she knew. But she had to try to get out. If she didn't . . .

She felt icy fingers of fear inch their way up her spine. Ice from fear. Heat from the fire above. Smoke to scorch her throat. Blood running down her arms and making her hands so slippery, she constantly had to hold tighter to the iron bar. Rats scampered over her feet as they, too, looked for escape.

She would ignore them all. She would pretend she was home, snug in her *grossmutter's* house, playing a wonderfully innocent hide-and-catch-me game.

So, keeping pictures of cool, white-capped mountain streams and swaying blue freesia in her head, she jammed the pry bar into the tiny opening in the hatch and pulled down on it with all her ebbing strength.

"Heave!" Captain Royce yelled to his men.

Vincent watched as Royce's men dug their bare feet

or boots into the decking, tugged hard on the line they had played out, and pulled *Sea Witch's* rowboat closer to *Buttress*. Somehow, it had been righted and a line tied securely into the metal chain link on its bow. It was filled with women and children, some crying, some praying, some staring blankly at naught. The male passengers from *Sea Witch* were in the water, kicking, treading water, trying to find a piece of flotsam to support their weight. *Sea Witch's* crew were scattered on deck like ants, held in check by the other captain.

"Heave, you scurvy lot! Heave!" Royce urged.

The men heaved, their arm and chest and leg muscles bulging, as if ready to pop. And close to hand, the first mate directed another contingent, who threw the noosed lines into the sea as close to a man as they could come. Before his eyes, Vincent saw some men sink beneath the waves. But others splashed their way over to the lines and grabbed hold.

"Put them under yer arms!" the first mate yelled.

Vincent didn't know how the men heard through the yowling of the gale. Whether it was divine intervention or merely second guessing, most of them quickly slipped the nooses over their heads and under their arms. One by one they were towed closer to *Buttress*.

And suddenly, without warning, the mainmast on the other ship ripped in two with a mighty roar. Vincent jolted forward as it teetered, swayed, then came crashing down on the deck.

And the men.

"Oh, Christ!"

Vincent raced below and unlashed his own men.

Geoff clutched at his arm. "But Scott! The storm . . ."

"Damn the storm. There are lives at stake."

Quickly, he outlined the situation. "Mind, you don't have to go to their rescue. None will fault you if you decide to stay below, but I'd appreciate the help. And so would those sorry crewmen."

To a man, his unit nodded.

"Right," Geoffroy said. "Let's go."

Between Vincent's unit and *Buttress's* crew, the rescue of *Sea Witch* became a little less frantic than it had been. With precision honed into them by strict British training, Vincent's men fit into the roles they were assigned. Grappling hooks flew through the air, most splashing into the water between the two ships. But two caught hold of the gunwales, then two more. Soon the mixed crew had managed to pull up the rowboat and its passengers, haul aboard the men in the sea, and breech the distance between the two boats. Whatever crewmen had not been killed were hauled aboard or helped across a hastily erected boarding plank.

"Good work, men!" Vincent said, going to each man in his unit to shake his hand.

"Aye, good work," Captain Royce agreed. "And many thanks, Lieutenant." He looked up to the sky, which was getting lighter to the North. "Only the tail end left to her fight now."

"But there is still the fire. Will you put her out?" Vincent asked.

"Nay, man. 'Tis caught too much already." Captain Royce checked over the rescued passengers. "You can tell your captain 'tis safe to come on deck now." He chuckled. "My cabin boy said they was all lashed to the timbers."

"We thought it best."

"Ah, but *you* came up to help, and then got your men when it was most needed. You'll have my commendation, Lieutenant. I'll send it to the General . . . Prentiss, is it?"

"Gage, sir."

"Gage, it is. Should help move you up in rank, you know."

"Sir, there is no need."

"Nonsense. There is great need for a man like you in His Majesty's troops. Initiative must be rewarded, Lieutenant." He saluted smartly, then patted Vincent on the shoulder. "If your men are not too tired, they could help with our new passengers. We've lost some." He sighed. "I hate this . . ." His arm flung out to take in the sobbing women and children wandering from place to place, seeking out whatever of their family was left. "Storms at sea are bad enough. But fire . . . Ha! What did the poet know? 'Tis not a woman scorned for which hell hath no fury. 'Tis this abomination which fire renders. Fire and hell. They breed each other. And leave naught in their wake."

He sighed and passed a hand across his eyes as if to blot out the sight of so many wounded and in despair. Vincent thought to lessen his worries. "Corporal Parkson will be at your service, Captain Royce," Vincent said. "There's someone I have to find . . ."

"Amidst this? 'Tis the luck of the Irish you'll need."

The luck of the Irish didn't do it. Vincent made three trips around the crowded deck—with his smattering of German, asking everyone if they had seen Hannah.

One wizened woman smiled weakly and sardonically at him. "Who? Hannah? Was ist her last name, *bitter*? Here, there are many Hannahs."

"I do not know her last name. But she is blond. With big brown eyes. Always bringing up the rear . . ."

"Ah . . . the orphaned one." She looked round her. "She ist not in my sights, no? Ask the others. Yost, that ist her last name. Yost."

She quickly dismissed him and bustled to help a young mother with four children grasping at her skirts. Vincent asked everyone for Hannah Yost. Most did not even recollect the name. Some, who did not even know English or could not understand his limited German, simply shrugged their shoulders as if it didn't matter, since there were already so many lost.

But it did matter!

The prayer service being said for the dead by the elders of the Mennonite faith—he had learned that much about these unusual people—must not include Hannah's name. He could not believe that a bright ray of light such as hers could be extinguished that easily.

He looked over to *Sea Witch*, burning steadily now, and walked over to the gunwale. Now that the storm had abated, the sea was calm and the air almost silent but for the mournful sounds around him. He was about to turn aside when something, some faint, hollow-sounding noise, alerted him and he turned back. He strained to hear.

It came from *Sea Witch*. A rhythmic banging. *Boom*. And a little wait. *Boom*. And another wait. *Boom*. *Boom*. *Boom*. Over and over. Each boom echoed faintly, like a wooden bell. He searched the remains of the masts and crossbeams, but they were not the cause of the repeated blows. Besides, the wind was so faint, and this was very loud. Very loud, to be heard above the moans and cries of the people. And very unusual, that wooden bell sound. There could only be one place from which it came. One place.

The hold.

Someone was there, on that burning ship, stuck in the hold, trying to signal. Someone . . .

He wanted it to be Hannah. He willed it to be her. In naught but an instant she had imbedded herself in a corner of his callous heart and he didn't—couldn't—let her go with just a prayer flung into the void. He had to get over to that cursed vessel and find . . . her.

"Prepare to get under way!" Captain Royce shouted.

With an instinct honed by years in the infantry, Vincent knew he would have little chance of convincing Royce—good captain though he was—that a rescue should be orchestrated on the off chance that someone was stuck in the hold. But there was one thing a good Captain needed in a situation like this. Enough food.

So Vincent shouldered his way to the bridge and asked the captain, "Will you not need the provisions on the other ship to feed these lot?"

"Aye. But I'll not endanger my crew. They are already exhausted."

"I shall go. And any of my men who volunteer."

Geoffroy agreed, and seven others. Quickly, *Buttress's* crew bridged the gap between the ships with a long boarding plank. Vincent loped over. Once on deck, he dodged flames and flying shrouds to work his way to the closest hatch, that in the stern.

He was right above the hold. Right above where the sounds must have been coming from.

His heart hammered faster than it should have from his exertion—faster, even, than it would have because of all the smoke. It beat so fast because the sounds he

47

thought he heard had stopped—if they had every truly been real. But on the off chance that they were, he battered the lock like a man demented. When he got it off, he and Geoff hefted the charred wood away.

"Bastards!" Geoff shouted as scores of rats raced out of the opening and scampered to the sides of the boat.

Like lemmings to the sea, they pitched overboard. Vincent stuck his head into the hatch. The ladder was scorched, but intact. He descended into the smoke-filled hold and shouted, "Halloo! Anyone here?"

"Are you daft, Scott?" Geoffroy asked. "Who could be down there?"

"I thought I heard something."

But there was nothing except the hollow echo of his own voice as it bounced off the walls of the hold and back through the smoke and flames below.

Chapter Three

Hannah tried so hard, prying until she screamed with fatigue. But the splinters in her palms dug in deeper. The blood ran in courses. Pain ripped up her arms, making her chest ache. The smoke got denser. She had long stopped seeing, and kept her eyes closed against the stinging, burning puffs circling her head and chest. She coughed often, trying to get smoke out of her lungs, trying to breathe in fresh air. But no fresh air came.

Finally, her strength ebbed and she slipped down a rung of the ladder. It was easier, then, to slip down another . . . and then another.

Easier to breathe below. Easier to see.

She stumbled back the way she had come, returning to her snug hiding place. If she were to die, she wanted it to be there, the only home she now knew.

She was tired. So very tired.

Hannah settled herself on the soft sacks and closed her eyes. She would say her prayers. But the German didn't come, only the Latin of the old, forbidden Mass.

She shrugged. God would sort it out in the end. *"Pater Nostrum . . . Ave Maria . . . Sacrila, sacrilorum . . ."* They rolled through her mind . . . snatches, really. And they were comforting.

Too comforting.

Her eyes jolted open and she cursed roundly, the way she had heard the sailors do. "Dolt! Do you want to lie down, stop fighting, give up?" She chastised herself but it was as if someone were chatising her. "No! 'Tis too easy! And you've never had an easy time in all your life!"

Get up, Hannah. Get up and try again.

But once she looked around the smoky interior of her hiding place, she knew she couldn't risk another try at the hatch. She had to find a different way to attract attention. She listened. Fewer feet pounded. Fewer voices cried or screamed. The wind howled less. The ship creaked more. There was a chance she might be *heard* this time.

But she had to stay below the layer of smoke.

On her tour of the ship she had been fascinated with the large sail locker, where extra pikes, whaling harpoons, and pulleys were stored. She headed for it and noticed the ship had quit pitching and rolling. It was easier walking and she reached her goal in a third the time it had taken to reach the hatch the first time. Inside the sail locker were several harpoons and pikes. She tested each one. Some were too heavy. Others, too short. Two rested easily in her hand *and* reached the deck over her head. Only one harpoon, however, reached if she were lying down. And she knew she'd have to lie down, if only to stay below the smoke.

She dragged it back to her hidey-hole and once again

stretched out. This time, however, she substituted sea chanties for prayers.

She began with *"A sailing ship came down the river. BLOW, boys, BLOW. And all her sails they shone like silver. BLOW, my bully boys, BLOW."* When her arms grew tired, she tried, *"We'll haul the bowline so early in the morning. We'll haul the bowline, the bowline, HAUL! We'll haul the bowline so early in the evening. We'll haul the bowline, the bowline, HAUL!"*

On each "Blow" or "Haul," she rammed the sharp end of the harpoon into the timber above her head. And with each pound she loosened dirt and chunks of wood. So she chanted and banged with her eyes closed and her prayer cap over her mouth and nose to keep out the dust and make it easier to breathe. Which was why, when the harpoon had weakened the timber over her head, she did not see the hourglass-sized piece of oak rip from the decking and crash down on her head.

"Those meal sacks, there. Take them above and transfer them to *Buttress*," Vincent ordered.

"Aye, sir."

"And when you're finished, get flour and sugar and water barrels."

He looked round the hold. He could not have been mistaken. He *had* heard that bell-like sound. Someone was here. And he intended to find out who.

"Mind you hurry," Vincent warned Geoff. "The fire could hit the magazine any minute."

"Well aware, Scott. Well aware."

Vincent pushed his way through the smoke-filled

51

interior of the hold and made his way carefully around the stores. Flames still ate into the timbers. But there was more smoke than fire. That wouldn't last, he knew. As soon as the timbers above them had been consumed, the fire would seek out other combustibles. Surrounding him were more than was comfortable.

Vincent was pleased to note that his men had made a heave-ho line, tossing sacks from one man to the other down the line, up the ladder, and across the plank. It was damned hard work, and damned dangerous, because of the blazing fires above. Any minute, shreds of burning sails could drift down on them. Rigging weakened by fire was like a cat-o-nine-tails set ablaze, and once it hit skin or hair, it burned deep, and painful. "Be wary! And keep your heads down, men! Away from the worst of it."

"Aye, Scott," Geoff answered.

Though Geoff wondered why his friend wasn't helping, he didn't ask. Scott was never one to shirk work. He had something he wanted to do, and it must be important, else he would have been right in line with the rest of them. That was the thing which set this lieutenant apart from the others, the thing which had captured Geoff's respect. From that, they had built a friendship, though they were different as roses and cabbages.

Scott's aristocracy might have kept him head and shoulders above the others, nose highest. Instead, that head and those shoulders labored as long as the men, and in most instances, longer. Not that he couldn't lift a tankard as well as any other man. He could and did. And he was as much a rake with the fair sex as his fellow officers.

Geoff frowned. More. There had been some real trouble in England. Trouble enough to have earned Vincent the title of Scandalous Scott. But Scott never talked about it, never, like some officers Geoffroy had known, bragged about the women he had compromised.

It puzzled him, that.

Scott took from women like a man who had been used to taking all his life. Yet, the camaraderie he showed his men, his concern for them, was real. No taking, only giving. Why, then, the difference? Though Geoff had joked about it often enough in the hopes of finding the answer, Vincent always shrugged Geoff off. He wasn't ready to settle down was all, according to Scott. But Geoff was convinced there was more to it than that. Someday, mayhap, Vincent would explain. Until that day came, however, it was a puzzler.

There was that brown-eyed girl on the docks, however. Something had attracted Scott, broken down his defenses. Too bad she had been posted as among the missing. It would have been very interesting to see what Scandalous Scott would do with *her*.

"Yo, Lieutenant Scott! What do we have here?"

Vincent's head jerked up and he hurried to the spot where Jones stood, scratching his head. The sight stilled him. A woman lying on her back, with blood running from her hands and a bright red stain on a cap she had laid on her face. A Mennonite cap. He moved slowly, his mouth dry and his heart aching.

When he took off the cap, for one moment he knew euphoria. Hannah. He hadn't been wrong. He reached out and touched her soft skin. She was real. He tried to will his heart to return to a normal rhythm. There was a deep cut and a huge knot on Hannah's forehead. *Dear God, after all this, don't let her be already dead.* Had he come too late? To find out, his first instinct was to lay a hand on her chest and check to be sure she was still breathing. The contact sent fiery warmth up his arm and a heat settled in his groin unlike any he had ever known. He jerked his hand away and glanced at it, puzzled. Never had he had a reaction like that. Not even with Clarisse.

Jones snickered and Vincent sent him a warning look.

"Still breathing," Vincent growled.

He picked up Hannah and carried her to the ladder. Smoke and flames billowed down. His men had been so busy, and he had been too much involved with finding the source of that sound—that he hadn't noticed how much of the ship was ablaze.

"How many of the stores have been transferred?" he asked Geoffroy.

"Twelve sacks of meal, flour, and sugar, six barrels of fresh water, a hogshead of molasses, and a barrel of rum."

Vincent could imagine Jones pitching that up first. The man was good in a fight, but he liked his liquor. "That will have to do."

"Aye, sir."

"How bad is the passage over to *Buttress*?"

"The boarding plank is being wet down with sea water. We can make it across if the deck isn't too bad."

Geoffroy was always one for understatement. A flash to their left warned them that they had not much time. The sides of the hold were going. Soon, the flames would eat through to the double-timbered magazine.

He had to hurry. But he could not carry **Hannah** up the ladder unless he threw her over his shoulder like a sack of flour. Apt, that. She was the most precious cargo on the ship.

"Take as much as you can carry," he ordered the men left in the hold. "Then don't look behind."

On deck, it was a nightmare. His unit had stripped to their waists because of the heat from the flames. One man dipped a bucket into the sea and tossed it over the others to keep them cool and unburnt. It would be treacherous, getting through those fingers of fire with Hannah's skirts billowing out. Vincent picked up a piece of scorched rope and quickly looped it round her legs, pulling tight to encase her. Her blond hair hung loose, blowing in the wind, whipped up by the heat pockets around them.

"Geoff!"

"Aye, sir."

"Get the men off the ship."

"Aye, sir."

Vincent searched for enough space, then lowered Hannah. He brushed her hair away from her face. Lovely heart-shaped wonder, it was. With the thickest pale yellow lashes, 'gainst cheeks reddened from the heat. He touched her nose, uptilted, with a slight bump in the middle, and felt his heart constrict.

Fighting every impulse to learn the texture of her skin, he wound her hair into a mass and jammed it under the blood-stained cap, tying the long strings securely under her chin. Then he picked her up again and made for the boarding plank. Dodging patches of fire and falling debris from the rigging, he slid more than ran the width of the ship. As he got to the plank, he heard a *pop,* then several more in rapid succession.

"The magazine!" Captain Royce shouted across the din.

Jesus, Mary, and Joseph!

They had to get *Buttress* out of there, or when it blew, everything they had done would be for naught. *Buttress* would go up like tinder, and every soul with her.

He bounded across the plank and fell in a heap on the deck, skidding against the legs of the captain and his mate.

"Raise anchor! Make ready to get underway!" Royce turned to his second mate. "Get us the hell out of here."

"Aye, sir!"

With the help of a young German boy, Vincent managed to get Hannah to the scuttlebutt, away from the activity of getting a ship ready to sail. He looked down at her. Her eyes were still closed. Her head still felt feverish. The bump was beginning to discolor and the cut needed stitches.

"Was ist das?"

Vincent didn't answer immediately because he heard fury in the voice which addressed him. Fury! From a man whose leader had shrugged off Hannah's "death" as if it were of no import. *"Das ist der kinder, Hannah Yost."*

"Kinder? Like sausage, you *Englishen* tie up *der kinder?"*

The man's boot reached out and nudged Hannah and Vincent surged to his feet. The first thing he saw when he glared at the middle-aged man was a sneer of animosity on his heavily bearded face. And something

56

else. Why, he actually thought—

In German, Vincent spat, "Get your mind out of the pig sty, Mennonite! I tied her to keep the flames from setting her skirts on fire."

"*Ja.* That is what my brother, our bishop, said." The Mennonite cocked his head, then smiled and stuck out his hand. "But I had to be certain, Redcoat. She is my responsibility."

"She almost died over there! How responsible is that?"

"I accept your censure. But we have many orphans in our group. Sometimes it is hard to keep watch over them. And Hannah is not one to mingle easily. I wish this were not so. I wish she would accept her lot with us." He smiled and his blue eyes sparkled with mischief. "But she is of the age. I was wild then, too. Most of our *kinder* are, before they profess their faith. When we get to Pennsylvania, she will be taught by her aunt and uncle. Then she will know. Then she will not fight against the grain. Then she will profess, be betrothed, marry, raise children. She will pray to her God, work on the farm, be a good Mennonite wife and mother. And God will reward her. It is a hard life, one which must be accepted, not forced." He clapped his arm around Vincent's shoulder. "We are not your enemy, Redcoat. Nor you, ours." He glanced down at Hannah. "I shall find the surgeon. She needs attention."

With that, he struck out for the hatch and disappeared below. Geoffroy came up to stand beside Vincent. "Did you understand all that?"

Vincent nodded. "Enough." He knelt and loosened the ropes around Hannah's skirt and untied her cap. As the sails crackled over his head when they filled with the wind, he ran his fingers over Hannah's cheek and smoothed back her hair. She was soft and very beautiful. And she was, as he had said, a *kinder*, a child. A child-woman.

Her eyelids fluttered, and their movement was duplicated in his chest. It amazed him, the reaction she kindled. Neither had spoken a complete sentence to the other. Yet, he felt tied to her, stirred so strongly by her—something foreign to Scandalous Scott's nature. It gave him pause.

Why her? Why, in all the world, had this Mennonite woman dug so deep inside him that he was in a muddle? There must be something about her, something other than her beauty. The answer stirred almost as soon as it was asked. Hannah was vulnerable, virginal, sweet, innocent. Vincent had seen so few women like that! Clarisse had set him on a course from which he had never tarried. Then this minx had stopped to peruse a few books, had wanted something so simple—not the jewels others of her sex sought. Not silks or satins or perfume or lace. Books. Such yearning bespoke a woman he had long sought, though he never knew he was doing so until she turned up.

My God, what have You done?

She was not for the likes of him. She was a Mennonite, a woman bound for a sect which eschewed everything for which he stood.

He was an officer in His Majesty's Second Fusilliers. And Hannah's people refused to serve, refused to bear arms, refused to fight. He hoped to God they were heading for a big city, where the militia would be a presence and could, therefore, offer then a *soupçon* of safety.

But the tall Mennonite had mentioned a farm. With the number in his band, that meant they needed acres of land. No big city that he could recall had acres of land to spare. No, the only place in Pennsylvania that they'd find their farms was on the frontier. The dangers they faced!

His throat constricted and he stared at the still figure of Hannah. Her arms jerked and she moaned.

"Bring me some water, Geoff."

"Aye, sir."

Hannah opened her eyes and the first thing she saw was a bright red jacket with polished gold buttons and miles and miles of gold braid. Next, broad shoulders; a determined chin; full mouth; strong, straight nose; lastly, eyes as grey as the fog in a cornfield before dawn, glowering at her.

"Was ist das?" When his glower deepened, she switched to halting English, which made him blink. "This time, you cannot find a smile for to give me?" she whispered. "Mayhap . . . angry you are?"

"Nay."

"You are certain? I did not the thanks give you when you . . ."

Oh, no! She pulled up her apron and patted her skirts. They were there. But *she* was . . . where? The last she remembered was . . .

"My pounding. You did hear it?"

"Oh, aye."

She pushed herself up on her elbows and looked around. The deck was teeming with her fellow passengers. Many were wounded, some crying silently.

A small band gathered on the rail, their Bibles in hand, praying and chanting the dirge for the dead.

"I did not die."

She said it with such surprise, Vincent fought to hold back his smile but failed. "No. You are very much alive."

Suddenly an angry, booming roar stilled everyone on the ship. Far behind them the sky grew bright with orange, red, and black. For moments, no one spoke. Some stopped breathing. The fire had finally found its way to the magazine and Vincent's words seemed ironic now.

Geoffroy came to their side and offered a bucket of water, a dipper, and a piece of toweling. Vincent dipped some water and offered it to Hannah. She drank greedily, then wiped her mouth and asked for more. When she had finished, he, too, drank his fill then wet the toweling.

"You have a bloody bump on your head."

Hannah's hand flew to her forehead and she fingered her injury. It didn't hurt until she touched it dead in the center. Then, she winced. The tall *Englishen* leaned over but she shook her head and looked around. "I can . . . uh . . . I can manage," she said, proud she had found the correct English word. "The elders . . . they would not view it good for me to allow you . . . um . . . privileges, not even the small and well-meant ones."

Vincent nodded and gave her the wet cloth. Out of the corner of his eye he saw the tall Mennonite headed their way with another of his kind, who had a medicine case in his hand. "Your bishop's brother has brought the doctor." He got to his feet and smiled down at her. "I will leave you now."

"Wait! Your name. Will you not tell it me?"

"Scott. Vincent Scott."

"Danke, Vincent Scott."

"You are most welcome, Hannah Yost."

The next few days on the ship were unlike those of the beginning of her voyage. Hannah had not a moment to herself. True to his word, Pieter Stultz took his responsibility seriously. He charged her with taking care of seven children, four from one family, three from another. Orphans because of the storm and fire. Orphans like her.

Her day began with prayers, then she and the eldest of the girls ... Elsa Foose ... went to fetch the morning's rations, usually a bowl of watery oat or corn meal gruel sweetened with a hearty spoonful of sugar, since there was naught much else to entice the children to eat it. After breakfast, she taught the children. The alphabet and simple words for the youngest. Passages from the Bible for the oldest. Then Pieter took the boys to another group, where he and some of the men taught the arts of whittling and simple wooden tool making. While they were gone, she and the girls helped sew new clothing for that which had been lost in the fire. Then luncheon of salted beef with cornmeal cakes, applesauce, pickles. Then more sewing. Then a swift circle of the ship three times to burn off some of the children's restlessness. Then counting games. Then supper. Then bedtimes stories. Then candles out by the time the night watch took over.

Though she was expected to sleep when the children slept, she usually tossed and turned until she finally gave it up and strolled round the deck a few times.

Always, she knew Vincent Scott watched her.

It had begun the first day. She had looked up from her breakfast bowl to see him lounging against the gunwale, his grey eyes boring into her. At luncheon, he took up a place several feet away, but she knew without turning that his gaze was fixed on her. And when she walked the deck, he circled it several steps behind her.

She had expected to be chastised for attracting the attentions of someone outside their Mennonite family, but she was teased instead.

"You have made a conquest, Hannah," Rebekkah Stultz said with a smile and a wink one day at luncheon. " 'Twill not be the first. Why, I can remember the days of my courting, when the young men of marrying age circled round us who were getting ready to profess our faith . . . Ah, it was a wonderful time! The singing. The dancing. The carriage or wagon rides. The bundling!"

Rebekkah was fifty, fat, and freckled. Her eyes squinted from fatigue. Her hands shook from over-work. Her steps were slow and plodding. It was hard to picture her as a young girl dancing with young men balancing this trait against that, always hoping that the young man who finally chose her for his wife was the one she most favored.

And to see her bundling once that choice had been made! No, Hannah could not imagine it.

But she could imagine herself bundling with Vincent. Oh, yes, that was very easy to imagine, since he was as handsome as any man she had ever seen. Certainly, he was heroic. He had saved her life, after all. And on her turns around the deck, she had heard the stories his men told about him. They made him sound dashing, yet cautious in battle; demanding, yet kind; favored by birth, yet unafraid to do hard work.

Yes, she could definitely see them together, bundling.

They would be fully clothed, of course, in the most modest of nightclothes. And each would have a separate blanket or quilt. Stretched out on the same bed, with only a board to separate them, they would talk long into the night about their dreams and how they would achieve them. They might lean over the board once for a chaste kiss. And they would sleep next to each other, knowing only a tug could dislodge the board and they could . . .

Her hands flew to her cheeks and she bowed her head.

Rebekkah laughed. "Don't worry, Hannah. Soon you will have a good Mennonite man to pay you court. In the meantime, enjoy the attentions of the Redcoat. It can do no harm, for we will be watching to be sure he keeps his place."

But the elders and sisters could not watch her thoughts. And there the Redcoat paid more than attentions.

Chapter Four

The Redcoat crept into her bed. His breath warmed her cheeks, sending thrilling pulses throughout her body, heating places Hannah had never thought would flame. His kisses plucked at her lips, always leaving her yearning for more. His hands pulled her close against him and she learned the long length of his body. His chest pressed against her breasts, and the sensation was wonderful.

But the reality of dawn always dissolved the Redcoat's hooded, sensuous grey eyes and left tiny, innocent dark brown or blue ones staring at her, waiting for her to get their owners some breakfast.

Seven days after the fire, Hannah was disconcerted to see the crews of both ships become restless, boisterous. Fights broke out on one hand, and jolly jokes and singing on the other. At night, when the children were abed, sea chanties and impromptu dances set Hannah's blood racing. There was an energy in the air. Potent. Palpable.

And Hannah didn't know why.

She sought out Hans, who had blended himself into the combined crews as easily as if they had never been separate.

Hans laughed at her fears. "The journey's near its end, Hannah. We all await the first sight of land. Near crazed, it makes us."

But it stilled Hannah.

She had naught but worries about what she'd find at journey's end. Here, on the ship, she had a place, if only a simple one. But *there,* in Pennsylvania . . . what did she have?

The uncertainty of her position and the black unknown that faced her made the forward rail her favorite resting place . . . the horizon, her favorite sight. But her eyes tired easily from squinting near every five minutes to bring the hazy, rolling demarcation line into focus. And during sunsets, they watered from fatigue and intense concentration.

Yet as she concentrated, thought, studied, pondered, she found no solace for her fears.

The only comfort she had was the steady presence of the grey-eyed Redcoat . . . Lieutenant Vincent Scott . . . ever near to hand, ever watching protectively.

"I shall not break," she teased him one night, taking a daring step closer to him, the first she had taken since he had become her shadow. They were alone, or as near to it as one could get on the deck of a great ship. The shadows hid them and there were no others of the Mennonite pilgrims near to hand. "Nor will I burst into flames. Nor disappear, Redcoat."

When she laughed delightedly, Vincent sighed. He had waited patiently for this moment, more patiently than aught she had of knowing.

When it came to women, he was *not* a patient man. He sought them out, flirting outrageously, he now realized, chagrined. He was bold, bolder than he'd ever had a right to be. And this girl had taught him patience.

No, his feeling of protectiveness had taught him that. But she was the reason for that feeling, and it gave him great pause.

"One horrific conflagration is aplenty on this voyage, Brown Eyes. Though breaking is possible, even now."

Especially my heart, he wanted to say. Especially at the thought that they would be soon parted, that tomorrow could bring the first sight of land, that he might die in battle, that she might succumb to a variety of ailments so prevalent on the frontier. Dear God! He might have only this moment, this last precious moment.

He edged closer to her and the salty tang of the air was replaced by a fresh scent of rose water, of Hannah. "Good Lord, I've died and this must be heaven."

"I doubt you would find it easy to climb that exalted path," Hannah teased. "A soldier you are, Redcoat. On your soul, there would be deaths which you wear. And the admonition, you know."

"The commandment, you mean?"

"Aye.'

"And does your commandment leave no room for self defense?"

Hannah frowned. Then she stared into his mocking eyes. "No. No room, Redcoat. Else from the burning bush the voice would have said, *Thou shalt not kill except for self defense.* Nay. The voice, 'twas most

67

clear. Most commanding," she teased.

"Yet the hand of the Lord and He, Himself, led the Israelites into battle, Brown Eyes. Many times. Many, many times."

"This is true . . ."

Her voice trailed off. She knew only what she had been taught . . . that killing was not of the Mennonite faith. But she had no ready reasons why this was so except for one other admonition . . .

"But Christ . . . Oh, what is the word? Absolved! Absolved all that. We are now to love one another."

"Ah, *that* I could do easily," Vincent said. He reached one finger out and traced Hannah's delightfully furrowed brow, then cupped her chin and turned her to face him square on. "Shall we give it a try?"

His face came closer . . . those smoky grey eyes wearing creases of merriment at the corners and glistening with a joyous sheen.

"Art thou sporting with me, Redcoat?"

"Nay, Brown Eyes. 'Tis no game."

Yet it felt more like a game to Hannah than things serious.

Until his lips touched hers.

"Oh! 'Tis like feathers. Soft."

Vincent growled and pulled her head closer. This time his lips moved more forcefully on hers, to let her know that he was not feathers, and he had more hardness in him than she dared know. Hardness in more places than she dared dream. Hardness which throbbed and ached because this kiss was all he might ever get.

Hannah's vision blurred. She blinked but all she saw was a fuzzy grey haze, so she closed her eyes and imagined the intensity which had just blazed hotly in the Redcoat's eyes. It was not hard to imagine. It blazed now in her, in places she hadn't known had feelings. It moved from the pressure of his lips into her skin and sinews, to the ends of her hair, the tips of her fingers, the mounds of her breasts, the juncture of her thighs. His mouth moved from one position to another over hers, never completely breaking contact, and she felt a languidness in her legs and arms that made her weightless, causing her to sway against him.

His chest was rock hard. And his heart beat as loudly as the snare drum which one of his men tapped rhythmically several times a day. Tappity, tappity, tappity, tappity. Faster and faster. And her own heartbeat bounded ahead, apace with his, until she was left gasping in wonder.

From this simple thing. A simple kiss.

Simple no more.

More complicated than a King's maze or a tangled fishing net. More complicated than the mysterious workings of her own body as it rested against his.

Without breaking their kiss, Vincent's hands moved up to take her own and bring her arms around his neck. She sighed into his mouth as she discovered how delightedly they fit together. Though he was taller than she, it was not too much that he towered over her. Her neck was bent back as he kissed her and she had to stand on the toes of her shoes to keep her arms around his neck, but her breasts lay under the hollow of his chest. Her belly rested against his waist. Her hips fit against his legs, almost encased by them.

And then something pulsed against her belly. And pulsed again. It was like a rod of steel, moving now almost insistently. She moved her hips away and Vincent's hand splayed on her bottom, pulling her tighter against that throbbing.

Suddenly, she realized what it was and she gasped.

Bloody hell! What was he doing? She wasn't some doxy from Marseilles! She was a girl. A girl who had obviously robbed him of all sense, all discretion. A girl who had stolen his heart. And he did *this* to her? Ah, Christ, he would have more than deaths through self defense to answer for in the hereafter.

Vincent tore his mouth from hers and quickly put them at arms' length.

Her eyes were still closed, their lashes thick and fluttering on her cheeks. Her cheeks glowed from friction caused by his unshaven face. Her lips were red and swollen, beckoning once more. At a fierce constriction of his heart, he reached trembling fingers to trace the damage his mouth and beard stubble had done.

Hannah slowly opened her eyes. She caught the Redcoat's hand, rubbed her cheek against it, and gazed into a grey abyss in which she saw . . . so many things for which she had no name. "Why did not my mother tell me?"

"Tell you what, Brown Eyes?"

"How it would be wonderful! And so many wonderful things you give to me. Shakespeare. Molière. Milton. This . . . there is a name for it?"

"Sex," Vincent muttered.

"Sex?" But there were only four things, counting the kisses. Not six. She shrugged. Six or four, it was all *wunderbar*. And she did not want to hurt his feelings.

He was so over-proud of his little knowledge of German. So she would thank him, pretty . . . the way her mother had taught her to do.

Spellbound, Vincent didn't move a muscle when Hannah placed a quick kiss on his lips, curtsied, and whirled away with a joyous, *"Danke* for the sex, Vincent Scott!"

Mouth agape, he was frozen to the spot. He hadn't meant to say *sex*. It had slipped out—in the heat of the moment, so to speak. But her reaction!

And then he realized what *sex* meant in German. Not a physical act, but a number. One two, three. *Ein, zwei, drei.* Four, five, six. *Vier, funmf, sex.* He threw back his head and roared with laughter. The minx! The sweet little minx!

"Oh, she's too good by half, Vincent," Geoffroy said with a chuckle and a hearty slap on Vincent's shoulder. "Scandalous Scott. Now I know where you got that sobriquet—racing after school girls and initiating them to sin! She's half your age, lest I miss my guess."

"Only five years younger, Geoff." Vincent shook his head. "Jesus! I feel as though I took an arrow through the ribs."

"Oh, you did. Shot straight out of Cupid's bow! If you are not careful, a few more of this kind of engagement with the enemy and you will receive more than an arrow through the ribs. More like a rifle at your back and a preacher at your toes. *Thank you for the sex,* indeed."

"Say one word to the captain and you shall be permanently stationed at the end of the line of march, where you can eat dust for dinner."

"Vincent, look around you. That little goodbye, flip of her skirts, and toss of her head stole the show this

71

night. Added one more black mark to the tote they keep on your exploits with the fair sex. You think the captain won't hear about it? Think again. And pray that her people don't boil you in oil."

Geoffroy was right. Enough of the crew and a few of the company had witnessed that last bit, though he wondered if Hannah's words had carried. Ah, hell! Of course they had. On the sea all words carried. From a half-league away, a man could sometimes hear things he ought not know.

Vincent broke out in a sweat. He had been completely flummoxed by this girl. Though by the grins on the faces round him, none e'er thought he'd been more than victor in this contretemps. Christ! Those black marks on the tote—his reputation—bah! It had been "earned" at the hands of the Good and Honorable Lady Clarisse Broward, daughter of the Earl of Braedeen. It had been "expanded" in anger and jealousy and rage. But until now it had never been added to by an off-hand remark as innocent as the girl who gave it. Sex. What had he been thinking of? She wouldn't know what he meant. Hell, he didn't know the German for it.

Reputations! Bah! Thus far he had shrugged his off as of no account. He had been burning with the need for physical release. The women had been willing. What was the harm to a little flirtation and a fillip between the sheets? In his social circle it was expected, endorsed by the Royals, no less. He had used and abused and thought naught of what he did. But he could see now that his deeds—especially this night— were as black as the apron Hannah wore. And as solid as the timbers under their feet.

But the events of the past weeks had taught him that even eight-inch timbers burned. Why, then, had he imagined he could play with fire and come out unscathed? A little kiss? It had been a conflagration of enormous magnitude. She had ignited his own magazine, torn down triple-thick walls seven years in the making.

Because of her innocence. Because she had passed up trinkets and jewels and rich velvet and brocade. Because lace didn't lure her. Because exotic scents held no interest. Because she had coveted a simple thing like books. Jesus!

Thank God they were docking in a day or two. Else if something like what had just occurred were to happen again, next time he might not have the will power to let Hannah go.

Tonight he could, must, would.

And likely regret it every day of his life ever after.

America was green. More green than ever Hannah had seen. More green than her Rhine valley. And blue. The bluest blue of sky and river and bluebells along the banks. And browns! Umber and ash and chocolate from timbers and field shrubs and wonderful beavers whose dams made the Delaware tributaries trickle into the mighty river. And yellows. Fresh hay yellow. Daffodil yellow in a wildflower that she had never known in her native Palatine in the Rhineland. Buttercup, a sailor said, when she pointed it out and asked its name. Wonderful name. Buttercup.

And red. From the purple of the redbud tree in full bloom to the scarlet of a flowering bush nestled among

73

the white dogwood leaves. God's palette was everywhere, and she reveled in its beauty as the *Buttress* slowly plied its way up the Delaware River to the docks of Philadelphia.

And once they approached the outskirts of Philadelphia she had to add one more red color to her list. Warm, cozy red brick. Every house, it seemed, was built from red bricks. Or at least fronted by them.

It was so different from aught she knew. In the Palatine there were half-timbered structures, mostly, with plaster between the timbers. Dirty white and dark brown, they quickly became. Then, in Amsterdam, the tall, skinny, wooden houses jammed together in rows to save precious land, of which the *Nederlanders* had little enough.

But here along the river, large homes sat squarely amidst enough acreage to allow for flower gardens near the central front door, herb gardens near the end kitchen door, and row on row of tiny shoots . . . vegetables by summer's end. She and her Mennonite charges waved to children who ran along the banks, shouting a welcome.

"It will be wonderful," she said, more to convince herself than to comfort the children, who were restless and worried. "See how friendly the people are? We will become a part of this land. Never fear."

But Lisle Stott clung to Hannah's skirts and sucked at her thumb, only risking a peek at the bustle of their landing. And once the taller buildings in the heart of Philadelphia came into view, Lisle ran sobbing to her mother and Hannah could do nothing to coax her back.

The docking took too much time, and too little.

Hannah had hoped to see Vincent again, exchange some small goodbye; but the *Englishen's* company and the other Redcoats were first off *Buttress*. Their quick-step march resounded hollowly in the quiet of the late afternoon.

Hannah sighed. Vincent had his assignment, his work to do. It was not likely they would ever again meet, ever again speak to each other. She would have to be content to hug secretly to her heart the things they had done, the way he had made her feel, and the knowledge that she had had some mysterious power over Vincent Scott's body.

She wondered if she would ever discover what that was.

Bishop Stultz rounded up the Mennonite band and led them in their first prayer in the new land. It droned on into the still evening air, counterpointed by the *Heave ho! Heave ho!* of *Buttress's* crew as they off-loaded the cargo onto the docks.

As Bishop Stultz shook hands with Captain Royce, Hans sidled up to Hannah. He tucked a small package in her hands and blushed when she hurriedly tore at the heavy paper to expose a small whittled Pan pipe.

"'Tisn't much, Hannah. But I wanted you to remember your friend."

Hannah put it to her lips and blew three notes which were far more melodious than the hymn they had just completed, though the Pan pipe was not in tune.

"I shall always remember you, Hans. It has been a very memorable trip, after all!"

Hans nodded. The words held more than their simple meaning, for there were many who had not survived the trip across the Atlantic.

"Safe journey, Hannah Yost."

"May everything you hope be Christ's gift to you, Hans."

Once again, Hannah brought up the rear of the Mennonite party, and received many frowns and shakes of the head from the other women. Hannah was about to sigh when she shook her head firmly. She would not think herself lacking simply because she had said goodbye to a friend.

Punctuality and solidarity were all to the good; but friendship and loyalty were solid Christian values, too. Had not Christ gone to His disciples to say goodbye before His Resurrection? Should she not follow His model? And had He not brought up the rear of the procession into Jerusalem? And on the back of an ass, no less!

By the time they had walked to the center of the city, Hannah wished she had an ass to ride. The city's heart was daunting. The docks had been as boisterous as those in Amsterdam. But she had expected the hustle and bustle to decrease when they left the port behind. Instead, the streets resembled pickle barrels . . . coaches and carriages so close to each other they seemed in danger of bumping wheels. In fact, one coach's horses actually reared up, whinnying in fear when a carriage and four careened around a corner. The frightened horses' front legs pawed the air before crashing down on the rumps of the passing matched roans.

The drivers of the carriage and coach pulled in their horses. The owners jumped out to assess the damage. And hot, loud, heated English assaulted Hannah's ears.

While the argument ensued, spectators crowded the streets and walkways, making it impossible for the Mennonites to continue. So Hannah saw everything, but only caught a smattering of the language. The smattering was enough. The sailors on *Buttress* had not used such profanity! She felt soiled by it.

She looked around until she found a small doorway to hide in, clamped her hands on her ears, and kept her eyes on the ground. Thus, she did not see when her fellow Mennonites pushed a path through the melee. And it was only when the shouting died down and the area began to clear that she looked up.

Oh, no! Not again!

Where were they? Not down the alleyway. Not on the next block. Not anywhere in sight.

Wunderbar. She was lost in Philadelphia. She could only speak a little English. And she had no money.

"Welcome to your new home, Hannah Yost. If you can find it," she murmured aloud.

Hannah waited for an hour near the spot where the accident had occurred; but no one came back for her. Finally, she admitted she was on her own. The only thing to do was to find someone . . . anyone . . . who spoke German, or could understand her very limited English.

How hard could that be? She had but to identify one of her own by the clothes they wore. A black brimmed hat for a man, a black or white prayer cap for a woman. Dark clothes. Plain. Unadorned. Anyone who looked like she did.

Or a sign in the window. A name which rang with the syllables of Germany. Even Dutch or French, she would settle for. She knew them both better than she knew English.

But silks and satins and lace predominated. And those who were dressed plain did not wear prayer caps but those frilly laced concoctions that perched on the head like giant moths. Fluttering here, fluttering there in the breeze. So Hannah knew they were not Mennonites; and from the way they talked, not even German.

The sun set and darkness overtook her before she realized it. Her stomach growled from hunger. Her mouth watered from smells wafting into the streets. She passed an inn and stared into the interior as its patrons methodically put one spoonful of food after another into their mouths. She was about to leave when she caught a glimpse of scarlet and gold in the corner. And a shiny black leather belt with a silver sword. Swallowing her fear instead of food, she hefted her belongings and strode purposefully into the interior of the inn.

An *Englishen* came up to her and asked her a question. He spoke so fast, the only word in his question which she understood was *want*. Frightened, yet determined, she pointed to the redcoat, shouldered the man aside, and skirted the tables until she stood directly in front of the *Englishen*.

Her hands shook. Her legs knocked together. But she swallowed her fear instead of food and tried to make the English come out right. "Lieutenant Vincent Scott," she demanded.

The Redcoat looked up, swallowed whatever was in his mouth, and examined her closely up and down. He smiled with his mouth but not his eyes, then began to chatter away at her. Truly frightened, now, that she would be unable to communicate with him the way she had with Vincent, what English she knew seemed not to be to hand. Would the words never come?

She shook her head at the Redcoat's unintelligible blather and repeated slowly, "Lieutenant Vincent Scott! I need. Now. Lieutenant Vincent Scott."

Chapter Five

Vincent had thought to settle his men into barracks, and was thus astonished to be given a fourteen-room, three-storied brick house on the square. It was stocked with fine furniture of maple, oak, and mahogany, their surfaces gleaming. Mirrors and crystal sparkled. The chairs and sofas that were upholstered had heavy brocade or tapestry covering thick, comfortable down or horsehair filling. Each floor had rugs, including those in the bedrooms. Turkish work predominated, their rich colors giving the large rooms warmth. In the dining room, blue woolens of every hue had been braided into a sturdy rug. Three bedrooms had intricately designed hooked rugs, whose surfaces were so uneven, Vincent could only assume they had been executed by the women and maids of the house and not by a professional. Probably by the very servants who now carried out his orders. Servants who threw him hate-filled glances before doing as he bid.

"What ho?" he asked Montmorency. "Why the coldness?"

"The house has been appropriated for Good King George's use. Which means us," the captain said, and chose the largest bedroom for himself and his *aide de camp*.

"Appropriated?" Vincent stared into the huge, angry blue eyes of a servant girl. "Appropriated from your master?"

"Mistress," the girl said. "The master is dead these six years." The girl flipped her skirts and went away, muttering, "Took the roof from over the head of a widow woman. Good King George, indeed!"

Vincent sighed. "Not such a good beginning in this new land," he said to Geoffroy.

"Bad, I'd say. With servants muttering 'gainst the king, what must the family of the widow woman be doing?"

Vincent had no time to think on it. He assigned rooms to his company, six men to a room, then sought out the comfort of the first real bed he'd known since leaving England seven months previous. He'd have to share with Geoffroy, who tossed and turned more often than a Marseilles whore; but that was small torture for nights of good rest.

The coverlet on the large four-poster bed was pristine and brightly colored. Tiny stitches outlined a quilt pattern he'd seen often in the French countryside, a weeping tree with fruit of some kind worked into the corners of each square. But it was the mattress which meant more to him. Soft as eider down, such as the kind on his bed back home.

He didn't stop to wonder why he suddenly felt bereft. That was an emotion well known to those who gave their lives to the military or the navy. Away from home so much of the time, a scent, a touch, a familiar object could set off a chain reaction which was too painful to contemplate. Better to steel his feelings and get on with his duties, he'd been told earlier on. And he'd done just that.

Steeled his feelings.

Encased them in steel and stone and ice.

How else survive the horrors of war, or the horrors of women's subterfuge?

So, once again, Vincent pushed feelings away from him and got back to the walking-through-life condition he was used to, the one he'd briefly abandoned because Hannah had somehow managed to pry open a crack in the steel encasement. But that was over. He wished her well, but he had to move ahead with his life, his work, his commitment to his king and his country. First, however, he luxuriated in a few moments of rest on the eider down before going down to the dining room to have his supper.

"And he has her tucked up in rooms on the third floor," a fat gentleman whom Vincent had never seen was saying to the assembled officers around the large deal table. The fat man snickered, stuffed a spoonful of stew into his mouth, and spoke while he chewed. "Trust MacTavish to find the only girl in town who can't yell for help. Since he's about to be posted to the Pennsylvania frontier, God knows when he'll get his hands on white flesh again, so he figures to get a good two weeks out of her before he has to make do with native whores. God, I wish she had seen me first."

Vincent helped himself to the dishes set up on the

sideboard—meat and potato *en croute,* cheese and macaroni pie, and boiled greens with fatback bacon swimming in the pot liquor—and took a seat being vacated by Lieutenant Randolph Chase. "A mute, huh? Well, he gets half what every man dreams of. Too bad most mutes are so unattractive . . ."

"Not this one! Take off that drab skirt and apron, muss up her tied-up yellow hair, and ignore her guttural German and MacTavish will have heaven on earth. She's probably a virgin, too, so young is she."

Vincent's knife stopped buttering the slab of dark brown bread. His fingers closed convulsively around the handle. "German? But you said she was mute."

"Not I. I merely said she couldn't yell for help. Well, of course she can, but who's to understand what she yells?" he chewed thoughtfully. "Though she does know a bit of English. Enough to ask for a man." He laughed. "MacTavish is a sly one. *In the dark one man looks like any other,* he says. And a brogue is a brogue. So he's waiting 'til the candles are gutted in her room. Then he'll sneak in and be this Scotsman she seeks. Ah, how I would love to be a flea in MacTavish's mattress for this night."

Vincent shoved back his chair and grabbed for the lace at the fat fool's throat. "Did you see her?"

"Aye." The fool's eyes bugged and he clawed at Vincent's tight grip. "Give off, Lieutenant, if you know what's good for you! You're strangling the life out of a King's agent!"

Vincent let up, but only a bit. "Describe her!"

"Corn silk yellow hair. White cap. Dowdy skirt. White apron."

"Her eyes, man . . . her eyes!"

The man seemed perplexed. "Eyes? Two." He looked round the assembled troops. "Help me! This is a madman, can't you see?"

Geoffroy stood next to Vincent. "Two eyes? Are you daft or merely stupid?" He pointed to Vincent. "The lieutenant, here, knows the number. Now tell him the color or I swear, I shall help him wring your neck."

"Blue . . . brown . . . green . . . who notices such things? What with her small waist and high, firm breasts . . ." He licked his lips. "Hungry, MacTavish was for them, too."

Vincent threw the man back into his chair. He turned to Geoffroy. "You don't suppose?"

"Give over, Scott! When has that girl not been in trouble since e'er you've known her?"

Vincent growled with rage. He raised his boot and kicked at the fat man's chair, sending it toppling over. Before the man could right himself, Vincent had his sword at the man's chest. He smiled and toyed with the buttons on the man's gravy-spotted vest. One engraved silver circle popped off, then another. When sweat gathered at the man's upper lip, Vincent snarled, "The inn where this assignation is supposed to take place. What did you say the name was?"

"The Hare and Hound."

"Street?"

"Commerce."

Vincent took off one more button for good measure, then shoved his sword into its scabbard. He was round the table and outside the dining room before he realized Geoffroy was at his heels. "I can do this myself, Geoff."

"Aye. I know you can. But I'm coming with you, just for the company."

There were five horses tied at a posting at the front door. Vincent assayed them and chose a huge grey gelding, mounting swiftly. The colored boy who had been left to watch the mounts made a grab for the reins, but Vincent yanked them out of his hands. "Tell the owner I shall return him unharmed. If you must, tell him I confiscated it for the Crown. But get the hell out of my way!"

Geoffroy caught up with him two blocks down the street, his own confiscated piece of horseflesh a black mare with a white star on her flank. He threw Vincent an astonished glance when Vincent urged his gelding to jump a wagon blocking the thoroughfare. It took Geoff another two blocks to pull up beside Vincent once again.

"Scott! Do you have any idea which way is Commerce Street?"

Vincent swore at the top of his lungs. He had assumed they should head toward the docks, but Commerce could be anywhere in this town of parks and squares and bank buildings. He reined up in front of a tavern, threw his gear to Geoff, and ran inside. Geoff heard shouting, and was half-prepared to go in with his pistol drawn to get Vincent out of any fracas the fool had gotten into; but before he made up his mind, Vincent returned in a flash and jumped on the back of the gelding, bounding down the street.

"Two rights and a left!" Vincent called behind him. "And pray we're on time!"

*　　　*　　　*

The kindly British officer had bought her a generous supper and arranged for a good-sized room at the top of the inn. It held a small table and chair by the fireplace, a chamber pot, a large mirror, and a huge four-poster bed with heavy linen draperies pulled to the side by silken cords. Hannah stepped round the bed and tested the mattress, which was firm, and nodded in pleasure. She thanked him profusely in German mixed with English. By his smile, she assumed he understood her speech, though he never spoke directly to her.

The maid brought a good supper of rabbit pie and boiled turnips with a tankard of ale, but Hannah asked for water. *Wasser*. . . water . . . with the appropriate hand signal; obviously the maid understood because she brought it quickly. Hannah smiled.

"*Danke.*"

"Dunk?"

"No . . . *danke* . . ."

Why did not the English come when she needed it? On *Buttress* she had not much trouble making herself understood. Well, at least not much when conversing with Vincent Scott. He knew enough German and she enough English to make intelligible sentences to one another. Anyone else, however . . . Hannah had to admit they would not probably understand.

Ah, well . . . she would be in these colonies for the rest of her life. Soon enough she would learn the good English.

Hannah emptied the pewter tankard of ale into the chamber pot and refilled it with the water, which she quaffed greedily. Then she began eating the aromatic pie. Hot, it was; but not so easy to chew. It was food, however, and Hannah was grateful for any little kindness.

She wondered how long it would take the redhaired *Englishen* to find Vincent. Not too long, she hoped. Though she had seen many soldiers in the streets, none was so tall as Vincent. With her German and a smattering of English, she had tried to sketch his height with her hands to the young officer. She assumed he understood, because he had nodded, then waggled his fingers at her and closed the door. She had heard some words spoken between him and the maid, and then the lock had been turned.

At first, her fear came quickly. But then she remembered the inn had been filled with men. Probably a good thing to be safe behind a locked door. If any of them were ruffians . . . or worse . . . and were to think her alone . . . she shivered and accepted the situation. So, when the maid came in with the chewy pie, Hannah made herself agreeable, asking only once, *Vincent Scott, he commen?* When the maid threw her a worried glance, then put her hand to her mouth and nodded, Hannah said, *"Danke,"* and settled in the chair by the small table next to the fireplace to eat her pie.

When she finished, washed her face and hands, and sat once more in the fireside chair to read one of her books. Somewhere a clock chimed the hours. *Sieben, acht, neun.* Seven, eight, nine. Her head nodded over her book. She yawned. She stretched out her legs, walked around the room, finally settling on the bed and closing her eyes.

Vincent would come. Vincent would come soon.

*   *   *

88

"Mmmph!"

Hannah's eyes flew open. She couldn't breathe. Something heavy held her down on the bed. Hops. She smelled hops. And a cloying perfume that could only be what her mother had called, *eau de putane Française* . . . the smell of a French whore. She batted at whatever or whoever was wearing that stifling scent and felt a strong mouth crush down on hers.

This was *not* Vincent Scott!

Vincent threw the reins of the gelding to the stable boy in the courtyard behind The Hare and Hound and raced through the back door into the candle-lit interior. A red-faced publican met him and blocked the way.

"No rooms left, Lieutenant. Sorry."

"The German girl! Which room is she in?"

A stealthy look came into the innkeeper's eyes. But his smile was all sugar and cream. "The German girl? I do not know what you are talking about."

"How much did MacTavish pay you to be discreet? I will double it!"

The innkeeper puffed out his chest. "Sir! I run a respectable establishment."

"And I'm Benjamin Franklin." Vincent drew his pistol and cocked it. The sound crackled loud in the hall. "Now, shall we start again?"

He and Geoffroy took the stairs two at a time. The publican had been more than obliging; but they still had a problem. MacTavish had the only key to the room at the very top, and Vincent doubted he'd open it willingly.

He stopped Geoffroy. "Get a good stout log, Geoff. We may have to ram our way in."

The words made him cringe. He could imagine MacTavish doing just that to Hannah. He swallowed back bile and continued on up the stairs, all the while realizing what he was doing was so uncharacteristic to be laughable—except that this was Hannah.

He had never interfered with another man's pleasure. Virgin or whore, he rarely saw the difference. A man scratched where he itched. He took what he coveted, pleasured when he could, and when he couldn't, still took. MacTavish was not less civilized than Vincent, nor more degenerate than most. If anything, he was more considerate. Others would have taken reservations and let the girl—Hannah, dear God!—be used by any who had the price for her.

Vincent had never done it, but he knew many who had. Lonely men, far from home and the civilizing nature of their mothers, sisters, wives, daughters. It did things to a man. Vile things, as vile as what Clarisse had done to him.

When he got to the door at the top of the stairs, he tried the knob. It rattled, but naught more. Though he didn't expect to get an answer, he tried for one, anyway.

"MacTavish! Damn you, open up!"

Were those footsteps? Coming closer? Had the man finished and saw his chance to make a few pence? Vincent braced himself for what he'd see, tried to contain his fury; he knew if he were not held back, he'd fly at MacTavish's throat. And he wouldn't let go the way he had with that stupid King's agent.

The door opened inward. He took one step inside and gaped. "What?" He whirled and saw Hannah, her hand extended in surprise, a small smile on her lips.

MacTavish lay in a heap, his body bound with silken cords, contorted into a very familiar shape.

Vincent growled and pulled Hannah into his arms. *"Was ist das?* How did you . . . ?"

"The cords from the bed, they were useful. A great farm, my *grossmutter* had. We all learned to rope and tie the baby steer and pigs." She gestured with her head to the man behind her. "He has not much strength to him when you know where is the good place to kick."

Vincent laughed until his belly ached. He found the chair by the fireplace, plopped into it, and pulled Hannah onto his lap. "How do you do it? What kind of angel lives on your right shoulder?"

"Who needs angels when they have a British fusillier?" Geoffroy said when he popped his head into the room. He flipped Hannah a jaunty salute and went to nudge the trussed-up man. "MacTavish, I presume?"

"Aye! Get me out o' here, man!"

"With pleasure." Geoffroy hoisted the man-bundle over his shoulder and hastened down the stairs, MacTavish swearing at the top of his lungs all the way down. Until Geoffroy used the log on his head. "And not another word," Geoff ordered the unconscious man.

Vincent leaned back and surveyed Hannah. He dreaded the kind of answer he'd get but he dared ask, "Did he hurt you?"

Hannah nodded. When Vincent growled and his jaw muscles tensed, she snapped, "He bit my lip!" She reached up and pulled it out. "Here, look!" Vincent traced it with shaking fingers, surprising her. She grumped, "His kisses were not *wunderbar.*" She nestled against Vincent's neck. "Why are things so confusing, so . . . so . . . complicated? Your kisses, I liked. I thought all kisses were such. But that man's . . . bah! He is swine." She wrinkled her nose. "He smelled of swine, too."

Suddenly, Vincent's stomach rumbled and Hannah jumped. He laughed. "I missed my supper because of you."

"The *hassenpfeffer* here is very bad. But filling."

"I think we'll take the leavings at my quarters. Can you sit a horse?"

She sniffed haughtily. "I am a Rhine maiden. I can ride, sit, or control a coach and four, Redcoat!"

"One big gelding is all we have, Brown Eyes."

When they arrived in the courtyard, Hannah walked round the gelding, patting his flanks and measuring his hoofs. "He *is* a big one, *Englishen.* Is he yours?"

"For now." Vincent flipped a penny to the stableboy and took the reins. "Let me give you a hand up."

"I shall hold the reins."

"Hannah . . ."

"You will walk, yes?"

"No. I will sit behind you."

Hannah shrugged and let him help her up. She whipped her leg over and sat astride, and Vincent gaped.

"You will hurt yourself."

"Now you are silly." She took up the reins and clicked in the gelding's ear. The horse whinnied, turned to survey the new rider on his back, bobbed his head, and clicked right back.

"Are you coming?" Hannah asked with mock impatience.

Vincent mounted quickly and allowed Hannah to rest against his chest. His hands he kept at her hips, cradling them as they cantered down the street. "Ah, Hannah Yost, why are you not like every other female?"

But he already knew the question was unanswerable. Thank God. Because she was different, she had intrigued him. Because she was real, she had pulled him close to where he had never been. Because she was herself, he blessed the gods who had brought him her.

The ride was perfect. Her in front of him, balanced on the back of that great steed, in absolute control of the situation at all times. Just as she had been in control in that damned room back there. Just as she had been in control on the deck of *Buttress*. Just as she had been in control of his days and nights since a month past.

While he ate the leavings from the bottom of the kettle in the kitchen, he and Geoffroy elicited the information they needed to unite Hannah with her uncle and aunt. He sent Geoffroy to their residence, to explain the delay. Hell, to try to mitigate the circumstances, knowing Geoff was able to soothe a charging bull.

Hopefully, he'd have success with Hannah's relatives.

Meanwhile, Vincent and Hannah sat in the front parlor, reading companionably next to the fire. When the front door opened and Geoff sang out his friendly *What ho!,* Vincent was astonished to see Hannah look up furtively, then stuff her book into the inside pocket of her skirt.

She held her finger to her mouth. "We are not allowed. You will keep my secret?"

"Of course."

Why not? He had already agreed to keep all her other secrets. The secret place in the hold. The fire. The kiss. MacTavish. What were three books, after all?

He liked Franz Yost immediately. Tall and fair, with a belly resembling a stuffed sausage, he had a jovial laugh and a booming voice which was warm and welcoming. Not so Magda Yost. She threw Hannah a warning glance which could have frozen the sun. Only a few inches shorter than her husband, she had a ramrod-straight back and a stiff neck. And her words were short, pointed, mean.

"We will take charge of the girl now," she said. "We will teach her her place in God's people. Once she knows this, she will be content to obey her elders, and to lead a life of piety and productive moments. No more will she wander. No more will she give displeasure."

"Hannah does not displease, Mistress Yost," Vincent countered.

"She may not displease you worldly *Englishen;* but she displeases her Gott." And with that, she gathered Hannah's bundle of clothes and shoved it into Hannah's hands. "We go now!"

When Hannah turned to give Vincent a silent goodbye, Magda yanked on Hannah's braid and pinched her arm. Hannah whipped her head around and marched quietly next to her aunt, out the door and down the walk. Without a backward glance, she got into the waiting wagon and settled herself between her aunt and uncle.

The wagon pulled away.

Vincent slammed the door, swearing under his breath at the realization that though he wanted to stop them, wanted to rescue Hannah from that woman, he had no right to do so. Worse, he had nothing to offer Hannah. She was too young to take to wife. And he was going to the frontier, into a situation fraught with danger.

"So are you, Hannah," he said into the dark as he blew out the candles in the parlor. "But I have Geoffroy. Who will be there for you?"

Part Two

Plans

Cuppimac

Pennsylvania-Ohio Frontier,
June, 1774

Cuppimac flattened himself against the rise of the hill and looked down into the valley. The growl-talkers were down there. In black suits and black brimmed hats to keep away the sun. They labored in the fields, using wooden plows to desecrate the land which Cuppimac still considered belonged to his people.

As did all the earth and everything on it.

And he would prove it to these growl-talkers. He would wrest it from them, take it through the spilling of blood. Avenge his people's slaughter, as he had done many times since that awful day fourteen years ago.

He felt a surge of satisfaction. And something more. A tightness in his groin. A tightness which from experience he knew could only be assauged when he had had his fill of white female flesh. A tightness in his groin and in his chest. But the chest tightness was easily soothed. After he had spent himself on the woman, would come the knife thrust. Deep into her belly. Or across her throat. It mattered not. Both had been done to his mother, grandmother, sisters, aunts, cousins. He only gave what he had been given. Took what had been taken from him.

But the men beside him—other renegades he had found in his quest these last six years—they had not the same sacred promise. They were there with him solely for the blood lust which overcame men too long without hope. Two were white men. From the Redcoats' people, not the growl-talkers.

Cuppimac had learned the difference during the great growl-talkers' war of ten years ago. They, the enemy of the Redcoats, had killed Cuppimac's people. He knew because of the scalps they had taken. Trappers and growl-talking soldiers. Not like the Redcoats, who paid a man in goods for his labors. No, these men-with-faces-of-hair paid no wages, gave no prizes or guns or whiskey if they did not have proof of an Indian's kill. Scalps, they had insisted on. Scalps, they wore on their belts. Scalps, they exchanged with their overseas governments for silver and gold. It sickened Cuppimac. Sickened him through to his soul because through the greed of the growl-talkers, Indians had been reduced to desecrating their dead, after all.

But these men from the Redcoats who had joined with the Indians, they were different. They kept to themselves, unwilling or unable to truly become one with their Indian companions. Huh! Unwilling or unable to converse with each other! What would their tales be? What had made them so fierce, even more so than the Indians in his renegade band? Some day Cuppimac hoped to know. Now, he took their help, though he often had to turn away from their viciousness.

He wondered at the roads which brought men to their destinies. His had begun in the woods. Roared into vengeance at his family's slaughter. Slammed into fruition the first time he had joined a renegade band and attacked a poorly guarded farm. But the people there had not been growl-talkers. So he had left them alive, merely taking their food, as much as he and his band could carry.

After all, his promise, his sacred promise, had not included all the men of the earth. Because he was on a sacred quest, only from those who had done great harm to him could he exact retribution. To do more, or less, would damn his afterlife. He had to go to the great god and the great hereafter in the Southwest with pride and satisfaction, doing what he had promised to do. He was not a slaughterer as these white men were. He was an avenger. There was a difference, though he knew the Redcoats who guarded the frontier settlements did not see the difference. They had put a price on his head. A great price.

So the Redcoats, he avoided.

Besides, they were not growl-talkers.

"Cuppimac, are we to strike?" Three Feathers asked.

A Pequot, Three Feathers was always hot for blood. It had been branded into him from his people's long, bloody history. He was a valuable man to have at Cuppimac's side. But he had to be held back, else his enthusiasm would give them away.

"At the height of the sun," Cuppimac said. "When the women and children bring the men their midday meal in the fields. Then they are least expecting

101

trouble. Then we strike."

"This will be easy," Three Feathers said. "They have no guns." He licked his lips and smiled cruelly. "Stupid white men, to have no guns."

Yes, stupid. Cuppimac could not understand this. The last farm they had attacked was also without arms. When they had ridden over the rise, they had expected to see the men run for their rifles and muskets, the women for hidden knives or blunderbusses. But the men had laid down their plows and whittling knives, removed their hats, and extended their hands as if in greeting.

As Cuppimac's people would have done that day in the woods.

He had not thought what the gesture implied. He was already on the slaughter run. It had taken a full week for the scene to be replayed in his mind until he saw it, actually saw it.

And still he did not understand.

Perhaps he never would. But what did it matter? His quest would not end until his death. That, he had promised. That, he would do.

But not today.

He pointed to the riders from the south who were cantering into the settlement.

"Redcoats," he said. "We break camp now."

"We can take them," Three Feathers said.

"Yes, we are fierce enough. But we will not. Kill one Redcoat and five more come to hunt you down. There are ten . . . fifteen Redcoats down there. Kill them all and there will be five times fifteen to hunt us, take our scalps, desecrate our land. No! We wait. There will be another time. Another place."

There would always be more growl-talkers. And where they were, he would be.

This, I pledge, Acoha my mother. This I promise, Abwenak, my father.

A sacred pledge. A sacred promise. He intended to keep them both.

Chapter Six

Germantown, Pennsylvania
June, 1774

"Must we go, Aunt Magda?"

"Of course we must! The *Englishen* are overrunning Germantown. We Mennonites cannot breathe without hearing their profane words or seeing their worldly garb. We must be separate, the Bible teaches. We are not of this world, Hannah. Thus, we must find a new place, where we can worship God in our own way, with our own people." Magda sighed. "Had your mother had more time with you, you would have been schooled to understand. I have tried over these last two years. But too much imagination, you have! You must dampen your curiosity. It is not good to be so bold. You must be separate, Hannah. You must adhere to the faith. You must profess, take a husband, be a good Mennonite wife. Perhaps in New Ephrata, you will find what the Lord has stored up for you." She pushed Hannah to her chores. "Yes, we must go."

"But Uncle Franz . . ."

"Will join us as soon as ever he sells his printing business. The good *Gott* grant . . ."

She choked off and ran for the kitchen. Hannah heard her banging pots and pans, making noise so Hannah would not hear the underlying sobs. Such a contrast Magda was now to the woman who had pinched Hannah's ear and dragged her away from Vincent Scott.

"For to get your attention," her aunt had said later. "For the making worry of us. For the *schandlicht* we felt."

Shame and disgrace overwhelmed them that night. But mostly *furchtlict,* fear.

"Over much we did, *ya,*" Magda admitted the next day, and apologized.

Hannah smiled, remembering. She had worn the mark of that pinch on her ear for several weeks. Yet, in the two years Hannah had been in Germantown, she had come to admire the people with whom her parents had entrusted her. Though her aunt had a craggy face and a hard crust, there was soft bread inside. She did care for her niece, more than Hannah had thought possible.

Hannah's bedroom, though plain and simple, was hers alone. Her aunt never interfered, never checked her drawers, her private things. So her precious books were safe. And how curious that was . . . that her uncle, whose business was printing, saw fit to have only those things of the church in his house. "For to read anything else by the faithful is *verboten,*" he explained.

106

But she had not professed, so she was not yet counted among the faithful. It helped ease her mind when she spent stolen moments within her pages.

And stolen, they had to be. Because as soon as she arrived, *ach, Gott,* the lessons in housewifery her aunt had given her! Milking. Smoking or sun-drying meat, fruits, and vegetables. *Putting by* the excess from the farm and garden. Pickling. Always, the pickling. By October, Hannah was certain everything that grew in or walked on the ground was pickled. Beets and cucumbers. Pig feet and beef. Onions and clover blossoms. And veal!

"For the sauerbraten, *ya, liebchen?*"

Oi, oi, oi, ya! Hannah's hands were permanently puckered.

Then, as soon as the cold came, Magda put by the rest of the world, this time by sugar cooking, and Hannah's wrinkles were left behind as her hands puffed to the size of small hams. Apple butter was a particularly back-breaking job. Standing over the large cast iron pot, the open fire beneath it kept *just so,* Hannah and Magda used large paddles to stir the apples from morn to night until they had turned a dark brown color. From a heaping pot in the morning, they could hope to get a third of a pot by nightfall.

Apple butter, apple sauce, apple slices. Apple hands!

Soon, however, with unending labor, the larder and cold storage bins were filled and the winter tasks began.

First, dying white muslin with skins from onions, seeds from wildflowers, roots and leaves of trees and bushes, and overripe berries. Hannah liked the berries best because she got to eat as many as went into the dye pot. Second, cutting up and sewing the dyed cloth into good, serviceable *plain* clothing. Then picking over old clothes, deciding what could be saved, what could be cut into strips for braided rugs. Ah! Braided rugs. After apple buttering, braiding was *pleasure-licht.*

But the best Magda saved for last.

As taught by her aunt, quilting—that mysterious job which looked so tedious—was joyous.

"With big scraps, we shall start," she had said that first time. "Take big stitches . . . like so."

"But the quilts all have those tiny stitches."

"Ah, but those who made them always began with big stitches. As do all things in life, Hannah. Small steps, people think you must take, then let them get larger and larger, until you CHOMP off a great chunk!"

Her aunt stabbed the cloth with her needle at the word *chomp,* and Hannah was astonished. She did not think there was so much passion beneath that stony visage.

"But, Hannah . . . the big stitches you make until you learn how to do not so large ones, then smaller and smaller . . . *ei* . . . then you will learn everything you need to know."

The stitches were not so hard with Magda's chatter and Hannah settled into the routine.

"So it is with life, Hannah. To accept the Faith, that is the big stitch. To profess, a stitch not so big. To become a part of the community, smaller still. Then betrothal. Then marriage. Then children. You see how the steps get smaller and smaller and the pattern is established, so? That is the plain life. That is the life of

108

the faithful." She corrected the line Hannah had started on the third square. "Straight keep the stitches, Hannah. Straight is the way and the life."

And the straight way led to New Ephrata, the huge tract of land in the Ohio-Pennsylvania Appalachians that the faithful elders had purchased. It would house several clusters of families, miles apart, including Magda and Franz's. Which meant Hannah. So preparations had been made and their belongings packed tightly on a large farm wagon. A waterproofed canvas topped the huge mound, and several of the Pennsylvania Mennonites helped Franz tie it down securely.

"Go with *Gott*," Franz said as he blessed them. "And be prepared for all things. 'Tis fraight with danger, the places of the mountains . . ." He turned to the Bishop with a gesture of supplication. "Prepare ye some ways to help survive any unexpected attacks."

Bishop Stultz nodded. "Not to fear, my brother. We have thought of that. Many ideas have we bandied about. Things to do to save *frau und kinder,* things which won't fly in the face of the Way."

The leave-taking was heart-rending, since Franz was not the only man or family to be left behind. Some men journeyed alone and would make a home for their families before sending for them. To balance them, some women and children left under the protection of the Bishop. Like Franz, their men would come later, after business was done or the farm sold for a profit.

Through all the sobs and farewells, however, Hannah had much to remember of Germantown with love . . . and wonder. She listened to the people around her, the men driving the wagons as well as the women and children who accompanied them. Their German was peppered with English now. So much so that it hardly resembled the German . . . actually the Low Country speech which was a mixture of German and French and Slav languages which had accompanied them to the new world.

Her people prided themselves on being "separate"; but they had not stayed over-separate. They were practical people. If they must trade with the *Englishen*, they must of leave learn their language, while not taking up their ways. True, German was still used in worship services. But now, English—broken up in the way the German sentences had once been—was the order of the day in Mennonite homes. Hindmost to the front, most of the time. This Hannah knew because of the books Vincent Scott had given her to read.

Vincent Scott. She wondered where he was now, what he was doing. She had matured in the two years they had been separated. She had grown five inches, and now stood taller than her uncle. *The trees, she is reaching,* one of the women had said. *Soon, to pick the apples without a ladder.* Not that tall, of course, but taller than most of the women. And her blond hair had grown longer—it reached her waist. Her arms ached every night from the brushing of it. Her brows were arched more, as her cheeks lost some of their baby fat and the cheek bones became more prominent. Her chin was more pointed, her mouth more noticeable.

She touched her lips, where she could, if she tried, still feel the imprint of Vincent's kiss. Somehow her lips had filled out with the rest of her. They were fuller, and she sometimes felt shy that they were so unlike her aunt's simple slash. So shy and uncomfortable was Hannah about them, that she often hid them with her hands. Would Vincent find them ugly? Did other men? She wished she had someone other than her aunt to ask these kinds of questions.

But she did not. She was still the *catcher-upper* in the small band. Still lagging behind. Still not a full member of the Mennonite community.

Mayhap it was because of the other things which had blossomed those two years. Her breasts were so large as to need binding. And her hips! She wished *Gott* would finish with her and have it done. If she ate more . . . *Nein!* Big as horses, she did not like. The figure like the hourglass was enough, already!

Hannah's thoughts were blasted when a young boy cried, "I must, quick! I must!" The whole wagon line halted while his mother hurried him into the bushes at the side of the road. And other mothers did the same with their *kinder.*

"How far yet?" Magda asked Bishop Stultz as he hurried along the line to get the children back into their wagons.

"Because of *de kinder,* we are making slow time. So, I calculate that we will camp this night and four more and by afternoon five days hence, there we will be!"

The "there" was *hut wunderbar garaigert.* Like the Rhineland it looked, with rolling hills and deep valleys of dark earth. Streams crisscrossed the land, streams which would bring good, clean water to the farms which they

111

planned. For now, however, while the children chased butterflies, it was enough for their parents to stand in the meadow and give thanks for their bounty.

But not too long. Five of the wagons held building supplies. The men quickly retrieved their tools and began the hard task of knocking together a permanent shelter.

Hannah didn't know how the time got away, but three large community houses, a barn, and several outbuildings were raised within weeks. She hadn't noticed, so busy was she with the children in her charge. She sang songs with them. Not songs from the *Ausbund,* but folk songs from the Rhineland. She played games with them and taught them their lessons, writing their numbers and words on the ground.

And when they napped, she explored their new home.

It was a fairyland. Copses hid fat mushroom rings. Walnut trees yielded delicious nuts. Rabbits and squirrels ran blithely through the woods, unaware of her presence.

But Hannah explored for more than the beauty of the place. She searched for another hiding place, where she could be alone, unhindered, to read her books and dream of the things that were left behind, those that were yet to be found. And to decide whether or not to make the big stitches in her life.

Magda did not hound, but she made several "suggestions" every day. Primary among them . . . Jacob Timmons.

"Jacob begins to grow his beard, Hannah. He has been asking after you. I don't know what to say, since you have given me no indication of your promise to be taken."

"Jacob has fine muscles, no? He will make the good husband for some lucky girl."

"Jacob is so quiet, so respectful, so nice-behaved, so *vernunftchlicht*. He has professed, this week. Not like that Willem. So loud. So *boischtrichtlicht*."

It took Hannah a few seconds to decipher that one. Magda had picked up the habit of stretching out German words, and even substituting some of the English sounds. In fact, sometimes the sounds were the only way to distinguish what the people in the community meant. Jacob was sensible. Willem, boisterous.

Jacob was also a descendant of Menno Jacobs, the founder of the Anabaptist movement which became the Mennonites. And it was true—he had a definite interest in Hannah. But was she ready to commit to a life of simplicity? She had gotten used to it, certainly. Used to the short hair and full beards, the only way to tell a married man of faith from a single one. Gotten used to plain clothes with no embellishments. Gotten used to shirts and trousers which tied together with ribbons, not buckles. Gotten used to boots and shoes, plain brown or black leather, sturdy for use on the farm. Gotten used to black or straw-brimmed hats.

Most of all, she had gotten used to the sameness of things. The only beauty was in the shining eyes of the people and the majesty of the land.

She no longer missed Philadelphia's finery . . . be-wigged or greased-back hair, tied at the nape with a ribbon. And she found it laughable, those cocked hats trimmed with gold or silver or colored braid, according to a man's station in life. And what use were gold and silver buttons on hat, jacket, gloves, shirt, waistcoat, breeches, boots, shoes? Where would she wear jewels? To slop the pigs? And what good were laces? For to give a treat to an inquisitive and hungry goat?

She could not hope for marriage in the English world. She would never be considered worthy. But here, in her aunt's world, she had dignity of place . . . and a man willing to love her.

So Hannah needed a hiding place to do more than read. But where, when Jacob and the others were as free to roam the land as she?

The answer came one day when a troop of British soldiers visited the settlement.

"Verschtechle! Verschtechle! Sicht bielen!" went up the cry. *Hide! Hide! Hurry up!*

The women and children ran to hide themselves, to be out of the clutches of these barbarians in uniforms made to frighten the hairs off young children. Or so the brethren thought. Jacob threw Hannah a glance of indecision, then raced down the hill and back to the settlement, there to take up his stand beside the other adult males. Eva Borke sped up the hill, shoving Hannah out of the way. Hannah fell into a bramble of bushes heavy with raspberries and got a mouthful of moldy leaves.

She spat it out quickly. "Eat dirt, Eva," she whispered loudly, enraged and sore from the scratches

114

on her arms. But when she went to get up, she saw something behind those bushes . . .

She looked around carefully. Alone? At last! Hannah pawed the ground round the base of the raspberry brambles, dislodging built-up leaves and kindling until she found what she needed . . . a hole big enough to slither through. On the other side of the bushes was a grassy knoll in almost a perfect circle. And best of all, the entrance to this new hiding place was so indistinguishable as to be invisible. *If* she tucked in a few extra branches behind her . . . which she did, quickly.

She basked in the silence of the grove, then rolled on the bed of leaves which looked as if it had been there since the beginning of time, so . . . so *erdig* . . . earthy . . . was its smell. She stretched out her arms and kicked her feet in the air.

"Ah! Peace!"

The raspberry bushes snapped. Branches broke as something was thrust into them again and again.

"Out. Out, now!"

If she lay very still, without moving a muscle, Hannah hoped whoever it was would go away! So she kept her eyes fastened on the movement of the leaves, but said and did naught. Seconds passed and the voice didn't repeat its order. Other seconds and no more sounds. She breathed easier. More seconds and she sighed, stood up, and brushed herself off.

Within a heartbeat, she was tackled from behind and thrown down to the ground.

"Oh, no!"

"Good grief!"

Man's hands turned her over and she stared up into the wonderfully precious smoky grey eyes of Vincent Scott.

Hannah gasped and brought her hands up to frame his face. "My Redcoat! How did you get here?"

"Brown Eyes! *Gott in himmel*, I thought you were an Indian. I could have killed you." He shook her. "What are you doing hiding here away from everyone . . ." His voice trailed off and his eyes grew bright. When he spoke again it was in a whisper. "No, don't answer that. You wanted another hidey-hole, eh?"

She nodded, overjoyed that he understood. "What do you seek here at the settlement?"

"Montmorency . . . you remember Montmorency?" At her nod, he shifted his weight, but didn't get up. He liked the feel of Hannah between his legs, under him. "He has us patrolling the far-flung settlements to be sure the settlers are safe."

"Safe." Hannah struggled to sit up and noticed that Vincent gave way reluctantly. "I am not safe with you here."

"Of course you are. I have rifle, sword, and hunting knife. No one can harm you."

"No! That isn't it . . ."

Though they talked in whispers, she was terrified that someone, somehow, could see or hear them. She searched the tops of the trees but saw no one hiding there. She was safe until someone noticed that she was missing. Then, if they found them together . . .

"I will be shunned," she said mournfully. "Alone with you like this . . . *Och, mein Gott!* I am of marriage age now. I cannot be with a man without a chaperone.

116

Especially you, my *Englishen* Redcoat. Especially you."

She traced his features once more, realizing her memories had not abated, were still powerful and true. He was handsome, with chiseled jaw, nicely arched brows, and aristocratic nose. His eyes, still like the fog which hung in the valleys of the Rhineland early in the dawn. His hair, brown with traces of a dark red like the mane of a chestnut horse. His strong body, a head taller than any of the men of the community. And his muscles . . . rippling beneath that scarlet jacket . . . were as hard as, or harder than, those of the brethren, who worked day and night behind the plow or in the barn, planting and building and tearing a settlement out of the wilderness.

So, she should not be here with this man who pleased her too much. But the fascination he held for her was too much to resist.

"What is shunning, Hannah?"

"To be separated from the community. To become an outcast, where even my aunt could not talk to me or sit beside me at table."

"They would shun you for merely being here with me?"

"*Nein.* They would shun me for sinning with you."

"But we are not sinning, Hannah."

"Not yet," she whispered brokenly. Her fingers touched the silky braid on his uniform and moved up to the stamped gold buttons at the neck of his jacket. She relished their unfamiliar textures, basking in her memories. The collar of his jacket gave off a smoky scent that she remembered was his alone. It made her feel a part of him, the remembering, the knowing without being told.

Hannah lifted her gaze to Vincent and the poignancy their dark depths contained nearly broke his heart. Hannah awed him. Her confession of need, in the face of what it would cost her to be with him, nearly drove him mad. He cupped her face in the palms of his hands, his fingers brushing back and forth on her cheeks as he smiled at her. She smiled back and he bent his head to kiss her lightly on the lips.

"I will not hurt you, Hannah. I will never hurt you."

"I know. It fills me with joy, the knowing."

Suddenly, the bell which called all the families to communal meals began tolling. It was the all-clear signal the elders had agreed to and its tolling meant the elders expected everyone to come to the settlement.

Hannah jumped away from Vincent and smiled. "I must go."

"We could stay here, pretend you didn't hear the bell . . ."

"Nein. They would come searching for me. Once again, I must ask you to keep a secret for me, Redcoat. Tell no one you saw me here in this private place."

"And once again, I will keep your secret as I have kept all the others."

"Danke, Vincent. *Auf wiedersehen."* As she spoke, she prayed that they would meet again. Someday, somewhere. But the rest of it, what would come if they did meet, on that she could not dwell. It saddened her too much. Hannah dropped to her knees and crawled back the way she had come into her new secret place.

Vincent was delighted at the sight of Hannah's round

118

bottom—so much more womanly now than it had been on *Buttress*—as it wiggled through the gap in the raspberry bushes. God, he liked that girl. Woman, he corrected himself. She was definitely a woman now. Yet she still had that shy smile. She was quick, intelligent. And she had the most amazing unadorned beauty. Being with her was so refreshing; it was something he wanted every day of his life. He would have to get Montmorency to give him this district to patrol. Seeing Hannah once in a while would give meaning to his boring days—though he knew damned well his nights would be aching in more ways than one.

He sighed, waited a few minutes, and then left the copse. As he hurried down the hill to join his regiment, he tried to catch a glimpse of Hannah, but the women all dressed the same and he could not distinguish her from the others. She was not there, he decided. Taller than those who were, he would have seen her had she been mingling with the rest.

The Mennonites served them dinner and Vincent searched for her among the women who waited on him, but she was not there, either. No unmarried woman was, he decided after hearing their chatter. He dared not ask after her, lest the elders know he had been alone with her. Shunning seemed a terrible punishment. He did not wish that on Hannah. He wished her only joy. But he could not imagine her with another man. That, he could not think about.

The regiment slept in the barn. As Vincent and Geoffroy prepared to keep first watch, Geoff stole a few moments to smoke a pipe, a new affectation with him.

"Scott, you've snapped at the men all this evening. What's wrong?"

"Why should anything be wrong?"

"A half a hundred Mennonites and *she's* not among them. Could that be it?"

"Who said she's not among them?"

Geoff perked up. "She is?"

"Yes. But I can't see her alone. It's embarrassing, Geoff! I'm like a schoolboy. Breeches too tight whenever I think of her. Bloody hell!"

"Is this the Scandalous Scott of bawdy fame? Pining after a girl?"

"Eighteen now, Geoff. And you should see her!" Vincent groaned and rubbed the front of his breeches. "Enough! I have to walk this off. I'll patrol the outer fringes."

"From that bulge, it will take three times round!"

It took five.

The next night, Hannah stared up at the ceiling of the communal bedroom she shared with her aunt and four other women. Her heart was full and bewildered. As soon as the Redcoats had ridden out of the settlement, the elders had instructed the children that men such as those were to be pitied because they knew not the ways of the Lord. But Vincent knew His ways. Vincent was very like Samson, strong and secure, a warrior for the right cause. Why, then, should she and the rest of the community ridicule men who would lay down their lives to keep the Mennonite community safe? Once more, she was questioning the Faith and the elders who preached it. Instead of accepting, obeying, she pushed at the rails, wondering what she would do when put to the test, the true test.

Thus far, she had been walking through her duties, performing her responsibilities with little or no thought to her future. Would she profess? Should she?

It was time to make a decision. She just didn't know which one it would be.

Chapter Seven

"*Ach,* Hannah, you make my heart *ubervoll.* To have professed. Ya, that is good. But to accept Jacob. *Ach,* that is better!"

If Aunt Magda's heart was too full, Hannah's was too empty. The decision to profess had kept her up nights, made her days in the grove a miasma of doubt. But in the end, it was not so difficult. She either believed in Christ or she did not. She did. And she was a part of this community. So, it followed like night and day. But when it was announced at services and she took the white prayer cap which showed her a part of the adult community, that had not ended it. Jacob Timmons had come that very night to offer for her hand. And she had accepted . . . like *that.*

Why should she not? Jacob had been shadowing her ever since they had arrived at New Ephrata. And there were few unmarried women in the community. What did it matter that there had never been any mention of love from Jacob? Hannah had never heard that love was necessary in a Mennonite marriage. A woman professed. A man offered. She looked him over, decided whether he would provide well for her and their children, and then decided.

Jacob would do that. He was a good man, a good farmer, a better carpenter. He liked children and played with them often. He was respectful to his mother and father. He was handsome, in his own way. With his beard just beginning to fill out, his uneven jaw took on softer angles and his mouth was not so sour-looking as it once had been. His eyes, too, were nice. Black like a fly's wings they were, with that same kind of sheen to them. His black hair was not yet cropped short—that would come after the marriage service. But it was thick and curly, like his beard would be. He was not so tall as Vincent. In fact, Jacob stood the same height as Hannah and he was stocky, like a bull. Strong like one, too. But most of all, he was *there*. She could do worse.

Then why did she feel so awful when Jacob came calling of an evening? When they walked in the fields together . . . without a chaperone because they were trusted, now that they were officially spoken for . . . they had so little to say to one another.

"The crop this year, by all the signs, it will be very good," Jacob would say. "Enough to feed us all and sell the excess in the city. And next year, we will plant tobacco for to trade with the *Englishen*."

Or . . . *"Mein mutter,* she wants for us to have a triple house. For them and us and Rolf, who is asking for Lisle's hand. We are drawing up the plans now. We will start it in two weeks."

Or . . . "The sow had a sour stomach today. We had to force-feed her and take away her piglets. She squealed up a storm."

How Hannah would have liked to hear something, anything else. She wanted to tell him about Shakespeare and read to him a sonnet. She wanted to tell him about the dreams she had had the night before. She ached to hear soft words and whispered jokes, such as the ones she had shared with Vincent Scott.

The only saving grace to the courting ritual was bundling. Hannah and Jacob were allowed to share a bed on Saturday nights.

In the community home in which Hannah and her aunt lived with five other families, a special room had been set aside. A room which had, until then, never been used. The bundling room was tucked into the eaves, far from the children's room and close to a chimney for warmth. In it, the men had installed a large bed with a double-thick feather mattress. And the women had quilted three coverlets for the bed, each piled one on the other. It was Magda's responsibility to shake out and rotate these quilts so one was not more dusty than the others. Little did Hannah know when she had been enlisted to help her aunt that she would be the first one to use the bed.

The first night Jacob came from his community house to theirs, he was welcomed with a *"sieben-und-sieben"* feast. Seven sweets . . . applesauce, apple butter, sweet small pickles, dried peach slices, pear fritters, currant conserve, precious raisins, and sugared buttered bread. Seven sours . . . sauerkraut, sour pickles, pickled pig's feet, pickled green beans, salted nut mixtures, soured cream, and sauerbraten. Washed down with cider from the cold cellar and accompanied by several kinds of dark bread and mounds of butter, it was the first *"sieben-und-sieben"* to be held in New Ephrata.

Following the feast, the children sat quietly while the men played their fiddles and half the women sang folk songs. The other half were in the large keeping room, cleaning up the leavings from the feast.

"No, Hannah," Magda said, taking a towel from Hannah's hand and shooing her away. "You are not allowed. This is your night. Go . . . go . . . sit with your intended. Enjoy!"

"But, Aunt," she said, "I don't know what to do."

"Let Jacob lead the way, Hannah. He will know what to do."

With a weary, shy heart, Hannah made her way into the communal parlor and found that a place had been kept for her next to Jacob. In the center of the room. Where everyone could see them.

She blushed but walked meekly to her seat. Jacob smiled and took her hand. He held it warmly during the entire hour of singing and fiddle playing. By the time it was over, her palms were sweaty.

But her mouth was dry. And her hair nearly stood on end when Magda came into the room, clapping her hands and saying, "Time for bed."

Dear God, not yet!

"Time for bed, *kinder.*"

Danke, Gott.

"Lisle, you turn down the quilts in the bundling room," Magda ordered. "And while you do it, remember . . . next, 'tis your turn."

"And me for the rail," Pieter Stultz announced. "Jacob, come help me fetch it from the barn."

Hannah sat helplessly as each of the children left the

room with a backward glance and a giggle. Her cheeks flamed. And she still did not know what to do!

Magda and Sophie Stultz, Pieter's oldest married daughter, came and put a wool-wrapped bundle in Hannah's lap. Hannah looked down at it and then up into her aunt's eyes.

"For the bundling. Each woman made stitches in it. And even some of the *kinder* added a stitch or two," Magda said.

Hannah opened it with fingers which had forgotten how to untie a bow! After three false starts, Sophie laughed.

"Just like me on my bundling night!"

She stooped and helped fold back the wool. Inside was a soft muslin night dress. Plain, but beautifully stitched. Its bodice was made of dozens of tiny scraps, each quilted into a pattern she had come to know as the "eternity" stitch . . . circles around circles, signifying life eternal.

"It's beautiful! Like fairy dust or choir robes in the Catholic Church."

Magda frowned. *"Nein.* 'Tis not of the world. Its beauty is in its purpose, *liebchen.* The quilting, later it will keep you warm. For tonight, you will wear it under your bodice and skirt."

Hannah's head snapped up. Of course! She had forgotten. They would be fully clothed this night. Only after their union had been blessed would they be allowed to . . . to . . .

Oh, good heavens, what had she done? Pieter came in carrying what looked like a table-sized rail; but Hannah knew it was no more than a foot wide and the length of the bed. He and Jacob carried it solemnly up the stairs . . . as solemnly as they could with giggles coming from the *kindergarten*.

"You may change in the kitchen, Hannah," Magda said.

The kitchen was dark, only one candle lit. And it was private. For the first time all evening, Hannah was out of the glare of staring eyes. But it didn't matter. She felt as though they were there, peeking over the rocks in the huge kitchen fireplace, floating on the beamed ceiling, peeping between the chinks in the half-logged walls. She shuddered and tried to forget they were there . . . weren't there . . . were only there in her imagination.

But her fingers wouldn't work any better in private than they had in the parlor. She made a mess of the ties on her bodice and from her impatience with herself, nearly tore away the plain black strands.

"You are making *widdersinnig*, Hannah," she told herself. "This is not so bad. Everyone else has done it."

But everyone else had done it with someone they considered special. And the only man she considered special wore a red coat and was out of her reach forever. She was settling for second best, she knew. Worse, she was giving Jacob second place in her heart.

And like being locked in the hold of the ship . . . no one knew.

Her hands stilled and she stared up at the ceiling, up to where the bundling room was, up to her future. And further up, through the earthly confines of the communal house, into the star-filled heavens.

She whispered, brokenly, achingly, *"Ach, Gott,* why did You send me someone I cannot have? And why did You give me someone I do not want enough?"

But like the other eternal questions which had plagued her all her life . . .

—Why was it necessary for her father to be taken?
—Why was it necessary for her mother to suffer?
—Why did good people have to die?
—Why were bad people rewarded in this life?
—Why was the sky blue and the grass green? And what were colors, anyway?

. . . these two particular questions remained unanswered except in the tiny warmth which washed over her, allowing her to finish undressing.

She slipped on the "practical" nightgown, made beautiful by caring hands, and smoothed it over her hips. *To hide this was such a shame*. But it would be visible another day . . . another evening . . . not many weeks hence. After the house was finished, they would exchange simple vows in front of the community in the parlor of *her* house, and the wedding feast would go on all day. And later, they would have a bed much like the one upstairs, only without the bundling board.

Once more fully clothed, Hannah thought to slip out of the keeping room and up the central stairs. But voices from the parlor told her Aunt Magda and the others were waiting. Had the gladiators felt this way when they walked through the tunnels to the games which would claim their lives or give them glory? And which was she to have that night and the rest of her life?

She already knew what the elders believed—that to live the Way was to begin the trek to eternal glory. But this bundling . . . was it not a strange way to begin it?

With a candle in his right hand, Jacob awaited her at the bottom of the stairs. He held out his left hand. Hannah looked at it as if she had never seen a man's hand before. She looked into Jacob's black eyes and saw more emotion there than she had ever thought possible. He trusted her and himself. His decision had been the correct one for him, after all. She could not disappoint him. So, laying her hand in his, she dutifully walked up the stairs behind the man who was to be her husband.

The bed was prepared. The bundling rail had been slid into the grooves at headboard and footrail. It divided the bed in half, and perched atop the quilts, which had been turned down on each side.

Jacob placed the candle on the small pie-shell table next to the bed, indicating that she was to sleep closest to the door. It was a ritual, one she knew was designed to give the wife access to the children and the house, so that if anything happened during the night, she would not have to disturb her husband to attend to it. Dutiful once more, she sat on the edge of the bed, removed her shoes, and slid primly under the quilts. Jacob covered her with them. She was only aware that he had taken his place beside her when the bed creaked and gave way on his side. She could not see over the rail. So she closed her eyes and waited for sleep to come.

"We start our house tomorrow, Hannah," Jacob said. He leaned over the rail and down, to brush a kiss across her forehead. "You will make for me the breakfast and dinner, *Ja?*"

"*Ja,*" she said.

He smiled and plopped back onto his side. "*Outen* the candle, Hannah."

"*Ja,* Jacob."

She raised herself onto her elbow and blew out the candle. Then, like the board between them, she lay in the dark, until Jacob's soft snores lulled her to sleep.

The rooster woke them both in the morning. And as

was usual, Hannah stumbled out of bed before she realized where she was. When she did, her head snapped back and whirled around. Jacob stood there with a sweet grin, his hands quickly tying together his pants and shirt. Her eyes dropped and she stooped to grab her shoes.

"Gruel and coffee in ten minutes," Hannah mumbled and hurried from the room, her shoes in her trembling hands.

After relieving herself in the comfort room attached to the rear of the house, she washed in a bucket at the back door, then joined the other women in the kitchen. Magda was already stirring the contents of a huge pot hung from a hook over the fire.

"Scrape the cinnamon, Hannah," Magda said, as if last night were like any other. "And mix with the sugar."

"*Ja, Tante,* like always."

Like always. Everything like always. Nothing changed. Every day another small stitch in the long road to the great stitch of eternity.

She set out a row of wooden spoons next to the wooden trenchers for the children. And when the gruel was finished, she helped her aunt spoon it into great bowls, one of which was taken to each man as he came down for his first breakfast. Each mumbled a short blessing, then quickly they ate. Quickly, too, they left for their chores.

"Today we will cut short our labors," Pieter said. "We will all be helping with the house raising."

It always amazed Hannah how prepared these men were to put up a house or barn or outbuilding or shed as quickly as they did. Every day since they had arrived, some trees had been felled, their branches and bark removed. Every day, boards and beams had been cut and hewn with great double saws and hatchets, and the boards and beams laid aside in the barn to dry out. Every day, nails had been forged, pegs whittled, windows made all of a size, doors banged together, stair treads cut to size. There were now enough supplies stacked in the barn to build several houses.

And today they would build hers.

It began after the cows and goats had been milked, pigs slopped, cheese set to curdle.

The men worked to clear a large section of the acreage across from the communal houses. Hannah was for a moment anxious that her precious raspberry patch would be destroyed, but the house was to the left of the patch and her secret grove was safe.

It always amazed Hannah how building a house was unlike building a barn, but not that unlike. The foundation went in first, each man digging furiously until a cellar was excavated in which a man could stand comfortably. Then the dirt walls were lined with large rocks which had come from the fields. To keep the rocks from falling, some of the men would chisel flat surfaces on them, others would chink the connections with a mortar of mud, clay, animal hair, and waste fabric. Then, beams to settle in all the corners and along the rock face. Then cross beams to square the first level of the house. Then flat timber to make the first floor.

Twenty men and boys working from dawn to mid-morning had the cellar finished and the first floor on.

Meanwhile, the women worked in the kitchens of the three communal houses to prepare the giant breakfast, lunch, and supper which their men would need. Chickens were killed, plucked, and boiled. A ham was dragged from the smokehouse and cut into slabs. Some children fed the chickens and brought in the eggs for the puddings and pies. Other children weeded the garden and brought in great baskets of peas and beans and greens to be boiled with bacon and ham. And the young women, those preparing to choose their own husbands as Hannah had done, were set to make the crusty brown bread which was always present on a Mennonite table. But today they would add raisins to it, because today was a feast day.

The cooking went on all morning, and Hannah and Lisle were allowed to bring coffee and tea to the men in the cleared field across the road.

"That's your house, Hannah," Lisle said. "Imagine, a house of your own."

"To share with Jacob's parents and brothers and sisters. To share with you, Lisle. My own, I would not call it." Hannah shrugged. "But, it is smaller than the communal one. And we each will have a small section to ourselves."

"How good that will be, *ja?*"

"Ja." *If you say so.* Hannah couldn't . . . or wouldn't . . . think that far ahead.

By mid-morning, the men came to get their second breakfast. Ham, bacon, beans, eggs, potatoes, maize fritters, and more gruel. And gallons of coffee and tea, whitened with their own cream and sweetened heavily with sugar.

"It is enough you have done, Hannah," Pieter Stultz said. "You must come and watch us put the walls up."

"Ja, she may watch," Magda said. "But her hands

may not be idle. She may sit in the shade, pick over the beans and shell the peas." She handed her niece a giant box of newly-harvested vegetables and two large wooden bowls. With that secret smile which all the women had had for Hannah that morning, Magda urged, "Go, go . . . make yourself useful while you admire the building of your new home."

It was a wonder, what the men were doing. Instead of building walls on the house, they built them on the ground, making one full skeleton before they hoisted it into position. Ropes and pulleys helped lessen the weight, but the men's muscles bulged under their shirts, and many wiped their heads over and over with large muslin handkerchiefs. And no wonder—it was late August and the sun was fierce!

By the time Hannah had finished the vegetables, three of the skeletons were erected. By lunchtime, all four.

"The roof tresses, is all," Jacob said to Hannah as they took their bowls and sat under the chestnut tree which would shade the front of their new house. He wolfed down his food as if he were starving. His bowl was empty before she had taken more than four mouthfuls.

"Papa, Rolph, and I, we will position the first of them and peg them good. Then all the men and boys will cover the walls with the boards. And last the roof. The windows and doors will come later. Papa and Rolf will help me with the putting in of them. It will be a good house, *ja,* Hannah?"

"*Ja,* Jacob. A very good house."

"And you will be happy there, *ja?*"

He asked it with such hope that Hannah realized he

knew she was less than enthusiastic about their betrothal. She did not realize he was so perceptive. She thought him a farmer, a man of the earth, little tuned to the thoughts and feelings of those around him. But he was demonstrating that Hannah did not know these people as well as she had thought she did. He cared for her. Truly cared. And he wanted her to be happy.

"*Ja*, Jacob, I will be happy there."

He let out an audible whoosh of relief and jumped to his feet. "Stay here and watch me peg the first timber, Hannah."

"I must help the others . . ."

"Please?"

She smiled into his sparkling black eyes. "*Ja*, Jacob. The first peg. Then I must help cook the supper."

He bent and gave her their second kiss. She did not even feel his lips. It was another soft brush of his beard, this time against her cheek.

So different from the kiss of Vincent Scott! So shy. So unschooled.

She finished eating her lunch and fed the leavings to the chickens and barn cats. Then she settled in the shade and watched her soon-to-be husband as he bounded up onto the rafters with his father and Rolf and helped hoist the roof tresses in place.

"Sending the mallet up," Pieter called.

The mallet was tied into a rope, which Pieter flung up to Jacob. The first throw missed by a foot and the men below laughed.

Rolf blew the air between his teeth in a loud sound which resembled a horse breathing hard. "The pigs can hope that you are at the end of the rope during slaughtering!"

"One more try," Jacob cried. "I will catch!"

"Make it good," Rolf shouted.

Pieter wound up and threw and Jacob reached for the mallet. Reached farther out than he had before. Reached and slipped, and fell off the roof.

It was the length of five stories that he fell.

Slowly. Like a dream that goes nowhere. Like a nightmare that never ends.

Chapter Eight

Magda adjusted Hannah's prayer cap and sighed. "He was a good man, Hannah."

"*Ja, Tante.* A good man."

"We will remember the joyous times with him. How happy a man he was."

"*Ja, Tante.* Happy."

"Hannah! Do you hear me?"

"I hear."

As *Gott* heard me. Heard what was in my heart and took the indecision away. Gave Jacob a joyous day for his last on earth, so that he wouldn't know unhappiness with a wife who did not love him. She would carry that knowledge to the grave with her. But the grave would not be with Jacob.

"You will wear mourning, Hannah."

"I know, *Tante.*"

"Since you are not yet married, it will only be for six months."

"I know."

"The other young men, they will be coming. One has

already approached me . . ."

"*Nein!* Not now. Not ever!"

"Hannah, it will heal, this sorrow. And Jacob would not want you to be alone, unwed. He would approve for you to accept another husband."

"Not now, Aunt Magda. I could not think on it now."

"All right. We will leave it for now."

But not for long, her voice warned. And Hannah was resigned to the betrothal ritual being performed all over again. She felt a coward inside but for the first time in her life she knew it took great courage to pick up the pieces and go on . . . merely go on.

She wanted to throw things, shout, scream, rail at God. But the community would be shocked by such expressions of feeling. A good Mennonite woman kept her passions bottled up, ready for her relations with her husband . . . which were *wunderbar,* according to what had been said . . . and what had merely been implied. And some passion was expected in her prayers to God, who gave all the goodness in life, all the joy . . . so Mennonite women gave Him back in full measure.

In all other things, a Mennonite woman kept tightly clasped into herself the true way she felt. She was stoic, silent, a rock on which the family could always depend. As they could depend on a good Mennonite man. There was no deviation from that decorum which characterized her people. They tolerated Hannah's "behindedness" but they would tolerate naught else. She must conform, as she already had. In that conformity lay peace and protection.

Do I have the courage these women show? I do not

feel it yet. Dear God, send it quickly or I will go mad.

Blessedly short was the graveside service for Jacob. Bishop Stultz read from Psalms. Pieter read from Matthew. Hannah did not hear the words. Like a rock, she stood beside Rolf and Lisle. Like a rock, walked stiffly into the communal house and to her place beside Jacob's mother in the "widow's room." Like a rock, received everyone as they whispered their words of condolence, shook their heads, and left her for the next one's words. They did not expect her to do more than smile and nod her head. So, that is what she did. Seventy-four men, women, and children. Seventy-four staccato sentences. Seventy-four nods and weak smiles.

She sat there silently all morning, holding Frau Timmons's hand, giving her a cup of coffee, a bite of bread, a piece of apple. At the sound of the midday bell calling everyone to the luncheon table, Frau Timmons smiled and stretched.

"We will join the others now, Hannah. Come, let us break bread with our families and drink a cup of sweet coffee for my sweet son, Jacob."

"I would like to be alone, *bitte.*"

"After midday meal, Hannah. Then you may mourn in your room. But now we must smile and get through this one last rite. It is fitting, Hannah. Christ had His last supper."

And Jacob had his and didn't know how bitter it was.

"And Christ knew He was going to die. How much better it is for us, not to know."

Hannah knew she wouldn't be able to swallow. She could not! But she did. She did because she was under

139

observation by rounded, worried, child-sized eyes that looked to her as an example. Hannah had come through the fire; she had survived being lost in Philadelphia, being pawed by that awful man in the inn. She could get through this.

Later in the raspberry grove, she closed her eyes, balled her fists, threw herself on the ground, and wept silently. The screams she held in, more for fear someone would find her hiding place than for decorum's sake. She did not rail at God. He already knew her heart. She did not talk to Jacob. If he was where they all intended to be, he knew her heart, too. She hoped it did not sadden him, that dreadful knowing.

She made a vow. A promise.

She would be true to her feelings, to what she thought was right, not what others did. There were no unmarried women in the community? There would be one. If she could not have the man she wanted, she would have no others. To accept another man's offer when she knew she didn't love him was *sin*. She would not, could not, allow herself to commit that sin merely because the community expected it.

She would be the *verrucktlicht* in this community. The crazy one. No more sinning against man and God. No more!

She slept then, and woke only when she heard the thundering sound of horses' hooves. The Redcoats coming back.

Vincent!

She smiled. He would know where to find her.

She sat up, took off her prayer cap, and shook it out. Her hands fumbled in her hair, tucking in wayward strands and brushing away pieces of leaves, dirt, and pine needles. She did not want to be dirty for Vincent. She settled her prayer cap back on her head and heard the first shot. And then the second. And the third. And dozens more.

Shouts and more shouts.

—*"Nein!"*

—*"Ach, Gott, nein!"*

—"Not the *kinder*. Not the *kinder!"*

Hannah peered through the bushes. She could not see clearly. What she could see were blurs of movement. Men on horseback, painted men. Indians? But not all Indians. Some were as farmers. They were shooting! Shooting as they rode through the settlement. Shooting every way, everywhere.

Why? Why?

They ran them down . . . the children, the women, the men. The *defenseless* men. Defenseless because they had been too busy wresting a productive settlement out of this earth. Too busy to do more than talk about defenses. None had been built. And now, they were . . . they were . . .

Hannah's soul screamed along with the slaughter of her people. She scrambled to get out of the copse. And stopped. To do what, when she got below? To be another of the victims?

Nein! She must survive. She must pray for her people's souls. She must tell what had happened. She must warn the others, those who would come after the community of New Ephrata. She must make them understand that they must . . . they *must* have secure hiding places and noncombatant traps. Traps for horses to fall into. Traps for men. Snares like those

141

they used to catch rabbits and squirrels. Something . . . anything!

She would get out of here. She would go back to Germantown. She would bear witness. And she would avenge their deaths.

Even as she thought it, Hannah knew there was no Mennonite who would seek vengeance. But is it vengeance to want justice? To want to see the killers punished for the wanton way they butchered innocent human beings? Turn the other cheek? *Nein*. Now, justice must be done. And she knew who to go to to wrest it from this sacrilegious slaughter.

Vincent.

But first Hannah had to hide like a frightened animal and smell the smoke of the burning barns and houses. She had to hear lambs bleating, screaming as the children had screamed. Had to smell the lambs being roasted to feed the ignominious infidels!

For three days, the renegades stormed their way through the settlement Their whoops and hollers did not abate, not even when they mounted up and rode off. They laughed all the way up the ridge to the southeast. Laughed so loudly, their voices echoed down into the valley which had once been New Ephrata.

Hannah had not eaten or drunk in three days. She had hardly slept, expecting any moment to be found by those barbarians. Expecting they could smell her from her leavings . . . the body had rhythms of its own.

But they did not find her. And after waiting patiently for several hours, afraid they might come back, she finally decided she had to take the chance. One more night and she would die of thirst, she was sure. So, taking her courage in her hands, she crawled out of her hidey-hole and stumbled down to the farm.

She avoided looking at the bodies around her. She did not have to look. The smell was all.

She found a few utensils and scooped water from the brook bordering the farm. Her overwhelming thirst slaked for the moment, she looked for food and found cold roast lamb left on the dead fire. Although it infuriated her to handle something so tainted with sin, Hannah ate it and some of the spinach which still struggled up to the sun.

Then she began to bury the dead.

It was an awful job, made worse by the memories which haunted everything she did.

That battered wagon in the shade of the willow had been made by Jacob for his little brother.

Yellow, the barn cat who was Magda's favorite, was now a heap of streaked red and yellow fur.

In the corner of their pen, twenty-nine piglets, every one with a name given by one of the community's *kinder*.

She almost stepped on a top Rolf had made for his and Lisle's first child.

She found its maker under the chestnut tree by the side of the new house, cradling Lisle in his arms. Lisle's skirt was above her waist, her stockings torn, blood on her thighs. And on the chestnut tree . . . Pieter . . . *Gott in himmel!* His arms were outstretched, pinned there with dozens of arrows. She closed all their staring eyes and whispered a prayer.

But Magda was nowhere to be found.

Hannah guessed that she had been caught unaware where she always was, in the kitchen of the house, cooking or preparing the meals. And the house had been burned down around her.

Ah, God, that poor, wonderful soul!

There were not many implements the marauders had left unbroken. Hannah dug with broken spade, slipping it into the soft ground of the kitchen garden. Still, it was draining work for an eighteen-year-old who had not eaten, drunk, or slept in three days. She mounded the dirt on the side, went four feet down and as far across as she was tall, then stopped, exhausted.

She could not do it! She was too weak, too much a woman.

She flopped on the open grave and had her first real cry. She cried for Jacob. She cried for Lisle. She cried for the children who would know nothing more. And she cried for herself, for her inability to do what needed to be done.

Ach, Gott . . . mei hilfen!"

If God heard, he had a sense of humor in the help he sent her. She felt a hard, dry nose nuzzle her and looked up into the watery eyes of Hambone, Rolf's old horse, who must have been let out to pasture since he was too old to do hard farm work. Where had he been hiding since the devastation started? Wherever it was, he missed being taken along with his fellow horses to God knew where, with the very worst of men.

Hambone threw back his head and whinnied.

He was here, he seemed to say. Hambone, her help? *Ja.* Too old to pull a plow through hardscrabble earth, he was not too old to pull one through soft, already cultivated ground.

It took them all afternoon. But by nightfall, they were finished and she could put a marker on the kitchen garden turned into communal grave.

144

She fed Hambone first, with what scraps of oats and grain she could gather from the fields, then haltered him and tied him securely to a tree outside her copse. Then she gathered all the food she could find, the best being that in the dry cold-storage bin near the kitchen well. She found dried beef and fruit, enough for two days. She packed it in a grain sack and brought it into the copse. For her supper, she had the leavings from the fire and more water.

The next morning, she said prayers for the dead, packed up her food, jumped up onto Hambone's back, and headed out into the wilderness. She had only one place to go, back to Germantown, where Uncle Franz was closing down his shop and preparing to join the community in New Ephrata. They had had a letter from him last week. He promised to be there by All Soul's Day, four weeks hence. She had three weeks, then, to get there before he set out. Three weeks to find the route they had taken from Germantown to New Ephrata. Three weeks to retrace their steps.

But she had not been watching closely and she did not know the proper way.

She knew only that she must go East. Toward the rising sun, always toward the rising sun. Toward Germantown and safety.

Chapter Nine

Vincent Scott smelled the devastation before he saw it. It permeated the air like spoiled chicken.

"Now, Scott," Geoffrey warned. "It might not be bad. They might be doing some slaughtering. 'Tis a farm, after all."

"'Tis New Ephrata, Geoff. I cannot take the chance!" He wheeled his horse and galloped next to his troops. "Be on the lookout! Stay alive." He cantered back to Geoff. "You take them in. I'm going on ahead."

But Geoff grabbed at his reins. "No, Scott, You'll not go alone. He might still be there, you know. And if 'tis bad, 'twill await your arrival."

"I have to know!"

"You'll do no good like this! We'll spur these men on better together."

Geoff was right. The troops had been lagging because they were exhausted. They had been chasing from farm to outpost to settlement—all in pursuit of an elusive character the British garrison at Fort Bedford had named Red Flame. It was a sobriquet the brigand had earned not only because of his red skin, but because of the conflagrations he had started and the blood he had spilled.

Why? What drove the man? What drove his followers? What horror lived in his mind, to do what he had done here to innocent children, unarmed men and women. Vincent felt a white hot heat explode in his head. Red Flame had begun to circumscribe a circle of destruction which encompassed only the German settlers. The English, he swooped down on, took their food and valuables, but left alive. Shaken by their experience they were, but alive to describe him and his band. But the Germans! Worse, the Mennonites. They had no weapons, could not fight back if they chose. And, of course, they did not choose.

Vincent did not understand this. Or perhaps he understood it too well. There had been a time in his life—the time with Clarisse—when he had chosen not to fight back, when he had taken no posture rather than an aggressive one. He had lost almost everything then. And that experience had fueled his desire to go into the military, a place where he had no choice, where to kill was necessary, where to lay down his arms was pure suicide. He could not tell which was the better choice. Certainly, his not choosing to fight Clarisse's charges had given him a feeling of self-worth. He had not lowered himself to her level. But it had brought ridicule and taunts from those in his circle of acquaintances who had also chosen—chosen to believe the lies from Clarisse's lips. 'Twas then he felt damned more by himself, by his non-choice, than in what she had done. And he was so furious at himself for what he had not done that his relationships with other women had forever after been tainted.

Until he'd met Hannah.

Ah, God! Over that rise was New Ephrata, Hannah and her people. Unarmed Mennonites. Facing Red Flame.

No, by God, they were not over the hill. For once, Geoffroy was wrong. The New Ephrata settlers had already faced Red Flame. Regardless of Geoffroy's words of caution, that much Vincent could tell from the stench and the grey smoke which hung in a pall over the place where the settlement should be. It was Red Flame's signature, his challenge if you would, telling those who were chasing him, *I have done it again. Catch me if you can.*

Vincent did not need a vivid imagination to know what he would find. Seven weeks ago a survivor had stumbled into Fort Bedford with news of a massacre at Twin Brooks. Mennonites, forty families, wiped out in a matter of minutes, he had said. The descriptions of the punishment meted out by Red Flame sent chills through the fort. No man wanted to be sent out on the chase after the renegade band who had done such grisly things. And when Montmorency had called Scott into his office, twenty-seven other lieutenants had breathed sighs of relief.

Vincent had stood there, resigned, yet at the same time excited. If he caught this devil—and Vincent was certain with the right approach he would catch the Indian—then Vincent could do something for Hannah and her people. So when Montmorency did not mention the assignment but instead handed Vincent a citation and smiled broadly, Vincent was caught off-guard.

Montmorency held out his hand, "Congratulations, *Captain* Scott."

Vincent shook his head. "I don't understand, sir."

"No more *sir,* Vincent. Gage finally heard about your heroism on *Buttress,* so he's given you the swift rise in rank that you deserve." Montmorency snorted. "Only took him two years this time. But at least he didn't completely forget who you are and where you've been."

Vincent knew that the sarcasm was for the six years Montmorency had been stuck at the rank of Captain. He had long been eclipsed by others, and the junior officers wondered if he'd ever see his Major or Colonel insignia. Geoffroy had intimated that Monty must have gotten the General's daughter in the family way. Why else the long wait?

"You'll have five units under your command," Montmorency said. "Who do you want as your lieutenants?"

"Geoffroy, sir. And Abbott, Walsh, Parker, and Billington."

"Good men. I'll see to their transfer."

"Geoffroy's promotion, sir?"

"Ah, yes. You tell him."

"Yes, sir."

"And Scott?"

"Yes, sir?"

"Don't call me sir."

"Yes, si . . . yes, Monty."

Montmorency's aide came in then, with a tray on which sat a large bottle of the best Jamaican rum and two tumblers.

"A toast, Scott."

"What shall we toast, Monty?"

"To the king and to the swift capture of the newest villain on the frontier."

"Here, here."

The rum spread warmth all the way to Vincent's toes and back, and he took a second large swallow to feel it course through his blood. His tongue felt numb but his fingers tingled by the time he and Montmorency had finished their third glass. Monty's words had lost their usual upper class crispness.

"Don' envy your new job, no sir, I don'" Monty said. "Not what we're here for, runnin' down those bess locked in Bedlam. Nay, I don' envy you one bit, Scott. 'Twill be hell."

And that was how Lieutenant Vincent Scott, of His Majesty's 42nd Fusilliers, had become Captain Vincent Scott, hunter of renegade Indians. Hell, not even that much. Only one renegade Indian and his motley group of followers.

Godawful duty it was, too. One hundred miles of frontier to cover between the fort and the settlements. Two hundred miles from the settlements to Philadelphia. With only five units of forty men each? It was a nightmare. In the end, they had stumbled on the swath of horror that Red Flame had scorched through the Pennsylvania frontier.

Vincent gave spurs to his horse, Nightwind, and yanked back on his reins. Nightwind reared and Vincent pulled him to earth with a crash of his hooves. "I don't give a damn what you said, Geoff, I'm going on ahead. Hurry the men along or I'll have their heads!"

"Aye, Scott!"

Geoffroy squinted against the noon sun and followed

Vincent's progress. He shook his head and sighed. "All right, men. Pick it up, now. Double time. The Captain's got a lady over that rise and he needs to know we care." He sent the message down the line. "Put some life in it!"

"Only to stumble on the dead," a voice drifted back to him.

Geoff wheeled and stormed down the line. "Who said that? Damn your eyes, man, what we do is give them a decent farewell. Hope that someone will do the same for you if you end up on a battlefield with your toes turned up."

"Aye, sir," the same voice said.

A young voice. New minted. Geoff expected to see peach fuzz on his cheeks and was proven right. Paltray, the son of an indentured estate grounds keeper. Thought he'd joined the army to live a life of adventure and ended up here, in the worst duty Geoff had ever seen.

Geoff snapped him a salute. "Lead the unit, Paltray."

"Oh! Aye, sir."

A reward and a punishment in one swoop. Vincent had taught him to deal with the men under him like that. It would keep the man wondering what had happened and keep his mind on the business at hand.

Ten minutes later, they crested the rise and looked down on what had been New Ephrata.

"Fan out and search, but keep a steady eye out," Geoff ordered.

It was an order directly opposite to everything the British foot soldier was trained to do. But Vincent had learned quickly that a coordinated hit-from-cover approach was Red Flame's style. So, Scott's regiment had long been drilled in diversionary tactics.

The men immediately followed orders. They had had seven weeks experience at this—they knew what to do.

But today was different.

Paltray came back breathless. "Can't find the settlers, sir. Not a hair of them. Could they have gotten away?"

"Did the Lord give you two heads and not one of them with an ounce of sense?" He waved his hand at the scene and snarled, "Red Flame's work, for certain. Now find his victims!"

"Aye, sir."

Geoff went in trace of Vincent. There was no sense looking for him in the leavings of the houses or the smoldering barn. He knew his friend. Like as naught, he would be in that raspberry patch he'd described to Geoff. Hannah's secret place. He'd be hoping against hope that she'd be there. Or wringing out of his guts a dirge for the girl.

Geoffroy clucked and shook his head. Too bad. Too awful. Vincent loved this brown-eyed lass. Wouldn't admit it, of course. But loved her, nonetheless. She had broken through that toughness he had with other women. She hadn't known she was doing it, but by her innocent goodness she had brushed softly against Vincent's heart and stolen it. Completely. Would that every man could find someone like her. But to lose her like this. Christ! If Vincent had been ice and iron before, Geoff hated to think what he'd be now.

Twelve paces to the left of the chestnut tree, fourteen paces up the hill. Geoff scanned the bramble patch. "You in there, Scott?"

"Aye."

"Coming out?"

"Aye."

Blood on Vincent's face and jagged rips on the shoulders of his uniform told Geoff that Vincent had barreled his way into the bushes.

"You searched the settlement?" Geoff asked.

"Aye."

"Anything?"

"Naught."

"Red Flame ever take prisoners before?"

"Over seventy of them? Don't be daft!" Vincent grasped Geoff's right hand. "My God, Geoff, where is she? Is she dead? Did that monster take her? Or did God come down and swoop them all up out of that monster's clutches?"

"Now who's daft, Scott? Get hold of yourself, man!"

"Why? So I can deal with—" His arm and eyes took in the mangled farm and all it had contained. "—with this? This hell which should have been a paradise? Why should I be the one to have control when all around me is in chaos!" He lifted his head and hissed into the heavens. "Jesus, God, why did You let this happen?"

"You know there's no answer to that, Scott. Never had been. Never will be."

"I know only that I must make someone pay for this. Red Flame. He'll know me by name before I'm through with him. By name, by God!"

Lieutenant Billington, over six feet and blessed with legs and arms which didn't move in coordinated ways, raced awkwardly up the hill to meet Geoffroy and Vincent.

"Sir," he said, snapping to a correct salute.

154

Vincent hurt so much he almost wanted to punch the young man, who was a good officer and deserved better. So Vincent steeled himself and became Billington's senior, a role he did not relish this moment. "Yes, Billington, what is it?"

"The kitchen garden, sir. 'Tis no kitchen garden, sir."

"Suppose you tell us what it is, Billington."

"Think you should see it, sir."

He looked at the anxious young officer, at the way his green eyes would meet neither Geoff's nor his superior officer's, and felt a moment of irrational hatred. "Out with it, Goddamn it!"

Geoff's gaze snapped around, filled with condemnation.

"Right," Vincent said. "We can't kill the messenger." He strode away from Billington and Geoff. "But I will kill Red Flame. Before I'm posted somewhere else, he'll know my steel." All kinds of steel.

The two hundred men in his regiment were gathered in small clusters around the spot where New Ephrata's kitchen garden once had been. Gathered round, but several paces away, they stood or sat. None snapped to attention when he approached, though most watched him warily. The others could not take their eyes off the mounded earth in front of them.

He had not paid it mind when he'd ridden Nightwind into the settlement. He had assumed it had been readied for a new crop. But this was August. What good farmer would plow up his garden in the middle of the harvest season? Yet a plow stood to one side. Beside it, a shovel. The plow and harness were for a work horse, obviously. And the shovel could have been left by anyone. But there was something else beside them, something he had never seen before. A flat, wide wooden board with a strange groove in the middle.

Vincent knelt to examine the something else when Paltray cautiously approached. He cleared his throat.

"'Tis a curious thing, sir. I've only seen one like it once before, when my father had a large root cellar to dig. See, this flat board affixed to the front of the plow will push a whole swath of dirt up and over to the side. Works almost like a huge shovel if the horse goes slow enough, and the man behind the plow works fast enough to push the dirt off the front of the blade."

The way he described it, Vincent saw the workings immediately. But he didn't want to believe its use.

"Show me," he ordered.

"I'll need a horse, sir."

"Get Nightwind," Vincent ordered another of his men.

The horse was brought quickly and Paltray snapped the harness to him. Then he brought the board in line with the plow and forced it onto the front, at a place where the groove made a tight fit for the plow. He stood to the left of and behind the plow and clicked to Nightwind.

"Jesus, no!" Vincent shouted. "Not in the garden. Pick another spot."

"Oh, of course, sir. I didn't think."

Working in a patch which was now a trampled mass of herbs and flowers, within minutes Paltray had dug a trench the width of the board.

"The deeper you go," he said, "the harder it gets to control. You have to shovel off the excess as fast as it builds up."

"But you can make the swath deeper?"

"Yes, sir. Deep as you want it to be."

Vincent hunkered down and stared at the kitchen garden mound. His heart felt shattered. There was no other explanation for what he was seeing, but he wished it nonetheless. Finally, when he could stand it no more, he whispered it into the air he forced himself to breathe. "A grave. A grave for all of them."

Geoff came and put his hand on Vincent's shoulder. "I'm sorry, Scott."

"That bastard. That vicious, mad bastard." He picked up a handful of dirt and let it sift through fingers which he no longer felt. "Who did this, Geoff? Who buried them?"

"One of the men, surely, Scott. Who else would have the strength?"

Paltray unharnessed Nightwind and set the plow to one side. He reached into his back pocket and removed a square packet. "I think whoever did it left this, sir. I found it jammed into the earth back there at the end of the grave."

Vincent took the packet and brushed at it absent-mindedly. "Gentlemen," he said. "We shall have a prayer service. Geoff, will you lead it?"

"Aye, Scott."

Geoffroy began with the simple opening of the Twenty-third Psalm and the entire company joined to complete it. Vincent said naught, felt all. As the holy words droned on, his fingers traced the indentations on the edge of the packet. Over and over, they formed shapes, until something transferred to his brain and he knew what he held. Then his eyes dropped to the front of the packet—the book—for confirmation.

"Sweet Jesus!"

He passed the book to Geoff, who stopped speaking in mid-sentence. The Lord's Prayer trailed off as each man realized that something of import had occurred. They watched as Vincent smiled broadly. Smiled, and threw back his head to shout.

"*Paradise Lost!* By God, Geoff, she's alive! She dug this grave." Vincent grabbed the book and kissed it, dirt and all. "A few pence, it cost me. Her treasure, she called it. *Paradise Lost.* Oh, my God! *Paradise Lost!*" He jammed the book into the kit bag hanging from his saddle, and turned to Geoff. "Finish the service."

"Aye, Scott."

So, Vincent thought, Hannah had dug the grave. Hannah. That sweet soul, doing that. Probably used up all her strength to do it, too. But she had to have had a horse. So she wasn't on foot, wherever she was. That meant he had to look for hoof prints. But this was a settlement. How would he know which hoof prints were hers, which the red devil's, which just ordinary farm comings and goings? He pondered it for some time, then realized he had been looking at the answer all along.

The newly dug and mounded earth.

Footprints and hoof prints.

Circling, circling round the thing.

Vincent walked away from Geoff. Keeping his eyes on the indentations near the mound, he searched until he found good, clean prints which showed clearly the complete depression in the soil which the horse had made. With one finger, he traced the shapes and found one very different from the rest. One of the shoes had a chip on the left, four on the right. One nail hole went deeper than the others, so it hadn't been a work horse, else these conscientious Mennonites would have changed the shoes long ago. He followed the distinctive tracks, hunkering down when necessary in order to discern this particular print from all the others in the yard. The worn-out indentations led to the chestnut tree. Whatever horse had been there had trampled the ground a bit. There were oats, some hay. And the leavings of a hasty meal.

Then he saw the dainty foot prints. Hannah's. He'd wager his life on them. She had stood here, probably filled a provision sack and hung it round the horse's neck. The hoof prints went deeper into the soil at one point, and Vincent could see her grasping the horse round the neck and pulling herself onto the old horse's back, throwing her leg over to ride astride as she had done in Philadelphia. The unusual tracks were easier to follow now. They went out of the compound, southeast.

Damn, he should have been allowed to bring an Indian guide with the regiment. By some magic and many years' experience, the Indian would be able to tell when she had left. Vincent, however, could only hope it wasn't too long ago, or he'd never find her.

His head came up and he stared into the distance. *"Ja,* Hannah. I will find you."

He strode back to Geoff and the men. "Find some food and make a meal," he ordered Billington. "Geoff, come with me." He led Geoff back to Hannah's grove and stared from it down into the burned-out farm. "She must have been here, Geoff, hiding the way she always did, reading her secret books, dreaming a bit. And then all hell broke loose. What had it taken to keep hidden? What courage in that small body! She would have been killed, had she rushed into the conflagration. Her thoughts. Can you imagine the pain she felt? Imagine the feeling of unworthiness, to stay alive when all others died. Imagine the strength and bravery and stiff-backed determination. To live! To live to bury the dead. Jesus! What kind of woman is she?"

Geoffroy smiled. For the first time Vincent had referred to Hannah as a woman. But he smiled most for the pride and respect which had crept into Vincent's voice as a counterpoint to the love a man like Scott probably had not yet recognized. "She's about the best kind there is, Scott."

"Aye. And she's out there alone, hundreds of miles from civilization, in country overrun by Red Flame." Vincent looked up into his friend's eyes. He read understanding there and he was grateful. "Aye. I'm going after her."

"Not alone. 'Tis our duty, too, to protect and defend the settlers."

" 'Tis your duty to hunt down the bastard."

"And we will. But you will not go alone. Take two of the units. Put Billington in charge of the other three."

Vincent hesitated, but the wisdom of the plan was obvious. Hannah could not last long out there alone. And Red Flame could be anywhere. In the clothing that marked her as a Mennonite, she was vulnerable. As he would be if he went for her alone. "You'll go with Billington?"

"Only if I'm out cold and tied to my saddle."

Vincent laughed. It felt good to have this man as friend. He was brave and loyal. And he was the best damned marksman in the regiment. "As Hannah would say, *danke,* Geoff. What unit is Paltray in?"

"Parker's."

"Give him the word that he'll be joining us and have Billington come up here for his orders."

"Will you eat with us?"

"Send me something."

"Aye."

"And, Geoff?"

"Aye?"

"Make it quick. I want to get a good start before the sun goes down. She's out there, Geoff. Alone. Vulnerable. And I'm going to find her."

Chapter Ten

When had she lost the trail? Hannah couldn't remember. She couldn't think, so tired and hungry was she. And Hambone. Poor Hambone. Putting one leg in front of the other was painful for the great, aged beast. Carrying her, more painful. But he had gotten her over the mountain onto a terrain that sloped downward, then leveled off. Mountain! She snorted in disbelief that she could think that. In the Palatine it would have been nothing more than a hill. But here, when she was trying to get to a destination which eluded her, it felt as high as the range of peaks leading to Switzerland.

Hambone was wheezing now. Snorting and stumbling. Hannah slid off his back and ran her hands along his flank and chest wall. A burbling, it was, coming from deep inside him. She blamed herself for his misery. When he should have been gamboling in the fields, enjoying his final days, he had been forced to endure hardships even a younger horse would have found difficult.

"Ach, Hambone! So great a heart you have. But not

163

so great your lungs." She ran her hands down his length, down his left rear leg, and lifted it gently. *"Ei, such dirt!"* Stooping, she scraped away at the leaves under her until she found a small, hard stick. When she began to clean away the debris which had accumulated on Hambone's hoof, he whickered and shied away. "Easy, boy. Easy. Please to let me get this out and you shall feel better."

But as she pried . . . more gently, now . . . she noticed a nail had come loose, then been bent by the pressure of miles of traveling. It hung at an angle and when she moved it Hambone screamed, pulled away from Hannah, and pawed at the air. She calmed him again. "One more look, boy." She groaned when a closer examination revealed what she feared. The nail had been driven in at an angle and now lay on a pain spot. She pulled her finger away. Blood lay on the dirt. Hannah had not been a farm maid for naught. She knew that she had to clean that hoof, douse it with witch hazel or lungwort tincture, and slather it with a concoction of herbs and pitch. If she didn't, pus would form and spread through Hambone's body. But she had no witch hazel. No lungwort tincture. No cleansing salve. She might be able to find sassafras. But would the horse allow her to clean that painful wound?

"Wasser, Hambone. Find *wasser."*

The word was like a magic incantation to the horse, who sniffed the air, whickered, and gingerly walked deeper into the woods. Within moments, they came upon a small stream . . . barely enough to wet the ground, but cool and clean.

Hannah ripped the hem of her apron and dipped it into the water. She picked up the wounded hoof and squeezed the water over the mess. Again and again, she did it, until all the dirt had been sluiced away. If she could only pry up the shoe, clean it, and hobble Hambone for a few days until the sepsis was gone. Sassafras leaves and roots . . . there were, thank God, enough of them around these woods to give him some comfort. But how was she to pry up that shoe? She had no tools. A stick would not do. And there were no flat, sharp stones of enough strength.

She stopped, took a deep breath, and felt the finality of it all. Even if she had the tools, she, herself, had not the strength.

She did what she could, binding Hambone's hoof with torn Sassafras leaves and a clean strip of cloth from her apron, and waited. Water was all they had. Water and nuts and a few not-quite-ripe berries she found. Hambone ended up eating the leaves around him, but they gave him belly gas. Finally, he lay down, closed his eyes, and took a great gasp of air. He was sleeping peacefully when Hannah left him at the side of the stream.

"He will not last another night, Scott," Geoffroy said, examining the horse.

"I can see that. But what I have to know is, how many nights has he already lasted? When did she leave him? And where the hell did she go? She's on foot now. In the roughest damn terrain around here. And there are all sorts of dangers. Wild animals. Trappers, ready for any piece of white flesh. Damn! Why didn't she stay with him?"

"And would here be any better than wherever she is?

She knows only that she's alone and has to get back to someone she knows. She's heading East. Back to Philadelphia, by God." Geoff shook his head. "She's a wonder. I didn't think she'd get this far."

"Let's hope to God she doesn't get much further."

"Are we making camp?"

"Not until nightfall." They were lined up and ready to march after Hannah when Vincent pulled out of rank and did what had to be done for Hambone. "She didn't even have the means to give him rest," he said. "My God, how does she hope to make it another hundred miles on foot?"

Hannah was getting mighty sick of berries and nuts. She should have brought a pot or something in which to boil water and make some tea. There was enough tansy here, and *lowenzahn*, the flower the Philadelphians called dandelion. But even if she had a pot, she didn't know how to make a fire without flint and tinder.

She looked up between the branches of the trees, to read the sky. Dark, soon. She had best find somewhere to make camp, somewhere safe to sleep. She dared not risk a cave or lying on the ground. When she had had Hambone, she had slept on his back. Now, she had to find something high, but the only things high were the trees.

She remembered a time when Bishop Stultz and Pieter had talked about survival along the trail. Pieter was the one designated by the community to travel between Philadelphia and New Ephrata . . . to bring mail and to make arrangements for the rest of the group to come to the settlement. Bishop Stultz cautioned that Pieter should keep to the trees to sleep.

The treetops, they are gifts from Gott. In the wilderness, the safest place, for sure. Limbs that are too light for large animals to jump onto can hold the weight of a person. You have but to stretch out correctly. Tie yourself, if you must. So falling out, you avoid.

Hannah examined her apron. Only half was left, since she had used the rest on Hambone. So, she would have to sacrifice the remainder. And then, if she needed it, her skirts would go, too. She found an elm—tall, strong, wide, and filled with outstretched limbs large enough to accommodate her body. But getting to its heights was precarious. She was weak, and climbing took so much of her remaining strength, she often had to stop and catch her breath. Once she was in the cover of the leaves, however, she felt safe immediately, as if she were in the hands of God.

But the limbs were not soft, nor comforting. The one she finally chose had so many bumps and knots, she was on the verge of cursing every moment. She had her strips in hand when she stretched out. But how in the world was she to tie herself and still remain lying down? She could tie her ankles. And she might be able to tie her waist. But what if her shoulders slipped off during the night? She might slip right out of the waist sling! Bishop Stultz might have had the tying right, but he had the position all wrong.

In the end, she chose a good limb, rising out of the main trunk at an angle that would allow her to rest her back against the trunk and stretch out her legs. To get the apron tie around the trunk and as high up on her body as she could, she had to use all the cloth she had

167

left. The torn-off hem of her skirt kept her bottom and ankles in place on their limb.

While waiting for sleep, she heard the mournful cry of a night owl, but couldn't tell what kind. Accompanying that was the howl of a timber wolf. She shuddered as its plaint was echoed to her left and right . . . and every direction around her. If there were owls and timber wolves, there would be bears . . . and other things as horrible. More horrible. As horrible as what had invaded the settlement. As horrible as *Holle* . . . hell.

They would go to hell, those men. But first they would have to be found. She wondered who would find them and hoped more than anything in the world that it would not be her Redcoat.

With the thought of Vincent and his smoky grey eyes on her mind, invading her refuge in the arms of the tree, she leaned her head on a knobby outgrowth, closed her eyes, hugged her arms around herself, and smiled. Sleep came more easily because of Lieutenant Vincent Scott.

He tossed and turned and finally gave it up. Throwing aside his trail blanket, Captain Vincent Scott strode over to the campfire and poured himself a cup of coffee from the never-ending pot. It tasted like dregs, was filled with them, but he drank it anyway.

"This isn't helping, Scott."

"I know, Geoff." He stared into the dark, into the woods surrounding them and breathed quickly when the call of a wildcat echoed eerily, rising higher and higher, then joining others of its kind. "Makes the hackles rise, that does," Vincent said. "And her, not knowing what she'll face at night, days—Aghh!" He threw his dregs on the ground, then immediately, absentmindedly, poured himself more.

"The men look to you, Scott. They've seen your icy control. They've heard how you brought all of us through the *Sorcière de Mer* fire. They know how you've brought them through frontier skirmishes. They know how good you are with sword and rifle. And they've seen you in hand-to-hand combat. But they have never seen you like this."

"And what is *like this?*"

"Nervous. You've lost that hard edge. Now, you're filled with emotion and that, my friend, loses your advantage. I know it. They know it. Only you seem to have forgotten it."

"I haven't forgotten, Geoff. But for the first time in my life I simply do not know how to separate what I know from what I feel."

"Welcome to the land of the living," Geoff said. "It's about time. But for God's sake, find a balance, Scott. Otherwise whatever good you could do for her will go for naught." He put a hand on Vincent's shoulder, took the tin cup out of his hands, and threw the untouched drink away, "Ironic, isn't it, Scott? When you finally begin to feel like a human being again, when you have some emotion that's real, the woman who has done it for you needs you sharp and on the edge, icy and calm. And unless you are that way, you'll lose. Worse, she'll lose and you'll lose *her.*"

Vincent allowed Geoff to lead him back to his bedroll. "You should have taken holy orders, Geoff."

"Good God, don't even think it! I like too well the

169

feel of a pistol in my palm. *Gute Nachte,* Scott. See? I'm learning, too."

But I have the most to learn, my friend. And none of it is easy.

Vincent waited until Geoff had settled down, then turned his back to the fire and stared into the dark again. So, he had to be icy and calm, sharp and on the edge, did he? Was that possible now? Was that possible when all he felt was despair and fear? Oh, not for himself. Certainly not for his men, who were honed to perfection. No, his fear was for Hannah.

They hadn't seen smoke from a campfire anywhere, and they had searched carefully in every direction before making their own camp. So, the icy, calm, sharp, on-edge Captain Vincent Scott had to conclude that she could not make a fire. And without a fire she was vulnerable to every damned wild animal that roamed this inhospitable land. Suddenly, a scream rent the air around him. Several fusilliers jumped up, grabbed their muskets and rifles, and looked around to see what they had to shoot.

"Not here, men. Back to sleep, now," Scott said.

Quickly, they dropped back to their places and settled their rifles next to them.

"Nice job, Scott," Geoff said. "The control in your voice will calm them down." The scream came again. "Wildcat, you think?"

"Aye."

"Fresh kill, maybe?"

"Aye."

Geoffroy sighed. "No, Scott. Not Hannah. You would know. You would feel it."

"I pray to God you're right."

170

*   *   *

If this were Yellow, he had grown a thousand times bigger. Or she was dreaming. But Hannah was so uncomfortable . . . and the screaming cat was so close . . . she knew this was no dream. 'Twas *ein alptraumlicht.* A nightmare. "Go away, *katzen.* Shoo!"

But the cat opened his mouth, shook his head, and screamed again.

"*Miauen,* yourself. Oh, please, please, go away!"

Hannah's fingers worked at the knots on her apronties, then stopped. She couldn't hope to jump beyond the cat. And she certainly couldn't hope to outrun him. He hadn't gotten all the way to her yet and the branches around her looked too fragile to hold him. She hoped.

From the way he was poised to jump, she would soon find out. While she held her breath and said a quick prayer, the cat fixed his eyes on her, put all his weight on his back legs, and sprang. She screamed, wrapped her arms around the tree trunk, and closed her eyes. She heard him land on the branch, heard him mew with delight, heard the branch bend, then snap, and heard his body crash from one branch to the other. But she didn't hear him hit the ground.

She opened one eye and peeked down. "*Katze! Ja.* Always land on their feet." He circled the tree. Round and round, pawing the ground, looking up. "Try it again, *katze.* But you will fail. And the next time . . . *ei!* . . . you may not be so lucky." The broken branches had ends which looked lethal. She'd have to watch very carefully when she climbed down. If the *katze* would let her climb down.

Hannah groaned. It would be her luck to be tied to

171

this branch until she took her last breath, just out of the reach of that great wild *katze* below. Well, she could not dwell on it. Either he would be there in the morning, or he would not. But if he were not, she promised herself that she would no longer sleep in the trees without a good long, strong stick with which to keep night marauders away. A stick, sharpened at one end. At first light she would find one, scrape it on a rock, and rub and rub until it was what she needed. At first light.

"Kätzchen! Wo bist du? Kätzchen?"

Hannah could only hope he had gotten tired of circling the tree and gone off in search of easier food. After letting herself loose from the trunk, she untied her legs and let them dangle. They prickled unmercifully for several minutes, numb, then painful, then throbbing. But she didn't know pain until she began to descend to the bottom. Her legs felt dead, then suddenly alive, resisting her weight with every movement. By the time she reached the ground, she was soaked with sweat and every muscle trembled.

But she had one thing on her mind and could not allow her weakness to deter her from today's task, from tomorrow's progress.

She found what she called her spear and spent several minutes sharpening the end on a jagged rock next to a stream. Then she rubbed it with sand to get the end to as deadly a point as she was able. When she was finished, she ran her hands over the bark and nodded.

"Gut! Come, *kätzchen.* Come and get your dinner."

Hannah gasped and stared at the spear. If she knew how to throw it, she could . . . but she could not risk this spear. It was too strong, too straight.

She searched for another stick like it and found five more. Diligent work gave her an arsenal. And her prey was scurrying through the underbrush. *Eichhornchen und kaninchen. Furry little stews.*

Practice almost lost Hannah her spears. But soon she was able to hit a circle on the ground. Not quite dead center, but close enough. A circle on the ground, however, was unmoving. And her furry stews streaked as fast as she could blink. But there might be another way. Something surer. And she could use the spear as a weapon of another kind.

So, she searched for berries, ate as many as she dared, and left the rest to pile on a square of her underskirt.

If she kept this up, soon clothes, she would have naught! Eve, she would be. But this, no Garden of Eden.

She sat cross-legged and tore four holes in the square, one on each corner. Then, more strips from her underskirt, long ones this time. Tied to the corners, so. A small sapling, bent down and held with another long, very thin strip. And leaves . . . lots of leaves . . . covering the cloth, almost burying the berries. More berries on top, with a few nuts thrown in for good measure. Cautiously, she reeled out the thin strip of cloth, took up a position in the densest part of the woods close to hand, and waited. And waited. And waited some more.

Ach du lieber! Would he never come? Were not these furry things curious? Lazy?

Hannah's back ached and she longed to stretch her

173

legs. They were cramping, as they had done the night before. But her hunger was more important. She knew if she did not get food, she would not make it to Philadelphia. Hah! She would not make it another week on only berries and nuts and water.

She must have dozed, for when she suddenly became aware of her surroundings, she felt a tug on the strip. She peeked up and over the bush in front of her. Grimacing, she pulled hard, pulled again, and the square flew up with the bent sapling. She ran to see what she had caught and laughed with joy when she found not one but two squirrels trying to claw their way out of her trap.

Hannah held her breath and killed each with one of her spears. She had no knife, so gutting and skinning them was difficult, but with the spears and her hands, she managed.

But she still had no fire to cook them.

Hannah almost cried. Her tears were right on the edge, threatening to spill from her eyes. But she bit her lip and fought to hold on. There *was* a way to make fire. She had heard of it in the Palatine. Rubbing sticks together. Rubbing hard until heat was produced and the wood caught fire. But how long would it take to do that? And would she have enough strength?

"*Ja*, you will! *Ausqerechnet sei!* You of all people! A Rhine maiden! You will have the courage."

The spear would work. It was already sharpened. All she needed, now, was wood to turn. But not just any wood would do. That much she knew from the years of making and laying fires in the fireplaces. The wood must be dry, else it would not heat quickly; all her work would be for naught. She had not enough strength left to waste it.

In her intense zeal to find good tinder, she knew she was deviating from the trail. But as long as she continued to go east every morning, she would be on the right track. So she put the tiny worry behind her and searched until she found three flat pieces of wood. All had lain in the sun until they were bleached almost white. When she broke off an edge from each, it came off in pieces. *Ja,* it would do.

What felt like an hour later, her arm muscles fluttered with fatigue. Pain shot up into her neck. Her fingers cramped. Her eyes blurred. But she dared not stop. To stop meant to start over again. She could not do that.

By the time she thought every muscle in her body had withered to dust, a sudden puff of smoke rose from the dry wood. Then a steady stream, small but so welcome; she nearly cried. And then suddenly . . . poof! . . . a flame. Hannah dropped the spear into the flame and pulled over some dried grass she had collected. She piled it on top, then the twigs, then more and bigger twigs. Finally, pieces of wood. While they burned, she created a fire pit . . . a circle in the grass she swept bare, then scraped down to the ground. She found rocks and piled them in a heap, leaving an open spot in the middle. Into that, she put more tinder and kindling, then brought over the flaming logs, one by one. Other logs, she piled on top. While they caught, she pushed one squirrel carcass onto one of her spears and held it over the fire. The smell nearly made her mad. As soon as the skin was seared she wanted to tear into the flesh. But she knew she had to be cautious. Half-cooked meat harbored too many ailments. She could not afford to

175

be sick, simply because she was starving.

Patiently, Hannah watched the squirrel darken. When the meat began to fall off the bone, she pulled it out of the fire, dropped it off the spear, took the other carcass, strung it like she had the first, and put it carefully over the flames.

She ate the meat before it had a chance to cool and burned her hands and mouth. But she didn't care. It was delicious. Tough and strong tasting, but filling and filled with strength-giving juices. She was almost tempted to eat the other squirrel, but knew she had to conserve her food supply. She would have liked to stay there, hunting, trapping, cooking her own food. But she knew she wouldn't survive long on her own. A place awaited her, and she had a message to bring to her people.

Death lay in New Ephrata. But life lay in Germantown.

So, she packed the squirrel in the sack in which she had caught it, wrapped it in its own skin, and stuffed it in with her precious books in the bottomless pockets of her skirt. When that was finished, she fed more logs into the fire and stretched out on the ground to sleep. But the first howl of a timber wolf sent her scurrying to the safety of a tall tree for the night.

When Vincent found the remains of a campfire in the woods, his heart leapt up.

"Can it really be hers?" Geoff asked.

Vincent poked at the ashes and held up a scorched piece of cloth. He looked it over carefully. "Dainty stitches, that. Not likely from any French or Dutch trappers or hunters. Yes, 'tis likely hers."

"If she had flint and tinder, why didn't she lay a fire before this?"

"I don't think she had flint or tinder. I think she's becoming a damned fine trailsman." He kicked at the sharpened branch laid near the fire, with the bones of a squirrel piled next to it. "Spears. Making fire with her own hands. I hope to God she thought to take some with her. I'd hate to see her palms in a few days if she has to prepare her fire every time from naught."

Geoffroy knelt to feel the stones around the base of the pit. "Still warm. Can't be more than a half-day ahead of us, now."

Paltray approached warily, and saluted. "We could probably catch up with her if we don't camp. We would be willing, sir."

"Thank you all for that," Vincent said, "but I've already decided. We would be taking our own lives in our hands if we tried to get through these woods in the dark."

"Ah . . . sir?"

"Yes, Paltray?"

"We could carry torches, sir. Lighted rush bundles. If we each have several, when one goes out, we could light another. That way, we'd make up hours of time, sir."

Geoffroy smiled at the young man. "If you keep up that kind of thinking, you'll skip up to lieutenant faster than you ever dreamed, Paltray."

"Oh, sir, that wasn't why . . ."

Vincent laughed heartily—and, damn! It felt good. "Gather ye rushes, men. We'll make us a flaming reel!" He looked into the darkness that was creeping on. "We're coming, Hannah. Have no fear."

Chapter Eleven

The next afternoon, the squirrel was only a memory nagging at Hannah's hunger. Should she stop and try to trap another? Or should she continue to Germantown and eat only what she could forage along the way?

She hadn't made up her mind when she got to a rise and saw a camp below her. Fear was so close to the surface, it flooded through her body, leaving her cold and shivery. She nearly backed down and took a circuitous route, when she noticed food tossed carelessly on a rock nearby. Hunger got the better of common sense and she climbed down closer to the camp. Though she searched carefully, she could not detect movement. Horses, pack mules, bedrolls . . . naught. She knew if she left the food there, an animal would claim it, certainly. And she would still be hungry.

It was lamb, roasted almost black. A small sack of coffee. Twelve hard, cold corn cakes.

She gnawed at the tasteless, yet filling, corn cakes while she stirred the ashes of the fire. Lucky, she was. Under the grey char, the wood was smoldering. For one moment she knew fear, but shrugged it off when she couldn't discover a good reason for it. So, feeding dry twigs atop the embers, she soon had a blaze.

"*Ach, Gott, danke* for this good fortune; but, *bitte, mein Gott,* may I never be required to make the fire again!"

She made coffee in an old tin pot she found and drank every drop. She reheated the lamb, breaking off the truly burned parts, and eating every bit. She nibbled on the remainder of the corn cakes as she rested against a large boulder and let the afternoon sun wash her fear and weariness away. Her limbs grew heavy. Her eyes teared. She yawned and stretched out on the ground. Only a little nap. That was all she needed. Just a few more minutes. . . .

"All right, girl! Where's our supper?"

Hannah's eyes flew open at the French accent. She stared into the angry blue eyes of a woman who pressed the sharp tip of a knife into Hannah's throat.

"*Ver zum Teufel are du?*" She must be a devil, Hannah thought in desperation. She must! Look at her clothes! Her hair! Her face! She raised her hand and another woman grabbed it and twisted it to the left.

"*Allez! Allez! Putain!*"

"*Ja!* Going, I get."

But not yet. Six men and three very angry women ringed Hannah. All the women held knives. And all the men carried long-barrelled rifles like those of the *Englishen.*

The blue-eyed woman tossed a chicken on the

ground and spat in Hannah's face. At her shocking behavior, Hannah pressed herself against the boulder, listening to all the women vent their fury at her in French. She could understand spoken French and she could read it . . . but speak it? She had less success with it than she had had with English before she had learned enough to make herself understood . . . at least by Vincent. For a moment her heart swelled with anguish, but she shook it off and tried to make herself understood half in English, half in German. *"Dejeuner . . . nein."* The women's heads whipped around at the word for dinner. But they frowned more harshly than before at the word for *no*. She realized then that they thought she was telling them the food was not theirs. It was no good. She finished in English. "I did not know . . ."

"Well, now you do!" one of them spat. Spat . . . on the ground . . . like a man would do.

In faith, the blue-eyed woman looked more like a man than a woman. Hannah tried not to stare at her breeches and dirty linen shirt. But there was no other place to look. Every one of the men and women were dressed such. Heavy leather boots to the knees. Suede breeches, mired with dirt and offal. Linen shirts that had once been white but were now stained with blood and oily sweat. Vests . . . some beaded, some embroidered, made Hannah wonder if Joseph's coat of many colors had been cut up and pieced together for this motley band. Most of the men had full beards. Two had lip hair. Unlike the Mennonites, however, the men's hair was not cropped short but worn long, some past the shoulders. And the women's hair was also unlike those of Hannah's people. Much of it was covered by odd bits of cloth looped over the top of the head and tied at the nape of the neck. Some of the women's hair was plaited, but most hung wild and free beneath the headclothes. Hannah looked down at her own dirty skirt and bodice, and fingered her own hair . . . she had long ago lost her prayer cap . . . and knew she could not pass judgment. Life on the trail did not allow time to wash and groom oneself.

Suddenly, shrieking and talking so quickly that Hannah could not understand, one of the women grabbed the front of Hannah's bodice and pulled her away from the boulder. The first woman, the one with the cold blue eyes, snapped her fingers and two of the others grasped Hannah's hands and yanked them behind her back. Another snap of the fingers and Hannah's wrists were tied together. Leather straps bit into her skin. *"Nein, bitte!"* she pleaded. But the women paid her no mind. They trussed her to a tree and left her there.

The sun went down, and the cold bit as deep into Hannah's body as the leather bands bit into her wrists. To divert her mind, Hannah listened as closely as she could to the conversation of the women, who did most of the talking. Though Hannah couldn't catch all the words, from what she did understand, she realized they were a mixture of French and Indians, brought together by the last war. Once full-time trappers, now they supplemented their winter trapping by hunting. And raiding farms!

Hannah shivered more in fear than cold. If they were the ones who had destroyed New Ephrata, she was in the midst of the worst of mankind. But if they were the ones, why was she still alive? From what she had witnessed at the farm, simply eating one bite of their precious foodstuffs would have earned her a sword through the gut. Yet, she had eaten everything and was still alive. So, they were not the ones. Of that, she was sure.

Of another thing, she was also sure. The women were furious at her. They had all been raiding when Hannah discovered the food they had left behind for their evening meal. Now they had to gut, skin, and cook that day's kill, when they could have rested and eaten what Hannah had consumed. They cackled as much as the chickens they plucked and spun tales about what they would do to the farm girl when they were through.

When they finished and the chickens were roasting on the fire Hannah had built, the blue-eyed woman drew near with a deerskin sack from which Hannah had seen several of them take a drink.

"You want water, bitch?"

"Wasser, ja. Bitte."

She laughed and poured it on Hannah's head. "'Tis all the *water* you will get. But I promise you, you will get something else very soon. Something you deserve for stealing our food."

She walked over to a large man with bulging muscles and long hair held in plaits down to his waist. She whispered in his ear. He raised his head and looked at Hannah. She whispered again and laughed. He stared at Hannah. Stared, and then nodded. Within moments, he rounded the circle of men and whispered animatedly to each.

There must have been some kind of signal . . . from the blue-eyed devil, Hannah had no doubt . . . because to a man, the circle rose and came towards her.

"Oui. Oui!" The women chanted and danced as they approached along with their men. "Take her. Take her. *Oui. Oui."*

Hannah shrieked when her bonds were cut and she was dragged from the tree by the blue-eyed woman. She screamed when the woman's dirty hand ripped her bodice from neck to waist. She moaned when a large, greasy, hairy hand grabbed her breast and squeezed.

"Nein, bitte. Ein jungfrau. Jungfrau."

"Yong fro? What is yong fro?"

But the greedy gleam in Hairy-hands' eyes gave Hannah enough warning. She clamped her lips together. To tell these men that she was a virgin was foolish. That would only whet their appetite, which looked fully whetted already, the way they rubbed the front of their breeches. *Ach, Lisle, what you must have suffered! Help me, little sister. Help me to be strong.*

Hairy-hands pawed at his breeches and dropped them to the ground. The blue-eyed devil laughed and kicked Hannah's feet out from under her. Hannah landed on the ground with such force, she had to fight to get her breath. Before she had time, her legs were pulled open, her skirts raised, and the man dropped to his knees in front of her. His hands touched her and her stomach lurched. Bile rose, but she bit it down and turned her head to one side. She stared into the excited eyes of the devil.

"Nein bitte. No, please. No."

The devil laughed in a high-pitched voice that echoed madly through the woods.

And the end of the world came in a blinding flash. Hannah smelled sulpher. Burning sulpher. She opened her eyes and found the blue-eyed woman behind her, holding Hannah's head up, pressing it back against the devil's shoulder, pushing the point of a hunting knife into the soft skin beneath Hannah's chin.

"Not on your life," Vincent said, and slammed his rifle butt into the dirty head in front of him.

Hannah screamed. The knife cut her as it fell to the ground. And Hannah found herself pulled backwards, behind the boulder, into Vincent Scott's arms.

"My Redcoat. *Danke.*"

"Save the gratitude until we get out of here, love." He cradled her head in his hands. Though he tried not to look, his eyes dropped to Hannah's bared breasts and his breath caught. "God! As dirty as you are, you are beautiful." He pulled up her bodice and kissed her quickly. "Now, stay here. Don't move. Don't look up."

In a breath, he was gone. And Hannah had to keep herself covered, her head down, and stay behind the boulder. But all around her were cries of pain, and shots from the rifles, and a madness of smoke and sulphur flames and a sickly sweetness that she knew was death.

Stay behind that boulder? Not on anyone's life!

She saw a clearing to her right and a large oak tree behind which she could hide, yet still see whatever was happening. She held her breath, dropped the ripped bodice, pulled up her skirts, and ran for the tree. A ping next to her feet sent sharp pieces of shale and tiny pebbles into her leg. She fell. Feeling for the place where she had been hit, she pulled her hand back to see blood coursing through her fingers. Vincent would have her head! But it didn't seem bad. Merely a deep hole. She scrambled to her feet, ran a few more steps, then fell to the ground and crawled the rest of the way.

Another strip of her skirt went to bind her wound. And the last of her underskirt, Hannah tied around her neck, to preserve what modesty she had left. Caked with grime was the bib she fashioned. But the cleaning of it and the rest of her clothing . . . as well as herself . . . would have to wait. She was far more interested in what was happening beyond the tree.

Five of the men were sprawled in various positions, their bodies contorted. Blood seeped through their clothes and their eyes stared up to the sky. The last man, the one who had pawed her, was positioned behind the women, firing his rifle from left to right as British troops fired at him. With a vicious growl, he threw one of the women into the line of fire and she crumpled with a strangled cry. When he made a grab for one of the other two women, both ran screaming into the woods. Hannah heard them slashing their way past trees and brush; and then she heard nothing. The man's head snapped back. He bent to pick up another rifle. Taking aim at a Redcoat along the line of trees, he cocked back something on top of the rifle and squeezed the trigger.

And nothing happened.

He cursed, threw it to the ground, and whipped out his hunting knife. With a mad cry, he lunged for the nearest Redcoat. Hannah turned her head when four shots rang out at once.

And she was glad she did because the blue-eyed devil was crawling away into the underbrush. With quiet determination, Hannah made her way back to the boulder, picked up the hunting knife which had been used to cut her, and moved quickly into the woods after the wench.

"Du Halten! Halten du!"

The woman turned and bared her teeth. She crouched and made gestures with her hands, daring Hannah to come closer. Hannah looked at the knife. It was not much different from a spear. If she threw it, she would probably hit the devil. But all her people's teaching flooded back at once and she couldn't throw it. She cried, *"Nein!"* and threw the knife to the ground. The devil saw her opening and sprang at Hannah.

Hannah expected the force of a bull to hit her; but of an instant Geoffroy lowered himself from a tree, lunged at the moving target, and brought her crashing on her face.

"At your service, Hannah," Geoff said. His kind, laughing face more serious than Hannah had ever seen it, he hauled the devil to her feet and pushed her forward. "Vincent will want to *talk* to this one. Shall we join him?"

"Ja. Danke."

Vincent watched the small parade prodded ahead by Geoffroy. While Geoff's eyes never left the murderous wench, Vincent couldn't take his gaze off Hannah. He had never seen her so dirty, so disheveled, so gorgeous. Her wheat-blond hair hung all the way to her waist, its plaits as well as its prayer cap covering long gone. Her eyes were rimmed with fatigue, but they shone brightly as soon as she saw him. Ah, God, he loved her! This waif, this ray of sunshine, this woman. His woman. The half of his soul that Clarisse had ripped from him. So simple, Hannah was. So purely wonderful.

And alive, thank God.

Paltray approached and Vincent rounded on him with anger. The young man didn't back down.

"Sir, I speak the prisoner's dialect, sir. I could help you question her."

"Aye, that you can," Vincent said. "Tie her to a tree and wait for me."

"Aye, sir."

That young man would go far, Vincent thought. And if he had the chance to see to a promotion for him, he'd do it quickly. King George could not afford to make men like him unhappy with their lot.

Vincent looked for Hannah and found her sitting under a tree, trying to keep her new bodice from blowing open. She looked melancholy. And then Vincent saw that her lips were moving and her eyes fixed on her clasped hands. A prayer for the dead, he did not doubt. For the men who would have raped her, the woman who would have killed her. There was a purity of soul about Hannah which was not present in any other woman he knew. And Vincent ached to have a piece of it reserved for him.

She watched him watching her, finished her prayers, and smiled at him. With that welcome, Vincent crossed the camp and plopped down beside her.

"You were foolish back there," he said.

"*Ach,* and I expected at least a *guten Tag!*"

Vincent laughed. "Hello, Brown Eyes. You have led us a merry little chase."

"I did not know you were coming, Redcoat."

"I would always come for you, Hannah. Always."

Everything split wide open at his words and Hannah threw herself into Vincent's arms. Tears held back for a week spilled over and would not stop. "Vincent! Vincent!"

He scooped her into his lap and held her. "Shh! 'Tis all right now, love. You're safe."

She wrapped her arms around his waist and let her head rest on his shoulder, breathing in the scent which she knew she would remember all the days of her life. Vincent's scent. Woodsy and male, and thoroughly wonderful.

"You saw the settlement?"

"Aye."

"You know what happened?"

"Aye."

"All of them, Vincent. All of them. Lisle and Magda and Pieter and Rolf and the Bishop. But, oh, *Gott, de kinder!* I had to . . . I had to . . ."

Her voice caught and she threw her gaze to the heavens and wailed. Dear God, how could he comfort her? What could he do? He saw the men watching him, embarrassment and fear written on their faces. Men hardened by battle were not used to its aftermath. Many of them were seeing for the first time what devastation did to those left behind, the survivors.

"Geoff," he called, and his friend came running. "Take over for me."

"Aye, Scott."

Vincent handed Geoff the weeping Hannah so he could get to his feet. Then, he took her back into his arms and slowly walked away from his units until he and Hannah were alone, in the shadows not far from the fire, but far enough for what he had to do.

He let her cry. He let her tears soak his jacket and shirt. He rubbed her back, her arms, her shoulders. He whispered in her ear—love words that he was sure she couldn't hear. But it didn't matter. Someday she would remember this night and the words would come back. Then she would know that one man loved her, loved her until his heart melted, broke, and was repaired again. By her, her tears, and her compassionate heart.

Gradually, she stilled. Hiccups and sniffles made him grin. But he never took his arms away from her. He couldn't. If he did, he would be lost.

Clarisse. How had he thought he loved her? How had he convinced himself that such a selfish, self-centered woman was the one he wanted to spend the rest of his life with? With Hannah in his arms, it seemed ludicrous. But at the time, he was convinced he knew his heart and his heart was filled with the vision of a black-tressed woman with big green eyes. She was his first love, his first experience with the pleasures of the bed. He assumed he was also her first. His proposal was met with a swift approval and they set the date for their marriage. Two weeks before the final banns were announced, he found her in his uncle's bed, playing wanton games with both his uncle and his cousin. His Clarisse, it seemed, was a harlot; and he was the only Scott who didn't know it. His uncle and father came to him and urged him not to make a rash decision. Clarisse was like many of the women of their class, they said, taking her pleasure where she wished. But that, they assured him, did not mean she would not make him a good wife. She had education, style, manners, beauty, intelligence, good breeding. They would have fine children. And she would bring a large dowry to his home; surely that alone meant something, since Vincent's inheritance was small and could not be

190

expected to last their whole lifetime.

Vincent listened, his stomach churning through the entire explanation. Through all the cajoling, he already knew what he was going to do. He did it the next day. He sought his solicitor, had him draw up papers which withdrew his offer of marriage to Clarisse, and joined His Majesty's Fusilliers.

Within hours, he was slapped with a breach of promise suit and Clarisse's solicitors pressed him to reconsider. When he would not, she took him to court. Brazenly, she told of how she had given him her faith and devotion, how she loved him and wanted only to make him a good wife. And all the while her icy green eyes dared him to speak the truth and make him and his family objects of derision. His betrothed in the bed of his uncle! It would take years before the Scotts would be spoken of again without fans being raised in front of tittering women's lips. Hang his uncle and cousin! He didn't care if they never saw the inside of Court again. But he could not do that to his mother and sisters, his brothers and father. So he kept silent, as Clarisse knew he would. And she was awarded half his estates as recompense for his calumny.

And his heart became ice until Hannah eschewed paint and baubles, lace and lavender, to pine for only books—Dear God, only books? Only the whole world! She healed him. Her innocence. Her guilelessness. Her love for her people and her prayers for these curs.

"Do you feel better now?" he asked when she sighed against his chest. He might have been asking it of himself, and the answer would be: *As long as I am with you, Hannah. Only as long as I am with you.*

"I do not think I will ever be completely well again."

"Time will heal, Hannah."

"That is what Bishop Stultz said when Jacob died."

"And who is Jacob?"

Her head bobbed up and her eyes widened. There was so much she wanted to say to this man, so much from her heart. But her tongue felt as though it were stitched to the roof of her mouth, so hard was it to get the words out. And when the words came, they were not what she wanted to say. Because she could not open her heart to him in the way she wanted to. She was Mennonite. He was the King's soldier. There were walls and rituals and orders between them.

"Jacob, he is . . . was . . . my . . . how do you say . . . marriage partner?"

Vincent's mouth went dry. "Husband?"

"*Ja. Nein.* That is with all the words before *Gott. Nein,* Jacob was my not-yet-husband."

He could swallow again, but it hurt. "Betrothed."

"*Ja.* Betrothed." She buried her head against his neck again. "He fell off the roof abuilding a house for our marriage." She felt she had to tell him everything. Why was that? Why did he occasion such full openness and honesty with her? "He died. But not before we bundled."

"Bundled."

"*Ja.*" She peeked up at him. "You do not bundle?"

"I don't know what it is."

"Sleep together in the same bed."

"You slept with Jacob?"

"*Ja.* This is wrong?"

"Is it part of your religion?"

She frowned and tried to remember ever having a sermon on bundling. "*Nein.* I think it is more custom

TO GET YOUR
4 FREE BOOKS
MAIL THE COUPON BELOW.

Heartfire Romance

FREE BOOK CERTIFICATE

GET 4 FREE BOOKS

Yes! I want to subscribe to Zebra's HEARTFIRE HOME SUBSCRIPTION SERVICE. Please send me my 4 FREE books. Then each month I'll receive the four newest Heartfire Romances as soon as they are published to preview Free for ten days. If I decide to keep them I'll pay the special discounted price of just $3.50 each; a total of $14.00. This is a savings of $3.00 off the regular publishers price. There are no shipping, handling or other hidden charges. There is no minimum number of books to buy and I may cancel this subscription at any time. In any case the 4 FREE Books are mine to keep regardless.

NAME

ADDRESS

CITY _____ STATE _____ ZIP

TELEPHONE

SIGNATURE

(If under 18 parent or guardian must sign)
Terms and prices subject to change.
Orders subject to acceptance.

HF 112

GET 4 FREE BOOKS

HEARTFIRE HOME SUBSCRIPTION
SERVICE
P.O. BOX 5214
120 BRIGHTON ROAD
CLIFTON, NEW JERSEY 07015

than religious beliefs. Everyone in the faith bundles. It is expected, honored, encouraged. Aunt Magda and the women even made for me a night dress with quilting in the very tiny stitches. It was beautiful."

Such ingenuousness! Vincent wanted to know more about this practice of bundling. But the question of what they had done remained uppermost in his mind. Hannah had been with a man. Or had she? "You truly *slept* with Jacob?"

"Why do you not believe me?"

"Oh, I believe you, Hannah. You are the only woman I believe completely." He tilted her head up and smiled at her. "Was it nice?"

"*Ja.* I think so. It was not much different from what I expected. So, *ja,* I suppose it was nice."

"Shall we bundle tonight?"

"Are you betrothing to me?"

"Will you have me?"

She examined his laughing eyes and saw something deeper than laughter behind his words. It mirrored what was in her heart. Though her faith would frown on her feelings, they were real. And she could not lie to this man who had captured her heart forever. "*Ja,* Redcoat. I would have you. *Zu lieben,* Vincent Scott. *Ju lieben.*"

Vincent kissed her, long, slow, deep. "Stay here, *liebchen.* I will be back to bundle with you."

Part Three

Promises

Chapter Twelve

The blue-eyed woman—her name turned out to be Valerie Despart—sniffed her derision of the British soldiers. "What can you do to me? I am a woman! You would not hurt a woman," she taunted in French.

Vincent scowled when Paltray translated. "You are a renegade and possibly a murderer. We hang murderers, woman or not."

"No! I did not murder."

"Ah . . . so you speak English."

Valerie cursed in at least four languages that Vincent was able to decipher. He advanced and held his bayonet at her throat. "We could hold a summary court. Right here. Right now. I don't think you would like that. From what we saw when we came into camp, you were the leader here. And we—" He threw his arm out to include everyone, and most heads were bobbing in agreement. "—We would not hesitate to account you guilty and hang you. Or would you prefer the sword?"

"We played with the brown-eyed thief. Nothing more."

"If we had not intervened there would have been too much more."

Valerie threw her head back and looked down her nose at Vincent. "If I answer your questions, you will keep me from the noose?"

Though he wanted to run her through with his bayonet because of what she had planned for Hannah, he needed whatever information she had about the massacre at the Mennonite settlement. So, he gritted his teeth and nodded. "I will try."

"This one," she jerked her head in Paltray's direction, none too pleased to see him grin. "This one asked after someone who is killing the bearded Germans."

"Do you know him?"

"Cuppimac, they call him. Though I do not know if that is his true name. They say it means *I will get even;* but I do not know if that is truth or Indian tall tale."

"He is Indian?"

"He is everything. His men are French, Dutch, British, Indian. Every rotten soul this side of hell rides with him. They plunder, rape, kill. But they are only after the bearded Germans. He will not allow them to touch any others. And he likes it. More and more, he likes it." She shuddered.

"You act and sound as if you fear him."

"I fear what he brings. What he has already brought. You. You, Redcoats. Many more Redcoats. And soon we . . . we hunters and trappers . . . will be mistaken for him. I do not look forward to that day."

"Why?" Vincent asked. "Does he only kill the Mennon—the bearded Germans?"

"It is said that men like that murdered his whole

198

tribe. Killed his parents. Gutted his brothers and sisters. He was not yet sixteen. He has been after justice ever since."

"Justice?" The word didn't half-describe what this Cuppimac had done. "Revenge straight from hell, more like it. These men do not bear arms. They are defenseless."

"Aye. But what matters it to him?"

"Where does he camp?"

"Better you should ask, *Where is the wind?* How would I know?"

Vincent had questioned prisoners before, many times. He knew the truth when he heard it. He wished the woman knew where the madman was. There were too many unprotected settlements, and Vincent expected too soon to see another massacre.

"Keep her shackled," Vincent ordered Paltray. "And don't take your eyes off her for one minute."

Vincent went to Wildfire and pulled off his pack.

"Geoff, have someone bring us water."

"Aye, Scott." Geoff studied his friend. "She's none the worse for wear?"

"Not a good choice of words," Vincent said. "But she's strong. Stronger than that bitch back there. Hannah will pull through." He grinned. "With my help."

"Ah! The civilizing influence of women. At least, one particular woman. When you get home, they shall hardly recognize you. You've changed, Scott."

"Aye. And I like the change."

Vincent carried his pack to Hannah's side. He dumped it next to her. "There's soap and a change of clothes in there. The shirt and jacket will be too big and the breeches won't have a prayer of fitting over your, uh, hips—" He broke off at Hannah's broad smile. "There's also needle and thread in the kit. You might be able to stitch yourself something from what's in there."

"You have the scissors?"

"There's a kit knife. Small, but I also have this—" He pulled his knife from his belt and held it out to her. She took it and dropped it on the ground. "I've Wildfire to feed and water and other things to do. I'll be back later and we can get to that bundling of yours."

Hannah smiled up at him. His voice was soothing to her soul. His eyes glimmered in the firelight and a feathery tingling washed through her. He bent to kiss her and she threw her arms around his neck and kissed him back. Like the time on the ship, this kiss was burning with feeling. Not like Jacob's cold peck on the cheek. Vincent's kiss was the kind every woman dreamed about and few ever found. She was looking forward to this night's bundling.

A young soldier brought her two buckets of water and laid them beside her with a smile. Another came with a lighted candle in a holder, which he put on a flat rock, smiled, and withdrew. And still another brought a horse, on which had been draped a large blanket. He tethered the roan, saluted Hannah, and backed away. Hannah peeked around the horse. The blanket hid her from view. She knew Vincent had sent it to allow her privacy and time to bathe as best she could.

She pawed through the supplies in Vincent's pack and was surprised not to find something personal. He had soap, as he said . . . a strong-smelling soap that reminded her of a clothespress which Pieter had made out of cedar. Along with the soap were some pieces of toweling and a strong scrub brush. There was also a powder that tickled her nose and smelled like pumice and applewood. A comb and brush with silver handles . . . not the plain wooden ones she was used to. Three ribands, probably to tie Vincent's hair behind his neck. And a bundle of clothing.

Hannah donned each of the items quickly, putting them on over her clothes, just to see how they would fit. There were two shirts and an extra red coat like Vincent's. This one was crusted over with much gold braid. She ran her hands over the coarse threads, liking the way the braid sparkled in the candlelight. Then she quickly drew her hand away. Such things were of the world. But they were very pretty.

One of the shirts was plain, the other had ruffles at wrist and neck. All three were, indeed, too large. The shoulders hung down nearly to her elbows and the sleeves trailed two hands' length below her fingers. But Vincent was wrong. The breeches fit almost perfectly. A little tight in the bottom and a little loose in the waist, but she could fix that easily enough.

After she washed every hair on her head and every toe on her feet.

The water in one bucket was icy, in the other, hot. She removed Vincent's clothing and folded it carefully so as not to get them dirty. Feeling as if the world were watching, she took her books out of her pocket and hid them beneath a rock. Then she gingerly peeled off her improvised bib, her torn bodice and underbodice, her skirt, her underskirt . . . what there was of it . . . her shoes and stockings. Into the cold water bucket, she poured as much hot water as it would hold. As soon as she was naked, she dropped her filthy clothes into the

201

hot water, lathered them with the soap, and left them to soak for a time.

She started on her feet and legs with the scrub brush, cleaning off layers of dirt and body oils and rinsing carefully with wet towels. She worked upward, and *ach, Gott,* it felt *wunderbar!* The dirtier the water got, the better she felt. Too often for the last several days, she had felt soiled by the world. It was as if she scrubbed away the pain and anger as well as the dirt, as if she were cleaning herself from the inside as well as the outside.

But the best feeling in all the world was when she dunked her head in the bucket and scrubbed her hair and scalp until it hurt.

"Hannah?"

"Not yet, Vincent! I will tell you when."

Vincent went back to the fire but his gaze was fixed on the candle-lit shadows which revealed what Hannah was doing. Every time she moved, he felt a rush of warmth flood his body. Bent over the bucket, she moved gracefully, innocently, not realizing that she was on display, even if one could see only her shadow. And when she stood to wring out the stuff in the bucket, her breasts bounced. But it was when she raised her arms to hang her clothing on the limbs of nearby trees that her contours were exaggerated beyond belief.

The men coughed, shuffled, some turned away. Paltray cursed and stalked off into the darkness. Vincent heard him puffing with exertion and could imagine him marching in place to take away the tenseness of his body.

By God, Vincent had to put a stop to this or he'd have mutiny on his hands!

He stalked back to the horse-divider. "Hannah, by God, you have to hurry!"

"So impatient for to bundle, Vincent! Only a few short moments, Vincent. I have but to put on your breeches."

Finally, she pushed aside the blanket and walked into the firelight, and Vincent nearly had apoplexy.

"Good God!"

She wore his dress shirt and breeches, but they had never looked like that. Every curve of her legs was revealed by the skin-tight fabric. Every hill and valley of her breasts was exaggerated by the way the cool linen clung to her wet skin.

But there was something wrong, too, and Vincent hid a huge grin behind his hand. She had miscalculated the ties on the breeches. The front gaped open a bit on the left and was stretched tight to fit holes above the mis-tied part. The shirt was tied primly at the neck, but the neckline was so large it hung crookedly.

There, however, her fool-like appearance ended. Vincent's heart hammered hollowly, fiercely, as he took in Hannah's attempt to make herself look plain in clothes which only made him and all the world know that naught could dress down that loveliness. The drooping neckline revealed the delicious roundness of the top of her breasts. The lace tickled across her skin and he wanted nothing more than to trace the place where it swayed back and forth as she walked. She had used his ribands to tie the sleeves in place. Looped around her upper arms, just above the elbows, the ribands made the arms of his shirt lay in puffed folds. And she had found something to hold the bottom of the shirt to her waist. The hem looked like a skirt, though one that didn't half hide her luscious bottom.

And her hair! It hadn't dried yet, but hung in damp waves across her shoulders and all the way down to her waist. Tiny tendrils blew gently against the sides of her face with each breath of wind. In the candlelight, she appeared to be crowned with spun silver and gold.

Nothing more feminine or seductive could he ever want to see. No wonder the elders of her faith demanded that their women dress plainly. Men would kill each other to get their hands on such as she.

He steeled himself not to show his feelings in front of his men, but it was too late. They gaped at Hannah and turned incredulous and envious eyes in his direction. When he swept them with as stony an expression as he could manage, they hemmed and hawed and suddenly found something very important to do. Most ended up in their bedrolls, tossing and turning. Vincent almost sympathized. There was nothing worse than that kind of ache. But this was Hannah, not some camp follower; he would brook no disrespect, not even from men as good and professional as these.

"Geoff, you'll have to take the first watch," Vincent said.

"Seems I'd best take all watches, Scott." He held up his hand when Vincent looked as if he'd give a thousand orders. "Don't worry. If anyone makes a move on Hannah, I'll string him up or shoot him."

He smiled at the woman in question. He, too, liked what he saw, but for a different reason. This was the woman who had turned Scott's life upside down and inside out. It wasn't her beauty that had done it, though. He had seen women more beautiful—though Scott probably wouldn't agree. It was her dignity, her grace, her smile, her acceptance of the worst that life brought and her zeal to get on with it. She would make Scott a good wife, if the damned fool could admit she would be better off with him than with her own people. But he knew Scott. First thing tomorrow they would be hell-bent on getting Hannah back to the nearest Mennonite settlement. Or wherever the hell she wanted to go. Scott wouldn't think twice, wouldn't put his needs before hers, would sacrifice happiness for duty. Scott needed some sense kicked into him! Too bad, Geoff thought. Too bad Scott would never feel it unless it was Hannah who did the kicking.

"Sleep well, Hannah Yost," Geoff said.

"*Ya,* I will," Hannah said. "Vincent and I, we will bundle together."

Geoff raised his eyebrows in a silent question.

"Don't ask," Vincent warned.

"Aye, sir. And you sleep well, too." He walked by Vincent and whispered meaningfully, "You are going to realign those ties, aren't you?" Then he whistled his way into the shadows and took up his post, a great grin on his face that he couldn't suppress.

His hands couldn't be fuller, Vincent decided. Now, even Geoff had the wrong idea. Well, he actually had the right idea—the correct idea—but it wasn't what Vincent wanted him to be thinking about right now. They could be attacked at any minute, though that possibility was remote. No, the dangers were right here, in the camp. Men's thoughts and dreams—and blithering, blabbering tongues. Vincent wondered how long before the story of this night rose through the ranks to the general himself.

"Damn!"

"There is something wrong, my Vincent?"

My Vincent. Dear God! "Naught wrong, Hannah." He went toward the campfire. "Are you hungry?"

"*Nein.* I ate all their food, you know. That is why they . . . they . . ."

"Why that witch is bound and gagged," Vincent said. He held up a pot. "Tea?"

"Oh, *ja.* That would be good before we bundle."

"Hannah—"

"*Ja,* my Vincent?"

"We have no sugar."

Hannah giggled. From the pained, confused expression of Vincent's face, she knew he had not said what he intended. "Plain is good for me."

They drank their tea silently, though Vincent had a thousand questions. The only thing he said, however, was, "We will sleep behind the horse and blanket."

"*Ja,* Vincent. Whatever you say."

He didn't know the protocol for this bundling, so he made it up as he went along. He took Hannah's hand and drew her to the spot he had chosen, the only place in the camp which had a good layer of moss on which to lie down. As ordered, his men had already spread out his bedroll. There was an extra blanket for Hannah and someone had rolled up a makeshift pillow for her head.

My, weren't they being considerate!

"This will suit, Hannah?"

"'Tis so much better than a tree, Vincent."

He helped her straighten out her blankets, then lay down behind her. He cradled her in his arms, pulling her back against him until her bottom fit in the cradle of his hips. She sighed when his arms came round her, and one of his hands rested under her left breast.

"What's this about trees, Hannah?"

"I slept in the tops of trees."

She told him about her escape from the claws and teeth of the wildcat and he pulled her closer. "Good God, I almost lost you."

"*Nein.* I think you and I, we are bound together, my Vincent. Like the two halves of something separated long ago. Now, we find each half and *krach,* a wholeness again. I do not believe *der gut Gott* will end such a thing."

"You are on more intimate terms with Him than I am, Hannah. If you believe it, it must be true."

"Ah, Vincent . . . He is with you, too . . . else how did you find me?"

"I don't ask those kinds of questions. I just thank Him when it happens."

"*Ja.* 'Tis *gut,* the *danke* . . . the thanking." She turned her head and kissed his cheek. "I thank you, Vincent. For everything."

He caught her chin and looked deep into her eyes. Hannah couldn't read what was in them, so misty were they. But she could feel his heart against her back. Its beat grew faster and harder, and his hand trembled. He opened his mouth to say something, then shook his head slightly, as if admonishing himself. Finally he bent his head and took command of her mouth.

Plain, it was not. Chaste, it was not.

This was filled with feeling, moist, hot, demanding, joyous.

His lips moved over hers, causing a friction which made it impossible for her to keep her mouth closed. When she opened slightly for him, the tip of his tongue tasted the inside of her lips, the edges of her teeth, the swelling he was creating.

She moaned at the beauty of it, and shifted her body to be closer to her Vincent. Her movement brought her breast in contact with the palm of Vincent's hand and he knew a moment of pure madness, pure joy. He cupped it, moving gently across its tip until her nipple puckered hard against his skin. In gratitude, his mouth moved more seductively over hers. He filled her with his tongue, felt hers dance against his, and moaned along with her. His thumb slid back and forth across that aroused peak, until he felt her breast harden and swell larger than his hand could hold. Both hands moved to it, brought it out of the wide, hanging neckline of the shirt, and he broke off the kiss and bent his head to nuzzle the soft mound which welcomed him.

When Vincent took her breast into his mouth, Hannah made a soft mewing sound that came from somewhere in the mysteries that were womanhood. "*Ach, Gott,* such bundling!"

Fiery heat slicked its way from the juncture of Vincent's mouth and her breast and she looked down to find the source of such wonder. His tongue washed over her nipple, then sought out its twin; more heat filled her to the pit of her stomach. She held his head there, there where the joyous feelings began, until she was satisfied that they wouldn't go away. Only then would she allow him to claim her other breast.

Was this what it felt like to have a babe suckling? *Nein.* This drive to grow closer to Vincent could not be duplicated by a mere babe. This was the wonder of being a woman, the joy of being with the man she loved.

Thank God she had lost her prayer cap along the trail. Having it would remind her too forcefully that she was very close to sinning. But how could such beauty be sin? And with Vincent? *Nein!* There could be no sin with Vincent. Bundling was accepted. *This* was the correct way to bundle, she hoped.

And when Vincent took both her breasts into his hands and moved his mouth from one to the other and back again, she was convinced. His sucking grew stronger, until she felt her breasts take on the contours of his mouth and her nipples rubbed against the folds behind his teeth.

She moaned and cried out, and Vincent knew he had to muffle her voice with his mouth.

This was lovemaking. This was what he was made for, what she had given him. This was cleansing, innocent joy. And he wanted more of it. He wanted to know every part of her body, without taking it completely. Because once he entered her, he knew he couldn't be gentle. He would have to yell from pure exaltation—and his men would probably wring his neck out of envy.

They *should* envy him. He was in heaven. Or would be.

When his hands left her breasts, Hannah felt bereft. But their trail made her rib cage tingle and the anticipation of where they were going made her breath catch in the back of her throat.

"The ties," he whispered raggedly. "The ties are askew."

"Askew? What is this word?"

Vincent showed her with his fingers and she gasped at the spurts of heat which jumped from his fingers to her stomach and on up to her breasts. And down. Down to the heated part of her where she knew he belonged, where she wanted him to go.

"You have the wrong ties in the holes. The flap doesn't hang correctly."

"You will fix them?"

"Eventually."

Chapter Thirteen

Hannah awoke to the song of a lark in the trees . . . awoke and remembered what "eventually" meant to Vincent. She smiled. 'Twas not difficult to remember, because the "eventually" was not long in coming last night.

And it remained even now.

Beneath the blanket which covered them, the pressure of Vincent's hand under the "askew" ties remained as constant and as wonderful as it had the night before.

Ach, the night before!

As he had undone the mis-tied flap, his fingers had feathered against her stomach until her muscles had contracted from sheer ecstasy. And then . . . she wondered if it had been by accident . . . his fingers had brushed against a sensitive spot which pulsed with a life of its own. She soon learned it was not by accident, for Vincent's fingers, and then his whole hand, rubbed delightfully against her. Up and down, back and forth, he had touched her, advancing, then retreating from

211

the hottest part of her. She gave herself up to the pure feeling, forgetting that they were separate persons, wanting this special, wondrous sensation to continue until the end of time. When she thought she could stand no more, when she thought she would go mad or giddy with delight, he advanced to the slickest part of her and slid inside.

She had gasped then, and his mouth had once more smothered her cry of joy. Because his tongue kept rhythm with his hand and fingers, she did not know what to feel more, his kiss or his caress. He took the decision away from her by giving her both, again and again. She did not know there were such sensations in the world. She did not think that Jacob would ever have discovered them. But with Vincent they were as normal and as beautiful as the love she had for him.

She remembered how her body had arched up to meet each sliding movement of his hand, each probe of his fingers. Arched higher and higher as a strange power took over and drew her into a world where only Vincent's touch and Vincent's kiss existed, where her body grew tense enough to explode in a million sparks of light.

He had continued to kiss and caress her until her breathing returned to normal and her body calmed slightly. Then, he had drawn away from her and looked down into her eyes.

"Was this bundling as good as the one with Jacob?"

"Mein Gott, such a question! We had on all our outer clothes and there was a rail between us. He did no more than kiss me on the cheek."

Vincent had gaped at her. "What?"

212

"You did not hear me? I will speak louder."

He put his hand over her mouth. "No. No, I heard you." He shook his head and continued to stare at her. "Why did you not stop me?"

"I thought you knew something I did not." She giggled. "I was correct, *ja?* A very *wunderbar* something, it was, too." She put her hand over his, which was still at the juncture of her legs, and he jerked it away. *"Nein,* Vincent. I like it there. Do you not like it, too?"

"Oh, Hannah, I like it very much there." His hand slid back to the place of the wonderful sensations and he rubbed it tenderly. "Very much." He kissed her. "Now, we should get some sleep."

"Ja, my Vincent. Sleep would be good."

She snuggled against him and felt his deep sigh of contentment. Soon, she felt his body soften and become heavy with sleep. Then, she allowed the darkness to engulf her, though she dreamed of what they had shared.

And now he was still there, with his hand warming her once again. She reached to touch his fingers. There were tiny hairs on the backs of his knuckles and she tickled them with her thumb. Such a difference, his body was, compared to Jacob's. So many more sinews instead of rounded muscle. So much more leg. More breadth of shoulder. To see how his bottom half was made, she reached behind her to feel along his flank. The hand that cupped her breast whipped around and slapped against her hand.

"Enough, vixen! We have to save something for when we are truly alone."

"We are alone now."

"*Nein*, Hannah. I hear my men stirring. There is coffee being brewed and breakfast sizzling in pans. We are most definitely not alone!"

She stretched and turned to him. "You liked the bundling, my Vincent?"

"*Ja*, Hannah. As I said before."

"But you pleasured me. I almost screamed from the joy. But you did not scream. You did not stiffen such as I. You were good . . . you did wonderful things to me . . . but I cannot tell if you liked it as much as I did."

Good God, she was serious! Did she truly not understand how men and women were aroused? How one kind of pleasure was as good as another—almost. Her "screams" the night before were spontaneous, natural. Not the *Oh, you're the best there is*. Not the *Ooh, how good. Yes, do that. But maybe also this*. Her body had become gradually hotter, gradually slicker, gradually stiffer. She had peaked slowly, but when she did, she gave every ounce of tension in her body its full release. And she did not know how glorious that alone had made him feel.

"I did not like it the same way you did, Hannah. But I liked it. And when we are completely alone, when there are no soldiers or camp followers around to interrupt or hear us, I will show you what it is like when I am pleasured as much as you."

"You promise?"

"I promise."

She rode astride, as she'd done before, accepting Paltray's offer of his horse. And Vincent rode beside

214

her, at the head of the two units.

It felt disconcerting to be amongst these brightly dressed soldiers. How had she, a member of the plain people, found herself with the like of them? They were far from plain. They were downright outrageous.

Like the plumes of birds, their uniforms dazzled the eye. Like the talons of hawks, their bayonets sparkled wicked and dangerous in the sun. Like the snap of wings, their rifles cracked when cocked. She felt as awkward leading them as a babe must feel when first learning to walk. Yet, beside Vincent, she felt like no babe. His eyes drank her in, until she wondered if he had found some new nectar in the night under the blanket. His gaze made her sit up straighter, hold her head higher, hug a secret smile to her heart.

She was proud of him. Proud of the way he spoke to Geoffroy. Proud of the way his men deferred to his judgment. Proud of how easy he was to please, and how strict, to keep order. He accepted only the best, the first, the fastest, from his men. And he awarded promptness and intelligence.

Lieutenant Paltray's unsolicited offer of his horse had drawn him a quick, *Good work, Lieutenant. The lady will be most grateful.* Then, Vincent had turned to another who wore the same kind of insignia as Paltray and snapped his fingers.

"Rogers, give the lieutenant your mount." Rogers jumped down from a great chestnut with a white star on his nose and handed Paltray the reins. "Paltray, for your generosity, you will ride. But for your further education in the workings of a regiment, you will be responsible for the supplies until we hook up with the rest of the regiment or until we get to Sandy Brook."

"Aye, sir."

"This is a good thing, this responsibility for the supplies?"

"A very good thing, Hannah. Paltray shows promise. He will make a good lieutenant some day. He must learn all there is to know about a unit and regiment. And part of that is to keep good watch over the supplies and equipment."

"It is hard, this job?"

"Very easy. But important. All jobs are important in the military."

"*Ja*. Also in a settlement. From plowing to scrubbing pans. All have their place. All contribute to the success of the community." She smiled up at him, pleased to have found something they shared besides the wonders of the bed and the joy they found in each other's company. "We are not so much different, Vincent, *ja?*"

Vincent hooted. His body shook with laughter. "Not so much. Only guns and religion and clothes and language."

She sniffed and wouldn't talk to him for a time. She was not convinced. Order was order. In *Gott's* kingdom was room for all kinds. Finally, because she was not happy unless she and Vincent were on good standing, she looked up and asked, "What is this Sandy Brook?"

"A temporary fort erected halfway between Fort Bedford and Philadelphia. There is unrest in the territory, talk of war."

"War with the Indians?"

"No. With the colonials."

"But why?"

"Taxes. Laws the colonials do not want to obey. A freedom they seek which alludes me, since no British subject has ever been truly free from the laws of the king and his council."

"I hope this war does not come."

"Amen," Vincent said, and was joined by Geoffroy and Paltray, the only ones close enough to hear the conversation.

Hannah worried all the morning. War meant great hardship for all the people. But more than that, it meant that Vincent would be in danger. From what she had seen at the settlement, killing was a form of hell on earth. No wonder the faith . . . a faith that believed man should make his home and family as close to a heaven as possible . . . would forbid such horror. But Vincent made war his profession. He seemed proud of what he did; and if the way he ran his units and led his men was any indication, he did it well. She had hoped . . . she had dreamed . . . that her love for him would make a difference . . . that he would want to leave the fusilliers and make his home with her.

How foolish. How naïve.

He was a grown man, with great responsibilities. She had no right to ask him aught. She had no claims on him. His offer of betrothal was in jest, pulled from him by her when she needed the stability only he could give. But she would not trap him. She would never trap him. When she was back in Germantown with her uncle, she would go on with her life the same way she had always gone on with it.

With one exception.

She would ask for a dispensation from the marriage bed. She could not marry with anyone else than

Vincent Scott. And if she could not have him, then she wanted no one.

It took them two days to get to Sandy Brook. Each night Vincent and she spent in each other's arms. He took her to the realms of ecstasy with his hands, his fingers, his mouth, his tongue.

Supper was tasteless, because she awaited the night and their coupling with unseemly eagerness. By the time Vincent took her hand and led her to their sleeping spot far removed from the other men, Hannah's skin tingled more every minute, merely from her great anticipation. And Vincent never disappointed her. He found more ways to tease her breasts and nipples than she thought existed. His tongue was butterflies one moment, butter, the next. His mouth, a bolt of silk or a length of suede. His fingers played her nipple like a fiddle or kneaded it like making dough. And when he slicked down and inside her it was sometimes the slow meandering of a brook or the pulsating rhythm of a thunderstorm.

If she tried to decide which of the sensations she liked best, her tongue would cleave to the roof of her mouth. There was no best. There was only better, and even better. She would never tire of Vincent's sweet lovemaking, she knew. She would remember it every night they were separated, which, she was afraid, would be every lonely night for the rest of her life.

Paltray was the first to hear the insistent beat of horses' hooves. He came up next to Hannah and Vincent.

218

"On the ridge behind us, sir. Horses. Riding hard. Lots of horses."

"Seek shelter," Vincent shouted. He raised his hand high above his head and made a circling motion which sent his men scurrying into the woods. He grabbed Hannah's reins and pulled her horse deep into the darkness of the trees. "If it's that devil from the settlement, I do not want him to see you. This time, stay down!"

"*Ja,* Vincent. I will. I have no desire to see him."

Geoffroy came up and shoved Valerie Despart behind a tree. He gave Hannah his rifle with bayonet attached. "If she moves, stick her."

Hannah's eyes opened wide and she began to shake her head. But then Geoff winked and she knew his words were only meant for Valerie's ears. Well, if the woman didn't know Hannah couldn't use the bayonet, mayhap Hannah could fool Valerie into obeying Vincent's orders.

"Do not move," she warned Valerie.

"*Ja.* I do not move," the blue-eyed devil sneered.

"Make mock all you wish, devil. Now, I am free and you wear ropes on your wrist."

Horses, dozens of them, thundered past. Hannah was relieved to see red coats on the backs of those who rode them. When Geoff came to lead the two women back, he wore a wide grin.

"The rest of Scott's regiment. And they have the horses the Colonel at Sandy Brook awaits."

"Good," Valerie said. "I am pure sick of walking."

"Hah! The officers and the men get first pick to ride. All prisoners walk."

"She can ride behind me," Hannah said. "We won't

need a saddle."

Geoff shook his head. "Vincent will not allow it."

"He will if I ask him."

But Vincent turned ashen when Hannah broached the subject. "No. Absolutely not. She'll probably bite your neck, then bolt."

"*Gut.* Then in front, she rides, *und* me behind."

"No, Hannah."

"How much longer to the Sandy Brook?"

"Two days hence." Hannah stared him down until he sighed. "This is why women are not in the militia."

"I do not think this is wrong, Vincent. But if you want to be certain of her staying prisoned, tie her hands in front of the horse's neck. Loose enough so she may sit up. But tight, so if she tried to get off, her wrists will bleed. That is punishment without cruelty."

Vincent grinned. "That is brilliant. But she will ride in front of *Paltray,* not you."

Hannah shrugged. She had won a skirmish. It was enough.

Sandy Brook was a makeshift fortification of stockade fences, a few log-walled barracks, several two-story logged and chinked houses, and over a dozen tents large enough to hold a full unit of forty men. There were streets and shops, even a building with a cross affixed above its double-door entrance. And people of every color.

Hannah's head swiveled when she saw a dark brown man helping a woman alight from a carriage. "Methinks he has been too long in the sun. He is done to a crisp."

Vincent doubled over Nightwind's neck, he laughed

so hard. "He's a colored man, Hannah. From Africa. Probably started out as a slave. Now, more than likely, he's an indentured servant."

"Slave? You mean he was owned, like furniture?"

"More like a work horse."

"Are there more slaves like him?"

"Hundreds."

"This is not *wunderbar,*" she said sadly. "We are all *Gott's kinder.*"

They drew up at a large house, where a British flag flew high atop the roof. The men lounging on the porch came to attention and saluted Vincent. He returned their salute and helped Hannah to dismount. He singled out one young man and said, "Tell Colonel Jennings that a regiment of King George's Forty-second Fusilliers, led by Captain Vincent Scott, are reporting for duty."

"Aye, sir."

"And tell him we bring the horses he requisitioned. They are quartered at the pasture."

"Aye, sir! He's been anxious about them, sir!"

"Then, go!"

The young man scurried as fast as his over-sized feet would carry him. Within moments the door opened and a short, plump British officer barreled his way past the men on the porch.

"Captain Scott! Welcome." He caught sight of Hannah and his mouth dropped. "What, is the king so pressed for recruits that he takes barmaids now?"

"Hannah Yost is no barmaid, Colonel. She's the sole survivor of a massacre at the settlement in New Ephrata."

"Good God!" The plump man with the thinning hair

and watery blue eyes bowed. "I apologize, ma'am. But in those clothes . . ." Merriment changed his very plain face into one of uncommon appeal. "Sergeant, fetch my wife from the minister's house," he ordered, without turning to designate which sergeant. "She'll have you fixed in a trice," he said, as he offered Hannah his hand. "We'll just wait for her in my office, where Captain Scott can tell me what happened."

"Best let Hannah tell it, Colonel. I only came in and saw the results, not the way it happened."

When they entered an inner chamber in the large house, Hannah surveyed the office of the first Colonel she had ever met. She supposed it was spare, for an *Englishen;* but it held more furniture than was in most Mennonite homes.

A fireplace, brocade sofa, low pie-shell table, and colorful fancy carpet defined an area for seating. Grouped around the room were comfortable chairs, both upholstered and plain. Candles in tall holders were placed carefully for an eye to good illumination, rather than mere decoration. But what held Hannah's attention was a large carved mahogany desk placed squarely against the side wall. It almost reached the ceiling, it had so many drawers above its desktop. And it spilled papers every which way . . . scrolls and plain sheets and parchment and ribbons with which to tie them. The opposite wall was fitted with row upon row of bookcases. Hannah had never supposed there were that many books in the whole world. She walked over and touched the titles. *Artillery and Armaments of the French Militia. Canterbury Tales. Troilus and Cressida. Don Quixote.*

"What is a kicks-o-tea?"

"Hannah is fascinated by books, Colonel," Vincent said. "May I show her?"

"Be my guest! I vow I have the finest collection of books this side of the Atlantic."

"Without a doubt," Vincent said.

He took the volume from the shelf and opened it carefully. The pages were worn, showing that the man not only owned them, but read them, too. Hannah liked that. Books were so precious, they should be used, not merely admired or possessed.

"Q-U-I-X-O-T-E."

"I can spell, Vincent."

"'Tis pronounced Key-ho-tay."

"Then why is it spelled that way?"

"'Tis Spanish. Don Quixote means *Herr* Quixote."

Colonel Jennings spoke up, "I believe a closer meaning would be *burgermeister*. A burgermeister who fences at imaginary windmills and all to catch the eye of the woman he loves."

"Ah!" Hannah though she might like this Burgermeister Quixote who was brave for naught but love.

"Can you read English?" Colonel Jennings asked.

"Oh, *ja*. Vincent, he gave me a Shakespeare and Milton. But I left the Milton on the grave of my people."

Vincent shook his head. "It is there no more." He pulled the book out of his pocket and handed it to her. "Lieutenant Paltray rescued it, Hannah. I have been meaning to give it to you, but we've been rather busy."

Hannah knew exactly what the "busy" meant, and she blushed and hung her head. "*Danke,* Vincent. This means much to me."

"Now, then," the Colonel said, "you shall have

another book." He wrapped Hannah's hands around the copy of *Don Quixote*. "May you have many wonderful hours reading it."

"Oh, I will! *Danke* . . . thank you."

Colonel Jennings took Hannah's hand and led her to the brocade sofa. "I would like you to sit and tell me what happened at New Ephrata so my secretary can take down all the information to help us catch the men who did this terrible thing. Unless, of course, it's too upsetting for you."

"*Nein.* I mourn the dead, but I must help you stop this man who does such wicked things."

The colonel's secretary came in, took a position at a small table, and picked up quill and parchment. In a monotone which did not begin to voice the deep pain such a telling brought to the surface, Hannah related all that had happened and all that she had done. While she spoke, the door opened and closed; but Hannah neither looked up, nor stopped her recital, until she finished with the incident of Vincent rescuing her from the trappers.

The quill scratched on the parchment. A clock ticked away the minutes. But no one spoke. From the tension in the air, Hannah wondered if they were breathing. Finally, someone crossed the room and put a hand on Hannah's head. She looked up into the moist hazel eyes of a woman as broad as she was tall.

"Do you have enough, Richard?"

"Aye, Rachel."

"Then I am taking this young lady with me. She has earned a rest . . . and much, much more." She turned to Vincent. "You and your officers will join us for dinner in our quarters. Half after six. Be prompt."

"Yes, ma'am." When Hannah looked up at Vincent, he smiled. "'Tis all right, Hannah. This is the colonel's wife. You will be safe with her."

"Oh, I know that, Vincent. I was worried about where we were to sleep tonight."

Vincent nearly choked. The woman said the most outrageous things! Yet, they were exactly the right things to seal his soul to hers.

He looked sheepishly toward Mistress Jennings, then thought, *The hell with it! We have naught to be ashamed of, naught to hide.* He lifted Hannah's chin and kissed her softly. "The colonel and I will figure that out, Hannah. Have no fear. I won't be far from you."

When Rachel Jennings took Hannah's arm and drew her toward the door, Hannah threw Vincent one more look which she hoped said everything she felt for him. Then she tried very hard to keep up with a woman whose girth should have slowed her down, but instead seemed to propel her like an avalanche through the streets of Sandy Brook. Hannah would not have been surprised if a few of the people in the street were not swept off their feet. She, herself, was breathless by the time they reached their destination, a two-storied, white-washed log house with nine windows in front, a fan carving over the door, and a pineapple carving on it.

Hannah was sure Rachel opened the door, but she didn't see her do it; for one moment she thought the door could not withstand the energy of this woman. Once inside, Rachel slammed it shut without turning around.

Clapping her hands together, Rachel called, "Hattie!

Rose! Prepare a bath in that new tub of the colonel's! Mind you, use lots of hot water and some of that French scented soap. Now," she added as she tugged Hannah up the stairs, "come along and we'll find something for you to wear that won't scandalize the Reverend Mister Bates. He's coming for dinner, too. Although . . . it would be very amusing to see his face if he ever caught sight of you in that uniform you're almost wearing in some places and poured into in others." She swept into a room of blues and yellows that had Hannah's eyes dancing from one embellishment to another, and never stopped talking. "This was my daughter's room. She's visiting her betrothed's parents. She looks about your size, so we'll have plenty to choose from. What color do you like best? Pink? Blue? Yellow? With that hair and your complexion, you should always wear pastels. They will do wonders for you. Now, what shall it be?"

"Black or purple."

"Black. Or purple."

"*Ja.* For the plain people, always black or purple, though sometimes we also wear the brown. For the skirts. For the bodices, white or blue or dark red. And a white apron. Long, with deep pockets."

Rachel plopped into a chair. "Black or purple or brown skirt."

"*Ja.* Long, to the ankles."

"With a bodice. And an apron."

"*Ja.* This is a problem?"

Rachel waved her hand at a chest at the foot of the large bed. "In there. That is all I have."

Hannah lifted the lid of the chest and her eyes were assaulted with a rainbow of vivid hues. With lace and ribbons and gemstones sewn to bodice and skirt, the clothes were exactly what the Mennonites called "worldly." They would not do. But they were so beautiful, Hannah couldn't help but touch them just to know what they felt like.

She closed the lid. "Your Hattie and Rose . . . they might have something for to suit me . . . *ja?*"

"Are you sure?"

Hannah looked longingly at the chest, and sighed. "*Ja,* I am sure."

" 'Tis simply not fair! I wished to give you something wonderful to make up for all that you have lost . . . all that you have been through. A gift. Just a small gift."

Hannah smiled gratefully at the kind-hearted woman. "But it is not necessary for you to gift me. Vincent has already given me the best and most wonderful gift any woman could ever want."

Rachel assessed Hannah and smiled. "The best and most wonderful gift any woman could want, hey?" She cackled. "Yes, I suppose you could call it that. At least, before you are married, you could."

"But not after?"

"Only if you're lucky, my dear. Only if you're very lucky."

"I *am* lucky, Frau Jennings. With Vincent, I am very, very lucky. And very blessed."

Hannah sat on a stool at Rachel's feet. She blushed and clutched at the hem of Vincent's shirt. There was something she needed, something she had been afraid to ask of Vincent. Perhaps this good woman would be the right one to help.

"Frau Jennings?"

"Call me Rachel."

"Rachel. I have a great question to ask of you. A great boon. One gift which would be very welcome to me."

"It sounds serious."

"It is. Most serious."

"Ask away, child. I will do whatever I can to help."

Chapter Fourteen

While Hannah took a long, leisurely bath in a contraption that resembled the inside-out of a horse, Rachel scoured Sandy Brook for the gift Hannah had requested. That left Hannah with time to think about what had happened and what she would do next.

The French soap delighted her nose. And the froth! She had never had soap made to froth like boiling bean soup. No wonder the elders insisted on naught but lye soap. If the Mennonite women were allowed such luxuries as this, they would have their minds on the pleasures of the bath instead of the Sermon on the Mount.

Yet Rachel did not think of it as important. She had handed Hannah a goodly supply of toweling and two large squares of soap and practically ordered her to use it all. Could it be that if *Englishen* women used this every time they washed, that they became so used to it, it made no impression? Were the elders worried about these little things, when there was no real basis for their worry? It was a puzzle and Hannah was not sure what the true answer was . . . or even if there was any "true" answer. Mayhap, in keeping separate, the elders had seized on insignificant things, things which set them apart, true . . . but things which were only important because they made them so.

Which left Hannah to wonder why she was wondering, why she was questioning the faithful. It surprised her that she made a distinction between the faith, which she embraced, and the faithful, the leaders of it. The faith came of Christ. The faithful, of an oppressive system against which they had rebelled. *The Martyrs' Mirror,* that collection of stories about the hardships and murders of the first of the faithful, made much of the differences in the Anabaptist beliefs and the Papists' idolatry. Made much of the gold and silver chalices, crosses, and vestments which the priests used when their parishioners starved; the graven images which led worshipers to think on the statue instead of Christ and *Gott;* the selling of paradise when faith and baptism were all that Christ required. These, however, were symbols of a greater problem . . . the problem of the poor, the Anabaptists, being subject to the rich, the Papists.

It bothered her . . . because if inconsequential things were only things and not snares for to take the faithful away from their thoughts of *Gott,* then what did she truly believe? And could she turn her whole life over to a system which she questioned?

Hannah found no answers in the froth in her bath. Nor did she find them in the underclothes Rachel had laid out for her.

There were two of everything. One set of soft, delicate silk. Hannah rubbed her cheek against each piece, loving the way it felt as it glided and tickled. But it was too worldly, too different from what she was used to. The other set was of fine linen, so fine, it, too, practically slipped through her fingers—until she got to the underbodice. There were things in the sides. Hard, long sticks sewn into the seams. Hannah shrugged. *Englishen* had many unusual items. It was not surprising to find sticks in underclothing.

Though the underclothing was ruffled and laced, Hannah accepted it. It would be under the skirt and bodice, after all. No one but she and *Gott* would see.

And Vincent. She hoped.

"Hannah! Are you decent?"

"I am Mennonite. Of course I am decent!"

"Oh, Hannah!" Rachel flung her way into her daughter's room and plunked a large, paper-wrapped bundle on the bed. "Every last pledget in the stores. But don't worry, there are more coming." She tore open the package. "I didn't suppose you had a support for them, so I bought three from the general store." She held up the sling which tied around the waist and into which Hannah could place her padded monthly protection. "I bought the smallest size for women. I hope they will be satisfactory."

Hannah blushed and hung her head.

"Oh, my dear! Have I embarrassed you?"

"*Ja*, Frau Jennings . . . Rachel." Hannah saw the distress in Rachel's eyes and hurried to explain to this generous woman. "It is just that in the community such things are discussed only in whispers and only with members of your family. That I have no family left means that I have no one to talk with about these things." She bit her lip and stemmed the tears which were always on the surface, and which she needed strength to control. "I am sorry for being so shy. I have never before spoken of such to anyone but my *mutter* or my aunt."

Rachel put her arm around Hannah's shoulders. "I am the one who is sorry, dear. Richard says sometimes I leap into situations before I look, that my mouth runs away with me. I try to slow down, but . . ." She laughed. "As you can see, I don't succeed very well." She hugged Hannah to her ample body, patted her on the back, and continued, "Now, let's get you dressed properly and we can go shopping. I dearly love shopping."

Hannah picked up the last piece of underclothing and dangled it from her fingers. "If you could tell me how this wooden-sided thing works . . . ?"

" 'Tis a side stay, dear. You wear it to give definition to your figure. Not that you need any more definition than you already have!"

Rachel pulled the side stay around Hannah's midsection and laced it up until Hannah cried for mercy.

"Are women not supposed to breathe?"

"They are supposed to stand tall. That's what the side stays are for."

"Side stays! Prisoners were treated more kindly."

" 'Tis fashion, Hannah. You will get used to it."

She would not. Hannah intended to ask to use the comfort room and she intended to remove the dratted side stays. Mayhap the elders had, after all, done a good thing in making Mennonite women separate.

Supplied by Rachel with enough pledgets from the military stores for six monthlies, Hannah and Rachel

232

set their minds to find something Hannah might wear that night. Hattie and Rose proved to be almost as large as Rachel. Hannah might have been able to take in the skirts and bodices, but they were far too short.

So, in her blustery style, Rachel took charge of "provisioning Hannah," as she called it.

"You cannot shop in your borrowed finery from Captain Scott," she insisted. "For the moment, you can wear my daughter's plainest dress."

Plainest dress turned out to be made of a pale blue linen strewn with tiny flowers. Violets, roses, buttercups, daisies . . . all so small they were hardly discernible from across the room. Its collar was low, but a scarf worn cleverly inside covered Hannah's bosom much more than Vincent's dress shirt. The cut of the dress, however, revealed Hannah's every curve, especially since it was, as Rachel said, "just a trifle small."

The sleeves were tight to Hannah's upper arms and flared into a triple layer of lace-trimmed ruffles which came to Hannah's fingertips. Not very practical in which to work! And the skirt! Yards and yards of fabric, almost twice as much as any of Hannah's skirts . . . and more ruffles at the bottom, with another layer of lace peeping through. A plain blue vest went over the bodice, hugging Hannah's midsection, and pushing her breasts over the curved top of the vest. Rachel tugged the long ribbons which laced it up, but could not get the ends to meet.

"You will just have to wear it like that." She tilted her head and stepped back to get a better view. "It looks fine, Hannah."

In the shops the only bolt of fabric plain and dark was a rough lightweight wool used for servants' skirts.

233

"Absolutely not!" Rachel said. "You will faint from the heat."

Hannah never fainted from anything. But the wool was a bit scratchy and she allowed Rachel to choose cotton in a buttercup yellow for the bodice and a walnut brown for the skirt. *And* a loden green and saffron checked pattern which was so small, Hannah made no fuss. There were several aprons, none as large as the one she was used to, and all embellished with ruffles; she found two which, with a little snip here and rip there, would be acceptable. There was, however, nothing which would do for a prayer cap. There were mobcaps aplenty, and some bonnets, but none of starched cheesecloth, lightweight wool, or stiffened cotton. In the end, Hannah ended up buying naught but yard goods. She and Rachel trudged home . . . cantered would be more like it, the way Rachel raced through the streets. Hannah was enervated, and a good thing, too. She would have to spend the afternoon sewing . . . and very quickly . . . if she were to be ready for the dinner party that evening.

But leave it to Rachel. She organized five of the servant girls in the camp who were handy with needle and thread and were used as dressmakers by the officers' wives. It was almost like an evening in the Mennonite community, when all the women came together to quilt and sew. These were girls more of Hannah's bent. Three were British, from Lancastershire, and had begun as indentured servants. Two were Continentals. Josette, from Normandy, and Constance, from Marseilles. All spoke English, but none had the same accent and soon Hannah felt very much at ease.

Since the plain skirts were easy to cut and sew,

234

Hannah left that up to the British servants. Constance and Josette, happier with the intricate stitches needed for the bodice, took one each. Hannah spent her time adjusting the aprons before she started producing prayer caps from the cheesecloth and cotton. The ruffles on the apron were the first to go. Hannah used them to make wide straps to crisscross in the back. And pockets. With judicious and creative sewing . . . piecing strips of the ruffles together so the finished product looked deliberately pleated . . . she managed to have enough for generous pockets for both aprons.

But the prayer caps took up most of her time. The pleating had to be just so, with enough room for her full head of hair. And the brim should come over the sides of the face, for to keep her from becoming more interested in what was happening around her than in her inner thoughts. The ties were important, too. They should be long enough to loop modestly in the front, but not so long as to make a worldly-looking bow. It was tiring work, but Hannah plied her needle with the skill Magda had taught her. Three hours later, she had two changes of clothing, but she still had to stiffen the prayer caps.

Rachel came to the rescue again.

"What will you need, dear?"

"Usually we mash dried corn to a powder, mix it with chalk and soak the caps for several hours, then dry them on special forms shaped like heads. You would have such things?"

"We have a starch made of milk and corn. But the forms you describe? The only one I know of is in the general store. Here, give me the caps and Hattie and Rose can starch them. We shall requisition whatever we need from the shopkeepers." She linked her arm through Hannah's. "Sometimes being the wife of the commander is a blessing. Other times . . . a curse."

"When a curse?"

"When they go to war, dear. When they don't come back."

"*Ja,*" Hannah said. "I know. That is what happened to *mein vater.*"

"He went to war?"

"He was forced to go to war. This is why we come to America. So as not to be forced to kill."

"But war is coming," Rachel said, sadly. "Coming soon."

"And will the soldiers come and take my people to war? Will they force them to bear arms here, too?"

"King George won't. He has generals and colonels and regiments and companies and units. He does not need those who would not willingly fight."

"And the colonials?"

"They have called for a Continental Congress. It is too soon to tell what they will do. But from what little I have seen of the colonials, they will only want men who are eager for this independence they talk so much about. They will not force anyone, have no fear."

But Hannah did fear. Not about the Mennonites being taken from their farms and thrown into the army or gaol, but of what dangers Mennonite communities faced. Renegades and Indians had already devastated New Ephrata . . . and others, according to Valerie Despart. With a great war, the British who were supposed to patrol the frontier would be in battle against the colonials. The Mennonite farms would be vulnerable once more. And with two armies needing supplies, she thought to herself, who knew how many times Mennonites would be "requested" to dip into their stores for to feed men on both sides.

Hannah's greatest fear, however, was for Vincent.

A captain, she had learned from the talk in Vincent's units, led his men into battle. Generals could conduct from the rear. Not so lieutenants and captains. If there was war, Vincent would be in front, dodging bullets and bayonets. Her Vincent. So visible in that red coat.

That evening at dinner Hannah could not take her eyes off Vincent. Though he was only one among five men who wore their dress uniforms, she thought him the shining example of the British crown. He had to compete with all the women, however. Gold braid and silver buckles were as nothing to necklines that disclosed rather than concealed, powdered hair piled high and heated with irons to unnatural curls, earrings of gold and jewels, rings of all colors and sizes. And these things were not confined only to the women. One gentleman had a ring on every finger of his right hand, including his thumb! How could people such as this be welcomed into the Lord's kingdom?

Yet the Reverend Mister Bates blessed the food much as Uncle Franz did. And the topic of conversation at supper was the sermon given at the last Sabbath service.

"Render to Caesar the things that are Caesar's and to God the things that are God's—is as important today as it was in Christ's time," Mister Bates importuned from his place next to Rachel. "Luckily, we here in Pennsylvania know that what is right for the king is right for the people. They will not bear arms, I tell you. They will not fight against the king, for they are about

the Lord's business and expect the king's servants—his army and courts—to be about his."

"But last Sunday you admonished us to love our neighbor," a bewigged and beringed woman said. "How are we to love our neighbor and go to war with him?"

"Ah . . . but that is where your Christian charity must prevail. Always, God wants you to love the sinner but hate the sin."

"And is war the sin?" Hannah asked timidly.

"Nay," Mister Bates said. "The sin is in not rendering proper obedience to civil authorities. The sin is in insurrection, mutiny, calumny. The sin is in not doing what Christ asked by not rendering to the king the just taxes and tariffs he and his councilors have begged from us. After all, they will be used to help defray expenses for the war against the French and the Indians, which protected all the colonies from French takeover. So, these insurrectionists are planning to deliberately break one of Christ's commandments."

"Which one of the ten is that?" Rachel teased.

"Coveting, my dear. Coveting what is rightfully the king's."

The eyebrows of the bewigged woman rose in mirth as she whispered to the woman across from Hannah, "Who covets that cow of a queen? More likely most would covet the court mistresses."

Queen and court mistresses? Hannah had thought the minister was talking about taxes and tariffs.

"Really, my dear," the man on the bewigged woman's right said, "you confuse our young friend. Tell her you jest or she will think you one of the revolutionaries."

The woman apologized but Hannah was left with a taxing problem of her own. She had assumed that the "worldly" never approached a situation from a religious point of view. Yet, they discussed Biblical matters as if they had great import in their lives. It was a confusing world she had stumbled into.

It was made even more confusing when musicians in the parlor began to play their instruments and Vincent came to ask her to dance.

"You look very handsome tonight in your dress uniform, Vincent," Hannah said as they walked toward the festivities.

"I liked it much better on you."

The seductive whisper made Hannah blush. She swept into the room with a quick laugh and a coy, "But do you not like my new clothes?"

Vincent made a thorough examination of the green and yellow check and nodded his head. "Much better than that old dark thing you used to wear."

"Alas, 'tis only temporary. I don plain dark brown and yellow tomorrow."

"But tonight you sparkle like a meadow in spring. Let us make the best of it."

"Oh, dear!"

"Another problem, Hannah?" Rachel said from behind them.

"The dances. They are not *bevolken* . . . Oh, what is the English? Folk! Lines and reels."

Rachel laughed. "I'm afraid we left lines and reels behind centuries ago. The closest we come is the minuet. They will play one of those soon. But the rage this year is the waltz. Vincent, you take her outside and teach her some of the steps. Go, go, you two, while I make arrangements for Hannah's sleeping quarters."

They were out on the wide side porch when Hannah asked, "I will not be staying here with Rachel?"

"The colonel already houses four officers and their wives and children who are here on temporary assignment. There is no room. He is having several tents erected for my regiment in the field next to the church. I have requested a small one be reserved for you, where I can keep my eye on you."

When he took the first dance stance, she giggled. "It seems, Captain Scott, that you keep more on me than merely your eyes."

"Hannah Yost, if I didn't know better I'd think you were flirting with me!"

"To make banter is flirting?"

"To look at me as if I were the main course on your breakfast menu is definitely flirting."

"Then you, too, are flirting with me!"

Vincent crushed her to him in an exaggerated turn of the dance. "My menu is more for a midnight libation, though breakfast entices as well. Ah, Hannah, how I love holding you in my arms!"

'Tis where I belong, Vincent, she wanted to say, but held her tongue so as not to put pressure on him. Though she often dreamed in the day about being his true betrothed, she had no such illusions that it would ever come to pass. They were in impossible positions, an impossible situation. That didn't mean, however, that she could not enjoy it while it lasted.

Enjoyment did not half describe the wonders of these unusual dances! If she and Vincent had previously been flirting with each other with their eyes, now they did so with their hands, fingertips, arms, bodies. Vincent held

240

her, so . . . and his hands were feather light touches. He turned her, so . . . and they were masterful. He whirled her in the intricate steps of the lively waltz and she felt his imprint on her breasts and belly one moment, only to have it withdrawn the next.

Round and round they whirled, until Hannah was dizzy . . . but not from the dance alone. Vincent's hand on her back, the way his fingers splayed along her waist, the heat that traveled from their joined hands, the way his voice sent whispers of wind against her ear, and the white hot tingling each time their bodies brushed against each other . . . those were the things that made her dizzy with desire—the kind of desire they had shared in Vincent's bedroll. And here it was open to everyone's view.

So confusing were these customs! Lovemaking in public, in fine party dresses and jewels, was acceptable. Behind closed doors or in a relatively private bedroll, indiscreet, *verboten*. The only difference she could see was that with the dance you were *vertikale;* with the bedroll, *horizontale*.

Mein Gott, such a silly difference! But on that a reputation rose or fell. How much more sensible, the bundling. For, of course, most couples advanced their bundling as their relationship progressed. Advanced to the point where there were sometimes "over the rail" babies produced mere months after the marriage vows were exchanged. But the babies were accepted as perfectly normal occurrences. Certainly, none at the community ever referred to them as illegitimate. Conceived through bundling or after the vows, *de kinder* were a gift from *Gott*.

That misty look in Hannah's eyes made Vincent

241

wonder what delights she imagined. He knew what he imagined. He imagined those shadows he had seen on the ground, the curves he had held and caressed—imagined seeing them unrobed for him alone. And immediately he felt a hardening in his groin which was a white hot throbbing ache that only Hannah could assuage.

There was no smile like hers, so genuine and guileless. No other eyes as brown as hot, rich chocolate. No lips so full and kissable. No body so lush in its modesty, so uninhibited and natural in its reaction to his lovemaking.

The reality was that he wanted this woman more than he'd ever wanted anything in his life. Including his military career. Including his share of the estate's largesse. Clarisse had taken almost everything from him. The military had given him back his dignity. Hannah had restored his soul. His wanting her was more than physical. It was the culmination of a yearning which had begun when he was barely as old as she. The only fear he knew at the moment was that the culmination of this quest would never reach its true fruition. It could come only if he and Hannah were joined in a perfect union of body and spirit, understanding and hope, trust and love.

How was this to be accomplished? She had her faith, her *raison d'être*. He had the military, the antithesis of her life to this moment. Could they bridge the gap? Would she want to?

God, he hoped so! He could not imagine a life without her. If he were to be relegated to such, he might wither—or what was more likely, turn into a block of ice so dense it would rival the greatest iceberg in

Scandinavia. He did not relish returning to that state of suspended life, that state that made him more corpse than corpus. He wanted this woman and the warmth, the life, she had brought him in such abundance.

"Are you ready to try out the steps inside with the assemblage?" He steeled his voice to hide the tremors of his body, the tremors that concentrated in that area below his waist where—when he was around Hannah— he seemed to have little or no control. He held his breath, hoping she would say *no.* Their entrance at that moment would reveal his discomfort to the entire household and he did not want to make her a subject of women's tittering and men's bawdy jokes. But he could not tell her that. She was too much the innocent to understand his condition and what occasioned it.

Hannah leaned against Vincent, her arms wrapped around his waist, her nose buried against his neck. It was as if he were her air, water, and sustenance—and she, drinking him in else she might not survive. When he asked her if she wanted to go inside, she leaned back to give him her answer. And in that small movement she learned what the dance had done to him.

She smiled, happy that he had been as affected as she. "I would prefer to find my tent, Redcoat. It has been a long, tiring ride . . . and my thoughts during this introduction to your life and your people . . . very *verwechslungen.*"

"That one I don't know, Hannah."

"*Verwechslungen* . . . mixed like cake batter. Whirling round and round in my head. More than confusion. Like a shooting star and a whirlpool, all at once."

"That describes how you make me feel."

"Ah, *ja*—me, too." She blushed and laughed. "*Nein.* Not how I make me feel. How you make me feel."

"I understood."

"We will find my tent?"

"We will say our good nights to Rachel and Colonel Jennings first." When they did so, Rachel drew Hannah upstairs to her daughter's room once more. "We did not think about your night clothing, Hannah. And you certainly have no time to sew up something plain now." She opened a smaller chest which sat under one of the windows. "I would like you to have this. It is plain, Hannah. Truly it is. At least as plain as I could find on such short notice."

Hannah fingered the delicate stitches on the bodice of a creamy peach-colored gown. Except for its color, it reminded her of her bundling gown. The bodice was quilted. Not patchwork, but an overquilting of *embroderie française,* depicting the mountain laurel, a flower found growing abundantly in Pennsylvania, and delicate wild roses like the ones Hannah had left behind in the Palatine. There were no ruffles, no encrusted braid—there did not have to be. The color and the handiwork made it a forbidden treasure.

"You have naught white?"

"Several But they are ruffled and very . . . how can I say it without embarrassing you . . . very seductive. Low necklines and clinging fabric. Stuff fit for a new English bride, not your kind of plain nightly wear."

Hannah sighed. Her fingers loved the texture of the fabric. Her mind reveled in the beauty of the design. "I would think of this and my prayers, naught."

"I would have given you something of Hattie's or

244

Rose's, but anything they have would be miles too big and leagues too short."

Rachel's shoulders slumped for the first time that day and Hannah realized how uncharitable she was being. "It is so lovely, Rachel. So much from your heart. I was overwhelmed for a moment and forgot my manners. *Danke,* sweet Rachel. I will accept such a beautiful gift with gladness in my heart for the woman who gives it."

Rachel's usual ebullience returned in an instant. "Oh, Hannah! Are you sure you cannot stay here with us? We would be honored to have a woman of your gentleness and quite common sense."

"Nein, Rachel. But thank you for asking. I must find my uncle and tell him and the others what occurred. And I must help them to understand that they must not attempt another settlement until this devil is caught."

"Richard has arranged that your captain go with you. You would like that?"

Hannah laughed. "You know I would."

"You love him, your captain?"

"Ja, Rachel. I love him."

"But you will not marry him."

"How do you know this?"

"By the forlorn way you admit your love. It is an embrace and a farewell all in one." Rachel folded the nightgown and handed it to her new friend. "As I give this gift, I give you an old Welsh blessing. 'With the wind at your back and a prayer on your lips, the Lord go with you and bring you the yearnings of your heart.'"

Chapter Fifteen

Vincent left Hannah at the flap of her tent with naught but a chaste kiss on the cheek. Her sad look almost stayed him but he smiled, pushed her inside, and made sure the tent flap closed after her before walking away.

Reluctantly.

He looked to the right and left as he walked, at the shifting eyes and vacant smiles from those he didn't know.

Who was he fooling?

Certainly not these soldiers, who examined the bulge in his breeches as nonchalantly as they examined the bug bites on their arms. Certainly not the men in his regiment, who lounged around the campfire and offered a chorus of: *Good night, Captain,* or *To the morrow, Captain,* or *All's well, sir.* And certainly not his good friend Geoffroy, who clucked his tongue and shook his head.

"May I join you, Scott?" Geoff asked. At Vincent's nod, Geoff offered his friend a pipe and a suede pouch of tobacco. "Just came in from the islands. Has some Virginia blend in it. Nice bite."

They pulled up camp chairs and a barrel in a group in front of the officers' tent, lit their pipes, and puffed leisurely. Then Vincent glanced over to Hannah's tent. What he saw there made his mouth drop open in awe. For one moment, he was flummoxed. Then, he choked on the smoke, jumped to his feet, and nearly fell on his face rushing to cross the field.

He threw open Hannah's tent flap and croaked, "Jesus, God, Hannah! Outen that candle!"

Hannah shrieked and held up her new nightdress to cover herself.

"Too late, *liebchen.*" Vincent blew out the candle in the lantern.

"What ist das? What have I done?"

Vincent crossed to her side and drew her into his arms. "You did naught but what I should have anticipated." He scooped her up and brought her to the bed. "You are certainly not the first woman who has come to Sandy Brook and gotten undressed for bed in front of lantern light. But I think you're the first who did it who isn't a camp follower trying to attract trade."

"What is this camp follower?"

"Someone like Valerie Despart, *liebchen.*"

"A *putain?*"

"Yes."

Hannah buried her face in shame. "What did you see?"

"The most glorious silhouette in the whole world. It was seductive, Hannah."

"But I did not mean it to be!" she wailed.

248

"Which made it more so. The innocence of you—it is not to be described. How you removed your apron and folded it neatly before putting it on the bed. How your arms stretched high—"

"I was yawning."

Vincent chuckled. "Your breasts were not."

"Ei, Gott! And the men saw?"

"I saw. Every movement." He sighed. "It was quite a sight. I liked it very much."

"Then why rush in here like . . . like the bull?"

"I wish that sight only for my eyes, *liebchen,* not for my men's."

"Ah!" She squirmed on his lap. "I have a confession, Vincent."

"Shall I get you the Reverend Mister Bates?"

"Nein. This is confession only for you."

"I shall listen with the wisdom of Solomon."

"While I was stretching, I was thinking of you . . . dreaming of our bundling . . . of the way I felt when you kissed me. So if I did wrong, it was only because you flame me, my Redcoat."

Good God, such honesty! "In a world that is completely corrupt, you are the only truly innocent thing I know."

"Not so innocent anymore, Vincent." She sighed against his chest, rubbing her cheek against the scratchy linen and the bumpy braid. "Uhmm. That is good, *ja?"*

"Very good."

She reached to touch his face and her nightdress dropped. Grabbing, she brought it back to her neck and gasped, "I forgot. I am not dressed."

"Of that, I'm well aware." His voice grew husky and

he nibbled on her ear. "So luscious. Have you been bathing in lemons?"

She stretched her neck to allow him access to other tender spots and was pleased that his mouth found them, sending stabs of heat through down to the tips of her breasts. "Rachel gave me powder for the night." She held one arm out to him. "You like how it feels?"

He brushed his mouth against her arm and smelled the scent, felt the softness. "I like." Sighing, his hand cupped her breast, found the hard nipple. "I like very much."

His fingers had wills of their own; they played with Hannah's nipple and music only he could hear came thrumming out and into his body. He pushed the fabric away and dropped his mouth to take in the symphony which was Hannah and was lost in a crescendo of feeling that exploded every ounce of sense he had.

"God, sweetheart, I want you!"

He placed her on her cot and looked down at her. Her nightdress was as a brook rolling over her body. Where her breast was bare, it caressed the underside of the delicate white mounds. Then it cascaded down over her stomach, undulated against her hips, dropped into shadow where the depths of her were, and finally flowed down the length of her thighs and over her knees to the floor.

The sirens of the deep were not so beautiful, so seductive.

And Hannah didn't even know she was.

Her eyes were wide in the darkness. Shadows cast by the dancing campfire outside made her skin lustrous silk and innocent one moment, velvety black and mysterious the next. She moved her leg and his heart

250

near jumped out of his chest. She was everything; and he wanted her.

He dropped to his knees and reached for the darkest shadow, the deepest depths. His hand pressed and retreated. His fingers sought and found. His mouth dropped to her belly and when she gasped—as he'd hoped she would—he felt her muscles contract all the way to where his fingertips rubbed gently. With one hand, he parted her legs, pulled aside her nightdress, and ran feathery touches up to her curls at the apex of her thighs. His head moved slowly, allowing her enough time to get used to one sensation before continuing on, ever downward, ever closer to the most wonderful part of her. And then he claimed it as he'd once claimed her lips.

Hannah's stillness drew his head up. He looked at her and found the shimmer of tears coursing down her cheeks.

"Hannah! There is naught evil or dirty in what we do."

"Ah, Vincent. This I know. There is beauty, always beauty. And so much beauty cannot be dirty, nor evil." She smiled slightly. "I wanted more of our beautiful bundling." A chuckle ended with a cry. "I always want more when I am with you."

He swiped at a tear and then another. "Then why are you crying?"

She touched his head and buried her hands in his thick, chestnut-colored hair. "Because by wanting so much your touch, your loving, I compromise you. I do not want to hurt you. I wish only for you to be rewarded for your courage, for the good work you do. But your men already think me a *putain*. By being here with me, your reputation . . . ruined, it will be!"

His mouth dropped open. "*My* reputation!?"

Dear God, she thought only of him. And he had not given her reputation one whit's worth of thought. He had wanted her and acted on that desire. And all the while she had agonized over what his being with her would do to *him*. And the world counted Clarisse a "lady," Hannah a peasant. The world did not know what a true lady was, nor where the true treasure lay.

In agony over what he had almost done to her, he gathered her to him, took her nightdress and drew it softly over her head. "I do not leave you because of my reputation, my love, but because of yours."

Her hand caught his chin and she kissed him quickly. "Vincent!"

He rose from her cot and smiled down at her. Outside, the campfire crackled. Insects buzzed. Crickets chirped merrily. Owls hooted. Boots clumped on wooden walkways. A fiddler swept up plaintive melodies. Men's voices rose and fell in waves of words that sounded far away. Inside, the firelight flickered on the tent walls. His heart thumped so loudly, he was sure she could hear. Hannah raised herself onto her elbows and watched him. She took shallow breaths that heightened as he moved away from the cot. And something so powerful it was frightening even to him overtook him and he dropped once again to his knees.

"I have to touch you once more. Just once more."

"*Ja,* Vincent. I want that, too."

He closed his eyes as his hands moved reverently over her body. He would remember this moment all the nights they were parted—all the days of his life. "Some day, Hannah. Dear God, someday I will teach you what it is like to make love. Someday I will take you to the heavens."

"If you could do that before death claims me, it will be wonderful, I know." She ruffled his head. "But it will not be enough unless someday you also show me how to take you to the heavens."

"Do the wishes of your heart come true, Hannah?"

"Some of them have, Vincent. But others, I still await."

"Do you pray?"

"Every morn and eve."

"Pray for that, love. For the wishes of both our hearts to come true."

He left her then, and she whispered into the emptiness of the tent, "I do not think the good God will honor the kind of wish I have for us, Vincent. But I do wish it . . . with all my heart."

When he returned to his tent, his camp chair had been picked up and put back on its legs. His pipe lay on the arm and a tankard of ale sat on the barrel next to it. Vincent plopped down into the hard seat, relit his pipe, and took a good, long quaff of the ale. He couldn't get comfortable and shifted until his groin wasn't aching quite so much.

Geoffroy snickered, then coughed.

"Don't say a word, Geoff."

"I wouldn't think of it, Scott. But what the hell are you doing back here so soon?"

"She was afraid for my reputation."

"I didn't quite hear that. Would you repeat it?"

"She—Hannah—was afraid for my reputation."

"You did say *my?*"

"I did."

"Good God!"

"Amen."

The silence was punctuated only by Geoffroy's sucking on tobacco that had long been extinguished. "When are you going to marry that girl?"

"I'd do it tomorrow if I could give her what she needs the most."

"Oh, great sage, pray tell me what that is."

"Stability. Permanence. A husband who might be alive for more than a month or a year." He sighed. "And a husband who could embrace this religion of hers." Vincent slammed the bowl of his pipe on the ground to remove the tobacco. He ground the smoldering blend into the dirt. "Jesus! Mennonites! That community of New Ephrata, damn them! They kept her so damned innocent in a world that is totally corrupt. When she needed weapons to guard herself against the corruption, they offered naught more than *Love thy neighbor*. Lord, I wish that worked with blood thirsty Indians like this damned Cuppimac, or greedy, rapacious trappers like Valerie's band of outlaws. But I live in the world that is, not what might be. Tell me, Geoff, how does a man who makes his living as a soldier become a husband to a Mennonite? To a woman whose religion thinks killing even in self defense is an abomination? To a woman whose leaders would sacrifice every woman and child before they would pick up a gun and defend them? How do we get past that wall, Geoff? When you get the answer to that one, let me know and I'll propose to the lady. For now, leave me the hell alone!"

Vincent tossed the empty pipe into Geoffroy's lap and stalked into the tent, leaving Geoff to ponder his words. It was a conundrum, that. Mennonite and fusillier. God, what a combination! But Hannah Yost and Vincent Scott were more than Mennonite and fusillier. They were like two perfect cogs. The pieces fit. Oh, not smoothly. Naught in this world, as far as Geoff could see, had ever fit smoothly. But Vincent and Hannah came as close as any two people could. There had to be a way they could make it work, but Geoff was damned if he could see it now.

Chapter Sixteen

When Hannah walked past the campfire the next day, Geoffroy called her over to a table at which he and Paltray were drinking coffee. "Paltray, get Mistress Yost a camp chair."

"Aye."

"And bring her some breakfast."

Paltray rushed to the back of a wagon, picked up a wooden plate, and thrust it out at the regimental cook. "I'll be right back, Washington. Give the lady a good helping of your best."

"The lady don't look like she eats good helpings," Washington grumbled.

"Then she'll need one, won't she?"

Washington's wizened face became more wrinkled when he grinned from ear to ear. "Yeah! She would, that."

Paltray brought over a chair for Hannah, then tore back to the wagon and returned with a plate heaped with biscuits, ham, creamed corn, and stewed apples. Hannah took one look and collapsed into the chair, laughing.

"Enough for the unit, there is," she said.

"Don't worry," Geoff said. "Whatever you don't finish, Paltray, here, will gobble up. He's still a growing boy."

Paltray blushed and stumbled back from the table. "Oh, for God's sake!" He stalked off, his shoulders slumped.

"You tease him often, *ja?*"

"Every chance I get." He chuckled. "He'll make a damned fine officer one day, but he's still a youngster and needs forming. Good-natured jesting will make a man of him. Soon's he learns how to respond to it, that is."

Hannah chewed thoughtfully. "It was like that at the settlement. Pieter worked with the young men. He teased them into shows of temper, then gently chastised them to show them the error of their ways. He was a good man."

"Most men are good."

"You believe that?"

"It surprises you?"

"It does." She tilted her head and scrutinized Geoffroy. "You are a soldier . . . like Vincent. But I do not believe that he thinks most men are good. I think he has seen too many who are bad. He has become . . . how do you say *ermatted* . . . weak? No . . . another *Englishen* word." She frowned and thought hard. "Tired . . . weary . . . ."

"Jaded!"

"*Ja*, jaded. He seems that way to you, also?"

"He has not told you about his life in England?"

"*Nein*. Was it *furchtbar?*" At Geoff's raised eyebrows, she chuckled. "Dreadful."

258

"Yes, at the end it was dreadful."

Though Geoffroy was not sure he should be the one to tell her Vincent's troubles, he decided that the damned fool probably would never do it on his own. So, although he fully expected Scott to call him out if he ever found out that Geoff had been the one to tell Hannah, he did it anyway. He related all of Scott's history—his family, its title, Scott's betrothal to Clarisse, the scandal that had never been fully explained, and Scott's sobriquet of *Scandalous Scott.*

Hannah sniffed. "How could he have earned that name? He is a gentleman. A true gentleman."

"Aye. It comes with being a Viscount's son."

"Nein. He is good, Vincent is. He worries about me all the time. And I am naught to him."

"You are everything to him, Hannah. Everything. And he hates it that he can do naught about it."

They were interrupted by Paltray, who thrust a broadside at Geoffroy.

"The colonials have met in a Continental Congress. A Continental Congress! What the hell is that? Oh, beg pardon, Mistress Yost."

Geoffroy read the broadside quickly and handed it to Paltray. "Avoid aggression, they warn the insurgents from Massachusetts. Yet, they promise aid if attacked. And that Galloway wants an American Congress to share power with Parliament."

"May I see?" Hannah asked.

Paltray seemed startled. "You read English?"

"Ja. Your Mister Shakespeare, he teaches me." She scanned the articles in the sheet of paper and read some passages twice. "What are Intolerable Acts?"

"'Tis complicated."

259

"But 'tis why you are here in the colonies, *ja?*"

Geoff nodded. As simply as he could, he told her about the Coercive Acts which had been passed by Parliament in March: The closing of the port of Boston; dissolving the government in Massachusetts and appointing Council members approved by the Crown; eliminating all but one annual town meeting and confining that to local matters only; restricting Massachusetts residents to trials in other colonies or in England, but not in Massachusetts at all; providing for billeting troops in private residences; and transferring jurisdiction of western Massachusetts land to Quebec, which was governed by the French and had no trial by juries or elected assembly. And he explained how the Massachusetts Governor, Thomas Hutchinson, had been dismissed and a Military Governor, General Thomas Gage, appointed in his place.

Hannah thought about what Geoff had told her and she didn't see any way out of the fear which overwhelmed her. In a voice barely above a whisper, she spoke tremulously, "If Massachusetts does not cap . . . capitulate, there will be war. And you will be involved?"

"Yes, Hannah," Geoff said. "Unless a miracle happens, we will be involved."

"Then I shall pray for a miracle." She laid her hand on Geoff's. "I wish you safe, too, Geoffroy. You are a good friend to my Vincent."

She pushed back from the table and strode off toward the Colonel's house. Geoffroy watched her progress carefully. Her dark brown skirt and pale yellow bodice were prim and proper. Her apron, a sign that she was not one of the officers' women. And because her figure was lush and could not be completely hidden by her austere dress, she attracted great interest. Some men saw only the servant-like costume and started to accost her. But when they looked higher and took in her face, they spied that telltale prayer cap—and the way Hannah held herself proudly, not at all like a servant wench who would welcome their advances—and both aspects of the woman stayed their forward motion. The men looked confused and stepped back to let her pass without incident. But Geoffroy frowned. Hannah could walk unmolested in the camp in the daytime, but at night? He had best see the Colonel or Scott and ask that a guard be placed on her at all times. Better yet, she should be hustled out of the camp as soon as possible, and someone from the army should be assigned to escort her home.

Geoff smiled, pleased with his brilliant ploy. Yes, that would do it. Scott on the trail with that woman for two weeks should cement the relationship. And if he knew Scott—and after five years serving under the man, he knew him better than the Viscount—Mistress Yost would be bound to a Viscount's son before General Gage ordered a shot fired.

With that in mind, Geoffroy went in search of Colonel Jennings and outlined the problems of having a woman like Hannah in Sandy Brook.

Meanwhile, Vincent had his own problems. The horses that were requisitioned for the post, it seemed, came with their own version of a harpy. Irish as the day was long, Cathleen Cochran—a tall spitfire with black

261

hair, green eyes, freckles, and a body which had caught the attention of half the fort—splayed her feet, slammed her fists against her hips, stuck out her chin, and glared defiantly at Vincent.

"Look at them, will you, now? Those are thorough-bred race horses, those are, in this pen. Observe their lines, the delicate legs on them, the aristocratic nose, the sheen to their coat. They have been loved, they have. And after looking at them, can you rightly think those are military horses, now? 'Tis a miscarriage of justice, I'm telling you. The horses bear my mark right here, you see?"

She ruffled back the hair on the flank of a particularly beautiful roan. Plain as plain could be Vincent saw a mark burned into the horse's flesh. He traced it with his fingers.

"Yeah, surely," the woman said. "The double *C*, don't you know? The double *C* for Cathleen Cochran. Me! And there's none that can claim different!"

Vincent sighed. The brand was what she said it was, but he had a bill of sale. And a job to do. He waved the bill of sale in her face. "The King says the horses are his."

"The King! Pah! That's a laugh for a fact. The King don't say naught, Captain. The King is in his court, dancing with the ladies, he is. That paper in your hand, it lies, don't you know?"

"No, I do not know. What it says—"

"I know what it says! It says that the blooming British army has bought itself twenty horses from the Earl of Dunswell. But I'm asking you, do the horses carry his brand or mine? And if mine, then whose do you think they be?"

"King George the Third's, that's whose."

"Not on your mother's head, they don't!" From the saddlebags on her own roan stallion, she pulled out some papers and waved them in *his* face. "Look at this, will you now? Papers. Newspapers. Describing the Cochran racehorses and the mark of the Cochrans. Describing how we're after beating the stuffing out of that stiff-necked Earl's own thoroughbreds. We've won every race against him in the last two years. Now there's a war of sorts of our own going on, don't you know? And I warrant the Earl's steward decided to even the score by substituting our best mounts for his work-horses. He must have figured the King's men would be so anxious to get *any* horses they'd not look too closely. He was right now, wasn't he?"

"Mistress Cochran, this is the most outrageous, but imaginative, nonsense I've ever heard."

"Nonsense?" She stuck her chin out and all but snarled. "Nonsense? Do you not believe your eyes? Then here!" She smacked his chest with the papers. "Read, damn your eyes! Unless you can't read, Captain?"

"Of course I can read!"

"Then don't you think you should have the truth of the matter now?"

Vincent knew if he didn't separate fact from fancy, then the army was in for a series of lawsuits. They had bought Dunswell horses. They had a right to Dunswell horses. But if these were not Dunswell horses, then they had no right to them. Damn and hell! Why had he volunteered to help settle this matter? Because his regiment had been in charge of the stupid beasts, that was why. But these were no stupid beasts, he had seen that right away. And if what Mistress Cochran said was true, then he had a fine kettle of mash on his hands. Unless he could get out of it quickly.

He kept her sputtering and hopping from one foot to the other while he read every last word of the account of the Cochran racing strain and its competition with the Earl of Dunswell. He compared the printer's rendition of the Cochran brand to the one on the flanks of several horses. She watched every last move he made. He began to realize it was not because of her unease for herself but because she didn't want him to make a wrong move with her horses. She spoke to them by name and they whickered and nuzzled her. By the time they had made a circuit of the pen and he'd seen the same thing happen to nine of the horses, he was convinced.

She smiled when he scowled, rolled up the papers, and pushed them back at her. "You seem satisfied, Captain, you do. Not too happy now, but satisfied I'm telling the truth, I vow."

"What good does this truth do me, Mistress Cochran? If I give you back your horses, I'm short twenty mounts."

"Ah, but if you own Dunswell horses, then take Dunswell horses."

"And where are we to get Dunswell horses?"

She smiled guilelessly and chuckled. "Well, now, I just happened to have come across twenty of the finest workhorses along the trail, so to speak. And lo and behold, they bear the crested brand of the Dunswells."

Vincent knew in a flash that this woman and Hannah had been made from similar molds. Cathleen Cochran, however, had had no mediating force like Hannah's faith to mellow her. Cathleen was cunning and cute, wide-eyed innocence in a calculating body; Vincent pitied the Earl of Dunswell, who obviously had more in this Irish lass than his title could handle.

Vincent returned Cathleen's infectious smile, then chuckled and finished up by laughing along with the delightful young woman. "So, Mistress Cochran, it looks as though King George's Army will own the Earl of Dunswell's horses regardless of what we have now."

"I was sure you would see it my way, Captain, I was. 'Tis so simple, after all. I'll just leave the Dunswell horses and take my own back and none will be the wiser."

"Oh, if I'm not mistaken the Earl will be the wiser very soon, Mistress Cochran. What shall I tell him when he or his steward comes galloping in here tracking after you?"

Cathleen Cochran winked saucily. "Tell him he's late to the finish line. As usual."

She fair skipped into the center of the pen to get her horses.

"Paltray!"

The man Vincent was beginning to call his shadow spoke up from just behind Vincent's left shoulder. It didn't surprise Vincent in the least.

Paltray saluted. "Aye, sir?"

"See that Mistress Cochran takes only the horses with the double *C* brand. And make damned sure that what she gives you bears the Dunswell crest. Count them, Paltray. She takes twenty. She leaves twenty. Then escort her to the next ridge."

"In what direction, sir?"

"Any direction she wants to go."

265

After she had read the broadside, Hannah had more than prayers on her mind. The gathering in Philadelphia of American assemblymen in their Continental Congress was too close for comfort. Germantown, her destination if she ever got out of this fortification, was just north and to the west of Philadelphia. From what Rachel had said, she knew Colonel Jennings intended to send an escort with her. What kind of a reception would a Redcoat receive in the hotbed of the revolutionary movement? For that matter, what kind of reception would *she* receive if she rode with him? She had already had one escape from men inflamed with passions. She did not doubt that one passion was as good as any other where *that* kind of behavior was concerned. So, she was vulnerable once again.

She would not, could not, let herself be a target for every stupid man who couldn't control himself. She had to find some way to protect herself, even if it was only to learn how to punch and kick in the right places.

She almost went to Rachel to ask for her help. But to seek such a thing from Rachel . . . *nein* . . . that was impossible. Rachel would make of it a whirlwind of activity and draw attention to Hannah. This, she did not want.

So, she made an about-face and skirted the edges of the tents, searching for someone who could teach her and keep it secret. Several soldiers perked up when she approached, but she knew she'd have more problems with them than she wanted.

Then something caught her eye. A young woman was in the horse pen. A young woman dressed in a skirt which had been split up the middle and sewn back together like full breeches. A young woman whose unbound black hair fluttered like a thousand butterflies in the breeze, whose hands steadied the horses as easily as any man's, whose eyes flashed with humor and intelligence. A young woman who had a pistol tucked into her waistband!

Hannah made up her mind in a trice. She noted that the young woman had two men with her and Paltray as an escort. They were riding out of the confines of the fort when Hannah sought out Geoffroy and asked to be allowed to go riding.

"I could use Nightwind," she suggested. "I know him well."

"And have Scott skin me alive? You'll take that chestnut you rode in here on. And an escort."

"But I see Paltray just leaving the fort. If I hurry, I can catch him."

"I'll give you a hand and ride with you until you're under his care."

Less than ten minutes later, Hannah and Geoff pulled up beside Paltray and the young woman.

"Mistress Yost would like a ride, Paltray. See that she gets back to the fort safely."

The young man puffed out his chest with importance. Two such assignments in one morning were a mark that he had come far since his landing in the colonies. "Aye, sir. I'll take good care of the Captain's lady."

"I shall be sure to tell him that," Geoff said. He cautioned Hannah. "Not too far from the post and not too late, else Scott might come looking for you, himself."

She nodded and waited for him to get far enough

away before she turned to Paltray. "Please stop a moment."

The young woman gave Hannah an exasperated gaze. "We have a good deal to go, and cannot be after taking time off, my lady."

"*Ja,* this I know." Hannah halted the chestnut and slid to the ground. "I hate the sidesaddle!" She undid the buckle and let the saddle fall to the ground. "We will pick that up on the way back, Lieutenant," she said. Then, she gathered her skirts, stood on the saddle, and hopped astride the horse's back. "Now, we may proceed."

At Paltray's horrified expression, the young woman threw back her head and laughed. "I like you, Mistress Yost."

"Please to call me Hannah."

"Cathleen, they named me."

"Very pretty. Very musical."

"Very. And not me at all."

"Oh, I do not think that is true. I think there is much music in your soul. You have the look of the *Feenlicht* about you."

"Feenlicht?"

Hannah laughed at Cathleen's pronunciation of the German. With Cathleen's accent, it came out *fenleeckit.* "The light of the fairies. With your wild, soft, black hair and your cat eyes. Very *Feenlicht.*"

"In my country the fairies are blond with blue eyes and they do devilish pranks."

"The physical coloring may be wrong, but I doubt not that the devil is in you, Cathleen. At least, I hope it is."

Cathleen gazed soberly at Hannah. "You did not

come merely to ride, now, did you."

"*Nein*. I have a boon to ask." Hannah sighed. "But before I ask it, I must a true story tell you. About where I have come from and why I am at Sandy Brook."

In a monotone, Hannah told it, trying not to relive the horrors of the three days of the massacre and the near-rape she had endured, trying to disclose the facts without involving her senses, her feelings. She could not do it. Within moments, she found tears flooding her eyes. Almost in concert, the horses slowed and Hannah finished the retelling under a tall oak tree.

Cathleen crossed herself. "Holy Mary and the Blessed Infant! And I thought the history of the Cochrans was cursed. At least we got out of Ireland with our lives and our honor."

"My people are honored, Cathleen."

"Aye, Hannah. In the arms of the Blessed Family, they be now. There is no more honorable place."

Hannah smiled at this young woman of a different faith, and the smile was returned with all the poignancy and understanding Hannah had hoped. They had found a common ground.

"I wish your help," Hannah said.

"What can I do?"

"I saw you in the pen with my Vincent and the horses. I saw you ride away, leading the men, not being led by them. You have the strength I need. And I ask only one thing . . . that you teach me how to protect myself."

"Cannot your Vincent do that for you?"

"I will be with him for only a short time and then I must go back to my uncle. The elders of my faith . . . they do not have the skills . . . they do not

269

believe we need anything more than faith and love. But I have seen and felt what it is like to have no protection at all. I do not wish to kill. I wish merely to be able to survive." Hannah looked up through the branches of the trees, into the brightness of the heavens. "I do not know if this is of *Gott* or of the devil. But I cannot believe that *Gott* wishes us to throw ourselves into the path of bullets and crazed men. I will turn the other cheek. But I only have two of them." She murmured a quick prayer, asking for understanding . . . and, if necessary, forgiveness. "Will you help me?"

Chapter Seventeen

When a shot echoed down the valley into Sandy Brook, all eyes turned toward the southwest and the direction in which it had seemed to come. Men raced to their standing muskets and rifles and took up a ready position. Vincent rounded up his men and discovered one short.

"Paltray should have been back by now. Where the hell is he?" he asked Geoff.

Geoff cursed himself for being six times a fool. "Sorry, Scott, but Hannah asked to go riding. I left her with him as escort."

"Dear God!"

Vincent ran at full speed to Nightwind. He didn't bother saddling the great stallion, merely jumped on his back and grabbed hold of his mane. Crouching low over Nightwind's neck, he urged him southwest. It was only when he was galloping past the pen that he realized it was also the way Cathleen Cochran had left Sandy Brook—he hoped to hell there wasn't a connection. If the Earl or his steward had come to get their horses and took out their frustrations on that Irish devil, Hannah was in the line of fire. Again.

He wasn't to the perimeter when another shot rang out. Then another.

His heart pounded in time with the horse's hooves as they crested the ridge and began the ascent into the woods. Since the shots continued, he followed their sound, becoming less frightened and more curious because of the staccato rhythm of the gunshots. He had had years of drill, years of attacks in warfare, years of shooting rifles and pistols just for the hell of it. This was no attack. This was target shooting.

Thus, when he got to a natural clearing in the woods, he wasn't surprised to see Paltray hovering around a young woman taking aim at a piece of wood set fifty yards away.

He was astonished that the young woman was Hannah.

And furious that the one showing Hannah how to aim the pistol in her hand was the Irish devil herself.

He brought Nightwind to a screeching halt that had the horse pawing the air. Vincent had no choice but to slide off his rump, landing in a heap at Hannah's feet. "What the hell do you think you're doing?"

Hannah couldn't help giggling. Vincent on his bottom, his legs spread wide, his hands holding up his torso . . . and still he tried to be the great, stiff-lipped Captain of the King's Fusilliers . . . when he really looked more like a scarecrow with all the stuffing shaken out of him. She smiled down at this wonderful man . . . at the fear slowly draining from his eyes, at his chest, which rose and fell rapidly. She was sure it was not all from his ignominious ride, judging from his frown.

She handed the pistol to Cathleen and stooped down beside Vincent. "Do you need a hand? One free I have, now."

Vincent couldn't believe his eyes or ears. She didn't have an ounce of sorrow in her voice, and her eyes danced merrily. She found him a laughingstock! She—she—

He grabbed her by the nape of the neck and pulled her to him. "Damn your eyes, you gave me the fright of my life." His mouth crushed hers and he drank deep, stopping only when he'd had his fill and could stop his hands from strangling her.

When his lips left hers, Hannah sighed. "Had I known this, the result would be, I would have tried target shooting long ago." She jumped to her feet and pulled him up. "*Mitcommen!* Let me to show you what Cathleen and Paltray have taught me."

"Paltray?" He rounded on the young man. "Count your promotion lost."

"But, sir!"

"Now, Vincent," Hannah said, "he did only as I asked him. And he took many punches for to help me keep myself safe. Why would you punish him for that?"

"But your elders, they would tar and feather us for showing you this—what did you call it? Abomination?"

"Such *nonunsinglicht!* Peaceful men, they are. They do not tar and feather. Only the abominators in the Palatine do such as this you speak."

"Hannah, you are evading the subject."

Her eyes skittered away and he could see the dancing lights in them. So, she thought this funny, did she? Her, with a pistol in her hand! Pieter should see her now. He would shun her for sure. But Pieter was dead. They were all dead. And Hannah wanted to keep herself safe. Vincent still remembered seeing that hairy hand on her breast, the dirty son of a—

"All right!" He gave his attention to the Irish devil, who had found herself a perch on a rock and was sucking on a dried piece of wild oats. "How much have you shown her?"

Cathleen twirled the oats in her palms and smiled. "A little demonstration you need now, Captain? Methinks Hannah will surprise you, if God be willing." She beckoned to Hannah. "Show him now. And go easy on him. He's a great brawny man, don't you know? But I can't think he's seen what you're going for to show him." She leaned back and crossed her legs. "'Tis a show I shall like, surely."

Vincent felt a movement behind him and spun around. Hannah was there in one moment, and in another, he had hit the ground. "What the hell?"

Paltray limped over. "She did the same to me, sir. Never saw the like of it. And it still hurts like the devil."

Vincent rubbed his neck but he had naught but tingles in his fingers. It was his groin that really smarted. He looked over to Cathleen Cochran. "You're responsible for this?"

"'Tis a little sporting which me sainted father, may he rest in peace, used to teach us. He had a theory, he did, that girl children should be able to box and dodge, good as the boys. And I was a quick learner, don't you know?"

Vincent got to his feet and tested the waters. He could walk and it didn't hurt more than tight breeches. He was sure, then, that Hannah had not kneed him as hard as she had Paltray. But his hand! "What did you do to my neck?"

"Punched it, she did," Cathleen said. "In the vitals, as me da called it."

"Here," Hannah said. She touched the area just under his left ear. "I tried not to hit hard. I hit something that did hurt you?"

"You hit something, all right. But damned if I know what it is."

"You should to hire Cathleen to teach your men."

"We hope we don't come that close to our enemy that we need to use our hands, Hannah. But if we do, we have our bayonets and our knives."

"But they will kill. This will not."

He realized, then, what she had been after. "A compromise. You wanted a compromise. To hurt but not kill."

"Not to hurt, Vincent. That, too, is a sin. But to stop an attack . . . like that of hairy-hands . . . *ja,* I do this compromise."

"And the shots?"

"For to scare them away so they do not come close enough to kill us." She picked up the pistol, loaded it clumsily with powder and ball, and cocked the hammer. "The heaviness, it is surprising, *ja?* And when it shoots! *Krach!* The ears, it deafens." She held it up with two hands, squinted one eye, and pointed it away from them. "That stick on the log . . . you see?"

"I see."

Crack! The stick flipped into the air. Hannah was thrown back into Vincent's arms by the force of the pistol. He put her back on her feet.

"You didn't hit the target."

"Close, I came. That is good enough. Remember,

275

Vincent, I do not shoot to kill."

Vincent put his arm around Hannah and hugged her to him. He kissed the top of her head and looked across at Cathleen Cochran. "Thank you," he said. "This woman is more precious than you know."

"I know," Cathleen said. "Good luck with her, Captain. You shall need it."

She was on her horse and leading her men out of the clearing before Vincent let his arms drop. He took Hannah's chin and lifted it. "It is good, what Cathleen taught you. But your people will not think so."

"I know, Vincent. But they have not seen what I have."

"Ah, God, Hannah! I have to get you out of Sandy Brook before you get completely corrupted."

The matter was taken out of Vincent's hands as soon as they arrived back at the fortification. Sandy Brook had gone on full alert and Colonel Jennings was hopping mad. He sent for Vincent immediately, because he had listened to Lieutenant Parkson and agreed with his assessment. Hannah Yost belonged back with her people.

"How soon can you be ready to leave, Captain Scott?"

Vincent's heart sank. Though he knew he could not keep Hannah by his side forever, he had hoped for at least one more night. He cursed himself and his need for her. His career was at stake.

His sanity and soul were at stake. And he knew it.

But he had an obligation to fulfill to his country and his king. He was not one to shirk responsibility, regardless of the cost. "Within an hour, sir. May I ask where I am to be posted?"

Having received his answer, Vincent couldn't wipe the grin off his face, even if he tried. He didn't try. He hurried to the officer's tent and tossed the courier's sack on his cot. Geoffroy handed him bulging saddlebags. Vincent took one look at the contents, checked his trunk and found it empty, and glared suspiciously at Geoff.

"You had something to do with this?"

Geoff shrugged. "Killed two birds, that's all."

Vincent turned his back so his friend wouldn't see how Geoff's friendship had affected him, but he also did it for one more reason. "You'll be joining me in two month's time. I managed to embellish your record a wee bit, told a few tall tales about your marksmanship, and offered the suggestion that the Reverend Mister Bates' daughter had batted her lashes once too often, making her father damned suspicious. By the time I finished, you'd think you were the devil incarnate—but the best fighting man King George could hope to find. *Goes hand in hand,* old Jennings said." Vincent turned back to find his friend standing perfectly still, his eyebrows raised and his gaze fixed at a far speck on the wall. He pounded Geoff on the shoulder. "We're to be in the thick of things, Parkson, old boy! Posted to General Sir William Howe when he arrives. Meantime, I get to escort the poor Mistress Yost to Germantown." Vincent sat on his cot and contemplated the astonished look on Geoff's face. "Aren't you going to say *thanks?*"

Geoff stumbled to his own cot and sat with a sudden

gasp. "General Sir William Howe! My God, do you know what this means?"

Vincent knew more than Geoff supposed. He riffled through the papers in the courier's pack and tossed a small, rolled-up missive to Geoff. "Colonel said to give this to you just before I left. Figure it will take you thirty seconds to digest it and a month to come down from the clouds, so you best read it now."

Geoff tore off the ribbon-tie and quickly perused the official document. "I don't believe it. I do not believe it! We've hardly been here three years and we've risen two ranks." He stood and snapped a sharp salute. "Colonel Scott, Captain Geoffroy Parkson reporting for duty."

Vincent waved his friend back to the cot. "I'm leaving you with the dubious honor of extending a promotion to Paltray, Geoff. And don't let it go to his head, will you? With war coming, there will be more promotions than we'll be able to track. Tell the lad he's being watched closely and you'll demote him for one Paltray mistake. Though I do think he'll be a good lieutenant."

"He should. He's been watching you so closely, I half expect him to put on your boots by mistake."

"'Twould be no mistake," Vincent growled. "He already walks in my footsteps."

The friends took time to raise a tankard before Vincent went to collect the most important member of his two-member entourage. He was posted to Philadelphia, Jennings had said. Posted so close to Germantown, it would be helpful for the Colonel if Scott would agree to escort the good Mennonite lady to her uncle. Agree? He would have fought any man who got in his way. He was whistling by the time he crossed the small field to Hannah's tent. And she was waiting, impatiently, but with a blazingly beautiful smile that told him she was as pleased by the decision as was he.

He said naught, only took her hand and led her to the horses and pack mule.

"Nightwind for me, Dulcinea for you. And that little guy back there is Stub, short for stubborn, and he is that!"

Hannah chucked the little mule under the chin and whispered, "A good boy you will be, Stub, will you not?" The mule blinked his eyes and snorted. "In mule words, he says *ja.*" She moved to stand beside the black mare Vincent had chosen for her. The horse had a white star on her left front flank and white streaks in her mane and tail. "She's beautiful. Like Cathleen. So wild looking. So free." She couldn't stop her hand from trembling when she patted the black mare's nose. "Dulcinea . . . Quixote's sweetheart. And who fights with windmills for you, *liebchen?*"

I do, Vincent thought. *For you.* At least for the next week.

While Hannah settled herself on Dulcinea, Vincent went to get her traveling bags and found she had three. Three! For two changes of clothes and a few baubles Rachel Jennings had given her. What did she have inside these things? His quick inspection had him grinding his teeth. And then he snickered and began to chuckle. He had been planning a week of bliss in Hannah's arms each night. And the Good Lord had given her the only protection which would stay both his hands and another part of his anatomy which seemed to have a will of its own every time he was near the good lady.

279

Pledgets and slings! Confounded Mother Nature.

He packed her things in the saddlebags on Stub and mounted Nightwind. But when a quick glance at Hannah showed her to be riding astride instead of sidesaddle, he choked. "In your condition, would you not be more comfortable with your legs together?"

Hannah's mouth dropped and she felt the heat of a blush rise up her neck. These *Englishen!* Was everything a topic for conversation? Did they know no modesty? Well, she would not be prodded into admitting her womanly responsibilities . . . not she!

"I have always this way ridden. For me, the other is awkward. I am no child, Vincent. I do not need to be led by you in what I do. I shall be perfectly comfortable. And if I am not, *I* will decide what to do."

Damn! He had stepped on her toes—more, he had poked his nose into places her community said it did not belong. After all these years, he should have known that Hannah's modesty was one of her best attributes. Yes, she had allowed him privileges which he had found astounding, but she had always done it with grace and an unaffected charm. Now, to start off their week together with this between them! What a damned fool he was.

"Accept my apology, Hannah. I did not mean to upset you."

She snapped her reins and cantered ahead of him. "Apology accepted!" she called back over her shoulder.

He knew better than to catch up to her now. Later, when they stopped to make camp, he would—what? *Damn you, Vincent Scott. How could you put such distance between you and her? Why couldn't you have seen this coming?* Because he was used to trollops, for

God's sake! Because Clarisse had chatted on about every damned thing her body did, making him a part of that ritual. And in the ten years since his father had first told him the differences between men and women, he had forgotten the manners his mother had fought so hard to instill in him and his brothers.

The civilizing force of women, Geoff called it. And when Vincent forgot it, as he too often did, it took someone like Hannah to make him realize just how much he needed—and wanted—it.

He wanted it so much the next three days drove him to distraction.

Hannah was completely chary of him. She shied away, hiding behind her precious books, reading, she said, *because it might be the last time that I can.*

She was beautiful in the moonlight, the sunlight, the shadows. She rode astride with no seeming discomfort, and he compared her to the fainting ninnies who had occupied his parents' estate during hunt season. She was tenacious and strong, delicate and totally feminine, studious and considerate, shy and sensuous. All at once and at varied times. There was naught he could find to fault her. But still, it drove him near mad to be with her and to have this nearly silent wall between them—a wall he had created, but one she was not trying to push down.

Why? Why? It gnawed at his vitals, the monosyllables they used instead of conversation. It preyed on his mind.

—She didn't love him.

—She loved him but was distancing herself because they would soon part.

—She didn't know how she felt about him.

—She was sorry for what they had done.

—She was delighted with what they had done and ashamed of having done it.

It was madness!

It was Woman, with all the secrets She kept from Man, and he'd be damned glad to be rid of her once they reached Germantown.

What was he thinking now, Hannah wondered, as they moved through the ever-changing hills which brought them closer to Germantown. That scowl on his face. That hooded gaze, so filled with tightly held-in fury. It was almost laughable. But she dared not laugh.

He had been in a foul mood these past three days. Ever since she had chastised him for searching her things and finding there what she had thought were private matters. Things not even husbands and wives discussed in a Mennonite home.

He had been accommodating enough to let her use the shovel when she needed to dispose of her pledgets. But he had stalked off in anger when she had turned her back on him each night, when she had set her bedroll more than an arm's distance away from him, when she had not fallen into his arms the moment the sun went down.

Were they so different, after all?

Were the elders correct? Were *Englishen* too free with their words, their actions, their thoughts, their bodies? Did they have no shame, no modesty, no privacy? Was it all . . . every function of life . . . a topic for discussion, for derision, for jest?

That is what it seemed like, yet Vincent had never been like that before. But she had never snapped at him before. She had been the follower, he the leader. Could he not see that her strength had been hard won and it was asking too much to ask her to give it up?

Yet, she would have to give it up when she got to Germantown. The elders . . . her uncle . . . they would never allow her the freedom she had with the *Englishen*. Mayhap there was a price to pay for that kind of freedom. Loss of modesty, loss of privacy, loss of dignity. *Nein!* Not dignity. She had always been accorded that. Vincent had always treated her with soul-shattering respect. And love. Always love. Or as close to it as she had ever known.

Suddenly they turned a bend in the trail and Hannah gasped in wonder.

"Oh!"

The trail opened into a wide clearing, as wide as New Ephrata's barnyard and kitchen garden combined. A cliff wall enclosed the clearing on the left in a shape like a horseshoe. Full-foliaged branches of elms and oaks and giant maples bent down in a vaulted ceiling from which dense ferns and tiny blue and pink and yellow and white wildflowers crept out of the dark of the woods. They grew in a lush carpet all the way to the edges of a small pond. And above, splashing merrily over the cliff wall, was a cascading river. It looked like hair, long, clean, foaming hair, and Hannah felt an overwhelming need to feel it flowing over her.

"Halten, bitte. Oh, please stop!" She dismounted before Dulcinea stopped and ran to dip her hand into the pond. " 'Tis not cold!"

Curious as to why the water was not ice cold like that in the Palatine, she looked up and through an opening in the trees which allowed the sun's rays to heat the pond, and probably the river beyond their sight. She splashed water into her face and laughed with delight. She had not felt this carefree since the hairy-handed one had . . . She shook off the image and drank in the beauty of this place, this one glorious place.

"May we camp here, Vincent? 'Tis still early, I know, but . . ." She swept her hand around the clearing. "It is so *wunderbar!*"

Kneeling there like that, with the sun dappling her body in muted shades of light and shadow, Vincent thought her an incarnation of some Greek maiden. Diana, maid of the forest. Narcissus, who looked in a pond, saw an image of himself, and fell in love with it. Vincent could understand, if the image were like Hannah's.

Thank God they were talking again. And if this spot had broken down the barriers, then he'd keep her here forever.

"Ja, Hannah. We will make camp here."

"Danke, my Vincent. *Danke."*

Hannah stretched out on the carpet of wildflowers and allowed the tension of the ride to drain into the ground. Her legs, always cramped after many hours in the saddle, slowly relaxed until there was only a small ache in the backs of her thighs. And the echo in her head stopped its normal clippity-clop, until she could distinguish at least five different kinds of bird calls.

It was paradise! The Garden of Eden could not have been more beautiful. America . . . what a glorious country that it could harbor a slice of the Rhineland here, a piece of the Netherlands there . . . probably bits of every country from which its pilgrims had come . . . and were still coming. Ah, no wonder its inhabitants would go to war to keep control of it.

Vincent sat down next to her, and for once, she didn't flinch. He picked a great bouquet of wildflowers and handed them to her. She smiled up at him and pulled herself into a sitting position, leaning her head on his shoulder.

"I like it here, Vincent."

He chuckled. "I noticed." He put his arm around her and she settled against him the way she had always done. "Are we speaking again, *liebchen?*"

She gazed into his eyes and her joy was mirrored there for him to see, take into his heart, and treasure.

"This place . . . it is ours, Vincent. Don't you feel it?"

He did not have to look at the clearing. His place was there, in her face, in her eyes. "I feel it."

Without knowing why she did it, knowing only that it seemed right, Hannah lifted her face up to him and kissed him on the chin, on the place where his skin was scratchy from the quick shave he gave it every morning with that funny straight blade shaped like a knife. It scratched her lips in a tingling sensation that made her hunger for more. She nibbled along his chin, up to the corners of his mouth. And as she did, she felt his chest contract, his arm muscles tense, his breathing become raspy. She dared a peek at his eyes and they were as she hoped, as smoky as the mist over the pond where the waterfall disappeared into dark depths.

How she loved the feel of him! It mattered naught that he had caused her unease these past few days. Things like that were expected when two people were intimate friends.

Intimate friends. What a strange expression. Lovers, it meant. Lovers.

She shivered at the implications of her thoughts.

She was Mennonite, *ja*. But she was also a peasant girl from the Rhineland. She knew of the world, which was why her parents had chosen to be separate from it. She knew of lovers. Of loving. She and Vincent had come as close as two people could without taking that leap over the rail.

Yet, she thought what it would be like if they did. Become lovers.

Now.

"Enough, Hannah," Vincent growled.

Had she spoken aloud? "Enough what, my Vincent?"

"Your nibbles have gone far enough, my Mennonite Brown Eyes."

"So, you have added the *Mennonite* now?"

"It helps me to remember to keep a distance between us."

Distance? He wanted distance? She searched his eyes and knew he spoke only what he thought she wanted to hear. So . . . all right . . . he was prepared to play this out any way she wanted it. *Gut*. Because she had something very different in mind from what they had had before.

Part Four

Fulfillment

Cuppimac

This time, it was not what he expected. The looting, the killing, the taste for blood was tedious. Tedious to swoop down on unarmed men. Tedious to have them offer no resistance other than to close their hands, raise their eyes to heaven, and pray in that growl-talk which made his hackles raise.

He was Cuppimac. He was a renegade. A thief. A murderer. A raper of women.

And they had made him so.

He now had a price on his head of such proportions it could have ransomed his people from the clutches of the Red Ones during the last uprising. But to ransom them, he would have to die. And when he died, his people would not get the ransom. The Red Ones— whoever it was who took his scalp—they would get it.

So, what he did had no meaning.

Except for his vow.

No meaning, save his vow of revenge.

No meaning in the eyes of the women he mounted. No meaning in the eyes of the men he slaughtered. No meaning in the throats of the children who screamed and then were still. No meaning in butchered cattle, lambs, hogs. No meaning in fires. No meaning in feasts.

There had only been meaning in those large brown eyes peering out of the bramble bushes. On the last moon, it was, when he'd seen her. That frightened face. Those gentle eyes which had instantaneously turned hard and determined. As his once had.

He had not told the others she was there. And when Lansford approached the patch, Cuppimac had ordered him back to the farm, back to the slaughter.

Why had he done this? He had pondered it many times. Now, he knew it was because he had felt the loss of his spirit guides and wanted somehow to get them back. An expiation seemed the only way. Yet, this month he had lost touch with the spirits of his father. His mother's spirit had long since deserted him. How, then, was he to journey to the afterlife in the Southwest if they were not there to guide him?

Why did he continue?

Because he had saved one life. One witness. One soul to plead his case, if ever he needed it.

And, perhaps, one voice to tell the world and bring the end he had begun to long for.

Cuppimac sat back on his heels and contemplated an ant moving on the ground, carrying, pushing, nudging a grain of corn many times larger than itself.

He sighed. That ant was his brother. They did the same job. Cleaned the earth. Toiled forever. Pushed, pushed, pushed at an object larger than themselves. Pushed until strength gave out. Rested, breathed, pushed again.

Yes, little brother. Work hard. Rush to finish. But watch your back!

With deliberation, Cuppimac ground a rock on top of the ant until it died.

That ant was his brother.

Who would give him, Cuppimac, the rest he had given his brother?

He craved it now. Awaited it. Yet he knew it could not come from these unarmed growl-talkers. It could only come from that yellow-haired, brown-eyed one. So he had sent his band on ahead, hidden himself in the trees, and watched her when she came out of that patch. Watched as she approached the farm, saw the horror, and did not cry out. Watched as she closed the eyes, dug the huge grave, did the same chores he had done. Watched as she went on the trail alone. Watched as she sheltered in trees, as he did. Watched as she learned to kill to survive.

She was his sister, his mirror spirit. She was as strong as he, as wise as he, as determined as he. Had those Red Ones not come to rescue her from the French, he, Cuppimac, would have killed them all.

Yellow Hair was his sister.

So he, Cuppimac, had been pushing closer and ever closer to Yellow Hair's and the Red Ones' settlements. Closer and ever closer to the territory the Red Ones controlled. Closer and ever closer to a fate which

291

Cuppimac instinctively knew was soon to come.

Pick up your rock, Red Brother, Yellow Sister. I come soon. I await its crush. For only then can I go to the land of my fathers. Only then see my mother's face. Only then know the fate that awaits me in the afterlife. Yes, pick up your rock, Red Brother and Yellow Sister. I come soon.

Chapter Eighteen

As was their usual custom, Vincent scoured the countryside to find firewood for the night. While he was gone, Hannah wove the wildflowers he had picked into a wreath for her head.

Lord, forgive me. She felt like one of the wood nymphs, the lovers of the satyrs . . . characters which peopled many of the folk tales from her home in the Palatine, an area just north of Switzerland, in what Americans called the Rhineland. The wreath was filled with every color of wildflower there was and she itched to put it on, like the women of her village had done every May when they danced round the pole. And when they stopped dancing, when the ribbon attached to the Maypole had been twisted tightly against the pole, the girls would let go. From all that dancing round and round, their equilibrium would be gone. They would teeter to and fro and have difficulty focusing. But the myth had it that once a girl did see clearly, the first eligible man her eyes could recognize was destined to be her husband . . . or lover, if that was their choice.

It was a dangerous myth, a paean to the gods of the forest, a myth which the God of Christianity had eclipsed. But it was a delightful custom and a happy-hearted time, those days in May in a village she thought she had long forgotten. Strange how, in the right circumstances, memories were triggered and old feelings rushed back.

She heard Vincent in the woods, his steps growing fainter and fainter. It had rained yesterday and he was probably having difficulty finding good, dry pieces for their fire.

Gut. She had much to do.

Setting aside her prayer cap, Hannah took down her plaits, untwisting them until her hair fluttered in the breeze like the dozens of butterflies flitting around her. She removed her clothing and tested the water on the inside of her wrist to be absolutely certain she was not mistaken about its temperature. She did not want to be frozen to death when Vincent returned.

Unlike the hated acts of Parliament, the water was cool but tolerable.

She found a section of bank that sloped into the pond, giving her easy access. With a hunk of Rachel's lavender-scented soap in one hand and her new flowered wreath in the other, she took one step, then another, allowing her body to get used to the chill. By the time the water swirled around her thighs, she knew she had to get wet all at once or give up on her grand design. So, she dropped the wreath into the water and let it float on the surface, took a great breath, held her nose, and launched herself into the center of the pond.

She came up sputtering.

Tolerable!??

On the edges, mayhap. Here, it surprised her that there were no ice chips on the surface.

Vincent, come back soon!

Else her skin would burn from the cold.

Within minutes, however, Hannah's body had gotten used to the bone-chilling water and she began to hum some tunes she had learned as a child in the Rhineland. They were *verboten* within the Mennonite community, but they were delightful songs about robins and flowers . . . and great battles and duels, all for the sake of love.

Du, du, du, liebst mir im Herzen. "You, you, you live in my heart!

Du, du, du, liebst mir im Sinn. "You, you, you live in my mind!"

Wie, wie, wie weiss nie fiel schmerzen. "How, how, how, I know great pain."

Weiss, nicht wie gut Ich dir bin. "For I know you are not good for me."

Du, du, du liebst mir im Herzen.

Du, du, du liebst mir im Sinn.

Wie, wie, wie weiss nei fiel schmerzen.

Weiss, nicht wie gut Ich dir bin.

Now why had that particular one come to mind? What significance did it have? In this place of wonder, all things, she was certain, had their place in the Order. The Order of the Universe.

You live in my heart, Vincent.

She soaped her hair and edged under the waterfall to let the water cascade down and rinse the soap out. Three times, she soaped it. And three times she splashed in the froth kicked up by the rushing waters.

You live in my mind, Vincent.

Remembering times in the Rhineland when she had frolicked with her cousins . . . those who had not joined the faith . . . she held her nose and ducked under the water. Cautiously, she opened her eyes and looked up to see her hair floating like a bedspread above her. When she surfaced, she felt invigorated, alive!

But, Vincent, how I know great pain.

Ach, Gott, why could not Lisle and Rolf, Jacob and Magda, Pieter and the *kinder* have been given this gift? Why had they been sacrificed? Why had she been saved?

For I know you are not good for me, my Vincent, my Redcoat.

She didn't want to think about that, about how her love for him was pulling her farther and farther away from the faith she had embraced, farther and farther from the people who were hers. He was her love. He was her heart. But the pain . . . *ach, Gott* . . . the pain of such discord, such variance . . . it was too much to grasp, too much to endure. She preferred *Du, du, du liebst mir im Herzen. Du, du, du liebst mir im Sinn.*

She ducked under the water once again, to the silence which she thought she could reach out and touch. Men and women . . . they floated in water in their mother's womb. Returning to it seemed so natural, so pure, so right. Her breath gave out and she began to surface. But her eye caught a dozen fish below, swimming under the waterfall on a current she could feel.

A current? In a pond?

She rushed to the top, took another great breath of air and dove to see where the current would take her.

She had no fear. She felt the mighty presence of her God. He had gotten her this far. She did not think He would abandon her now. Besides, He seemed to be beckoning her to explore this place. How could she say *nein* to Him?

When Vincent returned with his armload of sticks and branches, he stopped dead at the edge of the woods. He was seeing things! Things that had been eating at the edges of dreams. Things that caused him to wake from a sound sleep, sweating, hard with desire. He blinked his eyes. Was this heaven? Hannah, splashing with the birds. Hannah, with butterflies dancing round her head. Hannah, flicking drops of water at a wreath of flowers that bobbed on the ripples spreading out from her body.

Her body.

Good God, her breasts were gorgeous! He had never seen them in the light before. His hands had felt their glory. But *this!* This was perfection.

He watched, enchanted, as she soaped her hair and splashed under the waterfall. Repetition was the order of the day, he supposed, because she did it more than once. He did not want to give himself away. He could not chance destroying this innocent, wonderful moment. So he had to hold back a laugh of pure joy when she splashed into the middle of the pond and ducked down under the water, letting her wild, thick hair float on the surface. A golden carpet, it seemed. The sun glittered on it like a million dots of candlelight.

His breath was like a rock in his chest until she broke the surface, laughing as he had wanted to. But he did not want to laugh now. Now, he was lost in the timeless rhythms of man watching woman.

He imagined himself as the ripples, moving sensuously over her skin. He envisioned himself teasing her nipples until they hardened. He would search the roundness of her belly. He would caress the hollows of her body. He would discover delicate folds of skin, a tiny hardened nub, and a dark, moist opening that allowed him free entry. He pictured himself and Hannah entwined as lovers. They would give and take pleasure. They would relish the delights of their bodies. They would push themselves to consummation. They would exult in that exquisite feeling. They would soar into the realm the French called *le petite morte*, the little death. And they would sleep in each other's arms. And wake again. And make love again. And again and again.

He shrugged off his red coat and near tore off his shirt. Kicking at his boots, he lost sight of Hannah for a moment, but she couldn't have gone far. The pond was a small one. He had his breeches and underclothes off when he realized she had not yet come up for air. No! No!

He ran to the edge of the pond, calling, "Hannah! Hannah!"

He still had his stockings on when he jumped into the water and stroked for the spot he had seen her last. He dove, searching for her, and found naught. His lungs burned from lack of breath and he shot upward to gulp air for another search.

She was not there!

A whirlpool. A tidal wave. Some monster of the deep.

Flailing, feeling totally impotent, he swallowed a mouthful of water. It was no good. She was not there. Damn it to hell, she had drowned.

He made his way to the surface and screamed his rage and powerlessness.

"Hannah! God, Hannah!"

He felt a tap on his shoulder and whirled.

"You do not have to shout," she said.

"Hannah! Where were you?"

"I found something! Something *wunderbar!*" She took his hand. "Come, I will show you. But you must take a deep breath. Ready?"

Her eyes sparkled with mischief. He wanted to throttle her for scaring him half to death, but she thought it a game! And mayhap it was. So, he merely nodded, so grateful was he to see her alive.

"Then, we dive." She started to go under, then turned. "You can swim?"

He glared at her. "Yes, I can swim!"

"Gut. Kommt mit mir."

Under the surface of the water his sight adjusted to the shifting shadows. And when it did, Vincent almost sucked in water when he saw Hannah's naked bottom as she kicked her way through the depths of the pond and under the waterfall. It was like a beacon, that rounded *derrière*. And the glimpses he caught as her legs propelled her—opening and closing like scissors as she swam—dear God, if the water weren't so cold, he would be hard as the rocks beneath them.

Suddenly, she shot upward and he kicked to keep with her. His head crested the surface and he found himself in a pool almost the exact mirror of the one outside.

A cave. The sweet minx had found a cave. And a cave with limited light inside, so there must be another entrance to it, possibly from above. Another entrance? Dear God!

"Bears, Hannah!"

"Nein. Well, perhaps at one time, but not now. I searched. Only a few very small droppings, some very old bones and some fish scales on the ledge. Perhaps not even bears, Vincent. Perhaps some ancient Indians lived here, *ja?"* She walked out of the water and onto the ledge. "Come. There is an opening back here."

She was as unaware of her nakedness as a little girl. But he was not. Nor was he unaware of his nakedness. She had never seen him thus. He had supposed himself armored against scrutiny and criticism, but Clarisse had left a parting diatribe of his inadequacies. He had never honestly believed it. But it had never mattered before. So he did not move for a moment.

Hannah did not understand. What was he waiting for? A timid man was not her Vincent. Yet his shoulders rose and fell stiffly and she saw him hesitate after taking only one step.

"Kommt mit mir, Vincent. *Bitte."*

His eyes bored into hers as he put one foot in front of the other. She was locked to that smoky grey gaze, unable to move, to breathe. He willed her to do something; she could tell that from his intensity. But what could it be? What could be so important that he . . .

"Mein Gott!"

Her breath caught and held. Her heart pounded so hard she couldn't believe it stayed enclosed within her.

It had to leap out, it had to show him how much his presence affected her.

She inhaled his essence. With her eyes, she caressed his broad shoulders, so muscled from work they were ridged with sinew, hard with strength. The scattering of wet hairs on his chest, curling as they dried. The expanse of muscle that arrowed downward to slim hips, hard thighs, long legs.

And black stockings to his knees.

Oh, no! She wanted to giggle at the contrast, but one look at his fierce, piercing gaze and she knew it would be a mistake.

Instead, she ran her eyes over his body once more, loving the way he moved, the way his muscles rippled with power . . . harnessed but raw. His hands were clenched as he walked, further intensifying the image of strength. His hands moved forward and back in a direct line with his hips . . . and the chestnut-colored darkness surrounding his manhood, a manhood which was more than she had dreamed, more than she thought possible.

Awed, she sank to her knees almost in prayer and held out her hand in supplication. "Vincent. My Vincent! *Kommt mit mir!*" Come . . . to places unknown . . . to an ending and a beginning of this thing which eats at hearts and gives no rest until . . .

Vincent went to her. He touched her hand and felt her fingers twine in his. With his other hand he found the nape of her neck, tugged gently at her hair, and bent her head back. He swam in those big brown eyes. They seemed to glow in the dimness of the cave. Their depths shimmered with desire. He had expected condemnation and found molten hunger. And it—she—gave sustenance to his soul.

With a strangled cry of hope and love, he dropped to his knees beside her. Her hair blanketed them as he crushed his mouth on hers and tasted the sweetness that drove him wild.

"Hannah! I can't wait anymore— I have to— Dear God, I want you!"

"I, too, Vincent. I, too."

There was moss and lichen on the rocks, a bed fit for the gods, he thought. A bed for a goddess. He scooped her into his arms, stood, and carried her to it. When he laid her on the dark green carpet, he took a moment to sit back on his heels. A moment to etch her image in his mind. This would have to last his lifetime and he wanted to remember everything about her. But he was so filled with raw desire that he knew he'd shatter if he didn't touch her. The image could wait until later, after all.

He groaned as he pressed his body against hers. The feel of her breasts against his chest! The silkiness of her skin! The thrill as his leg brushed against those tight golden curls!

The temptation was too great. He remembered that *derrière*. He rolled onto his back and took her with him. His palms skimmed down her side and over her hips. She was soft. Warm. Delicate. He filled his hands with her bottom, making tiny circles to learn their contours. Larger circles, down to the beginning of her thighs.

"God, you feel good!" he growled. "So damned good."

He squeezed her bottom gently. Pulled upward, to position her. And hesitated.

Hannah felt lost in the warmth of his hands, in the warmth that spiraled outward, in the delight of this new kind of bundling. She snuggled against him, twisting her fingers in the springy curls on his chest. She nuzzled his neck, tickling his chin with her tongue.

When he slid her upward, she was just beginning to enjoy the magic he had created when he stopped. Her body lay completely on his. Her breasts and belly fit into the hollows of his body. Her hips rocked against his. Her legs entwined with his but didn't reach the tips of his toes.

And she felt his manhood throbbing rhythmically between them.

Then she knew why he lay still.

To give her time. To let her know that what they did now was her decision, and she alone could make it.

"*Dan* . . . thank you, Vincent," she said. "I understand."

"Hannah—"

She put her hand over his mouth. "*Nein.* Do not be sad or worried. We are protected by love. I choose this, Vincent. I choose you. *Du, du, du liebst mir im Herzen,* my love. You are my husband in my heart. There will be no other."

"I cannot give you what you deserve!"

"You can give me everything. Everything. *Kommt mit mir*, Vincent. *Kommt nach Himmel mit mir.*"

Her trust was life itself. He breathed it in. It flooded through him. Melted every resistance. Made his life to this moment worthwhile. She loved him. She trusted him. She gave herself freely. That was all he knew. That was all he needed to know.

Go into heaven with her?

He would go to his death for her.

Le petite morte.

There was no more hesitation in his touch. He kissed her. He poured all his love and all his gratitude into the pressure of his mouth and the touch of his tongue. He tasted her, and he allowed her the time to taste him. When she made tiny mews of pleasure, he chuckled against her neck.

"I love the way you react."

"I love the way you make me feel."

His mouth became his eyes and hands. He used it to caress. He used it to tease. He used it to taste. He used it to awaken feelings he knew she had never experienced. He licked her neck, trailed down to the hollow of her throat, felt it arch, felt a thrumming inside it.

"You sound like a cat," he whispered.

"Ummm. Do that again."

He did, gladly. And followed it with tiny kisses across her shoulder bones. From the right to the center. From the left to the center. Always to the center, to that indentation where he felt her heart beating faster and faster.

He smiled, pleased with her reaction.

Hannah looked up and caught that smile, caught the delight in his eyes, caught the concentration on his face. He was trying so hard to please her. And he did please her. Every touch tingled, teased, warmed, blessed.

If it was that good for her, she wondered, would it not also be good for him? Was she merely to lie here and do naught but allow him to take her where he would? She had asked him to come with her to heaven. She had a right to do what he did, a right to lead where he led, a right to please as he pleased.

His head began to dip lower, but she slid her hands down and drew him back. "My turn, my Vincent."

When she kissed his chin, Vincent chuckled. But when she continued to kiss him the same way he had kissed her, his body stilled.

"Close your eyes," she ordered.

"Aye, love."

With his eyes closed, all he could do was feel. Her lips brushing back and forth across his chin. Her tongue tasting behind his ear. Her teeth nipping on his lobe. Tiny kisses covering his neck. Fingers moving over his shoulders. Hands covering his chest muscles. A thumb innocently exploring his shoulder bones and brushing against his nipple. It did what he expected and Hannah stopped. Then her finger rubbed against his other nipple.

She sucked in her breath. "Oh! Look what it does when I touch you!"

His voice croaked, "I know what it does." His forehead rested against hers. "Shall I show you how your body works when I do that to you?"

"Ja!"

"You have to watch."

"Ja, I will!"

"Sit up, then."

She scooted up and he did the same. "Now," he said, "touch me again, the way you did." Her finger touched him. "Pretend 'tis a feather. Move it back and forth, gently."

Hannah did and it happened again! She looked over to him and grinned. But his eyes were closed, his head thrown back, an expression of . . . what . . . on his face. She jerked her hand away. "Oh, no! Did I hurt you, Vincent?"

His eyes popped open. "No, love. Shall I show you exactly how it feels?"

"*Ja!*"

He rested his left arm across her back so she would have a cushion. With his right hand and fingers, he cupped her left breast. "Watch, Hannah."

"I do."

Hannah watched as Vincent took his thumb and slid it up and over her nipple. Then round and round, just outside it, he made circles. Hot circles. And his fingers brushed across her nipple, making it pucker, causing shafts of exquisite feeling to spiral into her, down through her. She felt as if her bones had melted. But Vincent wasn't finished. His fingers plucked at her nipple, pulling it out gently, until all she could do was throw her head back and arch her breasts upward seeking more.

He gave her more, and Hannah reveled in it. His mouth closed over her nipple. He sucked in, taking more and more into the wetness, moving his tongue over her the way he had moved his fingers. She looked down. The beauty of what she saw ripped through her heart. Her fingers threaded through the damp richness of his hair, and she moved slightly until she could see the junction of his mouth with her breast.

She would hold no babe to her breast, know no other kind of suckling. This was all for her. All and everything. Everything and enough.

She touched the place where his mouth joined her body and felt a spasm deep inside her belly. "Vincent! Ah, my love!"

With almost instantaneous understanding of the mysteries Vincent was slowly revealing, Hannah wanted to know it all, and all at once. She levered his head away and kissed him, pouring all her love into the kiss. Her head swam with so many emotions, she didn't know one thought from another. She was all feeling, all want, all love. He had done so much for her, and she wanted to give him what she had received.

She moved her hands down his ribs and around to his back. "Lie on your stomach," she ordered gently.

Vincent knew what she was doing. Storing this up. Saving it in her heart and mind for the years to come. He could deny her naught because he was doing the same thing.

But when her delicate hands kneaded his flesh, he cried out with pleasure. A happy little sigh floated from her when she kissed him in the indentation of back and bottom. And he ground his teeth together. "Hannah!"

"Shh, love! 'Tis only the beginning."

Chapter Nineteen

Vincent sucked in his breath, steeling himself for this onslaught on his senses. Hannah was his love, but she did not understand what she was doing to him. And he could not tell her. He could not break the spell that in her innocence she wove so seductively. Saying naught, doing naught, was the hardest thing he had ever done. But for Hannah, he could and would face more pain than this.

But such exquisite pain. Such excruciating pleasure.

Her small, gentle hands skimmed over his hips and down to his legs. It felt as though every hair on his body stood at attention. Why not? The rest of him was.

He growled and it ended on a ragged breath as her hands washed over his bottom. He could picture her bent over, concentrating on finding every small indentation. The dimple on his right buttock seemed to thoroughly amuse her, so often did she go back to it. And when she did, her hair brushed back and forth on his skin. How could something so soft leave a trail so overwhelming.

She leaned close to his ear and whispered, "It pleasures you?"

"Yes!"

"*Gut!* Thus you pleasured me."

"And I will pleasure you more."

"Oh, I hope so. I truly hope so."

Their bantering ended then. Vincent ended it with a sweep of his arm to pull her to him in a searing kiss that left her lips swollen from his teeth and tongue. He turned her on her back and positioned her on the moss. His eyes darkened as he bent to kiss each swollen nipple. She loved seeing him there, loved having him there. But there was another place that called out for his touch, his kiss, his entry. She knew not what it would feel like, only knew the cautions she had received from her aunt about pain and fear. But she was not afraid with Vincent. He would never hurt her.

Vincent was not surprised that his hand shook as he glided it down her belly to find the place where the greatest sensations were. He was astounded that he could move it at all. He was rock-hard and molten, all at once. God, she had given him so much! He loved with a wildness that eclipsed time and place. It was eternal and ageless. It was godless—yet filled with God's love.

It was Hannah.

There was no other. There never would be.

"I love you," he said. "I adore you."

She was about to say *I know* when his fingers slicked into her and plunged deeply, filling her but not satisfying her. She knew there was more to come and wanted it with all her heart.

"I love you, Vincent," she said, and captured his

manhood as he had captured her womanhood.

She was shocked by its contrasts. Soft and cool like velvet on the outside. But inside, a shaft of iron, a core of fire. She tested the contours, but only a little. His indrawn breath and tensed muscles told her she had best move to other places.

Like his nipples. If he had made her feel so wonderful by suckling, would not he feel that wonder if she did the same to him? She watched the expression on his face as she raised her head and licked at one. Ah, *ja. Wunderbar.* And his belly . . . would it contract as hers had if she nibbled on it? *Ja.* With a great jolt. And his thighs . . . ummm . . . the hairs tickled but the skin tasted salty, clean. She moved upward and thought, *aber ja!* Her lips touched the base of the velvet once and moved on to the tip.

Vincent knew this was the culmination of his life, this woman loving him with child-like adoration. This woman, his heart.

He pulled her up, laid her back on the moss, and continued to love her. With his mouth he kissed her delicate rose-like bud. With his tongue he laved every fold that surrounded it. With his body he covered her. With his eyes he devoured her. With his hands, he opened her legs. And with one slow, easy, rocking motion, he entered her.

"I love you, Hannah. I love you!" he cried as he filled her. Completely.

And Hannah knew it was good. *Gut. Wunderbar.* Blessed. They did no sin when they loved thus. She felt the glory of a blessing enrich her soul as her entire being embraced her only love, her only husband.

Vincent.

Her life.

"I welcome you as my husband, Vincent. I welcome you before God and the angels."

Vincent's heart stopped beating. My God, my God! She gave everything to him. Held naught back. As cynical about life as he was, he felt humbled, awed, by such a gift. A great peace washed over him, enriching each sensation, fusing them to his soul.

Hannah.

His soul.

"I welcome you as my wife, Hannah. I welcome you before God and the angels."

He loved her with his body then. He rocked gently, settling into a rhythm that she began to return. Her arms encircled his waist, her nails scratched but he ignored it. Her legs wrapped around his. Her neck arched, exposing her glorious breasts. She moaned repeatedly, breathing deeply, shallowly, quickly. He pulled up her hips to fuse them with his as her body exploded into waves of soul-tearing sensation. They pulled him to a shore he had never explored, bathing him in a baptism of love—and commitment. They tossed him into the heavens and his body soared. With an insight he hadn't known until Hannah, he was positive he saw the beginning and the end of time.

Hannah floated somewhere between heaven and earth, where stars are created, where love begets love. And still it was not over. Her body was no longer under her control. Vincent's rhythm bore it along with his. It moved, shuddered, pulsed. Then trembled. They scaled mountains higher than her Alps, swam oceans deeper than the earth's. Higher and deeper. Higher and deeper. Moving ever onward in dozens of inner explosions that left her breathless, aching, and, finally, sated.

Oh, God, how she loved this man, her only husband. How she hurt to think this was all they would ever have. How it shattered her heart to know she would never give life to his child, suckle it at her breast, watch it grow. How it rent her soul to know that she would never sleep with Vincent in a bed, never cook his breakfast, wash his clothes, tend his wounds. Never, never grow old with him.

But the glory of what they had just shared was not eclipsed by sadness . . . it never could be. It was pure joy and deserved to be savored as it had happened, not used to bring condemnation to a future only God held in his hand.

Vincent wrapped her in his arms and held her close. "I love you."

"I love you."

"Sleep, *liebchen.*"

"Ummm. I already do."

He smiled and watched her fall into sleep. He marveled at the beauty in her face. She was a precious gift. He had been allowed to have the best. He had been given a love he was not convinced he deserved.

As sleep overtook him, he knew with absolute clarity that he would move heaven and earth to keep it.

Hannah woke, shivering. She snuggled against Vincent but could not get completely warm. The shadows in the cave had deepened and night was coming on. She stole a peek at the river, which seemed to have no beginning, and shook her head. *Nein.* She could not jump into that cold water again. She would rather perish here in the cave.

"Why that frown, Brown Eyes?"

She lifted her eyes to her husband and basked in the love she saw. Raising her hand she traced the outline of his wonderful lips, those that had given her such pleasure, brought her such love.

"'Tis cold, Redcoat."

"Aye. That it is."

"And I am not going back into that river."

Vincent chuckled. He loved the way her skin puckered from the cold, especially two delightful points which tickled against his chest hairs. When he and Hannah shared a bed, they would not use quilts. Cold made her more delectable.

"Mayhap we can both avoid the river."

"And freeze, starve, or become food for those bears of yours."

It amazed him that she was not shy, that she was bantering as they always did with each other. That she could be herself with him after such a lovemaking proved to him that she would never use artifice. She was natural and free and the most desirable woman in the world.

"*Liebchen,* the only food you will ever be is mine!"

When he made snuffling noises like a pig and gnawed gently on her neck, Hannah squealed. "Such shivers you give! Am I not already cold enough?"

He rose slowly to his feet and held out his hand to her. "Come, wife. I think there is a surprise awaiting you in this fairyland of yours."

"*Ja,* I come, husband. But very good, the surprise had best be." Her skin felt assaulted with tiny pricks of

314

ice. "Very, very good, *bitte.*"

Vincent walked deeper into the cave. As he'd expected, he felt a rush of air from high above. "Where is this opening of yours?"

"Here . . . around this corner."

The underground cavern was huge. The walls shone with a white sheen. There were ledges cut into one wall and a pit in the center of the cave where Vincent found the cold remnants of a long-forgotten fire. He looked up but whatever it was that made the cave had also made icicle-like projections which hung from the vaulting and curving ceiling high above. He could not see an opening for the smoke to escape, but he'd bet his life there was one.

He hunkered down and looked around the cave. If there was a fire, there had to be a way to bring in wood. He could not imagine the people who had used this cave taking in wood piece by piece under water, then waiting days for it to dry out. No, they would have had another entrance, cleverly hidden so they would be safe in this underground vault. He examined each wall and saw naught. Then something told him the entrance was not in this room, but far away, so far it would seem endless to those who did not know of the jewel at the end.

"Come, Hannah. We're going back to the river."

She groaned. "An icy bath, I do not like."

"Do you like marching better?"

"Will it make me warm?"

He put his arm around her and hugged her close. "I will make you warm."

"Oh . . . well . . . *ja,* this I like."

He laughed. "No, Hannah. No more lovemaking yet,

315

but this night will know no bounds for our love." He kissed her quickly and had to pull himself away from her hungry mouth. "Enough, love. We have to find the way out of here."

They went back to the beginning and then retraced their steps to the bend where Hannah had turned right.

"We are where we started."

"Yes," Vincent said. "But we are going to the left this time, not the right."

"There is no room there."

"Good."

"'Tis very dark."

"I'm here, *liebchen.*"

"And there are spiders."

"Don't tell me there is *one* thing that frightens you."

"I did not say I was frightened. But I do not like them slipping across my skin. And, Vincent, today I give them much skin!"

He hugged her to him as his body was convulsed by her humor. "Oh, *liebchen!* What will I ever do without you?" They both gasped and grew still at the same time. He looked into her eyes and saw such raw pain, it near broke his spirit. "Forgive me, Hannah. To mention these things—I am three thousand times a fool."

Hugging him was not enough. She needed to feel his body fully against her, needed to store up more memories. She stood on her toes and slid up, etching every inch of contact into a mind aching with awareness of what they had found, what they were destined to lose. *"Ach,* Vincent. Not to mention it would be foolish. We both know 'tis true."

He stood there holding his heart, his life, his soul. He stood in more pain than any human should have to bear; her gentle touch and kind words were a balm to his bruised spirit. "I wish it could be different, Hannah."

"I, too. But you are a soldier. I am a Mennonite." *Though not a good one.* "We have no common ground, Vincent."

"Save love."

"That may not be enough."

But it may. And he had to cling tenaciously to that thought.

"Get behind me, *liebchen.* Let the spiders slide on me."

"Oh, *ja,* Vincent. I do not argue."

They went to the left several yards, until Vincent ran smack into another wall. "Damn! I wish we had pitch torches!"

He felt along the wall to one side, then the other, and found a ridge just below shoulder height. It was only three fingers wide and seemed a place where many hands had worn down the white rock in order to guide the way to the hidden vault. It took much faith to put his hand in the ridge and allow it to take him and Hannah further and further away from the river. But faith had brought them this far. He did not think it would desert them now.

It seemed an eternity before they came to a bend in the tunnel and were dappled with a red glow.

"The setting sun," Vincent said.

"We face West, then?"

"Aye."

"The wrong direction!"

"Let's see." Vincent found the opening high above them and knew that was not what he sought. "Clever, these men who found or carved out this place."

"Why clever?"

"Air holes. To let smoke out, clean air in. Very clever. So the entrance must be carefully hidden."

"If there is one."

"Do you doubt, *liebchen?* You, the most trusting woman I know?"

"I do not trust the world, Vincent. Only you and *Gott.*"

He lifted her chin and kissed her. "That is enough."

A little farther into the tunnel and they came to another vault, but this one contained large rocks heaped against the walls. Some were as tall as a man and as wide as a horse, others no bigger than his fist. He studied them. It would be nonsense to suppose the entrance lay behind any of the piles of smaller stones. If that were so, the ones who had piled them would have to take down the pile each time they wanted to get into the cave. So, the man-sized rocks were more likely the hidden entrance. But which one? Since a worn ridge had helped him get here, he reasoned that it had taken many years to wear it down. So, too, would there be a ridge or indentation at the entrance, where men would have used a hand-hold to push the rock aside and pull themselves in. He examined each large rock, running his hand carefully over the edges and the smooth walls surrounding it. He felt—nay, naught. Yet—

"Hannah, come here! Close your eyes, *liebchen.*" When she did, he took her hand and guided it against the rock. "What do you feel?"

Her hand moved up and down. "Smooth. Cold." She ran it in circles. "Almost chiseled in places."

Suddenly, her fingers felt something close to her

waist. She ran her hand over it again . . . and smiled. Opening her eyes, she saw that her hand fit perfectly into grooves in the wall. She raised her eyes to Vincent's and he smiled down at her.

"They were small people. Smaller than me. Most likely many women," he declared. "This waited all these years for you to find. Amazing!"

She shrugged. Knowing what she knew, it did not surprise her. "I was led."

"*Aye.* You were, that. Thank God."

"Of course."

They laughed easily, forgetting they were cold and hungry and tired.

"Now, let's get this thing to work," Vincent said.

He pried at the rock, putting all his weight and strength into it, and near fell on his backside when the thing swung easily inward. "Who would have thought?" He examined the workings. "They chiseled out a depression and fitted an extension of the rock into it."

"Top and bottom, Vincent. Like a door!"

"Clever. Very, very clever."

"Do you know what Indians lived here?"

"Shawnee, Delaware, Iroquois."

"I read about the Iroquois. They have women as leaders, don't they?"

"Aye. Clever women."

Hannah beamed. "Something for you men to think on." She indicated the door, the tunnel, and the air hole. "This kind of cleverness."

"Women, pah!" he teased.

She threw her arms around him and rubbed herself against him.

"Women, yum!" He nuzzled her neck, then patted

her bottom. "Time to find our way back to camp, wife!"

It only took them a short time to realize they exited into the woods where Vincent had searched for firewood. Soon, they came out into the glade and Hannah threw her arms wide and danced in a circle.

"Paradise!"

Vincent slapped at a hungry bug. "Not quite." He picked up his red jacket and put it over Hannah's shoulders. "Warm?"

"Not yet. But I will be when you make that fire." She bent to pick up her clothes.

"Nay, wife. I like you best with your skin showing."

She ran her eyes up and down his body. "I like you best that way, too. So how will you get warm?"

"By working."

"We could bring whatever we needed back to the cave."

"And live there this night as if it were our own house?"

"*Ja*. Like husband and wife." She stood proud, requesting but not begging.

He nodded.

By loading the wood onto the pack mule's back, they were able to carry everything with them.

"You stay here, between the horses," Vincent ordered. "I'll get the fire started, then come back for you."

"We will need torches. I shall make some of rush while I wait."

"All right. But do not wander far."

"Leave me your pistol and rifle. I will use it if I have to."

"You're sure?"

"Positive."

When he returned much later, she handed him two squirrels and a dozen rush bundles for torches. He looked at the squirrels and then up at her.

"I shot them."

"I thought it was thunder."

She shook her head. When his surprised expression didn't soften, she stuck out her chin. "My stomach grumbled the whole time you were gone. And, I did not see that they were anything different from hogs or lambs."

"Compromises, Hannah."

"*Ja.*" She glared at him. "I have made many, of late."

He knew if he pursued this, he would regret it. "I'll skin them out here."

"I'll put the horses where they can get good grass to eat."

It gave her time to compose herself. She had killed and she had wanted him to understand how deeply that had affected her. But he didn't understand. He worried about her decision. But he didn't understand. Only someone of the faith could understand, she decided. Only someone who had had the same kind of experience. But there was naught she knew who had faced what she had faced, done what she had done. If she confessed all, her uncle and the elders would call it sin and ask her to beg pardon. She would be punished, perhaps shunned for a little while, but eventually she would be welcomed back into the community. What haunted her thoughts was that she had not yet decided whether she considered it a sin. She had not yet decided whether to leave it up to her uncle and the elders to make that decision for her. She had seen too much, done too much, stood on her own two feet for too long. She did not know if she could return willingly to the Way and the Faith, to the obedience and the subjugation.

Once she had looked on a man charred from the sun and been horrified to hear that he was a slave. Now, she began to feel as though she would have to become one herself.

That was not the Way. That was not the Faith.

She had changed. On the inside, where it didn't show, where she could hug it to her if she chose . . . or shout it to the rooftops. She had changed. And she wasn't sure whether the change was good . . . or evil.

Chapter Twenty

Their lovemaking that night had a poignancy about it that ended with Hannah sobbing into Vincent's embrace. He could not stop her. He did not try, because he was on the verge of tears himself.

She had given herself with gentleness and taken with gratitude. She had filled his soul, broken his heart.

He wanted to lie with this woman all the nights of his life. He wanted to hold her breasts in his palms forever. Wanted forever to feel her nipples contract from his touch. Wanted to taste them, flick his tongue over them, take them and their pink-circled flesh into his mouth and suck until she writhed beneath him. He wanted to feel her hands on his manhood. Wanted to feel her lips caress him so sweetly. Wanted to hear her cry of joy when he entered her. Wanted to feel the heat of her, the moistness, the strong waves of passion, the tremors of climax.

He knew he had given her great pleasure, immeasurable joy. But he had also failed her. He had filled her body, broken her heart.

They might have one more day together; they were on the trail to Germantown, and come sunset they would arrive at the first inn. He supposed he could get them a single room and give them another night together. But lying next to Hannah, knowing this was the last of their loving, he'd go mad. Nor could he sully her reputation by making her an object of gossip. Hannah's crying was an indication that she was on the brink of collapse. He could not do this to her. He could not give her one more experience of what they could not have. He would not hold her up to ridicule and censure. She deserved better than that. She deserved a clean break and time to become the woman her uncle expected her to be. To give her less was to value her less.

She was a precious gift worth more than anything material, more than the transitory pleasures of the body.

So he held her and let her express her sorrow, and his. Then, without a word, he left her alone to dress for the trail. He took his clothes and stumbled, shaken with grief, to the entrance of the caves, where he donned his own clothes, saddled the horses, and prepared them for the last day's ride.

Left behind in the shadows, Hannah very slowly plaited her hair, wound it round her head, and fastened it by forcing the ends into the coil. Then she drew her clothes over her body.

As each layer went on, a new awareness of what it represented filled her mind.

This bodice and underskirt replaced the ones Magda had made her. They stood for the inviolate border between the outer turbulent world and the inner peace of the faithful. This outer skirt and bodice were symbols of the history of her people. They held her separate and alone, but not without strength, the strength of all those souls who had gone before to give Mennonites the right to worship. Her apron stood for chastity—she did not hesitate to don it. She had married Vincent in her heart. That was, she believed, sufficient. But her prayer cap. Ah, that was different. The white proclaimed her a married or betrothed woman. That she had been betrothed to Jacob gave her the right to wear it. But after the six months of her mourning should she take it off? If she did, it meant that in her heart Vincent was dead. *Nein.* She would not take it off. Never. But if she did not, then the community would know that something had occurred, something she had not told nor confessed, and they would question her.

So be it. Vincent was her husband. That was the fact. She would have to live with the consequences.

Just outside the environs of Germantown, Hannah pulled *Dulcinea* to a halt and dismounted. She straightened her prayer cap, looked up at Vincent, and gave him a weak smile. Then she remounted the horse—this time, sidesaddle.

Another symbol.

Vincent looked away.

She reached over and took his hand and squeezed it. *"Ich liebe dich.* I love you. Always."

Hannah was surprised by the changes in Germantown. Many more Redcoats, most in units, some in regiments, all marching with bayonets fixed. And the

Americans . . . in groups or alone, they, too, carried arms now. When they huddled in groups, they spoke softly, and when a contingent of Redcoats came, they broke apart quickly, went inside, or walked away, sometimes throwing hostile glances over their shoulders. Glances which were also directed at her and Vincent. She noticed, also, that tempers flared. She saw many fist fights. And there were few women on the streets, as if they huddled inside, wary of what could happen at any moment.

The streets were crowded with men, however. Far more crowded than when she had left. Too, there were many more houses, and in only three months! Surely, the *Englishen* had overrun the place and brought their troubles with them. No wonder her people wanted so desperately to leave. But where would they go now? Back to New Ephrata? Back to land made sinful by the slaughter. She hoped not. She didn't think she could ever set foot on that land again. If she were forced to go, she would resist. And that would be the end of everything.

Because she could not go with Vincent. She knew that. From what she had seen on the streets only this morning, war was not a prediction, it was a fact. He would be in the thick of it. There was no place for her there.

She would be alone, with no skills and no trade, in a world torn asunder by war. She shuddered. There had to be another way.

They found Uncle Franz in his workshop, nailing up a barrel. When he turned and saw Vincent and Hannah, his face lit, then turned wary.

"Was ist das, Hannah? Why are you here with *him?"*

Hannah slid down from Dulcinea and took her uncle's hands. "Uncle, may we go into the house?"

"There is no furniture! It is there, on the wagon, ready for to go to New Ephrata."

"Then, to the Bishop's we could go, *ja?* I need a drink. A good hot cup of tea, *bitte?* And Colonel Scott, he is thirsty, too."

"Bishop Holtzen is closest. He is accompanying us on our journey tomorrow."

"So soon! I thought you were not due until two weeks."

"At New Ephrata, *ja.* But to be there in time, we must to leave tomorrow." He threw Vincent a look that said, *Come if you must,* and took Hannah's arm. Vincent dismounted and led the two horses as he trudged behind Franz and Hannah. "And how have you come to be here, Hannah-*schotzie?*"

"It is too long to tell and we will be too soon at Bishop Holtzen's. We will leave it to then, *ja?*"

She snuggled against his shoulder and felt bereft. She loved this man. And she was going to bring him great pain.

Greta Holtzen made them welcome and prepared two pots of tea. From the way she fumbled with the cups and saucers and threw despairing looks at Vincent, she obviously was not used to having an *Englishen* in the house. But then Hannah realized it was not Vincent that disturbed her. It was his field rifle and knife.

Quickly, Hannah went and took them from him. "I'll put them outside the door." Without thinking, she shouldered the rifle and tucked the knife into her skirt.

Her uncle was waiting for her when she came back

into the bishop's house. "Hannah! You handle these weapons of killing, so? This is not right!"

"There are many things that are not right, *Onkel*. Far too many things."

Franz took his niece's face in his palms and looked deeply into her eyes. The sorrow he saw there was so deep-seated, his heart seemed to stop. "Ah, Hannah-*schotzie!* Do not tell me these terrible things which darken your soul. Do not! Do not!"

"I'm sorry, *Onkel*. So very sorry. But I must."

Vincent and Hannah had only begun their story when Bishop Holtzen stopped them. "This is something which can only be told once. We will wait for the others." He sent his sons Georg and Maxim to the other families in the neighborhood. "Tell them," he said, "that I am calling a meeting of the community. An emergency meeting that will not wait for them to sup or finish work." He spoke into the room but not at anyone in particular. "When they all assemble, we will pray for the dead and give a warning to the living." When his sons left, he turned to those in his parlor. Greta and his daughter Sophie sobbed into their aprons in the corner. Hannah comforted them. Hannah, a girl two years younger than Sophie, comforted *them!* He shook his head. What had that girl faced? What were they all to face? "Franz, come with me into my study. We will pray together."

An hour later, the assembled community of forty-nine souls was in chaos. Hannah held her hands over her ears and burrowed into Vincent's jacket. He put his arm around her and whispered soothing words, but they did no good. She knew she had to break with tradition and argue with the elders. How could she not?

She was the only one who had witnessed what had happened and knew what they had to do.

She grasped Vincent's hand to gain some of his strength, took a deep breath, and stood quietly. Gradually, the others saw her and the room quieted. Faces turned to her and finally Bishop Holtzen cleared his throat.

"*Ja*, Hannah? You have something to add to our discussion?"

"'Tis no discussion, Bishop. 'Tis like a barnyard filled with laying hens but no rooster." When he flushed, she stared him straight in the eye. "Only I have seen the events I described. Only I know the dangers you face."

"*We* face, Hannah-*schotzie*," Franz said.

She nodded, conceding, accepting. "*Ja*. We face. But I cannot face that land again. 'Tis too far away from the *Englishen*. No, don't grumble. We may not want them crowding us in on all sides, but to have no protection from men such as that who destroy so callously . . . you cannot wish to face such evil. You cannot do it willingly, knowing the dangers. You cannot put your women and children in the face of that." She picked up a baby and held it aloft. "Do you want to see this soul destroyed?" The mother snatched it back and held it tight to her breast. Many men's eyes looked down. "No, I did not think so." Reaching out, she took her uncle's hand. "I buried seventy-six bodies back there. Men, women, children. I cannot do it again. Do not ask it of me or of yourselves."

"What, then, are we to do?" Sophie Holtzen asked. "You have not been here, Hannah. We are overrun with *Englishen*. We must keep separate."

329

"Find another place. Away from here. But close to a Redcoat fort, where we can get help if we need it."

"We do not ask for help from men who kill," Bishop Holtzen said emphatically.

He did not look at Vincent but Hannah knew what he was thinking. "Mayhap, in this case, we need the soldiers to show the renegades that they have resistance. We do not need the Redcoats to kill them." *I hope.* "But to do naught! To offer up sacrifices again and again. Do you really think this is what the good *Gott* wants of us? To die rather than to live?"

"We have died many times," the Bishop said. "Our *Mirror* tells us of those times."

"But it tells us something else," Hannah insisted. "It tells us that life is precious. All life. We do not take up arms. We do not kill. But you would walk into a settlement where death is guaranteed. That, to me, is only another form of killing. To sacrifice is to allow someone else to be killed. Yet, Jesus told us that we must be Good Samaritans. And we must love our neighbors as ourselves. If we do not love ourselves enough to seek protection, how then can we say that we follow His teachings?"

Sophie wailed. "But our homes are sold! We must leave tomorrow!"

Vincent cleared his throat. "There is one place where you could go and still be safe. One place where God has put a natural shelter where women and children may hide if an attack comes. One place where your enemies would have great difficulty finding you."

"Ah, Gott!" Hannah said, brokenly, and sat down. She sat with her eyes closed, realizing that Vincent was offering their paradise. If the community accepted it

he would haunt her every day in every shadow and ray of sun.

She would never be at peace.

But it gave the community a chance. And it was the only thing, the greatest, most generous thing, he could have done. If she did not already love him with all her heart, this alone would have convinced her.

Yet Bishop Holtzen was derisive in his examination of Vincent.

"We need good farming land," he said. "What do you know of farming?"

"My family farms two thousand acres in England. I worked the land before I joined the Fusilliers. I know land. This land is rich and arable. There are other things which recommend it. It has an underground river to fill your wells. It has a waterfall to power a wheel. There are good, straight trees for timber, butterflies to gobble up insects, small game to keep you in meat through the winter."

He took a breath because there were many interested expressions on the men's faces. But mostly it was the women to whom he spoke now. "And, there is a British fortification within three days' ride. Once I report that you have settled on the land, I will see to it that patrols are sent on an irregular basis, but at least once a week. If these devils see enough Redcoats visiting you, they will pass you by. It is not a guarantee that your women and children will be safe, but it is the best chance you have. Like it or not, war is coming. Though Hannah did not use the word, I can. To distance yourself from help is suicide. Is this what your religion teaches you?"

He turned to Hannah. "I will take my leave now, Hannah. You and your people have much to discuss."

To the Bishop, he added, "Send me word at the headquarters on King George Square when you have decided. But do not wait long to make your decision. I will have to get a settlement order for you. And it will take some time."

Hannah had no time to be with Vincent before he left. She wanted to say so many things, but could not. She was in the community now. She would not disgrace her uncle simply to say a good night.

She could not believe, would not believe, that it was more than good night. Their goodbyes would come another day, after the community was settled in the world's paradise. Greta Holtzen saw him to the door and returned to take a seat next to Hannah.

Suddenly, Hannah felt a hand on her hand.

"Take this," Greta whispered. "From your *Englishen,* it is." Greta closed her hand over a folded-up piece of paper. "That child you held so high is my first grandchild. *Danke* for what you said."

Hannah stuffed the piece of paper into the deep pocket of her apron. She smiled at her new bishop's wife and received a slight nod in return. Greta had done a secret thing and she could be chastised for it. But Hannah knew she had not done it for Hannah, but for her grandchild. She had paid back. That was all she would do. Now, she expected Hannah to remember who she was and where she was.

As if she could forget!

They both settled back to listen to the men talk of what the community must do.

The discussion could have gone on for hours, and might have, but Greta Holtzen suddenly sighed, raised her chin, stood tall, and said to her husband, "Ernst, I will speak with you upstairs, *bitte.*"

One half hour later they returned and Bishop Holtzen cleared his throat to get the attention of the community. *"Frau* Holtzen and I have been in prayer. We listened to the still small voice of the Spirit. We will go to this place the *Englishen* described."

Many of the women threw their arms around each other with cries of joy. Others simply sobbed. Most of the men nodded vigorously. One or two said naught, merely looking at the floor. Franz's eyes filled with tears and he turned his back on Hannah. From the expression on his face, she knew it was not from condemnation but from years of outward constraint. He wanted to keep his emotions to himself until he was ready to share them. But it was the children Hannah watched closely. The children. If *Gott* was good, none would bury their little bodies. They could be children . . . happy, laughing, boisterous. For now, however, they hung round their mothers' skirts, silent, their eyes big with fatigue, knowing from their parents' reactions that something momentous had happened.

They sent word to Vincent immediately. Then those who were expected to leave on the morrow gathered up their belongings and carried them or wagoned them to the homes of those who had a few more days. Franz and Hannah were welcomed into Bishop Holtzen's home, but Franz demurred.

"I wish to stop this last night in my own home," he said. "But Hannah may stay if she wishes."

"Whatever you want, *Onkel.*"

"Stay, Hannah. I wish to be alone."

"Ja, Onkel. I stay."

He gave her a small kiss on the cheek and left quietly.

He was a changed man, no more the jolly soul who had a ready smile and a turn of phrase that was always a light-hearted view of the world. She knew that Magda's death . . . the way she had died . . . and that she had died without him, simply because he had stayed behind to tend to business . . . must weigh heavily on his soul. Hannah wanted to reach out to him, but she also knew that the time was not yet right. The pain was too raw. Gentle words and kindnesses would only work when he had been in prayer with his God and been healed from within. That was Franz's way. Hannah would honor that and wait.

Greta gave Hannah the task of putting the children to bed. It was a wonderful gesture. It brought her back into the community and gave her to understand that she had been responsible for helping save these children's lives.

Hannah helped the youngest . . . Katrina . . . with her nightdress . . . and pulled the quilt up around the six children and grandchildren who were staying the night.

"Tell us a story, Hannah," Katrina said. "Tell us the one about the stepmother and the children she sends into the woods."

Though it was a folk tale, it was one which had been told to every child Hannah knew. Tonight, she needed folk tales. So, with tears in her eyes and hope for the future, she told them the story of Hansel and Gretel and then another about the wolf with big teeth. She told them without thinking and the children seemed to like them. But it was not until she was almost finished with the second that she began to wonder why children's stories were always about mean witches who wanted to eat little children . . . or giant beasts who wanted to do the same. After she finished the scary wolf tale, Hannah decided that she would never tell another like it.

Sophie stopped Hannah when she left the children's room.

"Will you stay by my room, Hannah?"

"I would be most grateful, Sophie. I will just get my things."

"Already, Georg fetched them up."

And Sophie had unpacked them. They were spread on the bed and beside them was a skirt and bodice exactly like the one Sophie wore, and a nightdress . . . very plain.

"Such worldly things, Hannah!"

It was a reproach and Hannah began to believe that Sophie had not extended this invitation to be gracious. As so often happened when a Mennonite woman was still unmarried at Sophie's age, there was great competition. Hannah, betrothed or married, would not have occasioned more than a passing interest. But Hannah in mourning . . . virtually an available female . . . cut down Sophie's chances. From Sophie's response Hannah realized she would have to settle her status with the bishop . . . and soon, or risk more intrusion than she cared to handle.

For the moment, she thanked Sophie. But in the morning, she sought out Greta and outlined her plan.

Greta backed up and her eyes grew wary. "Not marry!? Ever?"

"Not ever."

"Hannah, walk with me in the kitchen garden." When they got beside the barren hills where the produce had once lain heavy, she put her arm around Hannah's shoulder and asked, "It's the *Englishen*, isn't it?"

"*Ja*, Frau Holtzen. I love him very much."

Greta sighed. "I saw it in your eyes and his. It is so hard to love outside your faith, Hannah. It is so hard for the *Englishen* to give up what they have and take on ours."

"He will not become Mennonite, *Frau* Holtzen."

"I thought not."

"And I cannot go with him."

"But you want to?"

"*Ja*. With my soul, I want to."

"Have you sinned, Hannah?"

Hannah was prepared. She knew it was the first question Greta had wanted to ask. That she had held off until now showed how much respect the older woman had for the younger. "I have not sinned." *Not really. We pledged ourselves to each other. There was no sin.*

"Have you, then, shamed yourself?"

"There is no shame in loving him." She grasped Greta's hand. "You are a woman. You have known a woman's love. Help me with this, *bitte*. Please, help me."

"But you have not thought it out! What would you do? Where would you live? How would you support yourself in a community of families?"

"I have thought it out. I would take care of the children. I would teach them to read and write. I would teach the girls to sew and cook when you mothers are too busy. I would live with my uncle when he builds a house, and when he . . . when he dies . . . I will take in

336

orphans and care for them. I will support myself by doing sewing and cooking and cleaning for those women who are with child or ill. I would be useful! I just wouldn't be a wife."

Except to Vincent. I would always be a wife to my Vincent.

"Please, will you help me?"

Chapter Twenty-one

"It shall be considered, Hannah," Bishop Holtzen assured her. "I will not say I approve, but there is still at least five months left to your mourning for Jacob. We will wait three months, then the elders will discuss your situation. If we feel there is merit in your plan, we will agree. If not, you must submit to our wishes."

"But, Bishop . . ."

"*Nein,* Hannah! I will hear no more. It is enough already, for me to do this. Do not ask what I cannot give."

She had three months. Three months to convince them she could make a good contribution to the community and still stay unmarried. Of course, when she refused to remove her prayer cap after that time, she would face other problems; by then, she might have the answers.

Hannah helped the community ready themselves for the trip to the land near the clearing. The elders had decided to call the new settlement Damascus, after the road on which the Apostle Paul had had his conversion.

She sneaked away to meet Vincent, as he had asked of her in the note Greta had delivered.

They met in a coffee house near King George Square. The room was half-filled, the majority of the patrons wearing something red to distinguish them as loyalists. Hannah's entrance occasioned many heads to turn, but when they saw her dress, they smiled. The Mennonites had chosen to stay out of the confrontation. The Loyalists saw it as decidedly in King George's favor; Hannah knew it to be a resolve not to get involved with *any* political uprising.

As soon as she took her seat, Vincent covered her hand with his. "I had to explain."

"*Nein.* I understand. And I am grateful."

"I know what it would be like for me to return there without you. I didn't want to give you that kind of pain, but I saw no other choice."

Joy filled her heart. Vincent felt what she felt! That was enough. That was all! She smiled. "I know. But I can relive our moments together. And mayhap some day. . . ."

"I pray so." He ordered them coffee and two apple tarts. They arrived hot and flaky. "*Gut, ja?*"

Hannah giggled at his accent, though she didn't know why. Her English was worse than his German. But he tried, and that's all that mattered. "*Ja.* Very good."

He allowed her to finish her snack before he brought up the real reason for the meeting. He was on edge, wanting to take her upstairs and love her. As if he had a right. He swallowed back his hunger that no food could fill and wiped his mouth with his handkerchief. "Hannah, you must prepare them."

340

"I know."

"Teach the children to swim."

Hannah laughed. "Most of them already do. We grew up in a country with many lakes and rivers."

"Provision the caves. Make sure there is enough firewood and warm clothing. Enough food."

"Stop, Vincent. I have already thought about that."

"And one other thing." He handed her a pistol, some balls, and four powder horns. "I also have a rifle outside for you. And you will take my hunting knife."

She shook her head vigorously. "Vincent! Think! Where will I hide such things!? The elders pack the wagons. If they find these, they will throw them away and I will be shunned."

"All right, then. I will leave them for you in the cave. Under the third pile of small rocks inside the room with the swinging door."

"I cannot use them."

"They will be there. You know how to shoot to keep men and animals at a distance. If you are overwhelmed before help comes, use them! Please, Hannah. I cannot do my duty unless I know you are safe. Dear God, please."

"Leave them in the cave. But I cannot promise to use them."

"When the time comes, I have confidence that you will do what is right."

He took her to the back yard, to a stall in the stable where Nightwind waited, snorting impatiently. Inside, he put away his weapons and powder and pulled her into his arms and held her. Merely held her. Yet, his body reacted immediately. He was hard, throbbing against her, hungry for her. "I love you."

341

"And I love you."

He tilted her head up and gazed for an eternity into her brown eyes. He knew they would be the last thing he saw every night, the first thing he saw every morning. In his memory. Only in his memory. "Oh, God! How I love you!"

His mouth moved slowly over hers in a caress that was more poignant than a harder, more sexual kiss would have been. He worshipped her with his mouth. He blessed her with his tongue. He set up a rhythm which was echoed in the darkest reaches of her body, a rhythm that also pulsed against her belly, throbbing out his desire and hunger. It brought tears to her eyes and joy to her heart that she was loved so much by such a valiant and generous man.

"I will see you again," he whispered hoarsely. "In God's paradise, or, if He wills, in ours."

He staggered away from her, mounted Nightwind, and cantered out of the stall. He did not look back.

Men from the British headquarters came the following day to escort the settlers to Damascus. The first thing Hannah did upon arrival was visit the cave. There, under the rocks as he had said, were a knife, pistol, rifle, and ammunition.

And a wreath of mountain laurel.

There were no flowers on it, only the tiny berries of the fall. But she remembered it from the spring. Such a delicate flower, yet so tenacious it clung to life in the bleakest of areas. Ancient peoples had used it to crown victors of wars and games, their kings and Caesar. It had, therefore, become symbolic . . . only to the strongest of the strong was laurel given. Only to the survivor. Vincent had left it both as a reminder of the wreath she had made that day, and as a portent for the future.

Survive, it said.

She took off her prayer cap and placed the laurel wreath on her head. She would survive. *They* would survive. If the settlement was attacked, she would fight. Never again would she stand and accept slaughter when she could avoid or repel it.

The rock pile became a handy hiding place for her books, grown now to include the Quixote; a *Gulliver's Travels; The Pilgrim's Progress,* which she did not like at all but read because she thought it edified; and a collection of Milton's poetry, which she did like, though not as much as Shakespeare.

She read from Milton's *L'Allegro* . . . which was a bit bawdy, but reminded her of the community and what they planned for this settlement. Finished for the day, she put her books away, laid the laurel wreath on top, and piled the rocks over all.

She came out of the cave to find the men had already unloaded the cross timbers for the houses and barn. Others were busy in the woods, cutting stout trees to make sheathing and half-logs to cover the timbers. Some of the women cooked over open fires, others half-dug and planted a garden. Though late in the season, they had brought partly-grown cabbage, spinach, beets, potatoes. With any luck, some would take hold and grow larger. Those that didn't could be tossed into a stew pot.

"Hannah! Come here," Greta called. 'We looked for you."

"I went to the cave."

"Ah! You shall take the men exploring another time. Now you must begin your duties as child minder. The *kinder,* they must to plant their garlic and radishes."

If this was a test as to her dedication to the calling she sought, Hannah was prepared. She smiled and went to round up the children. With cajolery and play, she got all but the toddlers busy digging in the dirt.

"Today, you may dirty yourselves as much as you wish," she said. "And no one will scold." They looked at her in disbelief. *"Ja,* 'tis true." She handed out small wooden spades to the boys and pointed sticks to the girls. "The boys will dig this whole row on the outside next to the women's garden. And the girls will poke holes for where to put the garlic cloves. When that is finished, we will dig another row for *your* radishes. And each will plant his own seeds."

"What about the girls?" Beatrix Dunker asked.

"They, too."

"But you said *his* seeds."

She ruffled Beatrix's dark curls. "Don't worry. You will get your own radishes, too. And we will mark the rows with your name so you will know exactly where your radishes are growing."

"Mine will be the biggest," Beatrix asserted.

Hannah smiled. "I do not doubt it."

This was a girl equal to any man, so independent was she. But she would learn. In time, she, too, would take her place. Perhaps, though, she would be like Greta, who watched closely what they were doing. Quiet, Greta was. But that meekness hid a woman who had, in her own way, gotten her husband to agree to this decision. Hannah looked up and waved to Greta, who smiled and went to join the other women.

Later, after the children had completed their garden, had had their midday gruel, and were safely tucked away in the shade, napping, Hannah took the elders to the cave.

"Mein Gott, huge, it is," Bishop Holtzen said.

"Ja," Hannah agreed. "Large enough for all the women and children."

Grudgingly, Ernst Holtzen conceded, "Your *Englishen,* he was right in his offer. We may believe in nonviolence, but we do not believe in throwing ourselves into the fiery pits. We will provision this place. But first, we will pray here and offer its use to *Gott*'s plan."

For the next several weeks, half of the community worked a regular day on the farm, building the houses and barn, staking out corrals, feeding the livestock. The rest were assigned various tasks. Some, including Franz, trudged back and forth to Germantown, buying supplies and foodstuffs to stock the cave. Some cut wood and split it, both for the fires that were kept lit all day and all night, and for the cave, which soon had wood piled halfway up the walls on two sides. Some built moats and traps on the perimeter of the acreage. They disguised them with a layer of matting sodded to look like the surrounding fields. Some spent the day gathering hay and straw and dried grasses from the fields. And in the evening round the fireside, everyone braided and bundled the straw to make scary figures which they smeared with bog slime. They glowed brightly in the firelight, but when taken out to the fields under the moon, they cast an eerie green. These were hidden under layers of straw, ready to hand if they

345

should be needed as ghost figures.

One night Bishop Holtzen called a halt to the scarecrow making.

"It is enough," he said. "The community is ready for any attack. Indian, Loyalist, Rebel, or the devil himself. We will not fight, but enough of us may be saved to start again. And it is time to prepare for winter. The houses are complete—the furniture will be moved in on the morrow. Greta has the assignments for each of you. Now, let us pray that Damascus will not meet the same fate as New Ephrata. And let us pray for the souls of our brothers and sisters who lie in the single grave dug by a brave woman who has become a valuable addition to our community."

Though he did not mention her by name, many looked at Hannah and smiled. Such high praise! She was astonished by it. As she sat with the children, she saw Greta gazing at her silently but with great concern. One month of her probation was completed. November was almost over. Christmas would herald the last of her three-month trial period. Hannah had already noticed many unmarried men approaching her uncle; she was sure at least three had offered for her hand, including Maxim Holtzen.

And Sophie was still waiting.

From the scathing looks she sent Hannah, she would be a vocal opponent of Hannah's plan.

Or would she?

As the long monotone of the prayer droned into the night, Hannah felt for the first time that she might have some success in becoming the only unmarried woman in the community. If Sophie could be convinced to champion her cause, if she could agree to cajole her father, pester her mother, enlist her friends and cousins . . .

Dear God, you give great blessings, even in the form of jealous females.

When Hannah approached Sophie with her plan, the young woman stiffened her lip and shook her head.

"You think you deserve special privileges simply because you survived? You shouldn't have survived, you know. You should have been killed with the rest of them!"

"Oh, Sophie! Surely you do not mean that!"

"I don't know. Sometimes . . . why should I help you? You are no better than the rest of us. Why should you get what you want when we don't get what we want?"

"But if you do this, you can get what you want."

Sophie narrowed her eyes and pouted her lips. "How?"

"If I am dispensed from marrying, that leaves every eligible male for you, your cousins, and your friends."

Sophie's eyes widened in understanding, but she still didn't accede. "I will think on it," she said, and flounced away.

But she went directly to her distant cousin Gertrud, who always looked at Maxim with wide, adoring eyes. And the two of them went to Katrina and Josephine Japp, who had their eyes fixed on the Lendle brothers, two others of marriageable age who had visited Franz.

Hannah couldn't be sure her plan would work, but she had at least given it a better than even chance of succeeding.

She had less success trying to rid her thoughts and memories of Vincent Scott. How could she? Every week a contingent of Redcoats visited the settlement. As Vincent had promised, they came at odd times. With no one expecting them, the women had to scramble to prepare meals for them and to provide them with shelter for the night.

Sophie hated these unexpected visits worse than anybody. Busy scrubbing vegetables to add to the day's stew pot, she threw down her brush and glared at the unit lounging in the barn.

"Look at them! Making us work like this when we have so much else to do. Why can't they send us warning? Or why don't we have lookouts to tell us an hour ahead when they are coming? Then we wouldn't be so rushed all the time!"

Her anger set Hannah to thinking. An early warning of soldiers coming would help Sophie, but it would of necessity have to be set up all along the perimeter of the settlement. It would be difficult to do, since every man was needed on the farm. But if they did set up some system, it could also be used to alert the settlement to dangers, especially marauders or wild animals like bears or wolves. There were four young men in the community who were not yet strong enough to do heavy farm work and had been given the task of simple carpentry. If they worked in shelters in the trees, they could do their work and still keep watch for oncoming dangers.

Hannah went to her uncle with her plan.

It was difficult talking with Franz these days. He had wasted to a shadow of himself. Hannah had heard him talking with the bishop late several nights.

"I should have been there. I should have been there!" Franz had cried.

"And what could you have done, Franz? There were younger and stronger men there, and they did what we all would have done. They put up no resistance."

"But I might have found a way! Somehow . . . somehow I would have saved her."

"Christ could not save himself, Franz, and he was *Gott.*"

"Christ chose to die, Ernst. Magda did not."

"You do not know that."

"I know *her!* I know in my heart that she would have wanted to live."

"We all want to live. But we all must also face our time to die. Let it go, Franz. Honor her memory. Help the living."

"I cannot. I wish I could, but the thoughts keep rolling around in my head. If I had been there, I would have found a way to save her. I would."

And now Hannah was going to ask him to find a way to save others. She prayed she would find the right words.

Franz listened half-heartedly, then shrugged his shoulders. "What does it have to do with me? I am a printer. I do not know these things."

"I only know that we need this thing. I don't know what kind of thing it should be. Help me, *Onkel.* Help me find a way to save some lives."

His head jerked up. "Help you find a way?"

"Ja."

He stroked his beard and stared into the fire. "Find a way. Find a way." He patted Hannah's knee. "Let me think on it."

"Ja, Onkel."

The next morning he walked round the settlement yard and stared at the trees in the distance. He tilted his head one way and the other. He scratched his beard. He tapped his nose. He wrinkled his brow. And that night, at community prayer, he asked to speak.

"My niece came to me with a plan, a plan of an early warning system. She asked me to think of a way we could warn the community of trouble before it fell on us. I have thought on it and I have found a way."

For the next week the men were very busy. They cut timber and cross beams. They fashioned a tall tower with a ladder and a small cabin on top. They put it by the river, next to the spot where the water was swiftest, just above the waterfall. On the bottom they made a water wheel, and on the top they attached a windmill and a large bell.

When Hannah was allowed to climb into the tiny cabin she stared out at the land which was now theirs. It was a beautiful sight. Low, rolling hills of pine. Forests and meadowland. Rivers and lakes. And here and there bogs filled with wildlife, birds, and bees. Geese honked their way overhead, flying south. A hawk circled above a meadow, swooped down, and came up with something in his claws. Best of all . . . she could see for miles, in all four directions.

It was a stroke of genius: a watchtower disguised as a windmill. And whoever was assigned duty there could keep the mechanism working.

Franz joined her. "You thought to put men on the perimeter of our land, but that would have left *them* vulnerable. I sought to protect us all."

She put her arm around her beloved uncle and

kissed his whiskered cheek. "You have, *Onkel.* You have."

Three days later the bell tolled for the first time.

Stefan Lendle shouted. "Redcoats! A whole unit!"

An hour later, the Redcoats pulled into the settlement and were astonished to be handed tin cups of hot, sweet tea, and thick slices of cold apple pie.

Geoffroy Parkson dismounted and asked to speak with the elders. Hannah saw him and ran to hug him.

"What are you doing here? Why are you not in Philadelphia with Vincent?"

"I am here to warn your people about Cuppimac. He has been at work again. Getting bolder, now. Any farm will do, it seems. And he takes prisoners—women and children. We don't know what happens to them."

"Oh, dear God!"

Hannah was so distracted that she didn't realize for several minutes that Geoffroy had not answered her questions about Philadelphia and Vincent. By that time, he was busy with the elders and he mounted up his unit immediately, galloping out of the settlement without taking a meal.

Supper that night was fraught with tension. The elders had been in seclusion all afternoon. They shifted on their benches and kept their eyes on their plates. When Bishop Holtzen called for attention, they stiffened but looked up for the first time.

"The Redcoats have brought us bad news," he announced. "But not what we have not expected."

"Ernst," Greta interrupted, "should the children not be put to bed first?"

351

"*Nein*, Greta. They must know of the seriousness so they will do what they are bid, and do it without argument."

She nodded and sat back, though her eyes strayed to the children often.

"The man responsible for the terrible things at New Ephrata is heading our way," Ernst said. "The Redcoats believe that because of the unrest caused by these rebels, he is drawing his band closer and closer to Philadelphia to get the rich pickings there."

"But that's madness!"

"He will be caught!"

Bishop Holtzen held up his hands. "It *is* madness. He *is* mad, but he has not yet been caught. So, in his madness he is wily, like the fox, like all predators. He swoops. He plucks. He kills. He disappears into his habitat. Closer and closer he comes."

Hannah was reminded of the hawk she had seen. The great hawk, circling with his far-seeing eyes, swooping with his sharp talons extended, plucking his prey, flying to a hidden roost high in the trees. She shuddered, imagining the end results of that hunt, remembering the end results of Cuppimac's raid at New Ephrata.

Greta stood. "We will be prepared. The women and children will begin to do their chores in the caves. We will learn how to survive there. We will hide. We will survive."

The bishop sighed. "The Redcoat Captain, he thinks the Cuppimac one knows about the cave."

"No!" Hannah shouted. "How can he know? Why does Geoffroy think this?"

Bishop Holtzen lifted his coat and removed a roll of

bark from his breeches pocket. He unrolled it and used bowls to keep the sides from curling. "They found this at the last house he pillaged. On the top is a crude drawing of our waterfall and the countryside surrounding it. On the bottom, a detailed drawing of a hillside with a door in it."

"May I see?" Hannah asked.

Bishop Holtzen waved her over. She inspected the bark. The drawing seemed to have been burnt into the bark. Probably from hot sticks thrust into the fire, the way the boys made masks or decorated their wooden toys, she thought. She hoped against hope that Geoff and the bishop were wrong, but with one glance she knew they were not.

Cuppimac had left this at the last farm he pillaged. Geoff said he had been taking women and children. Mayhap this was a calling card, a grotesque imitation of those the *Englishen* left for each other. Hannah agreed that it meant he knew where they were.

But there was more in the drawing than the bishop had described. In front of the "door" in the hillside were figures that resembled people. Large women-shapes and smaller child-shapes.

Their Damascus watchtower had been erected to sight groups of men, but one man alone might penetrate that surveillance. Cuppimac left this to tell them he had. He had been watching them and knew the women and children frequented the cave. He left this to warn them.

He was coming. And there was naught the settlement could do to stop him.

Chapter Twenty-two

The only comfort Hannah allowed herself over the next few days was knowing that Cuppimac did not ride alone. *He* might be able to circumvent the watchtower patrol, but his band could not. It was small comfort, knowing what kind of men these were, but Hannah did not give away the information that the bishop had tried so hard to hide. Within the settlement, the drawings of the women and children were known to them alone.

The first snow fell eight days after Geoffroy brought them the dreaded news; it reminded Hannah of the fierce storms of the Rhineland, thick and wet and heavy. It piled up overnight until it reached the bottoms of the windows. The settlement looked as if a giant white quilt had been spread over everything, a quilt which isolated them from the rest of the world.

If Bishop Holtzen worried, he did not show it. He organized the farm and within two days the men had shoveled broad walkways to the barn, the outbuildings, the comfort sheds, the windmill, and the underground food storage bins. Then he began work on tunnels from the houses to the cave, tunnels underground so Cuppimac and his band would not know the women and children had fled *through* the earth to safety. And one last thing . . . he closed in the entire windmill with boards and built a comfort station to the side, just in front of the entrance to the cave. He tested it and nodded his satisfaction. The tunnels would end in the "comfort station," where the entrance to their cave was completely blocked from view.

Christmas loomed two weeks away. While the men were busy extending the tunnels, Hannah joined the women to prepare gifts for the children. The wool which had been carded, spun, and dyed over November was now brought out each night after the children were asleep. The best knitters made dozens of mittens, caps, bonnets, vests, stockings, and scarfs. Some women quilted doll blankets, others made the old-fashioned boy and girl sock dolls the Mennonites preferred, the kind with no faces, dressed in plain clothing. When the men brought in the wooden wagons, tops, and simple flutes they had fashioned, Sophie, their best artist, added a fillip of decoration to make each identifiable to the child who would own it come Christmas morning.

"No fights over these," she remarked.

Hannah chuckled. *"Danke,* Sophie. You make my day much easier."

Her day began around the keeping room table. Along with the alphabet and numbers that the children learned, she was expected to instill in them the knowledge that no problem was solved with fists or angry words. Children, too, were urged to seek guidance or intervention from the bishop or an elder when they felt cheated or abused. Easy to say, not so easy to do. The adults might refrain from altercations, but it was almost impossible to keep energetic, boisterous children from doing so, regardless of how many lessons she taught.

"You have a keen eye, Sophie," Hannah said. "The decorations are beautiful."

Sophie sniffed. "They are not meant for beauty, Hannah. We do not want to put worldly notions in the children's heads."

"No, of course not."

But they *were* beautiful.

After the gifts were finished, wrapped in scraps of cloth that would later be pieced together in quilts, tied with string, and hidden away, the work Hannah truly loved began: baking holiday foods, including raisin cake and apple stollen and dozens and dozens of dried fruit strudels. If there was one thing that distinguished a Mennonite from an Anabaptist, it was not the prayer cap nor the plain clothing. It was the Mennonites' hunger for sweets. They could not get enough of sweet things. So, pickles were sweetened as well as soured. Sweet relish was invented by them. And molasses-custard pies were a staple. But at Christmas the molasses was augmented with dried fruit and raisins to make a pie so sweet Hannah was certain it was the cause of her annual after-supper headache.

The community toiled hard, and when Bishop Holtzen announced that the tunnels were complete, shored up with timber, and solid as rocks, they frolicked just as hard. Fiddlers played, drums drummed, and flutes piped gay notes as folk songs filled the night air. Each person gathered around the two communal keeping room fireplaces and sang of the homeland they had left behind and told the tales of the Rhineland forest folk. And on Saturday, when supper was done, they sang sweet melodies that told of Christmas miracles.

But on Sunday, Christmas Day, the fiddles and drums and flutes were left behind and the people began their regular Sunday service at sunrise. At midday they had their usual hearty meal, then returned to their prayers, sing-song hymns, and hour-long sermons.

By mid-afternoon, the children were beginning to fidget. They knew as soon as the Sabbath service was over, there were magical things which awaited them. Hannah had her hands full keeping them quiet. There were so many *I must*'s whispered in her ear that she knew they were asking to be taken outside not to use the comfort room, but merely to let off some of that built-up excitement.

Beatrix Dunker's third request was greeted by her mother with a hardened eye. But Hannah smiled and shrugged, took Beatrix's hand, and wrapped her good and warm for the trip. For herself, she simply threw on her cape and trudged on the hard-packed snow beside the little girl.

Once outside, she asked, "Do you truly have to, Beatrix?"

The golden-haired girl looked up at her and wrinkled her button nose. Hannah could see the thoughts whirling in her head. *Should I be honest? Will Gott be angry if I lie? Will anyone find out if I tell the not-quite-truth?*

"I ask," Hannah said, "because I was a little restless and thought if you really didn't have to, that we could take a walk up to the windmill and back."

"Oh, yes!" Beatrix dropped her eyes and her cheeks reddened.

Hannah laughed, took her hand, and swung it high. "That's all right, *liebchen*. You only did what every one of us has done at least once. The seats, they do get hard, *ja?*"

"Very."

They walked quickly, knowing the elders would frown when they got back. But it was a good, brisk walk and it would make Beatrix sleepy enough to snuggle into her mother's side and take a little nap. Which was exactly why Hannah had suggested it.

They were only a few yards from the windmill when Beatrix pointed to the sky.

"Look, Hannah! The birds are like stars in the sky."

"So many!"

Too many. Rising all at once. Rising and cackling, not calling in friendly bird language, one to the other. Every kind fled into the woods to the North. As if . . . as if . . .

"*Mein Gott!* Beatrix, stay here."

"But . . ."

She shook Beatrix's shoulder and shoved her behind a large rock. "Stay here. Right here. Do you understand?"

"*Ja,* Hannah. I do."

With pounding heart, Hannah raced to the windmill. She craned her neck but could not see Maxim. "Maxim! Maxim!" She started up the ladder when an arrow thudded into the wood next to her ear. "*Mein Gott, mein Gott,* do not fail me." She reached the top, peeped over the opening, and saw Maxim sprawled on the floor, an arrow in his shoulder and blood seeping out. His chest rattled, but he still breathed. Without thinking, she reached in and dragged him inch by inch to the opening.

She had naught but her cloak, and this she used to wrap around his body. *There goes another underskirt!* Several strips made a sling with which she tied him to her waist. Then, she began the dangerous and tiring trip down the ladder. She prayed every minute, expecting an arrow in the back, determined to get Maxim to the house. She would not leave him here to bleed to death!

She was halfway down when she remembered the bell at the top. *Dummkopf!* But the rope hung long enough for her to reach. She grasped the ladder with one hand and held on for dear life. Then she pulled the rope. Once. Twice. Five times, their signal. She let it go and worked her way back down, one rung at a time. When she reached the bottom, she stepped into blood which had dripped from Maxim's body. She stumbled, took a step, stumbled again. He was too heavy!

She knew no one would come to help her. They had their own assignments. They would be busy. The women shepherding the children to the tunnel and into the cave. The men dragging out the scarecrows, ready to plant them in the field at first dark. The boys checking their traplines to be sure they could be pulled up . . . the snow would be heavy on them. They would need great strength to manage it, as much strength as Hannah needed to get Maxim to the house.

She could not risk the cave. Then Cuppimac would know that there was help there. They had to divert his attention from the cave at all cost. So, she dragged

Maxim's body to the rock behind which Beatrix huddled.

"Come, *liebchen*."

The child took one look at Maxim. Her eyes widened. Her mouth opened.

"Not a sound, Beatrix! Not one peep."

Hannah kept Beatrix close to her side and sweated and strained to get Maxim back to the house. Except for that one arrow, all was still. What was he waiting for? What was his plan? He had one, she knew that. She knew . . . she knew he struck the last time at midday. But midday was long past. Shadows were lengthened. The day would be over soon. Had he given them a warning, knowing full well they would be able to do naught? How like him.

Yes, she thought she knew him now.

They were bound together somehow. She had survived. She might be the only person who had survived . . . except for those women and children he had taken.

She shuddered and kept plodding back to the house.

When she got to the door, she collapsed. She had only strength enough to pound on the door. It opened and Bishop Holtzen gasped, pulled Maxim inside, then reached a hand for her and Beatrix.

"The others are in the tunnels. Go! *Schnelle! Schnelle!* I will take Maxim."

A giant trap door lay open in the center of the parlor. Its twin, she knew, would be open in the other house. The assembly would be broken into two groups, and half would have returned to the other house . . . to give no warning that they knew they were under siege.

"*Schnelle,*" Ernst urged.

But when Hannah looked down at the depth of the opening and knew she had to climb another ladder, her legs shook and cramped. She backed away. "You go. I will come as soon as I've caught my breath."

"Hannah!"

"Take Beatrix, *bitte*. I will be along. I promise."

"Bolt the door behind you."

"*Ja*. I do."

The bishop's head had no more than crested the trap when Hannah dropped wearily into the first chair. She noticed but did naught about the bloody trail left by Maxim. Nor did she see to her own blood-stained clothing. She had been thus once before. She was used to it now.

So, Cuppimac, she thought. *What are you doing now? And what can I do to stop you?*

If she were this maddened Indian . . . maddened by grief and revenge, but still mad . . . she would know her enemy very well. She would know that the Redcoats came to the farm at least once a week. She would know that this was a special holiday, that everyone would be celebrating. She would know that Maxim had been found, so the community was alerted. She would know that the stock would need to be fed. She would know patterns and daily routine. And she would know that, once having been alerted, the communities would bolt the door and stay inside, hoping to keep alive until the next visit from the Redcoats.

So, what would she plan if she were Cuppimac?

What had he done at New Ephrata that he could do here to accomplish his ends?

Her head snapped up and she moaned. She remembered Aunt Magda.

Cuppimac had burned down the house.

And Hannah remembered something else. She remembered the fire on the ship. She remembered how quickly the smoke had filled the hold because it had no place to get out. She remembered what it felt like to breathe in that acrid stuff and have it burn her throat, choke her. Her eyes whipped round to the trap doors. Just like those in the hold of the ship, they were. Strong. But when the fire came, it would consume them, too. And the timbers in the tunnels. Those stout timbers, dry and ready to be fodder for a fire.

And the smoke would slide down the shaft, float through the tunnels until it found the cave . . . and the women and children, the men and boys. They would be caught in the very place they sought for safety. They would choke, die.

But Cuppimac would not know that someone in the community had guns and a hunting knife.

She rose quickly, her mind made up by events beyond her control. She would not shoot to kill. But she would not allow anyone to torch these houses!

It took an eternity to get to the entrance to the cave and her precious pile of rocks. She pulled the large ones off the rifle and pistol, checked that they were still in working order, and picked up the knife. She tucked it and the pistol into her belt, dropped the balls and powder bags into the voluminous pockets of her apron, slung the rifle over her shoulder, and turned to go back up to the house.

"*Mein Gott,* Hannah! *Was ist das?*"

She turned to face the bishop and six other men, including her uncle. "He will burn down the houses."

363

"They are only houses. They can be rebuilt."

"The smoke will come down the shaft and fill this cave and the other. Maxim, the weakest, will die first. Then, the children. Then one by one, the rest of us." She shook the rifle. "This will keep him away from the house."

"It is a weapon of war, Hannah!"

"Bishop, I give my word. I will not shoot to kill. I will shoot on the ground to warn them away, to keep them from burning the house."

"I forbid it, Hannah!"

She turned to her uncle and told him what she had never said. "Aunt Magda died in the fire. He burned the house with her in it. She had no chance. Let me give us a chance."

"Ernst," Franz said, "let her go."

"If she goes, she will be under the ordinance. She will be shunned."

"Ernst, when this is over, we can discuss her punishment. For now, let her go." Bishop Holtzen turned his back on Hannah. Franz sighed. "We cannot help you. We have our own duties."

"I know, *Onkel.*" She kissed him on his cheek. "*Danke.* I love you."

"Take care, child."

"And you, dear *Onkel.*"

She returned to the house and prepared her pistol and rifle. She would have to take time to reload after every shot, precious time that could have been saved if she had one person to reload while she fired. But there was no one in the community who knew the faintest thing about weapons.

For two hours she prowled the house. The women

had taken every sweet and prepared food into the cave. The only thing Hannah found were a handful of raisins and that morning's eggs. She hated raw eggs, but mixed with a little cream, sugar, and cinnamon, it was a good drink. It was so dark that she worked in the kitchen by rote. Then she realized that Cuppimac would be suspicious if there were no fire. No candles, he would understand. But not to light a fire would signal that the houses were deserted.

The fire gave her some small comfort. The rest she got by believing that Cuppimac would not attack in the dark. She slept in front of the fire and woke later than usual. She near jumped out of her skin when the cows, whose udders were filled to bursting, began crying to be milked. It was not yet midday. She threw on a cape and slipped out into the yard. It took an hour, but she had the cows quieted and six barrels of milk left to carry to the house.

She had broken the routine, but only a little. She hoped it went unnoticed.

She carried all but one barrel of milk to the cave and left them for the others to find.

Then she took up her post by a window which gave a good view of the settlement. She noticed several of the boys racing to the barn from the other house. They had not come here because she was being shunned. Some looked back at her, but most ignored her. She sighed. It was beginning.

Chapter Twenty-three

The first wave swept down from the west, right into the front yard, expecting no resistance. But the boys' traps were aligned with what was, in any other weather, the road. The horses that were not directly in the middle of it raced like the others; then, at a shout from the barn, they plunged downward into the pits, their riders along with them.

Hannah laughed at the shouts of triumph from the barn. The boys had dug the pits so deep, no man could jump out. Once in, they needed a ladder or a lowered rope to get out.

The man in front . . . obviously the leader, Cuppimac . . . held up his hand and looked back. For a moment, he looked confused, but his confusion turned to anger and he pointed a finger at the barn.

Hannah knew he would get nowhere. The boys would have dropped into their own traps and scattered to dozens of tunnels, any one of which let them out at several spots where there were more controls for more traps. The farm was a rabbit warren of tunnels, and each led to more mechanisms that triggered traps and moats, wooden barricades that suddenly sprang up out of nowhere, and eerie scarecrows that glowed in the dark and could be made to "dance."

Cuppimac's men entered the barn and came back out quickly, shaking their heads. Hannah held her breath, waiting for Cuppimac to give the order to kill the livestock, but he must have shouted something else because the men remounted. His head swiveled right and left, then stopped. He stared at the house, looked up at the chimney, and dropped his eyes to the windows.

Suddenly, Hannah felt as if he were staring directly at her. Her hands shook. Her heart hammered. Her brow became covered in sweat. She picked up the rifle and found she couldn't focus on anything. She lowered it, sank to her knees, and sobbed.

How did Vincent do it? How did he fight for people he did not even know? What made him risk his life for men, women, and children he would never see?

Greater love hath no man than this, that a man lay down his life for his friends.

But what kind of love was it that Vincent harbored, to lay down his life for an unseen, unknown, faceless people?

And she could not even steady a rifle for those she loved.

Well, then, if not a rifle, then a pistol would do. But first, she had to make a hole in the window. She tapped as quietly as she could, but Cuppimac heard. His head whipped to her window and he stared. When the glass broke, he pulled up on the reins of his horse. The band stopped.

"Fire the house," Cuppimac ordered.

Hannah quickly balanced the pistol on the window ledge, pulled back the hammer and fired into the ground right in front of Cuppimac's horse. It reared and screamed and danced back.

"You said they had no weapons!"

"Have the British come in the night?"

"We lost Bridges and Culbert. I'm for trying somewhere else! What say you?"

Cuppimac turned and shot the last man to speak. He crumbled into the snow, which turned scarlet immediately.

Hannah fumbled to reload the pistol. She was not finished when the band began to move closer. She had no choice! She whipped up the rifle and fired. This time she took out a great chunk of wood from the nearest tree. It hit one of the men and he held up his hand to his cheek where it bled.

"*Gott* forgive me!" Hannah said. She had not meant to hurt anyone!

Cuppimac waved his arm and the band spread out, making individual targets. Big mistake, Hannah thought. Traps got two more horses and their riders. A barricade snapped the legs of one mount. Cuppimac shot it to stop its screams.

"Use your arrows! Fire the house!"

Dear God, she hadn't counted on that! She could hit a log. But could she hit an arrow in a bow? It would be close to a man's ear! Or . . . before he brought it up to his ear, it would be held downward to allow the fire to catch. If she could get it then.

"*Bitte. Bitte. Bitte.* Let me have this one!"

She used her rifle to cover the distance better. She

had to wipe the sweat from her brow so it wouldn't drip into her eyes. She took aim at the man who held the long bow. She waited until the fire was lit to give her a better target, then squeezed gently as Cathleen had taught her. Before the man had a chance to cock the arrow, it shot in an arc, backward in the air.

"Jesus!"

"With that kind of shooting, the British must be there!"

"They why aren't they rushing us?" Cuppimac roared. "Fire again."

She wished she could swear!

Powder, ball, more powder. Cock the hammer. Squeeze the trigger. There was a rhythm to it that eluded her. But she did the best she could. This time, she got the arrow as it arced into the air, heading for the house.

My goodness, she was good! But then, Cathleen had said she was the best she'd seen for a beginner. Too good, though, were these shots. Hannah had more than a fleeting notion that a steadier hand than hers was guiding her shots.

"Danke, Gott." And keep it up, *bitte.*

She wanted to shout for joy, but she was too busy reloading. She brought the rifle up to her shoulder, sighted the next ball of flame, and stopped. A flash of red on top of the ridge. Snow blindness? No! Another. And another!

The bow twanged and she sighted on the fire, squeezing the trigger just in time. And just in time the Redcoats swarmed over the ridge and came riding fast, shouting as they came, their bugler blowing for all he was worth.

Cuppimac and his band whirled away from the house. Now they truly had a fight on their hands.

The band scattered to the trees and the *Englishen* went after them. She heard shots and screams. Silence. More shots and screams. More silence. She slumped beside the window, waiting for . . . she knew not what. What she did not expect was to hear the back door open and footsteps tramp through the kitchen. She whirled and brought up her rifle, sighting along the barrel . . . and saw Vincent standing with his arms outstretched.

She cried out, dropped the rifle, and raced into his embrace. He picked her up and whirled her around, kissing her heartily. " 'Tis over, love. 'Tis over."

She covered his entire face with kisses.

"What a welcome! Shall we finish this upstairs?" His hands skimmed her body, cupped her breasts, kissed her hungrily. He found her bottom and pulled it up, into the hardness in his breeches. "God, how I've ached to hold you like this! Kiss you like *this.*"

His mouth brushed back and forth across hers and his tongue traced the outline of her lips before plunging into the opening she freely gave. It was demanding and loving, gentle and rough, and Hannah moaned because it wasn't enough.

She arched up to feel him, moved her hand down to touch him, and still it wasn't enough.

She tore her mouth from his and held his beloved face in her palms. "I thought I would never see you again."

"Christmas surprise."

"Thank God for Christmas."

"Amen to that," a hearty, deep voice said from the

other side of the room.

Hannah jumped away from Vincent's arms and turned to look sheepishly at her uncle.

"So, Hannah, this is why you do not wish to marry." He advanced on Vincent. "You will lay down your arms and embrace the faith, *ja?*"

"No," Vincent said. "I have a contract with my king. I am a professional soldier and intend to remain one."

Franz turned puzzled eyes to Hannah. "What will you do?"

"Later, *Onkel,*" Hannah said. "We will discuss this later. First, tell me . . . how are the others?"

"They survived. The boys, they were excited that their little ideas, they worked. But I think they may have worked too well. I think there will be someone who does not survive the traps. For that, the boys will have to beg pardon and receive punishment. But they will heal. They will be restored to full fellowship. As will you, Hannah, if you obey the orders of the elders."

"Is that what you have come to tell me?"

"*Ja.* They wait in the caves until they get the word from the Redcoats to come out. I will go and tell them it is time."

"No," Vincent said. "It is not time yet."

Hannah searched his face. His eyes were tinged with worry. "What is it?" She blanched. "No! He got away!?"

"Yes."

"Who got away?" Franz asked.

"Cuppimac, the leader," Vincent said. "My men are scouring the woods for him now. We have all the horses, including his. He won't get far. But it would be better for everyone to stay in the caves."

Franz took it stoically. "I will tell them. Hannah, you will come?"

"They will welcome me, *Onkel?*"

He held out his hands and waggled them in the age-old gesture of the old that meant . . . maybe, maybe not. "But Greta and Little Beatrix are anxious to see that you are all right. You will come, *ja?*" He put his hand on Vincent's shoulder. "And you will come, too, *bitte.*"

Franz went down the ladder first, then Vincent handed Hannah down to him, following after.

"Ingenious," Vincent said, surveying the new tunnel. "I will recommend this to every outpost and settlement."

"They all have caves?" Hannah teased.

"They could carve some out or use tunnels as escape routes."

"Ah . . . something we did not consider."

They reached the "comfort house" and pushed open the rock door.

"They are back in the largest cave," Franz said. "The children, intrigued by the river, they are. They have decided to catch fish for supper."

When they arrived in the cave, there were more glares and silence than welcomes. Sophie threw Hannah a malevolent, yet triumphant, look and flounced out to the tunnel leading to the river. Several of the other unmarried girls followed her.

The shunning continued.

"Franz," the bishop said, "tell your niece she is not welcome here."

"I told her she was. She kept them from burning the house, Ernst."

"She used weapons of killing. She disobeyed my order. She is not welcome here now. She may, however, join the children, where she can be useful until we have decided what her punishment will be."

Vincent wanted to step in and tell this pompous ass what he could do with his punishment, but Hannah's hand on his arm stopped him. These were her people. She had to decide on her own whether to stay or . . .

He hadn't had time to tell her his news. He had been too damned busy satisfying his hunger for her. And it hadn't been satisfied. It had merely been whetted.

"Do you want to go back to the house or with the children?" he asked Hannah.

"With the children," she said. She took his hand and led him away. "You do not understand, Vincent. If I had gone back to the house with you, they would suspect that we would be doing . . . what we *would* have been doing." She chuckled. "I was tempted, *ja*. But this is best." She skipped into the place they had first made love. "Besides, I can be a help with the children."

"How?" Sophie asked belligerently, breaking the code of silence. "By showing them *that?*" She pointed to Vincent's rifle, which had its bayonet affixed. "Weapons of killing! She brings weapons of killing to help with the children!"

"Oh, for heaven's sake," Hannah said, and snatched Vincent's rifle away, to put it on the ledge behind the first bend. Before she could move, however, Sophie's eyes widened, her arm came up, her finger pointed, and she screamed until it echoed madly off the walls.

Hannah turned at Sophie's scream. All she saw was a blur of motion, unconnected images. A wet, mottled

374

body rising in a roar from the icy river. An arm raised. A glint of steel. A red-streaked face. A mouth twisted open. Two mad eyes. She raised her hands in prayer. And his body . . . Cuppimac's body . . . pitched forward toward Sophie and found, instead, the bayonet affixed to the rifle in Hannah's hand, the rifle she had forgotten she held.

He looked down, then up at her. His hand dropped his knife and he pulled the bayonet out of his chest. With his bloody hands, he reached to touch her hair. He found, instead, the side of her face. He touched the corner of her eye.

"Brown," he said. Then he touched his own eye. "Like mine."

He put his arms around her, held her in an embrace, whispered into her ear. She stumbled backwards, unable to hear anything but what he whispered. It droned in her head, scaling upward, ever upward, until it reached a crescendo. Then it dropped again to an eternal, damning whisper . . . a whisper that entered her soul and engulfed her with a red mist until the cave was blotted from view and the world disappeared.

She awoke in the communal house on the bed in her uncle's room. Vincent sat in a chair by her side, holding her hand. And rimmed around the bed were Bishop Holtzen, *Frau* Holtzen, Sophie, Franz, and Georg.

She struggled to get up but was too weak. She found herself crying, sobbing uncontrollably.

"I did not mean . . . I did not mean . . ."

"I know," Vincent said. "It was an accident."

"Ja," Franz mouthed. "An accident."

But she could see in the eyes of the others the condemnation. They knew, as she knew, that had she not been holding the rifle, she would not have that awful whisper to haunt her for the rest of her life. She would not have these silent faces staring at her.

Suddenly, Sophie knelt beside the bed. "Hannah. I do not condemn you!"

Bishop Holtzen's stern voice sliced through the room. "Sophie! That is a sin for which you will ask pardon."

"If I pray and God tells me it is, then I will. She saved my life." She looked round the room. "She saved Maxim's life. She saved my life. She saved the children's lives." She took Hannah's hand and kissed it. "*Danke,* Hannah. May you always live with *Gott*'s blessing." With that, she rose and ran weeping from the room.

The bishop harrumphed. "I will take care of Sophie later. Right now, it is you, Hannah Yost, who is my concern. And the concern of everyone in the community. The elders have met. We have decided your punishment."

Hannah struggled to sit up in bed and Vincent supported her. "*Ja,* I will listen."

"The cost to us . . . the killing . . . it is too high, Hannah. We fear it is too high for even *Gott* to forgive. But we know that He will forgive us and you if you do these things we require. To stay in this community, you must confess your sins openly, at meeting. You must lay down your arms permanently. You must serve a penitent period of two years where you will live in a small house we will build. You will be alone, Hannah. Only one member of the community will be allowed to bring you food. But you may not have any conversation with anyone, not even your uncle. You may read your Bible and the *Mirror*. You may pray often. You may attend Sabbath services, but you must sit apart, in the back, with your face turned away from the rest of the community. Then, if you do no more evil to yourself or your brothers and sisters of the Faith, you will be allowed back into the community."

"Ernst," Greta said, "you forget something."

"Oh? Ah, *ja*. And you must accept for husband the man the elders choose for you."

Hannah grasped Vincent's arm and lowered herself to the bed. Tears welled up and spilled over. "I will think on it," she said.

"Better you should pray about it," Bishop Holtzen said. "Come," he said to the others. "We will leave our sister to pray. You also, *Englishen.*"

"*Nein,*" Hannah said. "I wish Vincent to stay."

"Hannah, you still disobey?"

"I have not accepted your conditions, yet, *Herr* Bishop. I wish Vincent to stay until I explain what you have said means and what I must do."

"Ah. *Ja. Gut.*"

When their footsteps retreated down the stairs, Vincent turned to Hannah. "You are staying, then?"

"We have been through this before, Vincent. I have no choice."

"Yes. You do."

She grasped his hand, searching his face for the things she had been praying for. "Give me some hope."

"I have requested a posting to Halifax, in Canada. There is a fortification there and the commandant has issued an order that all wives accompany the officers. Leads to good morale, he says. There will be little fighting, so you can breathe easier. It will not be the

377

kind of post I would have had with General Howe, but I will be assistant to the commander of the fort. A good promotion, so I advance, rather than retreat. And Geoffroy has decided to come with me. The people there are our kind of people—Scots.

"I am asking you to follow me. Become part of my people, Hannah. Live with me. Sleep cradled in my arms. Make love with me. Bear my children. Grow old with me. Like it says in the Bible. *Whither thou goest, I will go, and your people shall be my people?"*

"Not quite like that. But the meaning is all." She searched for an answer, a phrase she had not yet heard. "Vincent, are you asking me to marry you?"

"How can I do that? We are already married. But if 'tis a preacher you want, a preacher you shall have. What is your preference? Congregationalist? Church of England? Presbyterian? Episcopalian? Methodist?"

"I've always been partial to the Society of Friends. They, too, are pacifist."

"Heaven help me!" He kissed the palm of her hand. "It will be hard work up there in the cold of Nova Scotia. And I don't get much pay."

Laughter eclipsed the tears. "I don't get any pay at all! And Mennonites do not shirk hard work." She smiled at his wonderful, worried face. "That part about sleeping and loving and bearing children and growing old . . . could you repeat that?"

"I can do better." He held her hand and gazed contentedly into her eyes, saying,

Some glory in their birth, some in their skill,
Some in their wealth, some in their bodies' force,
Some in their garments, though new-fangled ill,

> *Some in their hawks and hounds, some in their*
> > *horse;*
> *And every humour hath his adjunct pleasure,*
> *Wherein it find a joy above the rest:*
> *But these particulars are not my measure;*
> *All these I better in one general best.*
> *Thy love is better than high birth to me,*
> *Richer than wealth, prouder than garment's cost,*
> *Of more delight than hawks or horses be;*
> *And having thee, of all men's pride I boast;*
> > *Wretched in this alone, that thou mayst take*
> > *All this away and me most wretched make.*

Don't take it away, Hannah. Don't ever take it away!"

"I never shall, Vincent. I love you now and always." Though she knew that by choosing Vincent, she would leave behind the rest of her family, that her name would be blotted from the family Bible and the history of the Mennonite community, as if she never were, she did not hesitate to give her love everything the Lord had sent into her heart. "Whither thou goest, Vincent, I shall go. And thy people, shall be my people. Thy God, my God."

It wasn't until they were riding out of the settlement, having been shunned even by Franz, that Vincent leaned over. "I forgot to ask you. What was it that Cuppimac whispered?"

"He said, *Thank you.*"

Author's Afterword

The first Mennonite community in America was established in Pennsylvania around 1748. For the next several years, many settlements were begun. All were destroyed by marauding Indians or French trappers, sometimes one or the other, sometimes both. The basis for these attacks varied from greed to retribution, from war to rumors of war. But the sole reason they resulted in absolute devastation was exactly what has been described in this novel: pure nonviolence. No Mennonite ever took up arms against his attacker.

The Germantown settlement thrived, however. Perhaps it was its proximity to Philadelphia which brought it some measure of protection. But it also brought the encroachment of the world. As is happening to all Amish and Mennonite communities today, its land was gradually bought up by English-speaking settlers who did not embrace the Way. This pushed the Eighteenth Century Mennonites further and further westward. Some moved all the way to the Ohio valley. Massacres were not unheard of, though none happened exactly as I have written.

On today's map, New Ephrata would be 60 miles east of Pittsburgh. Sandy Brook would sit somewhere just to the west of Amish country. And Damascus, between York and Germantown.

For those who wonder if the Mennonites still bundle, I have the word of a seventy-three-year-old member that they do. She regaled me with yarns of the days when she was younger (that would be around 1937) and there were fifteen "over-the-rail" babies born into her congregation in one year.

For those of you who wonder what the difference is between the Amish and the Mennonites—there are too many to list! For starters, the Amish are an offshoot of the Mennonite faith. So are the Dunkards, the Funkites, the Herrites, the Pikers, the Weavers, the Evangelicals, the Brennemans, the Wislerites, the Martinites, the Wengerites, the Hornings, the Reidenbachs, the Beachy Amish, the River Brethren, the Old Order River Brethren, United Zion's Children, Reformed Mennonites, Mennonite Brethren in Christ, and Old Order Mennonites. If I've missed any, I apologize.

Two wonderful introductions to the Mennonite and Amish communities should not be overlooked by those interested in learning more about the Mennonites and their more popular and better-known brethren. John A. Hostetler's *The Amish* (Herald Press, Scottdale, Pennsylvania) and Elmer L. Smith's *Meet the Mennonites* (Applied Arts Publishers, Lebanon, Pennsylvania), were inspirations for my further research among the people of York and Lancaster Counties in Pennsylvania. And for some of the idiomatic expressions which Hannah and her people use, I have A. Monroe Aurand, Jr. to thank. His "delightful bit of entertainment," *Quaint Idioms and Expressions of the Pennsylvania Germans* (The Aurand Press, Lancaster, Pennsylvania) had me laughing through each and every page. But most of all, I express my gratitude to Mickey and Jim Cox of Honeybrook, Pennsylvania, who gave me a long tour of the Mennonite countryside, helped me with my research, and showed me what it felt like to hold a gun and shoot it.

The Mennonites are interesting people, with fascinating customs and a wonderful faith resting firmly on family and love of God. In the research for this book I have come to respect their way of life, their beliefs, and their wish to remain separate from the evils and confusion caused by us *Englishen*.

PASSION BLAZES IN A ZEBRA HEARTFIRE!

COLORADO MOONFIRE   (3730, $4.25/$5.50)
by Charlotte Hubbard
Lila O'Riley left Ireland, determined to make her own way in America.
Finding work and saving pennies presented no problem for the independent lass; locating love was another story. Then one hot night, Lila meets
Marshal Barry Thompson. Sparks fly between the fiery beauty and the
lawman. Lila learns that America is the promised land, indeed!

MIDNIGHT LOVESTORM   (3705, $4.25/$5.50)
by Linda Windsor
Dr. Catalina McCulloch was eager to begin her practice in Los Reyes, California. On her trip from East Texas, the train is robbed by the notorious,
masked bandit known as Archangel. Before making his escape, the thief
grabs Cat, kisses her fervently, and steals her heart. Even at the risk of
losing her standing in the community, Cat must find her mysterious lover
once again. No matter what the future might bring . . .

MOUNTAIN ECSTASY   (3729, $4.25/$5.50)
by Linda Sandifer
As a divorced woman, Hattie Longmore knew that she faced prejudice.
Hoping to escape wagging tongues, she traveled to her brother's Idaho
ranch, only to learn of his murder from long, lean Jim Rider. Hattie seeks
comfort in Rider's powerful arms, but she soon discovers that this strong
cowboy has one weakness . . . marriage. Trying to lasso this wandering
man's heart is a challenge that Hattie enthusiastically undertakes.

RENEGADE BRIDE   (3813, $4.25/$5.50)
by Barbara Ankrum
In her heart, Mariah Parsons always believed that she would marry the
man who had given her her first kiss at age sixteen. Four years later, she is
actually on her way West to begin her life with him . . . and she meets
Creed Deveraux. Creed is a rough-and-tumble bounty hunter with a masculine swagger and a powerful magnetism. Mariah finds herself drawn to
this bold wilderness man, and their passion is as unbridled as the Montana landscape.

ROYAL ECSTASY   (3861, $4.25/$5.50)
by Robin Gideon
The name Princess Jade Crosse has become hated throughout the kingdom. After her husband's death, her "advisors" have punished and taxed
the commoners with relentless glee. Sir Lyon Beauchane has sworn to
stop this evil tyrant and her cruel ways. Scaling the castle wall, he meets
this "wicked" woman face to face . . . and is overpowered by love. Beauchane learns the truth behind Jade's imprisonment. Together they struggle
to free Jade from her jailors and from her inhibitions.

*Available wherever paperbacks are sold, or order direct from the
Publisher. Send cover price plus 50¢ per copy for mailing and
handling to Zebra Books, Dept. 4142, 475 Park Avenue South,
New York, N.Y. 10016. Residents of New York and Tennessee
must include sales tax. DO NOT SEND CASH. For a free Zebra/
Pinnacle catalog please write to the above address.*